By Susan Lewis

Fiction

Memoir

Too Close to Home

Too Close to Home

A Novel

SUSAN LEWIS

Ballantine Books

New York

A Ballantine Books Trade Paperback Original

Copyright © 2015 by Susan Lewis Ltd.
Reading group guide copyright © 2015 by Penguin Random House LLC
Excerpt from *The Girl Who Came Back* by Susan Lewis
copyright © 2015 by Susan Lewis Ltd.

Published in the United States by Ballantine Books,
an imprint of Random House, a division of
Penguin Random House LLC, New York.

BALLANTINE and the HOUSE colophon are
registered trademarks of Penguin Random House LLC.
RANDOM HOUSE READER'S CIRCLE & Design is a
registered trademark of Penguin Random House LLC.

Originally published in hardcover in Great Britain by Century,
an imprint of The Random House Group Limited, in 2015.

Grateful acknowledgment is made to New Directions Publishing
Company for permission to reprint an excerpt from UNDER MILK
WOOD by Dylan Thomas, copyright © 1952 by Dylan Thomas. Reprinted
by permission of New Directions Publishing Company.

This book contains an excerpt from the forthcoming book *The Girl
Who Came Back* by Susan Lewis. This excerpt has been set for this edition
only and may not reflect the final content of the forthcoming edition.

LIBRARY OF CONGRESS CATALOGING-IN-PUBLICATION DATA
Lewis, Susan.
Too close to home : a novel / Susan Lewis.
pages ; cm
ISBN 978-0-345-54953-2 (paperback) — ISBN 978-0-345-54954-9 (ebook)
1. Domestic fiction.   I. Title.
PR6062.E9546T66 2015
823'.914—dc23
2015028694

Printed in the United States of America on acid-free paper

randomhousebooks.com
randomhousereaderscircle.com

2 3 4 5 6 7 8 9

Book design by Virginia Norey

Too Close to Home

Chapter 1

Nothing was happening.

Everything was completely still, motionless, not a single rustle in the atmosphere, no stirrings within.

The only sounds, muted by closed windows, were the cries of white-bellied gulls as they soared around the neutral sky.

Jenna Moore, petite, dark-haired, and emerald-eyed, was sitting at the cluttered dining room table staring out at the winter-bleak garden. Looking at her, no one would have guessed she was the mother of four, the eldest being fifteen. Her smooth, playfully freckled features and girlish frame made her appear far closer to thirty than the forty she actually was.

It was Sunday afternoon and she was supposed to be making the most of some rare hours alone. The younger children—Josh, age eight, and the five-year-old twins, Flora and Wills—were on playdates down in the village, while Paige, fifteen last birthday, was somewhere with her stepfather on this sprawling misty peninsula, though Jenna wasn't for the moment entirely sure where. All she knew was that it never failed to warm her to think of how close Paige and Jack were. He was the only father Paige had ever known, since her own had abandoned them when Paige was barely a year old. They'd never heard from him again, though Jenna had felt genuinely sorry when she'd heard how he'd lost his life in a rock-climbing accident at the age of thirty. By then Paige was seven years old and Jenna was married to Jack, who'd accompanied them to the funeral and had sat with Paige for a long time afterward explaining how losing her real father wasn't going to make any difference to them.

"So you're my real daddy, really?" Paige had insisted.

"That's right. I'll always be here for you, and no one will ever be prouder of you than me."

"But why didn't my other daddy live with us?"

"He did for a while, when you were a tiny baby, but he wasn't really ready to be a daddy. He wanted to do other things."

"You don't want to do other things, do you?"

Jack had shaken his head gravely. "All I want to do is be your daddy, and Mummy's husband—and maybe a daddy to a brother or sister for you too. Would you like that?"

Paige had nodded eagerly, which had twisted Jenna's heart with longing. After two miscarriages she was starting to worry that she'd never give Jack a child of his own.

Blinking as an unexpected breakthrough of sunlight bathed the garden in a rich golden glow, Jenna began picturing Jack's and Paige's faces as they probably were now: intent, laughing, curious, and excited as they went about their task. This was the fourth Sunday in a row they'd been out capturing this special place in the world on film, and so far there had been no fallings-out that she knew of. In fact, between them they had gathered some impressive footage of surfers riding the waves over at Rhossili Bay; the flighty dance of marram grass as the wind gusted over the dunes; entrancing close-ups of old and young faces singing their hearts out in chapel; wild ponies roaming the vast open moors; golden plover, sanderlings, and little stints pecking and flitting about the wetlands; starfish, cockleshells, and feathers littering the shores . . . There was so much material now that Jenna could hardly remember it all. Today's mission was all about local folklore, Viking raiders, the Arthurian legend, smugglers, dragons, and damsels in distress. If there was fog clinging to the rocks of the Worm's Head, Jenna knew, Paige intended to whisper lines from Herbert New's sonnet to accompany the haunting scene. *Patient, folded wings; with lifted head, / Watchful, outlooking seawards sits the Form / Which, dragon-like, defies the approaching storm . . .*

The project was for Paige's ICT course—Information and Communications Technology: *Using your mobile phones, make a tourist video of the region to include everything you feel to be worthwhile.*

Jack was a big one for projects, sometimes seizing them as if they were his own until Paige—or whichever child he was supposed to be assisting—patiently, or occasionally hotly, reminded him that she was in charge.

Jenna couldn't help but smile at the way Jack tried to hide his hurt, or frustration, at being brought up short by his children, quickly covering it with pride that they were so gifted, or determined, or simply willing to learn from their own mistakes.

"Dad, I'm fifteen, for God's sake," Jenna had heard Paige grumbling as they'd returned last Sunday. "You're treating me like a baby."

"But you asked me to help," he'd protested.

"*Help,* yes, not take over. I need someone who'll do as they're told and maybe make suggestions if they're relevant. Not someone who thinks they know everything."

"But I do."

Paige hadn't been able to stop herself smiling at that. "But I'm the student," she'd reminded him. "I have to learn, and sometimes that means getting it wrong, or finding my own way to the solution."

This kind of response invariably brought Jack's eyes to Jenna's—such clarity and wisdom in one so young.

Paige had always loved to work things out for herself, whether a jigsaw puzzle as a toddler, new words in her storybooks as she started to read, or the complex challenges of the chemistry lab or maths class in school. These were the only two subjects at which she didn't do quite so well. Even so, her eagerness to grasp what was eluding her made Jenna worry at times for how hard she drove herself.

Still, she seemed well balanced, and had continued to thrive in spite of the life-changing move Jenna and Jack had decided on just over a year ago. It had been one of their biggest worries at the time, how it would affect their teenage daughter to be plucked from the heart of everything and everyone she knew to begin a completely new life in a country she'd only ever visited for a couple of weeks each summer.

Not such a very different country; after all, it was only Wales, where everyone, at least in their part, here on the Gower Peninsula, spoke English, and all the warnings of how insular and unwelcoming the Welsh could be to outsiders had proved total nonsense. Their neighbors could hardly be any friendlier, at least to them; the way they sometimes carried on with each other made Jenna wonder if she'd stumbled into the village of Llareggub, the infamous setting for *Under Milk Wood*.

This was a favorite book of hers, and recently of Paige's since it had become a set piece for her subject achievement exams, the GCSEs. As it was Dylan Thomas's centenary year, the whole region was celebrating his life and works in one way or another, and Paige had been chosen by her English teacher to take the part of First Voice in a school production to be staged at the Dylan Thomas Centre in Swansea. Such an honor had never been bestowed upon a female student before, but Miss Kendrick was of the opinion that Paige's understanding and enjoyment of the play made her such an obvious choice that she'd added Second Voice to the part as well. Since the casting Jenna and Paige had spent many hours listening to Richard Burton's famous performance, taking it line by line, nuance by nuance, getting to the heart of why he'd spoken, whispered, or growled in a certain way, and what he might have been thinking when observing the many oddities of the characters in the piece.

To say Paige was excited about taking this part was an understatement indeed. Drama was her thing; she loved to act, and this role was her biggest challenge yet. And she was going to be playing it not only in Wales but in Dylan Thomas's hometown.

As a family, they were loving being here, there was no doubt about that. In fact, in spite of not being Welsh—apart from through Jenna's father—it felt as though they were exactly where they belonged. However, it hadn't been their intention to move here after Jack had lost his job as the sales manager for a leading publisher. Their initial plan was for him to find another position in a similar field, but unfortunately it hadn't worked out that way. The industry was suffering. Dozens if not hundreds of people had been laid off across the country, and competition for the few positions that did come up was fierce. After Jack had suffered through months of nothing but apologies and rejection, his notoriously volatile temper had collapsed into a horrible despair. He stopped attending interviews, found it hard to engage with the children, and even turned his back on the easy and passionate intimacy he and Jenna had always shared. Despite his tendency to overreact, it had unnerved her considerably to see how hard he was taking his failure to start again. When things were going his way he was ebullient, larger than life, ready to meet any challenge head on with a certainty that he'd win. Over that time she'd felt him slipping away, diminishing in spirit and hope, and it had scared her. The Jack she knew and loved was still in there, she'd remained convinced of that, but reaching him, bolstering him, and trying to make him believe in himself again had proved an almost impossible task.

Then one day, without warning, he'd suddenly announced that they should relocate to Wales.

Jenna remembered her jaw dropping.

"We need a completely fresh start," he'd insisted, "with something of our own. We don't want to be at any other bastard's beck and call. We'll be our own bosses, answer only to each other, and when we start to expand, which we will, *we'll* do all the hiring and firing."

Jenna hadn't missed the way her highly successful, career-driven sister and brother-in-law had exchanged glances at this unexpected development. She didn't blame them, as she was skeptical too, but loyalty to Jack, combined with the overwhelming relief that he seemed so determined on this new start, made her say, "I think it's a very interesting idea, but what kind of business do you have in mind?"

"Publishing, of course," he'd replied, as if there could be no other. "Given my own employment history, and yours as a published writer and respected freelance editor, it's all we know, so we need to capitalize. And now, with the Internet, it's never been easier. We can base ourselves anywhere, have a website as big as we like, and sell whatever we choose. No, wait," he ran on as Hanna made to interrupt, "I've given it a lot of thought, and I reckon Wales is definitely the place to be. It's a land full of poets, playwrights, novelists, you name it, and almost none are getting the recognition they deserve."

"Would there be a market for them?" his brother-in-law had asked dubiously.

"Of course, if we present them in the right way. We won't be like all these other Web-based cowboys who make you pay to be published, then do nothing to promote the work. We'll have a totally different approach that deals with only high-quality product—that's where you come in, Jen. You'll be responsible for vetting the submissions and knocking the best ones into shape, and I'll sort out the website and business plan. It shouldn't be expensive to get off the ground, just the cost of designing the site and a few well-placed ads . . . Local media interest is a given, and chances are we won't even need to go to the bank for finance, which we probably wouldn't get anyway given how tight they are these days. We can manage everything ourselves, provided we sell this house. OK, I know that sounds radical, but the market's gone so crazy in London that it's got to be worth at least three times what we paid for it by now, and it's complete madness having it sitting there doing nothing when we could be making it work for us."

"But what about Paige?" Hanna asked, glancing worriedly at her niece.

"I'm cool with it," Paige assured her, apparently as carried away by the idea as her father was. "It'll be an adventure."

Jenna simply watched as Jack pressed a kiss to their elder daughter's forehead. "That's my girl," he laughed. "Never afraid to take a risk, and the younger ones will be fine. They'll settle in no time at all."

"What about you, Jenna?" Hanna ventured.

Deciding this wasn't the time to argue, Jenna had simply said, "I might need a while to get my head round it, but in principle . . ." She shrugged. "Why not?"

That was all it had taken for Jack to spring into action. In no time at all the house was on the market, a new business management team—recommended by Hanna—had assessed the project and helped to obtain funding from the Welsh Arts Council, and ads had gone into the local papers announcing the creation of a new e-publishing venture, Celticulture.

A little over a year later they were ensconced at the southern end of the Gower Peninsula in a ten-year-old detached house designed to resemble a barn conversion, which had to be at least twice the size of the Victorian end-of-terrace they'd owned in London. Instead of a street full of stamp-sized gardens and tightly parked cars, they were at the top of a quaintly sprawled village, overlooking a wild grassy moor that stretched all the way out to Port Eynon Point, where the sea glittered and smudged into an ever-changing horizon.

It was idyllic; "God's own country" was how Jack described it.

"You mean the back end of beyond," Paige sometimes grumbled, but if either Jack or Jenna called her on it, she'd quickly assure them she was only kidding.

"It's really cool," she'd insist. "Different, and a bit weird in some ways, but I can do surfing and stuff here that I could never do in London, and I'm making loads of new friends."

This was true; she'd taken to her new surroundings far better than they'd dared hope, and clearly enjoyed her new school, The Landings. Her new best friend, Charlotte Griffiths, lived barely a mile away, while her other new best friend, Hayley, was in Reynoldston, which wasn't far either. There were many others in their set, as they liked to call it: Lucy, Courtenay, Cullum, Ryan, Owen—Jenna was losing track of them all now, but what mattered was how readily they had accepted Paige and how happy she seemed. She'd even started to develop a hint of a Welsh accent, which Jenna loved to hear. It was so musical and friendly, with playful little inflections that fluttered like tiny wings straight to the very core of her heart.

Her Welsh father had never lost his accent, even after four decades of living in England.

How badly she still missed him; she couldn't imagine a time when she wouldn't. If she concentrated hard enough, she was sure, she could hear him singing, telling stories, whispering comforting words when she needed them. She could see him working in the garden, dozing in his favorite armchair, delighting in his grandchildren, who absolutely adored him. One of the fondest, most moving memories she had of him was the way his face used to light up with surprise and joy when she'd drop in to visit without warning.

"Ah ha!" he'd cry, his arms going out to wrap her up in the warmest, most wonderful hug in the world.

Almost three years had passed since he'd been struck down with a heart attack. He hadn't been ill, hadn't even shown any signs of slowing up or mentioned he was feeling unwell. He'd simply collapsed one day at the office and had never come home. It was like a cruel magician's trick: one minute he was there, the next he'd gone. She, Hanna, and their mother were still a long way from coming to terms with the loss.

Thinking of him now, as she often did in quiet moments, she hoped that wherever he was, he knew that she was living in

Wales. She could see his twinkly eyes shining with delight to realize that she'd returned to his roots. It would give him so much pleasure, especially since her mother had moved into a cottage at the heart of the village. Knowing him, he'd have wholeheartedly approved of Jack's plans for the new business, and would probably even have got involved in some way if he could.

Stirring as the next-door neighbors' cat jumped down onto the lawn, circling the children's trampoline, slide, and two-story playhouse before disappearing over the wall into the moorland, Jenna glanced at the blank screen of her laptop and gave a sigh of dismay.

"Take this time for yourself," Jack had told her after depositing the younger children at their friends' homes earlier, and before he and Paige had set off on their shoot. "We'll be gone for a few hours, so sit with it, see what happens. I bet something will."

He was wrong. Nothing was happening at all.

It never did these days, and she was annoyed with herself now for hoping that today might prove any different, when she knew very well that a creative flow couldn't just be turned on and off like a tap.

She was experiencing—*suffering* would be a better choice of word—a prolonged spell of writer's block, though she deliberately didn't call it that. She preferred telling herself that the story wasn't quite ready to be told yet, or the characters were still making up their minds which directions to take. It would help, a lot, if she actually knew what the story was about—or, more significantly, *whom* it was about—but she really didn't. It was as though she'd been abandoned by her own imagination. Actually, there was no "as though" about it—she *had* been abandoned by her imagination. It had run for cover following the awful reviews for her last book, taking the best part of her confidence with it.

However, blaming a handful of critics for a book that she'd known, even when she'd delivered it, wasn't as good as her best-selling first was hardly going to help get her past this crisis. Nor was the fact that her agent had recently reminded her that the publisher would be asking for a return of the advance if she didn't send something in soon.

So here she was, facing the happy prospect of having to repay something in the region of twenty thousand pounds in the next couple of months unless she could come up with a synopsis at the very least. Since this wasn't a sum she could possibly raise, and the only words she'd been able to conjure so far were "Chapter One," things weren't looking good.

In truth, the situation might not have felt quite so desperate if they hadn't spent virtually everything they had on setting up here. Jack's severance pay, her advance, the small inheritance she'd received from her father, and most of the proceeds from their London house had all gone into creating their new life. She couldn't deny they'd been extravagant, paying for the house outright, buying themselves a new car each—a flashy coupe for her and Jack, a sturdy dog-and-people-carrier for the family—and getting the children basically anything they wanted, including computers, iPads, iPhones, PlayStations, smart TVs, scooters, bicycles, and tree houses. There was even a jukebox in the sitting room, along with a pinball machine and a giant rocking horse Jack had won in a raffle. Jenna wasn't sure how low their funds were running these days, but she suspected it was lower than Jack was ready to admit.

"The business is due to launch in a month," he'd reminded

her only this morning, "at which point cash will start rolling in and we'll be sitting pretty again. Better than that, we'll be able to send a check to your publisher, leaving you free to write and deliver just when you want to. It'll probably turn out to be exactly what you need to get the juices flowing. No more deadlines, no nasty phone calls—just you, your characters, and all the time you could wish for to go on all the journeys you're dreaming about."

Time—a commodity virtually unknown to busy mothers, particularly those with three children under eight, each of whom had a character, set of needs, and schedule all their own, and a teenage live wire who'd lately started showing signs of a maturity that Jenna knew she should have been prepared for but wasn't.

Picking up her mobile as it bleeped with a text, she smiled to see the photo Jack had sent of Paige peering into a rock pool with her latest admirer, Owen Masters. *Should I be jealous?* Jack was asking.

I don't think so, Jenna texted back. *Will tell you more when you get back. How's it going?*

Shot enough for another feature film. Heading up to Arthur's Stone now. How about you?

How she longed to say she was on a roll, but even if she did, he'd know as soon as he looked into her eyes when he came back that it wasn't true. *Wondering if senna pods might help,* she replied, and smiled as she imagined him laughing.

A few minutes later the landline rang; glad of the excuse to leave her computer, she went through to the kitchen to answer.

"Hi, it's me," her sister declared. "Hang on, sorry, I'll be right with you."

Tucking the phone under her chin as she waited, Jenna

reached for the kettle to fill it. How she loved this kitchen! What luxury it was to have so much space to cook and socialize and watch the kids come and go. The house was just perfect; she couldn't love it more if she'd designed it herself, with its floor-to-ceiling windows all across the back to take in the garden and the view beyond, its characterful reclaimed beams through most of the rooms, and the highly polished sandstone floors.

The dining room was more like a conservatory off the kitchen, with French doors leading onto the garden, while the sitting room was her dream of how a sitting room should be, with an open stone fireplace at the far end, deep-cushioned sofas, tatty rugs, and endless clutter. The mess never bothered her; on the contrary, she rejoiced in it, which she knew was a reaction to all the years of having to live with her mother's obsession with order. Trails of toys, shoes, books, crayons—everything and anything—led off the sitting room into the playroom, and very often up the stairs to the bedrooms, where another sort of chaos reigned. Jenna and Jack's master suite was to the left of the three-sided gantry landing and was almost never off-limits. Josh's room was next to theirs and was poised to become sleepover central just as soon as the painfully shy Josh plucked up the courage to invite more than one friend at a time. Paige's own small suite was opposite and very definitely off-limits. The twins' room was next to Paige's, with a pink half for Flora and a blue one for Wills. From the landing that ran across the tall back windows it was possible to look down into the sitting room or to stand gazing out at the mesmerizing view—if anyone had the time, which they rarely did.

Even on gloomy days their house felt full of light, while on clear days it was possible to see all the way across the Channel to Exmoor. There was no sign of a distant land today, and hadn't been since long before Christmas.

"Are you there?" Hanna said breathlessly. "Sorry about that. The cat was on the windowsill. I thought she was about to jump. So how are you?"

"Great. How about you?"

"Frazzled, as usual. Got a deadline we have to meet by to-morrow. How's the weather down there? It's miserable here in London."

"It's just started raining again."

Sighing, Hanna said, "That's all it's done for months. I pity those poor people who've been flooded. This must be a never-ending nightmare for them."

"A couple of houses at the beach have lost their gardens," Jenna told her. "Jack reckons their foundations too, but no one's been in yet to check."

"That's terrible. Are they holiday homes?"

"Yes, I think so. Huge chunks of the seawall were smashed apart, so they didn't stand a chance, and you should see the muck the tide's washed up. The beach is like a rubbish dump at the moment. Anyway, I'm sure you didn't ring to discuss that."

"You're right, I didn't. I've just spoken to Mum. Have you seen her today?"

"No, but Jack dropped in on his way back from the shop this morning. She was all right then. Why do you ask?"

"She's just told me that she's going to start taking in washing and ironing."

Jenna's eyes twinkled.

"I've no idea where this ridiculous idea has come from," Hanna went on, "but I'm guessing she read it somewhere or maybe saw it on TV."

"She's just started *The Book Thief*," Jenna told her. "The foster mother's a laundress who also has a foul mouth, so let's hope no one round here speaks German."

"Oh, please no," Hanna groaned. "Do you think she means it? She's not really going to take in other people's washing, is she?"

Knowing how unlikely it was, Jenna grinned as she said, "I guess we'll find out soon enough."

Hanna sighed. "Do you think we ought to get her to see someone?"

"You won't have forgotten what happened the last time we tried. . . ."

"You mean the hunger strike?"

"And it's not as though there's anything actually wrong with her."

"She's just her own person," Hanna said, quoting their father, "and maybe a little bit on the autism spectrum. If you ask me, she's that, all right. Is she keeping to her diet?"

"Religiously. Everything organic, gluten-free, no refined sugars or artificial colorings . . . It takes forever going round the supermarket with her, and she's always online ordering some supplement or other. God knows how much good it's all doing."

"What matters to her is that Daddy put the diet together. She'll be on it now till the day she dies—or loses her marbles completely. Anyway, tell me about you. What's new in your world?"

As they chattered on, catching up on each other's lives, as they often did on a Sunday, Jenna watched the rain growing heavier, pulling a thick gray veil between the moor and the sea. Fortunately, the wind was nowhere near as violent as it had been over the past few weeks; if it had been, there was no way

Jack and Paige could have been out in it. During the worst of the storms they'd been forced to bring all the computers and company paperwork over to the house just in case their garden office got carried off by a particularly lively gust. Luckily, it had remained anchored to its spot, though a window had been smashed by a flying branch (already repaired by one of Jack's mates from the pub), and the stone path leading across the grass to its door had been washed away twice (both times reinstated by Jack himself).

"So you're still on schedule for the launch?" Hanna remembered to ask before ringing off.

"Absolutely," Jenna confirmed. "Putting us in touch with Martha Gwynne and her business management team was the best thing you ever did for us. She's amazing. Just wait till you see the website they've come up with. And they're full of ideas about how they're going to promote and market us."

"I'm thrilled she's working out so well. As a business consultant, she's one of the best, and it's lucky for you she's based in Swansea."

"And London. I think she's there most of the time, with a manager running things here, but as far as I'm aware, nothing gets finalized without her approval."

"Sounds like Martha. She has a home near you, hasn't she?"

"On the outskirts of Horton. You should see it. She invited us to a party there about a month ago. . . . I told you, didn't I?"

"You did, and the place is utterly amazing, with tennis courts, a pool, and its own stretch of beach. That'll tell you how successful she is, and how lucky you are that she took you on."

Jenna smiled. "Believe it or not, I think she likes working with us. Apparently we're not as demanding as most of her clients, or as egotistical or unrealistic. She's invited me for lunch a couple of times, as friends, but for one reason or another it hasn't worked out yet."

"I'm sure it will. She's a very easygoing sort, a refreshing change to all those executive females who take themselves so seriously—I admit I probably have to include myself in that. Anyway, how about the literary content for your new site? How's that coming along?"

"Actually, brilliantly. I'm being constantly surprised by how much real talent there is out there, and word is definitely spreading about us. Hardly a day goes by now when we don't get a new submission, and at least half the contributors are willing to be edited."

"So you've got your work cut out? How much are you charging for the editing?"

"It depends if it's full-on plot and character editing or just sorting out the spelling and grammar. The prices are very reasonable, though, and you don't have to pay anything at all if you just want to list your work. Obviously we have to vet those first to make sure they're not obscene or completely unreadable."

"So remind me again how you're going to make money."

"From the editing, like I just said, and advertising—Jack has done wonders with that locally, everyone from Howells the mobile butcher to some high-flying holiday rental company to the Film Agency for Wales has already bought space. Martha's team is handling the national campaign. I'm a bit vague about the details of that, but I think they're about to schedule a presentation to bring us all up to speed. Oh, and let's not forget that we're only taking a twenty percent commission on downloads; the other eighty goes straight to the author. Amazon takes seventy percent, and good luck getting noticed on their site. As a contributor, you're a dust speck in a busy vac, to use one of Mum's jolly little phrases. Anyway, I've just heard a car pull up, so it could be Jack and Paige are back. They'll be drenched, and I don't even want to think about the state the dog must be in. I'll call later to get more of your news."

After ringing off she quickly unlocked the utility room door, dumped an armful of towels next to the sink, and was about to run upstairs to start a bath for Paige—Jack always took showers—when her mother let herself in the front door.

"Didn't you hear me knocking?" Kay Roberts demanded in her usual clipped way. Her neat gray hair was glistening with raindrops, while the expression on her small, elfin face was caught in what looked like a dilemma, as though she couldn't quite decide whether or not to be cross. At almost seventy she was still an attractive woman, with a faintly lined complexion and quick, watchful eyes that were almost the same vivid green as those of her daughters.

"Sorry, I was in the utility," Jenna told her, turning back from the stairs. "Close the door, you're—"

"Yes, yes. Why wasn't it locked?"

"I thought it was."

"It doesn't need to be around here, you know. It's perfectly safe. They don't have any crime."

"No, of course not," Jenna agreed, knowing it was always best not to argue with her mother's version of facts. "The latch is a bit loose, so I didn't want the wind to blow it open. Anyway, I hear you're planning to take in laundry."

Kay stopped unzipping her lime-green raincoat, her sharp eyes shooting to Jenna's. "You've been talking to your sister. You know her trouble? She doesn't get a joke when she hears one."

Jenna's eyebrows rose. "Maybe it's the way you tell them."

Kay regarded her carefully.

"So, would you like a cup of tea?" Jenna asked, going back to the kitchen. "We've still got some of the fairy cakes the Brownies brought round on Friday if you want one."

"I believe they were very good," Kay called after her, "but I'll have one of my own, thank you. Where is everyone?"

"Josh and the twins are with friends; Jack and Paige are out making films. Actually, that sounds like them now. Would you mind going up to run a bath for Paige? But don't put any bubbles in—she likes to choose her own."

"Am I allowed into her bedroom? I can't get to her bathroom otherwise."

"On this occasion I'm sure she won't mind."

"You were always a secretive one too," Kay commented as she started up the stairs. "You made your father put a padlock on your door once."

"I can hear you," Jenna called after her.

"You're supposed to."

"And it was to keep Hanna out, not you. She was always stealing my stuff."

"Actually, it was me," Kay informed her. "We were the same size. Hanna's bigger."

Suspecting this was more of her mother's peculiar humor, Jenna pulled open the utility room door and quickly leapt back as a dog she barely recognized as Waffle, their daft golden Lab, skidded past to his drink bowl.

"Hey, Mum," Paige cried, bursting in after him. "It is totally crap out there. We're drenched right through. Is Grandma here?"

"Upstairs running you a bath. You need to get out of those wet clothes."

"I know, I know." Tugging down her hood to shake out her damp, wavy dark hair, she clicked on her mobile to read an incoming text.

"Where's Dad?" Jenna asked, grabbing the dog before he could spread the mud from his paws all over the kitchen floor.

"Still in the car, on the phone," Paige answered. "Please tell me you haven't eaten all the Brownies' cakes. I'm starving."

"There are a few left." Banging on the window to get Jack's attention, Jenna mouthed, "The dog!"

"Coming," he mouthed back from the driver's seat.

"Who's he talking to?" Jenna demanded.

"No idea. What shall I do with my coat?"

"Hang it next to the radiator, and put your wellies next to mine. With any luck Dad will clean them after he's finished with the dog. Waffle, will you please sit down?"

With instant obedience Waffle slumped to the floor and rolled onto his back for a belly rub.

"Dream on," Jenna commented as Paige laughed.

"You are too adorable," Paige told him. "No," she cried as he kicked at her legs. "I'm not touching you either. Oh God, look what you've done to my jeans."

"It's not like they don't already need a wash," Jenna pointed out. "Now give him a treat, then make sure he stays in here until Dad sorts him out."

A few moments later Paige came padding into the kitchen in wet socks, once again engrossed in her mobile phone. Her long, matted hair was hanging on either side of her pixie face, shielding the screen from any POS—parent over shoulder—advances.

"What happened to Owen?" Jenna asked. "Wasn't he with you?"

"Mm?" Paige responded without looking up. "Oh, Dad just

dropped him home. Thanks," she added as Jenna passed her a cake.

"Do you want a plate, Paige?" Kay asked, coming to join them.

"No, this is cool," Paige replied, blithely dropping crumbs over her front and the worktop.

"So have you decided what to do about Owen?" Jenna ventured.

Paige frowned in annoyance. "What about him?" she demanded, as if the conversation they'd had only that morning had never happened.

"You mentioned earlier that he was interested in—"

"He's *gay*, Mum!"

"So you said."

"And he hasn't come out yet, OK? I don't think he's even admitting it to himself, but no way am I making out like we're in a relationship just so no one'll suspect the truth."

"You're too young to be in a relationship with anyone," Kay informed her.

Paige's eyes darkened. "Grandma! I'm fifteen, for God's sake."

Kay nodded. "Yes, you are," she agreed, as if that were the topic at issue. "You know, your grandfather loved Dylan Thomas."

Paige looked at her mother.

"Where did that come from?" Jenna asked Kay.

"I saw the book on Paige's desk," Kay replied.

"You've been in my room?" Paige cried. "What were you doing?"

"You see, I told you I wasn't allowed," Kay informed Jenna. "A red circle with a white dash in the middle means no entry."

"I already told you, she was running you a bath," Jenna said to Paige. "Now you should go up before it overflows."

"Can I have another cake?"

"You'll get fat," Kay warned.

"Mum, look at her," Jenna cried. "She's barely a size six as it is. I don't want you turning her into an anorexic."

"Don't talk about me as if I weren't here," Paige retorted, "and FYI, I'm planning on being a size four by the end of this term."

"I hope you don't mean that."

Paige flashed her a smile. Helping herself to another cake, she took a bite, put the rest back on the plate, and made as if to give her grandma a hug, giggling as Kay instinctively drew back. "Oh, scary granddaughter trying to give Granny a kiss," Paige teased.

"Don't be unkind," Jenna chided. Paige knew very well that Kay had a problem with physical contact, and it really wasn't like Paige to be cruel.

"OK, I know where I'm not wanted," Paige told them. Grabbing the cake, she took herself off upstairs.

"I know it's her age," Jenna said quietly once she'd heard Paige's door close behind her, "but her attitude sometimes—"

"Is just like yours when you were fifteen," Kay interrupted. "And Hanna's, although she was worse."

"She was so sweet this morning," Jenna continued with a sigh. "We had a lovely chat while Jack was out getting the papers, and now . . ." She shrugged helplessly. "I never seem to know where I am with her. I don't think she's like that with Jack, or not so much anyway."

"You were never like it with your father, only me," Kay informed her.

Jenna avoided her eyes. *Not nearly as difficult as you always were with us,* she managed not to say.

"Ah, that sounds like Jack coming in," Kay remarked. "I'll go and give him a hand."

Watching her bustle off to make herself useful, Jenna found herself feeling suddenly sad. Having Kay as a mother, with all her awkwardness and lack of social skills, had never been easy, but that didn't mean there was no love between them. She knew, mainly because her father had helped her and Hanna to understand, that in her own special way her mother was every bit as devoted to them as he was. It was simply that Kay had never been able to show her feelings in the way other mothers could—or wives, come to that, although her father had remained silent about that. All she and Hanna knew was that he'd always seemed very happy with their mother, and throughout the thirty years they were married they'd never spent much more than a night apart. And a very real intimacy must have happened at least twice, or she and Hanna wouldn't be there.

Looking round at the sound of the utility room door opening, she broke into a smile as Jack emerged, dark hair mussed by a vigorous rub with the towel, and cheeks still reddened from the wind. Though it would be hard for most to describe him as TDD, as Paige would put it—totally drop-dead—Jenna had never had a problem with that. As far as she was concerned, he was just perfect, with his wonderfully flamboyant air, constantly merry eyes, and the kind of charm that stole hearts wherever he went.

"So have you seen any of what we shot?" he asked, hauling the dog back as it made a dash for anywhere but the utility. "You have to wait in there till you're dry," he instructed Waffle.

"We got some really good stuff again, and she's a natural with the commentary."

"She's gone to have a bath," Jenna told him. "I'll see it later. Who were you on the phone to?"

"When? Oh, just now." He came to help himself to a cake and gave her a quick kiss before popping it in his mouth. "I'm thinking of going over to Cardiff again tomorrow," he said, hovering in the doorway on his way to take a shower. "I need to go to the bank, and while I'm there I thought I'd try to line up a few more advertisers. Anything you need while I'm over that way?"

"You mean apart from a few good ideas? Actually, one would do."

"You can't buy ideas," Kay announced, drying her hands as she came out of the utility.

Treating Jenna to a playful wink, Jack took himself off upstairs, leaving her to watch her mother staring after him. "What?" she prompted as Kay turned back to her.

"He didn't answer your question," Kay informed her.

Jenna almost asked, *What question?* But since she knew, and really didn't want to get into it with her mother, she simply said, "It wasn't important."

Upstairs in her room with butterfly lights glowing round the bed's fancy headrail and the Vamps' "Last Night" pulsing from the iPod speakers, Paige was in front of her computer, wrapped in her dressing gown while FaceTiming Charlotte.

"So did you manage to shoot much?" Charlotte was asking as she rubbed a purplish face mask over her troubled complexion.

"Yeah, loads. Have you finished yours yet?"

"No. I should have come with you, but then we'd have ended up with everything the same. So Owen showed up, you said in your text."

Jenna sighed. " 'Fraid so. I mean, I really like him and everything, but he's so, like . . . you know. What's that stuff you're using?"

Charlotte held up the tube and read from the back. "Apparently it contains antimicrobial willow bark, mango, and blueberry to minimize blemishes and to clear away excess sebum."

"Excess what?"

"Sebum," Charlotte giggled. Turning around, she wiggled her bottom in front of the camera.

"I am *soooo* glad you're wearing knickers," Paige laughed.

"Be grateful. Oh my God! That reminds me. Have you seen the latest episode of *The Valleys* yet? It is totally insane. That girl—you know, the one who looks like Kelly Durham? I forget her name. Anyway, she only took her knickers off in the middle of a nightclub."

Paige pulled a gagging face.

"Just what I thought," Charlotte assured her, "but I can't stop watching it. So, what are you doing later? Do you want to come over?"

"Would love to, but I've still got loads of homework to get through. Have you done the geography stuff about ecosystems yet?"

"Yep. You'll sail through it, provided you get the answer to question one right, which is seaweed. English is more Dylan Thomas, so no problem for you there. Maths is going to totally fuck with your head, but when does it ever not? And business studies is starting to really piss me off. Let me know how you get on with all the crap about sourcing finance—I could do with some help."

"Like I'm going to know."

"Bet you do."

"Yeah, right. So I'll see you at the bus stop in the morning?"

"Worse luck. Let me know if you hear from Oliver before that."

Paige's insides melted to liquid. "Don't," she groaned plaintively. "No way am I going to hear from him. He doesn't even know I'm alive."

"Course he does."

"Course he doesn't, unless . . . Oh my God, Charlotte, you haven't told Cullum? He's his *brother*. He'll—"

"Give me a break! Would I do that to you? I'm just saying, I reckon he's interested."

"He's eighteen."

"And?"

"And he's going out with Lindsay French."

"I heard he's chucked her. I'll try to find out."

"No! You can't ask Cullum!"

"Is that what I said?"

"You don't know anyone else to ask, and if Oliver finds out we're, like, *stalking* him . . . Oh God, I'll want to kill myself."

Laughing, Charlotte said, "I've got to go and wash this stuff off. I'll speak to you later."

As the line cleared, Paige dropped her head in her hands and groaned again. *Oliver. Oliver. Oliver.* She could hardly stop thinking about him. It was like she was becoming obsessed, and she'd never even spoken to him, for God's sake. Had only really seen him twice. He'd noticed her, though, last Saturday, when a crowd of them had gone to support the Swansea College rugby team against Worcester. He had looked so totally drop-dead in all his gear that she'd nearly fainted.

Maybe she had, because she couldn't remember anything that happened after he'd caught her eye.

Chances were he'd been looking at someone behind her.

Or maybe he'd spotted her and something had happened for him too. He might, even now, be wondering who she was, trying to think of a way to ask his younger brother about the girl he'd brought to the game. . . .

She had to stop thinking about him, get him out of her mind before she ended up making a total idiot of herself. He was three years older than her, for God's sake, and was so completely out of her league that it would be like pairing Zayn Malik up with Ugly Betty. Not that she was anything like Ugly Betty, who in real life was a total babe, which *she* definitely was not. Besides, there couldn't be a girl alive who didn't have the hots for Oliver Pryce; he could have his pick of anyone, and though it made her want to die just to think of it, she knew in her heart that he'd never choose her.

Remembering her bath, and feeling a dizzying rush of excitement at the thought of Oliver coming to watch her, she was about to get up from the computer when someone instant-messaged her.

Hey. Can you talk?

Frowning, she looked at the name. *Julie Morris.* She couldn't think of anyone called that. *I'm cool. Do I know you?* she typed back.

Is it true about you and Owen Masters? the sender asked.

Paige frowned as her pulse started to drop back to normal. *Tell me who you are,* she typed back.

I'm a friend.

But I don't know your name. Do you go to The Landings?
Yes.
Which year?
Same as you.
So Julie Morris isn't your real name?
I'm not supposed to go on chat rooms and stuff so I've made up this name in case my parents check. Long story. Will share if we become friends.

Intrigued, Paige asked, *So why do you want to know about Owen?*
Just interested. Do you like him?
He's OK.
I think you should go out with him.

Whoever this girl was, she obviously didn't realize Owen was gay, and no way was Paige about to tell her. *He's not really my type.*
So who is?
That would be telling.
Does he go to our school?
No. Do you have a boyfriend?
No. Thanks for the chat, have to go now.

Paige blinked as the connection ended, and started going through everyone she could think of in her year who could be Julie Morris, but couldn't come up with a single one who'd ever said she wasn't allowed to go on chat rooms at home. On the other hand, the girl might not want to admit it to anyone, and Paige supposed she didn't blame her for that. Whatever, it was the girl's call, and since Paige could hear Josh and the twins running up the stairs shouting her name, she quickly shot into her bathroom and locked the door.

Chapter 2

"Are you OK?" Jenna asked, glancing at Jack as they strolled along the beach at Port Eynon.

"Sure. Why wouldn't I be?" he replied, slipping an arm around her.

"I just wondered. You seem a bit . . . distracted. I thought you might have something on your mind."

He pulled a face as though considering the possibility. "No more than usual," he assured her.

She wondered whether to broach the subject of their finances, but simply watched him stoop to pick up Waffle's ball and hurl it up into the dunes. As the dog bounded after it her phone bleeped with a text.

Forgot to bring my dinner money. Px

Sighing, she showed the message to Jack. "She left in such a hurry this morning. . . ."

"Tell her I'll pop it in on my way past," he said.

After relaying the message Jenna linked her arm with his as they strolled on, taking in the bracing air and watching the lively break of the waves. Back at the house the kitchen was still in chaos after breakfast, all the beds needed making, and there was a pile of ironing that could take her all week to get through—it wasn't going anywhere, so she'd tackle it all when they got home. More important was spending this rare time together with no one else around.

Reaching for his phone as it rang, he clicked on without checking who it was.

"Jack Moore speaking," he announced cheerfully. "If you're trying to sell me something . . ." The voice at the other end stopped him, and after a moment he laughed as he turned his back to the wind. "Sorry, Martha. Sure, it's OK to talk. I'm just out walking the dog. What's up? Or hang on, I can't hear you properly in this gale. Can I find some shelter and call you back in a few minutes?"

As he rang off Jenna said, "It'll be about the website."

He was frowning thoughtfully as he nodded. "I expect you're right," he agreed. "Do you want to go on? I'll meet you back at the car."

Looking down at Waffle, who was eagerly snatching up and dropping the ball at their feet, she said, "I'll take him as far as the Salt House."

Jack glanced ahead to where the five-hundred-year-old ruin sat forlornly on the edge of the seawall, an old-timer not quite able to yield to obscurity. "No farther," he cautioned, "the tide's on its way in."

"No farther," she promised, and after telling him to send Martha her love, she used the ChuckIt! Josh had given Waffle for Christmas to fling the ball hard along the beach, sending it soaring past the old lifeboat slipway and on past the storm-damaged cottages to where Sam Thomas, one of their neighbors, was walking his springer, Dylan.

"Meet Dylan Thomas," he'd say to anyone taking an interest

in the dog. "He's not much good at poetry yet, but he's definitely got the hang of the pub."

After giving them a wave, Jenna turned to watch Jack striding over the rocky sand back toward the port. It was a shame Martha had rung when she had. It wasn't often they found time to walk together in the mornings. When they did, it invariably got the day off to a good start, though she had to admit most days had turned out to be good since they'd been here.

It had a lot to do, she was thinking as she turned to walk on, with being in an Area of Outstanding Natural Beauty. "What's not to love?" she'd often remark. She'd learned from her father, a long time ago, that the Gower Peninsula had been the first place in all of Britain to be awarded the highly prized accolade. And really it was no surprise, for with its dramatically rolling moors and marshes, rambling stone villages and centuries-old chapels, all hemmed in by miles of golden sand and spectacular coastline, it was more than a feast for the senses; it was a wonder, a fantasy even, come to life.

Sadly, since the winter storms the coast had not been at its best, with the dunes ravaged by apocalyptic waves, tons of sand sucked away into the sea, and more rubbish on the shores than could be found in the tip over at Sketty.

The kids were enthralled by the booty the tide washed up, and had even talked their father into sending for metal detectors to help them track down treasure. They hadn't had much luck so far, but all three young ones remained determined to discover something as historically amazing as the two Napoleonic cannons that had turned up in Porthcawl, or the ten-thousand-year-old forest uncovered at Newgale.

Bracing herself as her mobile rang, certain it was going to be the twins' school since Wills had thrown up before Jack had whisked them off this morning, she saw it was Verbena, her friend, neighbor, and trusted editorial assistant, and readily clicked on.

"Jenna, I'm sorry, I won't be able to come in today," Bena apologized in her usual harassed way. "I've just had a call from the school. Looks like our Aiden's gone and broken his arm, so I'm on my way to the hospital. I feel like I bloody live there with that boy, I swear I do. This is the third time in as many months that we've been at the emergency room with him."

"How did he do it?" Jenna wondered, relieved that it wasn't her own accident-prone eight-year-old, though sorry for Bena.

"Apparently he fell off a desk. Don't ask me what he was doing up there in the first place, because I don't know, but he'll have been up to no good, that's for sure. Just wait till his father hears about it—he'll probably break the other bloody arm knowing him."

Unable not to laugh, Jenna said, "Well, if there's anything I can do . . ."

"Oh no, you're fine, thanks. I know how much you've got on with your own little hellers, and with the launch coming up, so I'll be back tomorrow."

"But if he can't go to school . . ."

"He's going, whether he wants to or not, and he will if he has a cast on his arm. Besides, I'm not letting you down at this crucial time, and I have to admit we need the money."

Inwardly grimacing at the pittance they paid her, Jenna said, "I promise you'll get an increase as soon as we can manage it."

"I know that, and really it's not why I'm doing it. It's bloody wonderful getting my head round all those poems and short stories and the like. I thought I was never going to use my brain again after I became a mother. Anyway, I'll call later to update you."

After clicking off Jenna decided now was probably as good a time as any to start taking the beach shots Paige had felt were missing when they'd sat down last night to review yesterday's shoot. Some of the sequences had been highly entertaining, especially those that Owen must have captured, since they featured Paige and/or Jack pretending to be smugglers, or Druid bards, or creatures of the Tylwth Teg.

Consummate actors, the pair of them.

"Just get me some stills of the rocks and seashells," Paige had instructed before leaving that morning. "Nothing fancy— I only need them to remind me of shapes and colors and stuff. Oh, and if you can hold the phone up to record a couple of minutes of the sound of the waves, that would be brilliant."

"Anything else, Mr. de Mille?"

"What?"

"Never mind. Sounds like you're making an epic."

"I might be." Treating each parent to an airy kiss, she'd swept out of the door, heavy book bag on her back, phone in one hand, slice of toast in the other, and Flora screaming a tantrum in her wake about wanting white bread in her lunch box, not brown.

After capturing what she hoped would satisfy her elder daughter and throwing the ball a few more times for an indefatigable Waffle, Jenna turned back toward the port, her mind starting to empty of family affairs and fill with her professional commitments for the day ahead. Emails, Facebook, Twitter, LinkedIn, and the regular post would probably take up most of the morning—she should also check Bena's terminal to see if anything needed urgent attention there. She must then call one of their more prolific short-story writers from Fishguard to discuss his latest contribution, which luckily needed very little work. He'd be happy to hear that. Not so happy would be the first-time novelist whose third draft required even more cuts than she'd already agreed to, so Jenna wouldn't be surprised if the ex-headmistress put her foot down and withdrew her work. It would be a pity if she did, not only because she showed real promise as a writer, but also because she had an extremely engaging Jean Brodie–ish tale on her hands, with a strong central character and a dry humor that should help her book to sell very well. They just needed to get the pacing and structure sorted out, add a little more punch to the denouement, and they should be there.

If only she could make some progress with her own work. Maybe she was a better editor than she was a writer.

A few minutes later she hooked Waffle onto his lead and walked him up into the center of Port Eynon. Since this consisted of one small roundabout, the Seafarer fish-and-chip shop, the Captain's Cabin café, and a gift shop, there was no problem spotting the car. It was the only vehicle in sight.

Oddly, though, there was no sign of Jack.

Looking up and down the dunes, then across to the main car park and seafront campsite, both of which were deserted, she decided he must have either popped into the gents' or been waylaid by one of the villagers.

After waiting a few minutes she took out her phone to call him. "Jack, where are you?" she asked his voicemail. "I'm at the car and can't get in."

When there was no immediate call back she began wandering up through the whitewashed cottages toward the church, where the towering statue of a lifeboatman held endless fascination for the children. She glanced at the Smuggler's Haunt as she passed, but it was closed at this time of year, so she hadn't expected to see anyone there. A little farther on was the turning to the Ship, where Jack occasionally went for a pint and chat with some of the locals. Though it seemed unlikely he'd be there now, she walked the twenty or so yards to check, and found that the doors were firmly locked and no lights were on inside.

Baffled, and not sure whether to be worried or annoyed with him since it was starting to rain, she retraced her steps to the car.

"Jack, where the heck are you?" she demanded into his voicemail. "Call me back now. I need to get home."

"Thanks, that's really kind of you," Paige was saying as Charlotte handed over enough cash to pay for both their lunches. "I thought Dad would've been here by now. I suppose he forgot. Typical. They're so wrapped up in the business now that the rest of us could leave home or become famous and they probably wouldn't notice."

"Think of the freedom," Charlotte reminded her. "And don't worry about the money. You can always pay me back tomorrow. Where shall we sit?"

As she and Paige searched the crowded canteen someone suddenly bumped Paige from behind and sent her plate flying off the tray.

"Oh my God, I am *sooooooo* sorry," Kelly Durham cried in a tone that made sure everyone knew she was anything but. With her perfectly round face, eyelash extensions, piercings, tattoos, and dyed blond hair, Kelly was an arresting-looking girl ("common as muck" was how Charlotte usually described her; "a right slapper" or "fat cow" was what others said, though not one would have had the nerve to utter it to her face). What everyone knew about Kelly was that she was part of the famous Durham family from the Killay area of Swansea—not exactly posh, but definitely not as downbeat as some parts—and no one, but no one, ever messed with the Durhams.

Paige's eyes went to Charlotte, whose cheeks had turned as crimson as her own. She could feel everyone turning to look at her, waiting to see what she'd do.

"Fight, fight, fight," a year nine boy shouted from a nearby table, banging it with his fists and stamping his feet.

Having zero intention of getting into any kind of scuffle with Kelly, who not only was bigger but had a ready army of supporters at her side—the Durmites, as they were known—Paige simply got down on her knees to start clearing up the mess.

"Tell me, Paige," Kelly said in her singsongy voice, "how's your gimpy boyfriend these days?"

Since Lee Forest, a boy with a limp she'd once defended while he was being picked on by Kelly, had left the school soon after the incident, Paige had no idea how he was, though she wouldn't have answered anyway.

"Is it true," Kelly continued, "that you've been calling me names?"

Paige's heart turned over.

"We heard she had, didn't we?" Kelly enquired of her acolytes.

"Yes, that's definitely what we heard," Bethany Gates confirmed.

"So do you want to call me these names to my face?" Kelly invited Paige.

Feeling the heat of fear and humiliation burning through her, Paige carried on clearing up her meal, half expecting to be kicked at any moment.

"Seems like she doesn't have the guts," someone sneered.

"I never called you names," Paige said as the others began clucking and calling her chicken.

"What was that?" Kelly asked. "Did it say something?"

"TA! TA!" someone hissed. Teacher alert.

As Kelly's crowd moved on, treading in the lost lunch as they went, Paige sat back on her heels, her face pale, her heart thudding, her eyes bright with anger.

"Don't," Charlotte whispered.

"It's all right," Paige assured her. Even if she could think of what to say, and she couldn't, she knew it would only make matters worse if she came out with it.

"I'll go and ask for a dustpan and brush," Hayley offered, coming up behind them. "You can share my lunch if you like."

"And mine," Charlotte insisted.

Paige attempted a smile. She wasn't hungry anymore, but it was sweet of them to offer.

"You know why she's picking on you, don't you?" Hayley said when they were settled at a table as far from the Durmites as possible. "It's not only about that kid you stuck up for. It's because she's jealous."

"Of what?" Paige demanded incredulously. "There's nothing to be jealous of." She was looking at Charlotte. "Why does she think I called her names?"

"She doesn't," Charlotte replied. "She's just trying to pick a fight."

"You know what she's like," Hayley went on. "She has to show everyone she's in charge when she totally is not."

"Don't you reckon she's like that girl on *The Valleys*?" Charlotte whispered to Hayley. "You know, the really chavvy one who took her knickers off in a nightclub?"

"Actually, yeah, she does look a bit like her," Hayley agreed.

"A total double-bagger," Charlotte declared, keeping her voice down.

Though she laughed along with them, Paige was careful not to let Kelly see in case it offended her in some way. She definitely didn't want to be on the wrong side of Kelly Durham, but she had no idea how to escape it, especially when she truly couldn't stand the girl. Kelly was always so full of herself, strutting around the place with her shellac nails, orange tan, and gaggle of chavvy mates like they were in charge of the world. They were forever shoving younger kids out of the way, or making them hand over their tuck, or forcing them to do stupid stuff like eat grass, or let the air out of their own tires, or promise to blow up the chemistry lab. No one ever had, obviously, but Kelly and her gang seemed to get some sort of kick out of making them feel they had to.

As the others tucked into their food while chatting about the gross waste of time it was learning Welsh, Paige glanced around the room in search of someone who might be Julie Morris. No one was looking her way, and since she had nothing to go on to give her a clue, she soon gave up the search.

"It's just someone playing silly buggers," Charlotte had stated earlier when Paige told her about it. "I'd just ignore it if I were you."

Paige was half inclined to agree, but on the other hand, she couldn't help being concerned in case someone was feeling lonely, in need of a friend, and didn't know any other way to reach out. She'd hate it if that was her; it must be the worst feeling in the world to have no one to talk to. She'd seen it happen at her last school when one of the boys in her class had been cruelly tormented for being overweight, so she'd gone out of her way to make him a friend. Everyone had more or less left him alone after that, and she'd never let on to anyone that she almost regretted doing it because he turned out to be a bit of a liability. It was one of the reasons she hadn't been that sorry to leave.

"Look out, here comes Owen," Charlotte warned in a whisper.

Paige looked up and smiled as he approached. She might not want to be his girlfriend, but she had a very real fondness for him, and he had the sweetest face, a bit like an angel's with his sky-blue eyes, rosy cheeks, and dark blond curls.

"Is it OK if I sit here?" he asked, coming to hover behind an empty chair.

"It's yours," she told him, wishing for his sake that he had a little more self-confidence.

Clearly pleased, he put his tray on the table and squeezed in next to her. "Have you finished?" he asked, noticing her empty place.

Leaning forward, Hayley said, "Kelly Durham, the bi—"

"I wasn't hungry," Paige quickly cut in, treating Hayley to a meaningful stare. Hayley had obviously forgotten that Owen's sister, Olivia, who was in year eleven, was mates with Kelly Durham. Though she knew Owen wouldn't mean any harm if he decided to repeat things to his sister, she didn't want anything getting back to Kelly that might blow up in her face later.

"So have you viewed any of the stuff you shot yesterday yet?" he asked, digging into his pasta.

"You've got pasta *and* chips," Charlotte accused.

He looked down at his plate, clearly not understanding the fuss. "So?"

She shot him a withering look. "It's all right for those who don't put on weight at the mere sight of a carb," she said tartly.

"Yeah, I guess it is," he agreed in a way that made Paige and Hayley laugh. Turning back to Paige, he said, "So have you?"

"Some, but not all," she replied. "My mum really liked the bits you shot, but since they were mostly of me and Dad messing about, she would."

"I thought we did them specially for her."

"We did. I've just got to put them into a separate file so I can send them to her. We've got ICT this afternoon, so I might be able to do it then."

"By the way, I thought your sister was brilliant in assembly this morning," Hayley told Owen. "The way she plays the violin . . . She's like a bloody professional."

Owen nodded and continued to eat.

"Don't you reckon she is?" Hayley asked the others.

"Definitely," Paige and Charlotte agreed.

"She practices all the time," he told them.

Paige couldn't help wondering why he always seemed so reluctant to talk about his sister, especially given how close they were. They came and went from school together and were often together during breaks; Paige was sure they'd eat together if Olivia ever came into the canteen, but she never did.

Moving up to make more room as Cullum and Matt came to join them, Paige snatched a chip from Matt's plate and almost instantly wished she hadn't, because of how hungry it made her feel for the rest.

"Have you been picked for the team this week?" Cullum asked Owen.

Owen nodded. "Second row."

"That's where you belong, mate. Matt's on the bench."

"Knee's still not right," Matt reminded them. "Coach reckons I could be fit again by next— Paige! Get your hands off my chips, will you?"

"She hasn't had anything to eat," Hayley told him.

"So go and get something and stop half-inching mine."

"Who are you playing this week?" Charlotte asked Owen.

"Bishopston."

"Don't forget to go after that clown who did this to my knee," Matt told him.

"I'm on it," Owen promised, glancing at Paige's mobile as a text came in.

Sorry Dad didn't bring money. Change of plan. He's not going into Cardiff today. Did you manage to borrow from Charlotte or Hayley?

Everything's cool, Paige texted back, looking up as Mrs. Haynes, their form tutor, called out from the door, "Paige, you're helping to set up the charity-bag pack for the year eights, aren't you?"

"Yes, miss," Paige replied.

"Good. If you've finished your lunch, could you come over to the study center for a minute? There are a couple of things we need to go through. It shouldn't take long."

As Mrs. Haynes continued to hold the door open, Paige got to her feet. "You're on the committee too," she reminded Matt.

"Yeah, but she didn't ask for me."

"Do you want me to come with you?" Charlotte offered, apparently sensing Paige's reluctance to walk past Kelly Durham's table on her own.

"No, it's OK," Paige replied. After all, what could Kelly do with Mrs. Haynes standing right there?

The answer was clearly nothing. In fact, as Paige passed their table neither Kelly nor any of the Durmites even lifted their heads to watch her go by.

For some reason that felt almost as bad as if they'd jeered and called her names.

Chapter 3

"Am I still in disgrace?" Jack asked cautiously as he peered into the office, waving a white handkerchief to prepare the way.

Looking up from her computer, Jenna rolled her eyes and tried not to smile. He could be completely maddening at times, even thoughtless, definitely impulsive, and occasionally irrational, but she wouldn't do a thing to change him. "You should be," she informed him. "I was soaked to the skin by the time I got home."

"But what was I to do?" he protested. "I couldn't just leave the poor thing running loose. Anything could have happened to it."

"You mean in all that traffic down in Port Eynon?"

He pulled a face. "Have a heart."

She laughed and shook her head. Since Irene Evans's ancient poodle had become the object of many rescues lately, she could only wonder now why she hadn't thought of it when Jack had disappeared.

In fact, it was generally agreed that the lonely but canny old lady urged the half-blind, arthritic little beast out of the garden on purpose in the hope of luring a hero or heroine into her cozy little cottage for a nice cup of tea, a homemade biscuit, a bit of a chat, and *oh, just a tiny job that needs seeing to, if you have the time.*

In Jack's case this morning she'd had him unblocking her bathroom sink and sorting out her Internet connection. She'd even talked him into driving all the way to Mumbles later to take the dog to the vet, which was where he'd just returned from. Precisely why the poodle couldn't see someone closer to home Jenna had no idea, nor was she particularly interested to find out. She had a lot to get through today and didn't want Irene Evans, sweet as she was, hijacking any more of it. "You could have answered your phone," she reminded him, going back to the notes she was making.

"As I said, I had no idea I'd managed to switch it to silent," he replied, dropping a pile of Sunday's papers on a side table before sinking down at his own desk. "But I did text."

It was true, he had, and thanks to the erratic reception in the port it had turned up a good hour after he'd sent it.

"And let's not forget," he went on, "I was just as wet as you by the time I got home."

This was also true, for when he'd returned to the car and found no sign of her, he'd spent twenty or more minutes walking up and down the dunes searching for her and Waffle—half afraid, he'd insisted, that the tide had swept them away. "And have I asked you why you didn't answer your phone?" he grumbled, opening his inbox.

Jenna blinked in surprise. "I guess that would be because it didn't ring," she replied.

"Then you need to get it checked, because I definitely tried calling. Is this correct? Did we really receive three more submissions while I was out?"

"Two poems by the same person," she confirmed, "and a pornographic short story about dragons and maidens that I've already trashed." At the beginning they'd found most of the lewd submissions—and there were plenty of them—either hilarious, sickening, or downright mind-boggling; these days they rarely got past the first page before binning them. "Martha rang while you were out," she told him.

His head came up. "Really? How come she didn't call my mobile?"

She shrugged. "Maybe because it was on silent? Anyway, she said she's sorry she had to cancel today, but she should be free tomorrow morning around ten."

He frowned, keeping his eyes on her even though she wasn't looking at him. "Was that all?" he prompted.

"Were you expecting more?"

"I guess I was hoping she might have had more news on the upload problem. She didn't mention it?"

"Correct, she didn't."

Scowling, he returned to the task at hand, not speaking again (other than on the phone, volubly and at some length, to one of his golfing buddies) for at least half an hour. Then he said, "Remind me what Bena's full name is again."

"Verbena Forse. Why?"

"I'm doing the About Us page. Do we have a photo of her?"

"She'll have one, or we can take one when she comes in tomorrow."

"We'll need a short bio as well. I've got yours. Great shot of you, by the way. Do you think we should include Martha?"

Jenna frowned. "Would she want to be included? I mean, she's an adviser, not an actual member of the team."

He shrugged. "I guess you're right, but we wouldn't have got this far without her and her team."

Since this was true and had been acknowledged so many times it needed no further airing at this point, Jenna sat back in her chair and stretched and yawned. "Fancy a cup of tea?" she offered.

He nodded but didn't look up. "Tell you what, I'll make it," he suddenly declared, noticing the time. "Your mother should be here any minute with whatever she's tortured in the oven today."

Jenna had to laugh. In spite of loving to bake for when the children came in from school, her mother's choice of gluten-free, low-fat, no-sugar recipes rarely won her efforts many fans. "Actually, she's on one of her socials with the Women's Institute today," she informed him, "so we probably won't see her until teatime."

"Your mother's on a day trip?" He smiled, getting to his feet. "Blessings. I can hardly wait to find out what she brings us all back. What was it the last time? A miniature china watering can for me, a clockwork ballerina for Paige, a pack of doggy-doo bags for the twins . . . I've forgotten what she brought you and Josh."

"A tea towel for me and a CD of *Land of My Fathers* for Josh, but it's the thought that counts."

With an ironic tilt of his eyebrows, he took himself back through the garden to the kitchen, where she could see him filling the kettle while clicking on his phone to answer.

She loved watching him like this, a romantically shadowed image through all the rain-spattered glass, knowing he could be seen, and sometimes putting on a bit of a show to entertain her. It was so pleasing to see how relaxed and happy he was in Wales, at least most of the time, clearly delighting in the many new friends he'd made, clubs he'd joined, new sports he was learning. Sailing, surfing, fishing, and even flying had made it onto his agenda lately, though he'd yet to have his first pilot's lesson. It was doing him so much good here that she didn't even want to think about how he'd handle it if their business didn't succeed.

So she wouldn't think about it, because it wasn't going to happen. OK, it was probably going to take a while longer to get off the ground than he was expecting, but new ventures often did, and it wasn't as though they were looking to make a fortune from it. All they needed was enough to get by, so they could carry on living this idyllic life with the children while helping to bring some very real artistic talent to a marketplace.

Reaching for the Sunday papers, she reminded herself that this was what really mattered to her about Celticulture, that they were using it to win recognition for those who truly deserved it. And many did, that was for sure. Perhaps not always in a big way, but even those who probably weren't going to soar to the dizzying heights of stardom were excited about having their work professionally represented and published in electronic format. She could sense it every time she spoke to them on the phone—she even felt it coming through in their emails, along with impatience to get going—and loved every one of them for it. In her wildest dreams she sometimes even dared to envisage their exclusive list being recognized as a fertile source for major new talent—though she accepted that they were probably going to need a goodly amount of Welsh fairy dust to make that happen.

Feeling her heart sinking at how much of that very dust her own creative efforts needed, she opened the Culture section of the *Sunday Times* to the latest charts and almost immediately wished she hadn't bothered. Sitting there, right at the top of the hardback fiction list, was a name she knew well.

Natalie West.

She'd met this renowned author only once, at a publishing party in London where their joint editor had introduced them.

"Oh, so *you're* Jenna Moore," Natalie had drawled, looking down at Jenna from her imposing height. "I haven't read your book, but I hear it's been selling."

"Yes, I believe so." Jenna had smiled, not sure whether this towering (literally) author was being insulting or not.

"Mm, you can never tell what'll work," Natalie murmured, her busy eyes hunting the room for more interesting guests. "*Poetry Emotion*. Not a title I'd have chosen myself, but then I'd never have wanted to reduce Byron and Shelley to the indignity of popular fiction."

Shocked by the rudeness, as well as the unjustified attack on her work, Jenna had simply stared at her, at a loss for words.

"You have children, don't you?" Natalie asked.

"Yes, four," Jenna automatically replied.

"Well, I'm sure you're a wonderful mother." And with that she'd swept off into the crowd.

"Wow. Is she like that with everyone?" Jenna had whispered to her editor as they watched her go.

"Only those she sees as competition," the editor had replied, "or more talented than her, so try to take it as a compliment."

Jenna might have managed that, and might even have put it out of her mind altogether, had Natalie West not decided a few

months later to review Jenna Moore's second book for one of
the national papers—and totally decimated it. OK, Jenna had
to admit it wasn't her best work. She was sure that if she'd had
longer to produce it she'd have made a better job of it, but even
so, she truly didn't believe it had deserved the kind of derision
Natalie had poured all over it.

It had just seemed spiteful and unnecessary, especially since
no one, apparently, had even invited her to submit a review.

It could easily be said that Natalie West was responsible for
Jenna's writer's block, though Jenna had no wish to give the
woman such power over her. In fact, she'd rather not think
about her at all, especially when West's style of writing, in her
opinion, contained very little charm or nuance and her characters were almost entirely unsympathetic or stereotypical. And,
again in Jenna's opinion, it was nothing short of a travesty that
someone with such a stunted talent should be enjoying the
kind of success that she did.

Dumping the Culture section in the bin, she purposefully
cleared her mind of the bitterness and looked up to find out if
Jack was on his way with the tea yet. He was still on the phone,
pacing up and down the sitting room, waving an arm as he
spoke, clearly engrossed in his call. She wouldn't bother telling
him about Natalie West's latest success when he came back.
He'd only become angry on her behalf, which could easily turn
into a row between them, and what was the point of that when
she was OK with it, really? Her life had moved on, or it was
here, anyway, with him and the children—and her mother—
and since they were happy, healthy, and totally in the right place
for them, that was all that mattered.

*   *   *

"Honestly, I reckon Owen should just come out and tell everyone," Paige was saying as she and Charlotte waited for the school bus to pull away from their drop-off point. "It's not like he'd lose any friends. We'd all be there for him."

"Course we would, but you can't blame him for not wanting people to know. You weren't there when Darren Brown came out the year before last, but Owen was, so he saw what happened. Darren got tormented rotten, and not only by the Durmites, though they were definitely part of it. The other boys were really mean, pushing him around, calling him disgusting names, stealing his stuff . . . They managed to get him thrown off the rugby and football teams, and you know how Owen loves his sport. It was so bad for poor Darren that he ended up leaving the school."

Having heard about Darren Brown, Paige had to concede that maybe Owen was right to keep his secret, even though she was certain most people knew, or at least suspected. She guessed as long as he was in denial they could be too, and what business was it of hers to try to change things? None, was the answer; she just wished people weren't so prejudiced and narrow-minded, and that he could live his life the way he deserved.

Spotting Waffle bounding along the lane toward her, she broke into a smile. "Here he is, the best boy in all the world," she laughed, ruffling him savagely as he reached her. Since he came most days to meet her from the bus, she wasn't surprised to see him, only pleased.

Making a fuss of him too, Charlotte said, "By the way, how's your knee now? Still hurting?"

Checking the graze, which started to sting as soon as it was mentioned, Paige said, "It's fine." It had happened during netball when Bethany Gates had tripped her, sending her crashing to the ground. Since Bethany had sworn it was an accident and the coach hadn't actually been watching at that moment, the game had simply continued.

"You should have said it was Bethany," Charlotte stated belligerently. "She did it on purpose. I saw her stick out her foot, and Kelly Durham punched a fist in the air when you went down, like she'd bloody scored or something. If you ask me, they planned it."

Though Paige suspected the same, she couldn't prove it, and even if she could, she was hardly going to start whining to the coach when she'd only end up paying for it later, so she simply shrugged it off. "I'll just have to keep an eye out for her next time," she said, waving to a neighbor as she drove out of the lane and turned down toward Port Eynon. "Are you coming over later? We can work on the penicillin history project together."

Charlotte grimaced. "It's my granddad's birthday," she reminded her, "so we're going there tonight. When does it have to be in by?"

"Not till next Tuesday, so plenty of time. I'll hold off until we can do it together, and do some more on my video tonight."

"It's going to be brilliant," Charlotte told her. She gave Paige a playful nudge. "Fancy Mr. Thomas saying you have a natural talent for making films. He never gives anyone a compliment normally. I reckon he *desires* you."

"Oh, puh-lease." Paige gagged. "He's totally gross and his breath stinks."

"Just a bit. How does his wife stand it? Anyway, my video, of course, is total shite."

"That's not what he said. You just don't have enough material, but you can always use some of mine if you need it."

"I might take you up on that." Charlotte was checking a text. "My mum wants to know where I am, so I guess I'd better go. I'll FaceTime you later if I get a chance. Good luck with the . . . Oh my God, oh my God," she suddenly cried. "I almost forgot. Did you get the text from Cullum?"

"You mean about going surfing at the weekend?"

"Yeah, that one. When I saw him last period I asked who else was going and it only turns out that Oliver and Liam might be there too. So we have to go."

Paige's insides were in free fall. Oliver was going to be there. And Liam, whom Charlotte was totally crazy about. "Definitely," she agreed. "I already said I would anyway."

Grinning, Charlotte hefted her heavy bag over her shoulder to start in the opposite direction. "You're in love," she teased. "You're going to kiss him, shag him, marry him, and have his babies."

"You mean that's what you're going to do with Liam," Paige called after her, her smile so wide it almost hurt.

"Bring it on!" Charlotte laughed. "I'm ready for it whenever he is."

"I'll tell him that."

"And I'll tell Oliver. He'll be like, 'Oh my God, Paige Moore wants to do it with me? Let's get a room.'"

Though Paige was still laughing and buzzing with excitement as she started toward home, no way was she going to allow herself to believe anything would ever happen between her and Oliver Pryce. It just wouldn't, not in a million trillion years. She was too young for him, and he already had a girlfriend, and even if he didn't he wouldn't look twice at her. But if he did . . . He definitely wouldn't, but if he did . . . If he saw

her again and remembered her from rugby . . . It might turn out that he'd been thinking about her too, wondering who she was, how he could get to know her. It would be, like, totally amazing, actually out-of-this-entire-world amazing and awesome and utterly brilliant, if they actually started going out. Oh God! She could hardly even think of it. Everyone would be like, *No way is she with him,* but it would be true. *She,* Paige Moore, would be Oliver Pryce's girlfriend. Kelly Durham and her gang wouldn't dare to have a go at her then. They'd back off big-time once they realized she was moving in a different league than they were, going out with someone who was at college and had a car. Or more likely they'd want to be her friend, crawling round her, sucking up like little pigs, but she wouldn't even bother looking at them, never mind letting them into her crowd. They could just drop dead and go and find someone else to have a go at, because no way in the world would Oliver allow them to carry on messing with her.

"Come on, Waffs," she cried, feeling suddenly elated as she broke into a run along the lane. "It's freezing out here, and I'm starving."

In no time at all she was passing Butler's Farm and the half-finished new build next to it, crossing the patch of grass they called a green, where random white stones marked the border and sheep were often found grazing, and skirting the three grand Victorian houses that had been knocked into one to form an upmarket B&B. Next to them was a shabby old bungalow belonging to a couple from Llanelli who hardly ever set foot in it, and next to that was a long quaint stone house with wide arched windows, two tall chimneys, and a massive oak in the front garden. This belonged to her grandma, who didn't appear

to be at home, since her car wasn't there and no lights were on. However, after running up the lane past more cottages and houses tucked in behind wild bramble hedges or shiny black gates, she spotted her grandma's car on their forecourt, so it was no surprise when she let herself and Waffle into the kitchen to find Kay busying herself with the ironing. Weirdly, ironing was one of Grandma's favorite things to do.

"Hi, darling," her mother said, interrupting a phone call as she looked up from the tea she was making.

"Hey," Paige responded, dumping her bag and grabbing a biscuit for Waffle. "Hey, Grandma, kiss kiss."

Kay gave one of her awkward smiles. "Kiss kiss to you too," she replied, sweeping the iron along the back of one of Jack's shirts. "Good day at school?"

"Same old."

Kay frowned. "Same old what?"

"It was OK," Paige assured her, slotting a slice of bread into the toaster before shrugging off her coat. "How about you?"

"My day was very good, thank you," Kay replied seriously. "I went with the WI to visit one of the cockle-processing plants in Pennclawdd. There are two, and strictly speaking they're in Crofty, but the cockles come from the Burry estuary, which Pennclawdd sits on the edge of, and the families that own the plants all come from the village too. They've been harvesting cockles there for hundreds of years—"

"Yes, Grandma, we've been there with the school. So did you bring any home?"

"Of course, and a recipe for laver bread, which is actually seaweed. We tried some while we were there and it's delicious."

"Are you going to make it, or will Mum?" Paige asked warily.

"Oh, I expect I shall. Your mum's always so busy, but she's going to make us a seafood pasta this evening using some of the cockles I brought."

Though Paige didn't much care for cockles, she wouldn't hurt her grandmother's feelings by admitting it, so she simply said, "Cool. Can I have a cup of that tea, Mum?"

"Please?" Kay prompted.

"Please. Where's Dad?" she asked her mother as Jenna got off the phone.

"He went to give Barry the builder a hand with something," Jenna told her, "and knowing them they'll stop at the pub on the way back. Good day? What happened to your knee?"

"Oh, I fell over in netball. By the way, Mr. Thomas was totally blown away by the footage me and Dad shot for my ICT project. He reckons I'm going to have a really good film when it's edited together. He might even show it to the Welsh Tourist Board if it turns out to be as good as he thinks."

Jenna's eyebrows rose. "That's fantastic," she declared, coming to hug her. "Next thing we know you'll be turning one of Celticulture's books into a movie."

Liking the idea, Paige said, "That would be so cool, wouldn't it? Especially if it was *Poetry Emotion*. I agree with Dad, I reckon that would make a brilliant film, or TV series."

"We can always dream," Jenna said with a smile. "Do you have much homework?"

"Some. What time are we eating?"

"About six, unless Dad calls to say he's going to be late."

"Which would be typical. How come he didn't go into Cardiff today?"

"Irene Evans needed some help with her dog, so he decided

to put it off till Thursday. Ah, that'll be Colin delivering some wood," she declared as someone knocked on the utility room window. "I'll just go and—"

"Paige! Paige!" Flora cried, dashing into the kitchen, her skinny blond ponytail spilling out of its pearly band and pink-rimmed spectacles steaming up with excitement. "You have to sponsor me," she declared, grabbing Paige's hand. "Mum already did and Grandma. It's only ten p and it's for charity."

Allowing herself to be dragged from her toast into the sitting room, Paige said, "What do you have to do?"

"I'm doing it too," Wills told her, from his upside-down position against the wall. "The boys have to stand on their heads for twenty seconds without toppling over."

"And the girls have to do fifty skips without being out," Flora finished. "She's sponsoring me, not you," she told Wills, "because I asked first."

"That's not fair. I was practicing. *Mum!* Tell her Paige's got to sponsor me too."

"It's all right, I will," Paige assured him. "Where are your glasses?"

"I took them off so they wouldn't get broken."

"You're cheating," Flora cried. "You're not supposed to put your feet against the wall, is he, Paige?"

"*I'm practicing,*" Wills yelled. "Mum said she'll come and hold me steady in a minute so I can try without the wall."

"How many skips can you do?" Paige asked Flora, lifting her up and treating her to a boisterous hug.

"I did thirty-nine just now," Flora replied proudly as she hugged Paige back. "I would have done more, but I got a bit tired."

"She's useless," Wills declared, coming down from the wall.

"You are," she shot back.

He poked out his tongue, so she did too.

"You're such a baby," he jeered. "Look at you, having cuddles."

"You're just jealous. Isn't he, Paige?"

"Definitely," Paige agreed. "But I don't mind giving you a cuddle too," she told Wills, starting toward him.

"No way," he squealed, diving over the arm of the sofa. Suddenly he yelped, "Ow! Ow, ow, ow!"

"What's wrong?" Paige sighed.

"I hurt my arm," he wailed. "Look, it's bleeding."

Quickly putting Flora down, Paige went to check the injury, which didn't look serious, but what had caused it probably was.

His blue eyes rounded with horror as she picked up his broken glasses.

Flora gasped. "That's the fourth time—"

"Shut up!" he shouted. "No one asked you."

"But it is, and Mum said—"

"If you tell her, I'll beat you up."

"You have to tell her," Paige pointed out.

"Not if you mend them."

"I can't, the arm's broken off. They'll have to go back to the optician."

"You take them."

Paige laughed. "Like I'm really going to do that. I don't even have a car to get there, never mind the money to pay."

His little face started to crumple. "I hate them anyway. Who cares if they're broken? They're just stupid."

"What's going on?" Jenna asked, coming into the room with Paige's toast, lavishly buttered. "Wills, why are you crying, sweetheart?"

"He's broken his glasses," Flora told her.

Jenna's eyes closed. "Again, Wills? What's the matter with you?"

"It wasn't my fault," he cried. "I didn't mean to do it, did I Paige?"

"No, he didn't," she told her mother, taking the toast. Deciding to leave them to it, she went to grab her school bag and made for the stairs.

"Can I come with you?" Flora cried, jumping up and down. "Please? I'll sit on your bed and be quiet, I promise. I won't get on your nerves."

"Later," Paige replied, running up to the landing.

"I'm just popping out to get Josh," Jenna told her. "If you feel like giving Grandma a hand with the ironing, don't let anything stand in your way."

"I've got homework," Paige reminded her. Quickly closing her bedroom door, she dumped her bag on the bed and went to turn on her computer. How totally, unbelievably amazing it would be if there was a message from Oliver. The mere thought of it set her heart skittering about like a bunch of trapped butterflies. She had no idea what she'd do if there was; she guessed it would depend on what it said. But since there was absolutely no way in the world she was going to find anything, she should get a grip on herself and start chilling out.

She was right, there was nothing from him, and it was totally dumb to feel depressed about it when they didn't even know each other, for God's sake.

Hearing Waffle scratching at the door, she went to let him in. She gave him the last corner of her toast and put some music on before checking out one of the many chat rooms she belonged to. There was loads going on about all sorts of stuff, most of it to do with sex, which she rarely contributed to, but it could be hilarious to read.

Horny honcho here looking for cam-to-cam with a horny girl, message me.

Want more than just chat, join our virtual world for adults.

Please talk with me and tell me what you like best.

Someone called Bobby popped up to chat with her, but she quickly closed him down, then clicked through to YouTube to watch Oliver's video for the gazillionth time. It was totally amazing. He was the most brilliant singer ever, writing all his own stuff and performing it like he was a real professional. She loved it when he closed his eyes; it was like he was feeling really passionate and deep, and she could imagine him being that way with her as they kissed and he laid her down on the bed and did stuff she loved to think about but knew she'd probably never have the courage to do. She felt so connected to the words as he sang them that he might have written them just for her.

Every time you smile, you make my heart go wild,
Every time we kiss, I feel your sweet tenderness.

She wished she could tell him how amazing she thought he was, that she was certain he was going to be famous one day, but even though she'd been on his Facebook page a hundred times or more, she'd never plucked up the courage to send a friend request. Instead she read the exchanges between him and his friends, not always understanding them, but relieved to see that they were mostly about sports, or music, or stuff they were studying. Though it said he was in a relationship with

Lindsay French, there were no pictures of her or messages that she could find, so maybe they weren't together anymore. She liked to think they weren't; it was easier that way.

After watching the video three times, she clicked on to another chat room and was just about to join in a row about Ellie Goulding, one of her favorite singers, when someone private-messaged her on Facebook.

It was Julie Morris.

Hey, how are you?

I'm cool, Paige typed back. *Are you going to tell me who you are now?*

Like I said yesterday, I'm a friend. I mean, if you'll let me be.

But that's just weird, being friends and not knowing who you are.

It's complicated, but I promise I'll explain when I know I can trust you. I heard Bethany Gates pushed you over in netball.

Not dumb enough to trust someone who could easily turn out to be Bethany Gates herself, Paige replied, *Who told you?*

I just heard. They're real b*s that lot.

Though she'd like to go a lot further with what she thought of the Durham gang, she decided it was best to get off the subject just in case. *Where do you live?* she asked.

Just outside Oxwich.

Do you have any brothers and sisters?

There was a long pause before the answer came back. *Yes, I do, and you've got a sister and two brothers.*

How do you know?

It's on your FB profile.

She was right, it was.

I understand now why you don't want to go out with Owen.

Paige frowned at the screen. *What do you mean?*

Just that I get it. There's no point if he's gay.

Stiffening, Paige typed, *Who says he's gay?*

You, on your FB page.

Paige's heart missed a beat. She hadn't posted any such thing. Quickly going through to check she saw the post with her own profile picture next to it, and her heart stopped beating altogether.

Owen Masters is gay. I am not his girlfriend, so everyone can just stop thinking I am.

"Oh my God," she murmured in a panic. How had this happened? She definitely hadn't put it there herself, but Owen was going to think she had. She had to ring him.

She tried his number over and over, private-messaged and texted him, but he didn't respond, and by now all sorts of horrible comments calling her a two-faced bitch, a total fucking waste of space, even a c——t, were flooding onto her FB page.

Chapter 4

"So where are you now?" Jenna was asking as she opened the car for Waffle to jump into the back.

"Still in Swansea," Jack replied.

"Did you remember to take Wills's glasses?"

"Yep, they're already fixed." He went off the line for a moment, saying something to someone else that she couldn't quite hear.

"Are you still at Martha's office?" she asked when he came back.

"I am, and she says hi."

"Don't let's forget about that lunch," Martha shouted out.

"Don't worry, we won't," Jenna called back.

"OK," Jack said, "I'm about to drive over to Cardiff to check out what this email's all about from the Arts Council."

Jenna slipped into the driver's seat. "Tell me what it said again."

"Hang on, I'll get it up on the screen."

As she waited Jenna reversed out of the forecourt and started down through the village. It was a dismal morning, with every shade of gray glooming the sky and a cloying mist shrouding the fields, but at least the rain had stopped, so she was grabbing the chance to take Waffle down to the beach for a run.

"I can't find it now," Jack grumbled irritably, "but it's on my phone somewhere, so I'll forward it to you when we've finished. Basically they've invited me to drop in for a chat the next time I'm in town."

"Do you think they're going to increase our grant?"

"It might not be about that, but it could be an opportunity to bring the subject up. It was all very casual, signed from someone called Lewin, or Lewis, but I thought we shouldn't hang about."

"Absolutely not," she agreed. "Remember, you're going to be there on Thursday anyway."

"True, but as I don't have much else on at the moment, I thought instead of going up to London at the weekend to see my mother. I'll go straight from Cardiff today and come back on Friday."

"What about the bank?"

"I can always change that."

"And Wills's glasses?"

"Oh hell, I forgot about them. Tell you what, I'll pop over to The Landings and drop them off with Paige. How was she this morning, by the way? She was in a strange mood last night, I could hardly get a word out of her, and the way she yelled at Josh over nothing at all . . ."

"It's probably her time of the month," Jenna sighed. "She always gets moody then. Or it could be the pressure of schoolwork. She has GCSEs next year, remember? Even so, it can't be good for her to spend so much time shut up there in her room, always reviewing, or doing homework, or chatting with her friends. We hardly see anything of her these days."

"That's great news about her video, isn't it? Her teacher thinks she had some excellent material."

"I hope you're not giving yourself all the credit."

"No way. I mean, I played a part, obviously . . . Hang on, Martha's trying to get my attention." To Martha he said, "What for? I don't know . . . OK, OK, I'll put her on. She wants to talk to you," he told Jenna.

As Martha came on the line Jenna was passing the church in Port Eynon, turning down toward the seafront, where she could already see foaming whitecaps charging for the shore.

"Hey," Martha said in her usual cheery voice, "how are you?"

"I'm fine, thanks," Jenna replied. "How are you?"

"I'm cool. Kind of busy, but that has to be a good thing."

"Absolutely. So how's the upload problem coming along? All fixed now?"

"More or less. Actually, it's why I wanted to talk to you. I was going to email a list of instructions, but if it's convenient for you I'll come over and show you how the changes will work."

"That's great, but I can always come there."

"It's no problem. Let's say tomorrow or the next day. I'll give you a call when I've looked at the calendar. Maybe we can fit that lunch in while we're at it, have a nice cozy chat, just the two of us."

"I'll look forward to it."

"Good. Here's Jack."

Before he came back on the line Jenna heard him talking to Martha in a tone that didn't sound too friendly, until he suddenly laughed and said, "Of course I don't have a problem with you seeing my wife, and no, I'm not feeling left out."

"I think you are," she heard Martha tease.

Apparently ignoring her, he said to Jenna, "I should go now, but I'll call you later, let you know how it goes in Cardiff."

By the time the call ended Jenna was parking the car in the middle of the port, where—surprise, surprise—Irene Evans's poodle was standing with its back to the road and nose pressed up against a steel waste bin.

"Oh, Charlie," she sighed, going to attach the dog to Waffle's lead, "I guess we'd better get you home before any harm comes to you." Opening the back of the car for Waffle to jump down, she let him run on alongside as they headed into the jumble of white cottages.

"Hello, Irene." She smiled warmly as the old lady opened her front door. "Look who I found by the beach."

"Oh my goodness, he got out again," Irene cried, clasping her wrinkled old hands to her powdered cheeks. "I didn't even notice he'd gone. Thank you for bringing him back. Will you come in and have a cup of tea? Clare, isn't it?"

"Jenna."

"Of course, it's just that you look like a Clare. Pretty name, Jenna. Where is it from, do you know?"

Unable to be rude when the old lady was so sweet, she said, "Well, my dad, who chose it, told me its origins are Arabic and it means 'heaven.'"

"Oh my, that's just lovely, so it is. Heaven. Do you know what Irene means? It means 'peace,' so I think we go very well together, don't you?"

"We certainly do," Jenna agreed with a smile. "I'm afraid I have to be going now. I want to walk the dog before the rain starts again."

"Yes, yes, of course. I don't want to keep you. I've just boiled the kettle, though, so if you want to change your mind . . ."

"That's very kind of you. Perhaps another time."

"You're always welcome. Same goes for that lovely husband of yours. How is he? I haven't seen him for a while."

Deciding it might not be kind to remind her that he'd been there only yesterday, Jenna said, "He's fine, thank you. I'll tell him you asked after him."

"Yes, please do that. I've been away, you see, at my daughter's in Swansea. She brought us back this morning, me and Charlie. It's lovely seeing her, she's very helpful, but there's nothing like your own home, is there?"

"No, nothing," Jenna responded, confused, until she realized that Irene's sense of time was probably as dodgy as her memory. "Do you have everything you need?" she asked. "I'm going to Tesco's later if—"

"Oh, I'm all stocked up, thank you, my love. Our Ginnie saw to that before she left. So I've got plenty of biscuits if you decide you'd like a cuppa when you get back from your walk. By the way, you know, don't you, that a peewit on the Bryn means snow in seven days?"

Surprised, Jenna said, "Why, have you seen one?"

"No," Irene replied. "Not this year."

Unable to suppress a smile, Jenna squeezed the old lady's hand and headed off for the beach.

Half an hour later, dripping wet and thinking she'd like nothing better than a cozy little chat with Irene in front of her gas fire, Jenna was on her way to the vet. Waffle had cut a paw on a shell and was limping badly. "If you haven't already got them," she was saying to Jack on the phone, "I can pop in and pick up Wills's glasses."

"I've just given them to Paige," he told her.

"Oh, OK. How was she?"

"She seemed fine."

"Did you ask if she was all right?"

"Was I supposed to?"

"You said yourself that she was in a strange mood last night."

"And you reminded me of why that could be."

Since she had, she said, "Did you get Josh's text about ten minutes ago? He's been picked for the school football team on Saturday."

"No kidding. Way to go, son! He'll be as proud as Punch."

Her heart flooded with love as she imagined Josh's delight when his name was called. In truth, he wasn't all that good a player, but it never seemed to put him off trying, even though he spent most matches sitting on the bench.

"Are you going to come and watch?" she asked.

"I should think so," he replied. "I guess it depends if I'm back in time."

"You said Friday."

"Which is definitely what I'm aiming for."

"You know how much it would mean to him to see you there."

"I'll do my best. Let me know how you get on at the vet's."

"OK, will do. Have to go now, Paige is trying to get through."

"Hi, Mum, it's me," Paige said into her mobile.

"I know. Are you all right?"

"Yeah, I'm cool. Well, actually not really. Do you think you could come and get me?"

"What is it?"

"I just don't feel well. I've spoken to Mrs. Haynes, and she says it's all right for me to go home. When do you think you can get here?"

"Well, I'm on my way to the vet with Waffle right now—he's cut his paw—then I have to take Josh to the dentist and collect Grandma's prescription, but I should be able to come after that. Can you hang on for a couple of hours?"

Utterly fed up, Paige said, "I suppose I'll have to."

"Oh, Paige. If it was an emergency you know I'd come straightaway."

"It's OK. I get that everyone else is more important than me."

"That's not—"

"I'm ringing off now. Don't bother coming, I'll get the bus home." And before her mother could argue, she ended the call.

Charlotte and Hayley were watching her worriedly, using their slight bodies to shelter her from the wind. They were huddled behind the head teacher's study, where they'd come to get away from the snide remarks and name-calling that had been going on all morning. It was lunch break now, but it would soon be time to go back inside, and Paige wasn't sure she could bear to.

"I know it's running away if I go home," she said miserably, "but everyone's being so vile, and it's not as if I did it."

"We keep telling them that," Hayley assured her.

"They ought to realize someone hacked into your account," Charlotte declared hotly. "Are you absolutely sure it wasn't this Julie person?"

"No, I'm not sure," Paige cried. "How can I be when I don't even know who she is? I just don't know why she'd do it, that's all."

"Tell us again what she said when you asked her," Hayley prompted.

"That there was no way she'd do that to me. She wants to be my friend, she said, and she thinks it's terrible that someone would pretend to be me."

"That's rich when she's pretending to be someone else," Charlotte snorted.

"I don't see what she'd gain from it," Paige pointed out.

"What does anyone gain, apart from turning the whole world against you?" Hayley put in.

"Thanks for that," Paige retorted.

"Sorry, I was just saying . . . Anyway, I don't think it was Kelly Durham, or not her personally. Remember, I sit next to her in ICT, so I know how crap she is when it comes to understanding anything about computers."

"It doesn't have to have been her," Charlotte pointed out. "It was probably one of her psycho mates."

"Like Harry Adcock," Hayley agreed. "He's a total genius with computers. He even writes his own programs, so he'd know how to do it."

Paige looked past them to where a group of year eleven students were going into the study center. Owen's sister wasn't amongst them, or not that she could see, but when she'd passed Olivia in the corridor earlier, on her way to Religious Studies, Olivia had given her such a filthy look that Paige had wanted to curl up and die.

As for Owen, he hadn't come in at all today, so at least he was being spared all the spitefulness and prejudice that scared him so much.

If only he'd return Paige's calls or texts.

"He's got to know I'd never do anything like that to him," she exclaimed in frustration.

"But you did keep saying you thought he ought to come out," Charlotte reminded her.

"Yes, but not like this, and whose side are you on?"

"Yours, obviously. I'm just saying, that's all."

"You think I did it," Paige accused.

"No way!"

"God, I can't believe this is happening. It's like everyone's turning against me, accusing me of being a two-faced bitch . . . There are even people posting who I've never heard of."

"They're just sickos jumping in for the ride," Charlotte assured her. "You have to ignore them."

Paige sighed. "I just hope Owen's reading what they're saying. He'd know then that everyone's too busy turning against me to bother about him. Try texting him again," she told Charlotte, unable to bear Owen's silence.

Obediently Charlotte took out her phone and pressed to send the same message she'd sent four times already. *Owen, please don't think it was Paige, because it wasn't. She's been hacked. Ring me when you get this. Cxxx*

As she finished, the bell rang for afternoon lessons to begin.

"What have you got now?" Hayley asked Paige.

"Double English," Paige replied. "And there's a rehearsal for *Under Milk Wood* after school. Miss Kendrick'll go mad if I miss it."

"So what are you going to do?"

Paige's face was pale as she stared off toward the science block.

"Don't you sit next to Cullum for English?" Charlotte reminded her. "He's OK."

Paige nodded. "Unless he's decided he hates me too. He's good mates with Owen, don't forget."

"What he said to me this morning was that Owen will come round once he realizes you had nothing to do with it."

Since that sounded as though Cullum believed her, Paige took heart. "I should stay," she stated, suddenly determined not to miss the rehearsal. She really wanted to play this part, had almost learned it by heart already, so she'd hate herself if she ended up letting the Durmites spoil it for her.

She looked at her phone as a text arrived from her mum.

Do you want me to come for you or not? XX

Texting back, she said, *No, don't bother. I'll be fine.* She didn't add any kisses; that way her mother would know she was still pissed off about being made to wait.

As they started back toward the main doors Paige felt as though the whole school's eyes were on her. Everyone obviously knew by now, no matter what year they were in, that Owen Masters had been outed on Paige Moore's Facebook page. No doubt they'd all been online to have a look, and even add their own snide comments. She wondered how many of them believed she'd been hacked. Probably none.

What mattered most was that Owen should believe it, because she really didn't want to lose him as a friend.

As they approached the lockers to sort out their books for the afternoon Paige spotted Kelly Durham and her gang hanging around close to hers, and felt a desperate urge to shrink out of the way before they noticed her. She wouldn't allow herself to do that, though; she had to find the courage to stand up to them.

Spotting her, Kelly immediately gave an exaggerated glance at her phone followed by a pantomime gasp. "Oh my God, have you seen this?" she asked her friends, while keeping an eye on Paige to make sure she could hear. "She must have been *hacked* again."

As the others shrieked with laughter and turned to walk away, Paige felt herself turning hot and cold all over. What was on Facebook this time? What sick lies was someone telling? Why were they doing this to her?

"Got it," Hayley murmured as Facebook came up on her phone. Her eyes widened with horror as she read the latest post on Paige's page.

My best friend Charlotte is a minger who sucked Mr. Thomas's cock.

Charlotte's face was ashen as she and Paige looked at each other.

"Don't worry, I know you didn't do it," Charlotte assured her.

"I swear I wouldn't."

"It's OK, I know."

"Charlotte!" someone called along the corridor.

They all looked up to see Kelly and her gang still hanging about outside the loos.

"You can come with us if you like," Kelly told her. "I mean, who'd want to be friends with someone who says stuff like that about them? I know I wouldn't."

As Paige's heart twisted, Charlotte scowled angrily, then shouted back, "Just fuck off." Grabbing Paige's and Hayley's arms, she turned them around to go off in the opposite direction.

The following morning, after dashing through the school run and walking the dog in his protective boot so the stitches didn't come out, Jenna was handing Martha a coffee while removing a bucket of Legos from the kitchen sofa to make room for her guest to sit down.

"We have biscuits," she declared, whisking a plate from the countertop. "I'm afraid they're mostly of the jammy dodger or peanut butter variety, but there are a couple of rich tea and a custard cream in there somewhere."

Laughing, Martha was about to have a rummage when her mobile rang. She checked the screen and grimaced. "Sorry, I've been waiting for this call. Do you mind?"

"Please, go ahead," Jenna urged, and reached for her own mobile to check her messages as Martha wandered from the kitchen into the sitting room. Apparently the call was confidential.

They'd spent the past hour in the office with the new website displayed on Jenna's screen as they talked through everything from fonts to page layouts to navigation systems, until eventually Jenna's head had started to spin. Not that she didn't appreciate Martha taking the time to walk her through the most recent changes, as a member of her team could easily have done it; it was simply that trying to digest so much technical information in one go didn't come easily to her. This was why Jack ran that side of the business, leaving her to concentrate on artistic content, though she was touched that Martha apparently felt it important to keep her in the loop.

"Sorry," Martha apologized, coming back to the kitchen. "I'll turn it off now."

"Oh, you don't need to do that," Jenna protested. "I understand how busy you are."

"But it's lovely to have a break once in a while," Martha assured her. Returning to the sofa, she picked up her coffee and crossed her plump, shapely legs as she sat down. She was an ample woman of around forty with chaotic blond curls and the kind of face that, while not classically beautiful, was enhanced by her sleepy eyes and her constant air of cheerfulness.

"Do you think she's sexy?" Jenna remembered asking Jack after they'd first met her.

He'd looked at her askance. "I suppose she could be," he'd replied, "if you like them that large."

"I thought you did."

"What? How do you figure that, when I'm married to you?"

"I'm thinking about the girlie magazines you like looking at. They're all pretty busty. . . ."

"Yeah, because they don't get cast for how petite they are."

"They turn you on."

"Only when we look at them together."

Wondering why she was recalling that conversation now, Jenna settled at the other end of the sofa, aware of Martha looking around the kitchen with an almost girlish enthusiasm.

"So how are you enjoying Wales?" she asked, a hint of mischief in her tone. "I expect it already feels like a lifetime since you moved in."

Remembering the pristine kitchen in Martha's glamorous seafront villa, and trying not to wince at the clutter in her own, Jenna rolled her eyes. "Tell me about it. But we're very happy here. The kids have settled in even better than we'd hoped, and Jack just loves it." She gave a wry laugh. "You know what he's like—Mr. Sociable. He's made so many friends I'm losing track of them all. One day he's sailing, the next he's playing golf or helping out with some fair or festival. That's when he's not working on the business, of course, which takes up most of his time." She wondered why she'd felt the need to assure Martha of that, as though Martha were the boss rather than their adviser. "I take it he told you about the invite from the Welsh Arts Council to drop in anytime?"

"He did. And he went yesterday?"

"That's right. No feedback from the meeting yet, but it's probably a bit soon."

"I'm sure it'll be good," Martha declared confidently. "They're a great bunch, and they love anyone who takes an interest in our little principality."

Jenna smiled and tried to think what else to say. Jack was in London now, visiting his mother, but Martha didn't need to know that.

"Tell me about you," Martha suggested, her merry eyes seeming genuinely interested as they came to rest on Jenna's. "How's the writing going?"

Jenna grimaced. "The less said about that the better," she answered dryly. "Actually, I'm thinking about paying back the advance to try and buy myself some peace of mind."

Martha appeared concerned and sympathetic. "I guess with four children to take care of, a home to run, and a new company to launch, it can't be easy to find time for yourself."

Jenna sighed. "It's not, but on the positive side I'm loving working on the submissions, and as for everything else . . ." She cast a sardonic look around the kitchen. "As you can see, I don't get too fussed about everything having to be in its place. I used to, before I was a mother, but by the time the twins came along I realized it was a losing battle. You have children, don't you?"

Martha nodded as she helped herself to a second rich tea. "Yes, two. A boy, David, who's almost fourteen, and our youngest, Julia, is twelve. They're at boarding school, near London."

"Do you miss them?" Jenna ventured gingerly.

Martha's smile seemed resigned. "Of course, but I work such long hours, and, being a pilot, Martin's away half the time . . . It's better for us all this way." She looked round as the doorbell rang.

"It'll be the postman," Jenna said. "I won't be a moment."

By the time she returned Martha was on her feet studying the children's paintings and poems stuck to the fridge.

"They're so sweet," she commented, "and talented."

Jenna laughed. "I'm not so sure about talented, but they like to think so, and I guess that's what counts. Ah, Mum will be pleased," she declared, bringing a wallet of photos out of a padded envelope.

"Are those actual prints?" Martha asked with mock incredulity. "You almost never see them these days."

"I'm sure we wouldn't if my mother didn't insist on keeping albums."

Apparently entranced by the idea of prints, Martha said, "May I? Are they of the children?"

"I'm sure most of them will be," Jenna replied, handing them over, "and please don't feel you have to be polite."

"No, really, I'd love to see them."

Suspecting they were going to show a very different kind of family from Martha's own, Jenna could only wonder what Martha was thinking as she went through a messy birthday party, a chaotic sandcastle build, a trot around the woods on ponies, and Paige striking a few pouty-model poses before going out to a disco. Though Martha paused every now and again and either smiled or frowned curiously, she made almost no comment until she'd handed them back. Then she said, "I think it's wonderful that your mother keeps a record, like this. I wish we'd done it for ours."

"But you have them all on computer?"

"Of course; it's just not the same. I see Jack doesn't feature in many, so I'm guessing he's the photographer."

"Usually. But the younger children like taking photos too. They're just not very good at framing or focus, so we tend to edit them out before ordering prints."

Martha smiled. "Your eldest daughter—Paige, is it? She's very pretty."

In spite of rolling her eyes, Jenna felt a rush of pride. "She doesn't seem to think so, but I guess that's part of being her age. Would you like another coffee?"

"Oh no, thanks, I really should be going." She glanced at her watch. "I'd hoped we might make that lunch today, but once again time's running away from me."

As they walked out to Martha's car, Jenna said, "Thanks again for coming all this way. It was so much simpler to understand the changes than if you'd sent a set of instructions."

"I'm afraid one will be on its way," Martha warned, "but hopefully it'll make more sense now you've seen how it works." She held out a hand to shake, her pretty dimples showing as she smiled. "It was lovely to see you."

"To see you too," Jenna replied, meaning it. Hearing her mobile ringing, she made to turn back before realizing how rude it would seem.

"It's OK, go ahead," Martha encouraged, taking out her own phone as she got into the car. "Give me a call if there's anything, won't you?"

After assuring her she would, Jenna ran back to the kitchen and picked up just in time. "Hi, darling, sorry," she said. "I was just seeing Martha out."

"Right. Good. How did it go?" Jack asked brusquely.

"Fine. She's very good at explaining things."

"She's supposed to be. So what did you chat about, apart from the technical stuff?"

"Nothing much, really. The kids, photographs . . . She thought Paige was very pretty."

"She's right, she is. So it went well?"

"Were you expecting it not to?"

"No, of course not. I just wondered, that's all. Was Bena there?"

"No, she had to take Aiden back to the hospital this morning. She'll be in later. How are things going with you? Is your mother . . . ?"

"Hang on, sorry, I've got another call coming in. I'd better check who it is."

After clicking off her end Jenna picked up Martha's empty coffee cup and carried it to the sink. She was glad to have spent some time with her, though she had to admit she didn't feel she knew her any better as a result of it. In fact, thinking back over the morning, she was starting to sense that there might have been more to Martha's visit than the demonstration of a new computer system. Though what that could be presumably only Martha knew.

It was Friday evening. Jenna and the younger children were around the table having their tea when the back door opened and Jack burst in as merrily as Santa on Christmas Eve.

"Daddy! Daddy!" the twins yelped, and immediately dashed to throw themselves at him.

"We weren't expecting you for at least another hour," Jenna commented, putting down her fork as she got up too.

"Dad! I came in third in spelling," Josh shouted out proudly.

Jack beamed. "Way to go, little man." He balanced a twin on each arm as he kissed Jenna.

Catching the beer on his breath, her eyebrows arched knowingly.

"It was just the one," he promised, "but I'll have another now I'm home."

"Another what?" Flora asked, rubbing her fingers over his stubbly chin.

"Beer," he growled, pretending to bite her.

"I'll get it! I'll get it!" Wills insisted, sliding to the floor.

"Grandma's gone to t'ai chi," Flora informed him.

His eyes sparkled with laughter. "Has she now? I expect she'll be very good at it."

"We do t'ai chi in school sometimes," Josh announced. "It's really slow, so Grandma should be OK. Oh yes, and it's good for breathing, and she needs to breathe at her age, doesn't she?"

Laughing as he went through to drop a kiss on Josh's head, Jack said, "She certainly does. And where's Paige?"

"Where she always is," Josh complained, "upstairs in her room."

"We've called her," Flora told him, "but she's ignoring us. I started on a new reading book at school today."

"You did? What's it called?"

"Um . . . oh yes, I know. *A Wee Bit of Trouble.*"

His eyes rounded with amazement. "You mean they've written a book about you?"

Flora squealed with laughter and flung her arms round his neck. "I'm not trouble," she insisted.

"Yes you are," Wills assured her, bringing a beer for his father. "I finished my book too, Dad, and I'm already on page three of my next one. And I did a painting for Mum, didn't I, Mum?"

"You did, and it's your best one yet," she replied. "A lovely abstract. I think we'll put it up in our office."

"I'm going to do a painting for Mum too," Flora declared. "Mine will be of Waffle."

Hearing his name, Waffle lifted his head and wagged his tail.

"Has anyone fed you tonight?" Jack wanted to know.

As though understanding, Waffle got to his feet and wagged a little harder.

"His paw's nearly better now," Wills informed him. "He can probably take the boot off next week."

"Has anyone fed him?" Jenna asked, looking around.

"Paige might have," Josh offered. "She usually does."

"Go and check with her," Jenna instructed. "And tell her Dad's home, so she has to come down for tea."

"I'll go," Flora cried, dashing for the stairs before anyone could beat her to it. She had no competition; the boys were nowhere near as interested in what might be going on in Paige's room as she was.

"I'm here!" Paige shouted over the landing. "And yes, I've fed Waffle. Someone has to or the poor thing would starve."

Relieved she'd emerged, no matter what kind of mood she might be in, Jenna called out, "Do you want mash with your lamb chops or chips?"

"Whatever," Paige retorted, scooping Flora up as she reached her.

"Will you tell me your secrets?" Flora whispered in her ear.

"Only if you'll tell me yours," Paige whispered back.

Flora's eager nod quickly turned to a frown. "I don't have any," she confessed.

Laughing and hugging her, Paige set her down in the kitchen and regarded her mother.

"What?" Jenna prompted, raking a healthy helping of mash onto Paige's plate.

"Nothing," Paige replied. "Is that mine?"

"Yes. The other one's Dad's, so you can take that too."

"Ah ha, here's my little beauty queen," Jack declared, reaching for Paige as she brought his plate.

"Oh, Dad," she groaned. "I am so *not* a beauty queen."

"Now, that's just where you're wrong. How can you not be when you look just like your mother?"

"She's ugly," Josh muttered.

Paige turned to Jenna. "Is he talking about you or me?" she demanded.

"You!" Josh shouted.

"She's not ugly, she's beautiful," Jenna admonished.

"How can she not be beautiful when I already said she looks just like her mother?" Jack added.

Paige rolled her eyes. "He is *sooo* corny. I don't know how you can stand it."

"It's hard, but I manage," Jenna admitted.

"Dad?" Josh said, drawing out the word. "What's a condom?"

"What?" Paige shrieked. "How do you know about things like that?"

"I heard someone talking about them in school."

"But you're only eight," Paige protested, "and anyway we're eating, so we definitely don't want to talk about *that*."

Loving the way Jack's laughter made Paige's eyes shine, Jenna returned to her own meal just as Josh was saying to Paige, "Everyone's coming to watch me play football tomorrow. Will you come too?"

Eyes glued to her mobile, she said, "Can't. I'm going surfing with my friends."

His face fell.

Seeming to pick up on his disappointment, she added, "Sorry."

"It's all right," he said, shrugging.

"It would mean a lot to him," Jenna said quietly.

"Mu-um," Paige said through her teeth.

"I know!" Josh cried brightly. "Why don't we all go surfing after the game? We can meet Paige there. Where are you going?"

"No way am I going surfing with you lot," Paige stated firmly.

"Why not?" he demanded.

She regarded him as if he were crazy. "You mean apart from all the potential for embarrassment?"

As Jack and Jenna burst out laughing, Wills said, "Me and Flora can do body boarding, can't we, Mum? Mum, where's my board?"

"In the garage."

"Can I go and see it?"

"When you've finished your tea. We had a lovely email from the school today about Paige," Jenna told Jack. "Apparently Miss Kendrick, the English teacher, is putting Paige's short essay about daffodils in the school magazine."

Jack's eyes lit up. "That's marvelous," he declared. "I've told you before, you're following in your mother's footsteps with your literary talent."

"My essay's hardly in the same league as a *novel*," Paige pointed out. "And it's just dumb putting it in the magazine. No one'll want to read it."

"You'd be surprised," he responded knowingly. "What's happening about our tourist video?"

"It's *my* video, and I'm still editing it. I only have two ICT lessons a week, so it won't be ready for ages."

"We've got daffodils in our garden," Wills piped up. "Can we pick some, Mum?"

"I don't think so."

"OK. Mum? What's a condom?"

"Don't tell him, please!" Paige cried, covering her ears.

As Jack and Jenna laughed again, Wills said, "But I have to know or I won't ever learn."

"It's something people use when they're making babies to stop them catching diseases," Josh explained.

Astounded, Jenna said, "I thought you didn't know what one was."

"And I wouldn't exactly describe them that way," Jack added. "What they're—"

"No, Dad, don't, please," Paige begged. To Wills, she said, "Mum and Dad don't really know what they are. If they did, there wouldn't be so many of us."

Jack gave a shout of laughter. "Touché, Paige," he conceded.

Clearly trying not to laugh, she simply shrugged and carried on texting as she ate.

"So who are you going surfing with?" Jenna ventured as Flora came to sit on her lap.

"Just some friends," Paige replied. "You know, Charlotte and everyone."

"Which beach are you going to?" Josh asked.

"No way am I telling you. You'll turn up."

"But we're not embarrassing, are we, Dad?"

"We try not to be," Jack assured him.

"Can we take Waffle?" Flora asked.

"Of course. We wouldn't leave him at home, would we, boy?"

Closing in for a head rub, Waffle whopped Paige with his tail.

"You're Waffle's favorite," Flora told Paige.

"Because I feed him."

"So does Dad. He does it most, don't you, Dad?"

Jack was reading a message on his own mobile.

"Dad!" Flora cried.

"What?"

"I said—"

"Sorry, I heard you. I think you're right, Paige is his favorite."

"Is she your favorite too, because she's the oldest?"

"We don't have favorites," he insisted, which was true, they didn't, though Jenna did sometimes wonder if Paige might have the edge for Jack.

"Paige is my favorite," Flora decided. "And Mummy and you and Josh and Wills and *Waffle*. Oh, and Grandma."

"Speaking of grandmas," Jenna said, "how was your mother?"

Jack sighed and put down his phone. "No change. I think she was glad to see me, though."

"What's the matter with Grandma Moore?" Wills asked.

"She had a stroke," Jenna reminded him.

"What's a stroke?"

"It happens when blood can't get through to the brain."

"She can't speak, can she?" Flora asked.

Jenna shook her head.

"So how do you know when she's hungry?"

"Or when she wants to go to the toilet?" Josh added. "Or what she wants to watch on telly? I wish Flora and Wills would have a stroke so they didn't always get to watch what they want. I'm never allowed to choose."

"Yes you are," Wills cried. "And anyway, you've got your own television."

As the predictable row broke out Paige picked up her plate and took it through to the kitchen. To Jenna's relief she'd managed two-thirds of it, more than she'd got through the past couple of nights.

"I hope you're not leaving us," Jack called after her.

"I've got homework," Paige replied, keeping her back turned.

"Please tell me you're not spending all your time in chat rooms," Jenna commented, following her out.

"I go on them, like everyone else," Paige retorted. "What's wrong with that?"

"Just as long as you're not using any sites you know we wouldn't approve of."

"Don't worry, I'm not stupid."

Jenna eyed her warily. It was true, Paige wasn't stupid, but as her mother, Jenna was never going to take anything for granted.

"Mum, stop looking at me like that," Paige complained. "I just chat with my friends, and kids from other schools who are studying the same subjects. It's all perfectly legit."

"Make sure it stays that way—and if anyone you don't know tries to get you to do anything . . ."

"It's cool, OK? I know the rules, I'm not going to let myself be groomed or stalked or anything that you're thinking. Oh God, will you listen to them? Why do they always have to scream?"

"Because they're young. You were once, but now you've grown up into a grumpy teenage girl who tries not to laugh at our jokes but can't really stop herself even when she's totally embarrassed and wishes we were anyone's family but hers."

"It's spooky how you read my mind," Paige informed her. Treating Jenna to an exaggerated smile, she disappeared off upstairs.

It was much later in the evening, after hot-water bottles had been filled, stories read, and goodnight kisses dished out, that Jack returned to the kitchen to find Jenna checking her to-do list. "Paige seems in a better mood tonight," he commented, going to put the kettle on.

Jenna nodded. "Thank goodness. It's lovely when she laughs, isn't it? I always feel myself relaxing, which is when I realize how tense she can make me."

Coming to fold her in his arms, he said, "You're a wonderful mother, Jenna Moore. She's lucky to have you and she knows it."

Jenna's eyes were shining as she gazed into his. "It's her daddy she loves best," she told him. "But I don't suppose I blame her for that."

He kissed her deeply, easing her back against the worktop, where they might have gone further had a little voice not called out from the landing. "Mum, Wills said there's a monster under my bed."

By the time Jenna had resettled Flora and returned to the

kitchen, Jack had left a note letting her know he'd taken Waffle down to the beach.

"In the pitch dark?" she demanded when he answered his phone.

"There's a moon, and I brought a torch."

"Are you sure you aren't in the pub?"

"Would you mind if I was?"

"Only if you were trying to hide it. How long are you going to be?"

"Another ten minutes, no more."

"OK. I'll open a bottle of wine to drown our sorrows."

"What sorrows?"

"The fact that the Arts Council didn't increase our grant."

"They might still come through," he insisted, "so open that wine and put a Do Not Disturb sign on the bedroom door."

Laughing, she said, "Much notice anyone ever takes of it."

As she rang off she reached out to answer the landline.

"Jen? It's Marcus here. How are you?"

"I'm great, thanks," she replied, feeling her usual warmth for Jack's younger brother. "How are you?"

"Pretty good. We're still planning to visit again in the summer if that's OK. The kids had a blast the last time we came."

"So did ours, and of course it's OK. We loved having you here."

"That's kind of you to say, but if that new business of yours is up and running by then . . ."

"We'll still want you to come, so don't think any other way. Jack's out at the moment, I'm afraid, but you can reach him on the mobile, or I'll ask him to call when he gets back."

"Thanks. I only want to know if he's still intending to drive up and see Mum tomorrow."

Surprised, Jenna said, "He's just come back from there. Didn't he tell you he'd changed his plan?"

"Uh—no, uh, sorry—I . . . I had no idea. Well, if he's already seen her, I guess that answers my question."

"Would you still like him to call?"

"No. I mean yes, if he has time."

"He always does for you. Give my love to Penny and the kids, won't you?"

"Of course. Same goes for all of you."

After ringing off she tiptoed up the stairs, emptied the laundry baskets in Josh's and the twins' rooms and stood quietly outside Paige's for a moment, listening to the music inside. It was the same song she'd heard on other occasions, though whether it was coming from the iPod speakers or the computer she had no idea. It hardly mattered. Whoever the singer was, he had a good voice, strong yet mellow, slightly haunting in a way. She wondered if he was the latest teen sensation, or someone Paige knew. So many kids were putting videos and soundtracks online now that it could quite easily be a local lad hoping to make it big.

She'd ask if it wouldn't out her as an eavesdropper. Since it would, she tiptoed away. Deciding to forget the laundry for tonight, she went to her own room to start lighting candles. It was a while since she and Jack had made love—either they were too tired, or there was a child in the bed, or she was already asleep by the time he got home. Tonight, however, she was very much in the mood to make it happen.

Chapter 5

Daffodils have a jaunty exuberance, unlike primroses whose own exuberance is shyly sunny, or roses who can be guilty of a haughty grandeur. Daffodils, being the traditional flower of Wales, are always worn on St. David's Day and they light highways, byways, woodlands, parks and gardens with the buttery radiance of their smiles throughout the spring months. They seem to say, here I am, winter's over, love me, pick me, share me, just don't ignore me.

Paige couldn't remember any more than that; she wasn't even doing very well recalling this first part of the short essay she'd written about a month ago, *"In Praise of the Daffodil."*

Miss Kendrick was mad about the flowers and never stopped going on about them at this time of year, when the whole countryside was covered in them.

Paige had to admit they were lovely. They had a way of making a person want to appreciate nature—this was something else she'd written in the essay, but she couldn't think now how she'd made it fit in. It didn't matter, since no one was about to test her on it; she was just trying to focus her mind on something other than how excited and fearful she was about the day ahead.

Oliver was definitely going to be there at the beach. Cullum had confirmed it to Charlotte last night. So was Liam. She and Charlotte had been on FaceTime for hours after Cullum's text, and again this morning as they'd decided how they were going to wear their hair and whether or not they looked fat in their wetsuits.

They were in Charlotte's mum's car now, heading through Burry Green on their way to Llangennith. Paige was in the back, gazing out at the millions of daffs brightening up the route and trying not to feel sick. She had to keep herself calm by thinking about anything but him; unfortunately, she couldn't think about anything else. She was asking herself a gazillion questions, such as: Would he remember her? Was he hoping she'd come today? Was he going to like the way she'd loosely plaited her hair over one shoulder? Would he think she looked cool and sophisticated, the way the model had in the magazine she'd copied it from? He probably wouldn't notice her at all. *Please God, don't let me do or say something stupid so I end up making a total prat of myself.*

She'd hardly slept, she was so worked up about this. Making it a thousand times worse was the fact that she'd actually sent him a friend request last night.

Why had she done that? How could she take it back?

"I don't expect he's even seen it yet," Charlotte had reassured her on FaceTime earlier. "He might not be someone who goes on every day the way we do."

"He's probably wondering who the heck I am," Paige had groaned. "If he even knew my name in the first place—and I

bet he didn't—he'll think I'm really weird for suddenly changing it to my mum's maiden name."

"Well you could hardly ask him to connect to the page that's
under attack from the Durmites."

"At least they haven't posted anything since that horrible
thing they said about you."

Charlotte appeared to have forgotten it already. "Do you
think we should be wearing one-pieces rather than bikinis
under our wetsuits?" she asked.

"I'm definitely wearing a bikini and a T-shirt. Should I tell
him I've watched his video?"

"If it comes up, but I wouldn't cough to how many times or
he'll think you're a stalker. Which reminds me, have you heard
any more from that Julie person?"

"Not really, and she's not a stalker. I think she's just lonely."

"But she still hasn't told you who she is, and for all you know
she might not even be a girl. It could be someone's dad or
brother getting off on pretending he's a schoolgirl."

"Then how would he know all the stuff that's going on with
Owen and the Durmites?"

"No idea. I'm just saying I still think it's weird that she won't
tell you who she is."

Paige thought so too. Even so, she'd been online with Julie
for over an hour last night, chatting about all sorts of stuff that
only girls would chat about. Favorite bands, movies they rated,
makeup they'd tried, how strict their parents were, what it was
like being part of a big family—Julie always seemed to like
hearing about her family. Not that Paige was dumb enough to
tell her anything really personal; she was never going to do that
until Julie fessed up to who she really was.

She looked down as her phone bleeped with a text.

You are such a fucking loser. Think we haven't figured out your new FB name? What a pathetic mummy's girl you are, you filthy swot!

It was from Kelly, the fourth that morning. She wasn't even bothering to hide the fact that she was the sender, which was why Paige was feeling quite certain now that Kelly and Julie were not the same person.

Another text arrived.

Have you had this one yet?

Paige opened the attached picture. It turned out to be of a giant penis. Knowing how hilarious the Durmites would be finding this, she quickly closed down her phone. She wasn't going to let them spoil her day, and besides, she could never get any reception at Llangennith anyway, so she wouldn't need it.

As the pale blue expanse of sea came into view she sat forward to rest her arms on the back of Charlotte's seat. They'd already passed the King's Head, so they were only minutes away.

She wasn't thinking about the Durmites. They meant nothing to her, and she definitely wasn't going to tell Charlotte about the texts; if she did, they'd end up talking about them, and she just wanted to forget them.

"I'd feel happier if there was a lifeguard on duty," Charlotte's mother commented with a sigh.

"It's not dangerous," Charlotte assured her. "No one's ever drowned here, have they? No surfers anyway."

"Are you sure about that?"

"Definitely. And we've been here a hundred times, Mum. It's not like we don't know it."

Since this was true, Lucy Griffiths said no more as she drove them into a caravan park and wound down through the site to a sprawling car park behind the dunes. There were plenty of other vehicles around, and people coming and going, some of whom Paige vaguely recognized, but most she didn't.

"Do you know if they're here yet?" Paige whispered to Charlotte as she tried to spot Oliver's black Ford Fiesta.

"They must be," Charlotte replied. "Cullum texted before we left to say they were already on their way."

Going to retrieve her surfboard from the back of Lucy's wagon while struggling to hold her plait in place against the wind, Paige found her spirits lifting at the tangy taste of fresh salt air on her lips. The sound of the sea was a low, constant growl all around them, threaded with seagull cries and the odd blast of music coming from someone's car. "Did he say if Owen was with them?" she asked, feeling a clench of nerves as she thought of it. If he was, it would be the first time she'd seen him since the horrible Facebook posting, as he hadn't been at school at all after that.

"No, but he said last night that he was pretty sure he'd be coming. It's all right, you don't have to worry. You know what Owen's like—he's too sweet to bear a grudge, especially for something he's got to realize by now that you didn't do."

Knowing she'd feel more confident about that if Owen had returned her texts and messages, Paige stood aside as Lucy fussed around Charlotte reminding her not to take any risks, or to get too cold, or to talk to strangers.

"I'm not six," Charlotte protested.

Laughing, Lucy embraced her. "Just teasing. But *don't* talk to strangers. Are you OK, Paige? Got everything?"

"I'm good," Paige assured her, feeling slightly envious of Charlotte's only-child status. Not that she didn't love her brothers and sister when they weren't driving her mad, which was actually most of the time; it would just be nice to have her mum and dad to herself once in a while.

A few minutes later, after waving Lucy off, they were starting along the path through the dunes, boards tucked tightly under their arms, heavy bags draped on their shoulders.

"Have you noticed something? We seem to be the only ones heading in this direction. Everyone else seems to be leaving," Paige remarked.

"They probably started early," Charlotte responded. "God, it's bloody freezing, isn't it? Let's hurry up and get there. Just tell me, are you sure my bum doesn't look big in this?"

Obediently checking, Paige said, "Don't be daft. You're a supermodel, so how can it. Does mine?"

"Yeah, huge," Charlotte decided.

Paige's eyes rounded.

"Like someone who's size six has a big ass. Do me a favor."

Giggling, they tramped on through the sand, careful not to collide with other surfers who were heading away from the beach.

"I reckon they know something we don't," Paige whispered.

"There's Cullum!" Charlotte cried, spotting him coming up over the mound. Matt and Ryan were with him, but there was no sign of Owen—or of Oliver and Liam.

"Surf's lousy," Cullum told them as he approached. "Waste of time. We're heading up to the café."

"Did you bring any money?" Charlotte asked Paige.

Paige almost didn't hear. She'd just caught sight of Oliver, and he looked so amazing, so totally drop-dead in his wetsuit with his dark hair blowing about in the wind and his teeth gleaming white as he laughed, that she thought she might faint.

"Uh, I've got a fiver," she mumbled, and quickly turned away before anyone realized where she was looking.

He was here! He was actually coming toward her with a group of his mates, and any second now she was going to say hello. *Oh my God. Oh my God.* She was so elated and terrified she hardly knew what to do. Would he mention her friend request? Maybe he'd already accepted. What was she going to say if he had? She wanted to sound intelligent and witty and like someone he'd enjoy talking to, but she wasn't sure she knew how to do that.

"Come on, if you're coming," Cullum shouted.

Paige spun round. Realizing Charlotte had turned back with the others, she hurried to catch up. *Please God, don't let Oliver think I've been waiting for him.*

"He's here," she whispered as she reached Charlotte.

"No way!" Charlotte responded ironically.

"Do you think he saw me?"

"How do I know?" She cast a glance over her shoulder to check how far behind he and his mates were and almost choked with shock. "OMG! OMG!" she hissed. "Liam only just winked at me. I need oxygen. He is so totally amazing. Do you think he's watching my ass?"

"Ssh, they'll hear," Paige warned with a laugh.

There was a burst of mirth from behind, and she immediately tensed. She hoped he wasn't telling his mates that she'd sent him a friend request. If it turned out that was what they were laughing at, she was going to collapse and die. If only she hadn't done it, she might not be feeling so stupid and self-conscious or thoroughly sick of herself right now.

Though the café was crowded, Matt and Ryan managed to snag a couple of tables by the window as another group left, while Cullum headed straight to the hatch to order. "I'd treat you," he told Paige and Charlotte, "but I've only—"

"It's OK," Charlotte assured him, grabbing Paige's fiver. "Cappuccino for you?"

"With chocolate," Paige replied.

Since there was only one barista, they had a long wait for their drinks, but eventually they were all seated around the tables, with Oliver and his mates at one end and Paige and Charlotte at the other. It was a disaster, but since they could hardly ask Cullum and the others to swap places, they had no choice but to make the most of the fact that they were actually in the same caff as Oliver and Liam. Whether Oliver and Liam were feeling the same was doubtful, since they barely even glanced in their direction as they chatted and laughed with the rest of their mates. But then, during a rowdy group debate on who was going to score for Wales in the Six Nations match that afternoon, Oliver caught Paige's eye and smiled. She nearly passed out, and had to thank God for reflexes, because it was the only way she managed to smile back.

"Did you see that?" she murmured to Charlotte as soon as he'd turned away.

"Are you kidding?" Charlotte whispered. "He's definitely got the hots for you."

"Are you sure he wasn't just being polite?"

"If that's what you want to tell yourself, but no way did it look like that to me."

"Oh my God. What do you think I should do?"

"Ask him for a shag."

"Be serious."

"OK, then I don't know."

"I can't just go over there and talk to him."

"Maybe he'll come over here. Cullum, you tosser! That's my cup."

"Sorry," he laughed, putting it down and picking up his own.

"Hey, Charlotte!" someone called out.

Realizing it was Liam, Charlotte's eyes almost popped out. "OMG, he's telling me to go over," she muttered to Paige, already getting to her feet.

Desperate for Oliver to invite her too, Paige could only watch and feel foolish and envious as Charlotte made her way to the end of the table, where Liam pulled up a chair for her to sit down.

Minutes passed as Charlotte amazed and impressed Paige with the easy banter she seemed to fall into with Liam, while Oliver, appearing oblivious, talked to another of his mates. In the end, starting to feel like a total lemon, Paige leaned in toward Cullum and said, "So how come Owen isn't here?"

Cullum's eyebrows rose incredulously. "Why do you think?" he countered.

Realizing it was because of her, Paige felt herself flush. "I thought . . . I mean, you've told him it wasn't me, haven't you?"

"Course I have, but he said he still wasn't going to show today if you were here."

Paige couldn't think what to say.

"Actually, now we're on the subject," Cullum ran on, "we're all going back to my house afterward to watch the Six Nations. I've told Owen we really want him there, so if you could kind of, you know, back off when we leave here . . . He's had a tough week, and I think he needs to find out who his real friends are."

Paige's heart was twisting; there was a buzzing in her ears that made it almost impossible to hear herself as she mumbled,

"Yes, of course. I mean, don't worry, I wouldn't be able to make it anyway." She wanted to leave now, to get as far away from here as it was possible to go, but Lucy wasn't due back for another couple of hours, and with no phone reception she couldn't call her mum.

She tried to catch Charlotte's eye, but Charlotte was too busy enjoying herself to notice. Cullum was talking to the others again, his back half turned as though deliberately shutting her out. She didn't understand it. He hadn't been like this when they'd sat together in English during the week, or when they'd rehearsed *Under Milk Wood*. Not that there had been a chance to discuss anything then; Miss Kendrick was too much in their faces to allow what she considered idle chitchat.

Feeling too wretched to carry on sitting on the edge of things, she gathered up her bag and headed for the ladies' room. Instead of going in, she turned toward the exit, and after collecting her board she started out of the campsite. It wasn't that far to the King's Head, probably about a mile along a narrow country road, and once there, with any luck, she'd be able to call her mother to come and fetch her.

It didn't happen that way, because even when she got there her mobile still wouldn't work and the pub was closed, so she couldn't get inside to use a landline. She didn't know what to do. It was too far to walk all the way home, and she was so cold she doubted she'd make it anyway.

With tears pricking her eyes she laid her board down and went to try the pub door, just in case.

It was definitely locked.

In desperation she walked round to the back of the building and climbed to the top of the car park, holding up her phone, willing it to catch a signal from somewhere, but there wasn't even the glimmer of a single bar.

She shouldn't have left the café. It was a stupid, childish thing to have done, especially without telling Charlotte. By now Charlotte would be wondering where she was, wanting to know why she'd gone off without saying a word, and Cullum would probably tell her. What would happen then? Would everyone start looking for her? They'd probably just assume she was in a sulk and would show up again when she was ready.

How childish they must already be thinking she was.

Nevertheless, a part of her was desperate to go back, but she was going to feel a total idiot traipsing up to the café with her board, like she'd just taken it for a walk or something. Where would she say she'd been? Maybe *I took off in a huff because Cullum clearly doesn't believe my Facebook page was hacked?* Or *My feelings were hurt because everyone wants Owen to watch the match later, not me?* She could always say she'd needed to make a phone call, so she'd gone to try to find a signal. She shook her head. Like she'd really take her board for that!

It was the best she could come up with; even so, she still couldn't bring herself to go back. Cullum obviously didn't want her there, which no doubt meant Matt and Ryan didn't either, and no way was she going to push herself in where she wasn't wanted.

Dropping her bag on a random picnic table, she stared helplessly at her phone again. She wondered if Oliver was worried about her, or if he'd even realized yet that she'd left. Over half an hour had gone by, so Charlotte would no doubt have checked the ladies' room by now, which meant they had to be wondering what had happened to her.

If they were, they certainly didn't notice her as they drove past in Oliver's Fiesta a few minutes later with their boards strapped to the roof. She didn't catch a glimpse of Oliver, but Cullum was definitely in the passenger seat and Charlotte was in the back. Another car with more boards on top was close behind. She saw Ryan and Matt in that one, and was sure it was Liam at the wheel. If she hadn't been tucked inside the car park, which meant they were almost past by the time she saw them, they might have seen her too. As it was, they were gone in seconds, and she suddenly felt so alone and so horribly abandoned that it was as though she had no place in the world to go.

She tried telling herself that was nonsense, but it was how she felt, and the fact that she couldn't get hold of her mum and dad was making it worse. They'd had a horrible row last night. She had no idea what it was about; she'd just heard them shouting, so she'd put her earplugs in and turned up the music. She hated it when they rowed. Not that it happened often, but when it did it was like everything felt wrong and scary and like they totally needed to get over themselves. At least they'd seemed all right this morning, what little she'd seen of them, but her mum had said that they definitely weren't going surfing after Josh's football match, so there was no chance they might drive by at any minute.

She had to get a grip and remind herself that she wasn't a child, so she could figure this out. She was sure Mr. Dixon, one of the science teachers, lived in this village, but the trouble was, even if he did, she had no idea which house was his. She could always knock on someone's door and ask. Or she could sit here and wait until the pub finally opened so she could go in and use their phone.

Feeling close to tears again, and colder than she'd ever been in her life, she dropped her head against the drizzle and almost didn't look up as a car came chugging steadily down the hill. Thank goodness she did, because the instant she saw it she leapt to her feet, waving madly.

"Grandma! Grandma!" she shouted, running out of the car park.

The little yellow Fiat kept going, past the village hall, around the bend, and out of sight.

Paige ran faster. She had no idea why her grandma was here—maybe Charlotte had rung as soon as she'd got reception and now everyone was searching for her.

As she reached the bend she fully expected her grandma to be long gone, tootling obliviously along the road toward the beach, but to her relief the Fiat was pulling up outside St. Cenydd's Church.

"Grandma!" she shouted as Kay got out of the car.

Kay looked around in bewilderment.

"Grandma! It's me." Paige was almost there now.

"Goodness, Paige, what are you doing here?" Kay demanded. "I thought you were surfing."

"I was. It's a long story. Oh, Grandma, I'm so glad to see you," and she promptly burst into tears.

A few minutes later, having delivered the leaflets she'd come to drop off for the parish, Kay was once again behind the wheel of her Fiat with Paige's surfboard jutting out of a rear window and Paige herself wrapped in a fleecy blanket in the front seat.

"Do you want to tell me what happened?" Kay invited as they started up the hill.

Paige was staring down at her lifeless phone. No texts or calls from Charlotte. How mean was that? She was going to watch the match with everyone else, and obviously wasn't sparing a single thought for her best mate! "Not really," she answered miserably.

Kay continued to drive.

That was the weirdest and sometimes loveliest thing about her grandma: she never asked too many questions. She was the only person Paige knew who seemed comfortable with not talking for hours on end. Not that it was going to take them that long to get home, only about twenty minutes—although considering the way her grandma drove, it might be closer to thirty. She did everything so precisely, obeyed all the rules, and always seemed startled when others failed to do so. Road rage seemed to pass straight over her, even when someone behind was flashing their lights and honking their horn to make her speed up or let them pass. She just kept on going, hands on the wheel at ten and two, eyes straight ahead, and expression as neutral as if she were thinking no thoughts at all.

Paige longed to be able to switch her mind off the way her grandma seemingly could. Then she wouldn't have to keep thinking about Oliver, or Charlotte, who had totally betrayed her, or Owen, who should have known she'd never deliberately hurt him, or Kelly Durham, who despised her for no good reason. Everything was just totally horrible. She wished they'd never moved here now. She couldn't bear it that all her friends were getting together to watch rugby, *at Oliver's house,* and she wasn't allowed to join them.

Fighting back more tears, she glanced at her grandma, and amongst all the angst and self-pity she felt herself flood with affection. Kay was a funny old stick, as her mum would say, a woman who was definitely her own person, but she was always there when one of her family needed her, and she never made a fuss about anything. Paige wondered what she did when she was at home on her own, if she felt sad or happy with her life, how much she missed Grandpa. She never talked about him, but maybe that was because no one ever asked.

"Grandma?"

"Yes?" Kay's eyes were tight to the road.

"Can I ask you a question?"

"Of course."

"How did you and Grandpa meet?"

With no hesitation, Kay replied, "It was when we were at college. He was studying to become an engineer and I was doing a bookkeeping course."

"But how did you actually get together?"

Clearly having no problem with recall, Kay said, "Your grandpa noticed that some people weren't very kind to me, so he made me his friend."

Paige's eyes widened. "Why were people unkind to you?"

"Because I wasn't really like them."

So she knew she was different. "Did it hurt your feelings when they were mean?"

"Yes, very much, but they never seemed to realize it. Or perhaps they didn't care."

"What did you do?"

"I tried to ignore them, but it was Grandpa who really sorted them out."

"How? What did he do?"

"He used to give them one of his stares."

Paige giggled. "You mean the secret weapon," she said, having heard about his famous look from her mother.

"That's the one. He could make people feel very foolish with that look."

Paige laughed and felt so glad for her grandma that she'd had Grandpa to take care of her that she wanted to hug the older woman.

If only Grandpa were still around to take care of *her*.

"Yes, Mum, I can hear you," Jenna was saying into the phone as she made her way from the football field to the car. "Josh had a good game, if that's why you're ringing. We were hoping they might make him man of the match, but it went to someone on the other team in the end."

"I'm sure Josh was more deserving," Kay responded loyally.

Knowing he wasn't, Jenna looked down at his happy little face, bobbing proudly along beside her, and wanted to go and thank the coach all over again for including him today. It had meant the world to him. She was just grateful that he hadn't scored an own goal, because it had been a very near thing.

"Are you coming home now?" Kay asked.

"Not yet, I'm taking the twins into town for new shoes. Can I get you anything while I'm there?"

"No thank you. I did my shopping yesterday. I think you should come home."

Frowning, Jenna said, "Why?"

"Because I've just dropped Paige off and she was crying when I found her."

"What do you mean, found her? Where was she?"

"In Llangennith. I know she was supposed to be surfing, but she was a long way from the beach and there was no sign of her friends."

"Did she tell you what happened?"

"No."

And her mother wouldn't have pushed it. "She's obviously had some sort of falling-out with Charlotte," Jenna decided, experiencing a flash of annoyance as she spotted Jack in his car talking on the phone. *Who the hell is he talking to now?* "I'll give her a ring."

After disconnecting, she settled the children in the back of her car and, leaving them to squabble over who had to sit in the middle, took Waffle over to Jack. As he saw her coming he opened the driver's door and told whoever he was talking to that he'd get right on it and ring them back.

"What are you doing?" he asked as Jenna ushered Waffle into the passenger seat.

"You need to take him home."

"But I've arranged—"

"I don't care what you've arranged. The dog needs to go home while I take the children."

"Jenna, for God's sake . . ."

"Don't 'for God's sake' me. Whatever your plans are, you can change them."

"They're expecting me."

"Who?"

"Bill and the lads. To watch the match."

"Then call back to say you can't make it. The dog needs to go home and apparently Paige is upset."

"What about?"

"I don't know, but as her father, you might like to find out and see if there's anything you can do to comfort her."

"Oh, come on. Whatever it is will have blown over by the time I get there. I'll take the dog back, then carry on."

"Why are you so insistent that you have to watch the match with the lads?"

His face tightened. "Because it's what we arranged."

"Well, now you can unarrange it and watch the game with Paige and Josh. He doesn't need to come with me—he had new shoes last week."

Sighing and holding up his hands in surrender, he said, "OK, if it'll make you happy . . ."

"It will." Aware they were being watched by other parents, she went to get Josh.

"Dad's going to watch the game with *me*?" Josh gasped in delight. "That is so awesome!" Throwing off his seat belt, he dashed over to his father's car.

"I want to watch it too," Wills cried, trying to follow.

"You have to come with me," Jenna told him.

"But I don't want to. Please don't make me."

"You need shoes and we won't know what size you are if your feet aren't there."

Finding that funny, Wills laughed and settled back in his seat.

"Are you still cross with Daddy?" Flora asked, her dark eyes sweetly magnified by her glasses.

"You don't miss a thing, do you?" Jenna commented, getting into the driver's seat.

"Are you?" Flora pressed.

"No, I'm not," Jenna lied. "I'm only happy that Josh had a good game and that I've got my lovely twins coming into town with me."

"You didn't even stand with Daddy while Josh was playing," Flora pointed out.

This was true, she hadn't, for the very good reason that she might not have been able to stop herself carrying on their argument from last night, and the last thing she'd wanted was to turn them into a public spectacle. What she'd needed, then and now, was to find out the real reason why he hadn't returned home until after midnight when he'd said he'd be back in ten minutes. His excuse was that he'd got chatting in the pub and time had run away with him, which often happened with him, and ordinarily she simply let it go. This time she hadn't, and she wasn't sure why. Maybe because he didn't appear to have been drinking, and she was sure he'd smelled of perfume.

Perfume, for God's sake!

"The only reason I could possibly smell of perfume," he'd retorted when she'd leveled it at him, "is because Andy Ritch's missus was in the pub and you know how she always reeks of the stuff."

Actually, she *didn't* know that about Judy Ritch. "So is that who you were with?"

"No! She gave me a hug before she left."

"So if I rang her now, she'd confirm that?"

"Jenna, for Christ's sake, you can't go calling people up at this time of night. And where has all this suspicion suddenly come from? What exactly are you trying to accuse me of?"

Since she wasn't entirely sure herself, she'd turned away and gone into the bathroom, where she shrugged off her dressing gown and tossed the filmy negligee she'd put on—three hours earlier—into the laundry. She'd then dragged on her pajamas, collected up all the spent candles, and dumped them in the waste bin.

By the time she'd returned to bed he was already asleep, or at least was pretending to be, but she hadn't wanted to carry on the scene anyway, so she'd simply turned her back and switched off the light.

Being Jack, he'd assumed it was all forgotten this morning when he'd ventured downstairs for breakfast, and had appeared genuinely surprised when she'd moved away from his embrace. In truth she hadn't even known she was going to do so, had actually told herself at some point in the night to let it go, but for some reason she was finding herself unable to.

Where had he really been last night? And who was so important that he'd missed the last five minutes of his son's football match to go and take their call just now? She should have asked to see his phone, and probably would have had they not been standing in full view of half their neighbors.

As she drove across the bleak, glorious landscape of the Bryn, where the randomly wandering wild ponies immediately grabbed Flora's attention, she felt tempted to call the pub to find out if he really had been there last night. She wouldn't do it, not only because of the gossip it would stir up, but also because she wasn't certain she wanted to hear the answer. She was remembering now how Irene Evans had seemed so certain that she hadn't seen him for a while, and how perplexed his brother had sounded when she'd told him Jack had already seen their mother this week.

As her heart churned with dread of what this could mean, her hands tightened on the wheel. *Damn him! Damn, damn, damn him.* How could he put her in this position, making her feel worried, insecure, jealous, when she'd never been any of those things before? They were so close, had always been each other's best friend, had never had secrets from each other—or so she'd believed.

Dear God, please don't let things be about to change. They were happy together, adored their children. They were about to launch their own business, had the house of their dreams, enjoyed the kind of marriage so many of her friends only dreamed about . . . She couldn't lose it all now—she couldn't lose it *ever*.

Using the hands-free to connect to him, she half expected to be bumped to voicemail, but he answered on the fourth ring.

"Are you home?" she asked.

"Just got here. Paige is in her room." He didn't sound angry, but neither did he sound very friendly.

"Have you spoken to her?"

"Not yet. I'm not sure how to make her come down. Any suggestions?"

"She will if she wants to. If she doesn't, it'll probably help just to know you're there."

"What's wrong with Paige?" Flora asked from the back.

"Nothing, sweetheart. You keep counting the ponies." To Jack she said, "There are hamburgers in the fridge, buns in the bread bin."

"Thanks."

"Can we have hamburgers?" Wills wanted to know.

"Yes, for tea, when we get home."

"I'm hungry now."

"We'll get something in town."

"Dad!" Flora shouted. "I counted sixteen ponies."

"Very good," he praised. "Can you work out how many legs that is?"

Amused, and annoyed, by the way he'd so easily distracted her, Jenna said, "I don't want this to go on."

"You think I do?"

"No. I hope not, anyway."

"I don't."

She knew if the children weren't listening he'd probably say more, but because they were it would have to wait. "I'm sorry I jumped to conclusions," she told him.

"I'm sorry too. I should have come home earlier. I wish I had, because unless I'm gravely mistaken I think I missed out on some candles."

"You did, but we have more." Kind of glad she'd made the call, she rang off.

Putting aside the hot-water bottle her grandma had given her before going off to deliver more leaflets, Paige got up from the bed. She was feeling a bit better now, more able to face up to everything that was going wrong in her life.

It had helped, a lot, that she'd had a long chat with Charlotte a while ago. Apparently Charlotte had been worried sick about what might have happened to her and hadn't been sure whether to call her mum.

"If I hadn't heard from you in the next ten minutes I was going to," she'd vowed when they'd finally connected. "Cullum told me what he said to you, the tosser. It's bloody typical of him to come out with things the wrong way."

"So are you at his house now?"

"Yeah, and Owen's here, so I'm going to try and have a chat with him. It's just stupid the way all this crap is getting out of hand. When he sees for himself that none of us have turned against him—well, he's got to know that already or Cullum wouldn't have invited him—he'll definitely come round."

Desperate to believe that, Paige said, "How's it going with

Liam? You were totally amazing the way you went over to him, like you knew him already."

"I must admit I felt really comfortable with him right off. He's, like, totally easy to be with, and we can't stay virgins all our lives, can we?"

As they giggled Paige said, "Have you spoken to Oliver at all?"

"Not really. He's a bit, I don't know . . . kind of moody, I guess, and . . . What's the word? *Deep.* That's it, deep. That's how he comes across to me, anyway. Don't get me wrong, he has a laugh and everything, but there just seems to be this other side of him. I'll keep an eye on him during the match and let you know what I think after."

Loving him even more for being moody and deep, Paige said enviously, "Please don't tell me you're the only girl there."

"No way! Hayley, Courtenay, and Nicole have just turned up and more people are on their way, apparently, so I expect some of them will be girls."

Struck completely miserable by being left out, and by the fear that Oliver might fancy one of the other girls, added to the fact that he had a girlfriend anyway (except where was she?), Paige said, "It really sucks that this is happening. It's making me feel like a total loser." That was what Kelly Durham had called her.

Maybe Kelly was right.

"No way are you a loser," Charlotte objected. "It'll all get straightened out with Owen, I promise. I'm going to find him as soon as we get off the phone."

"Before you go, what's the house like? Is it as big as Cullum's always making out?"

"Oh my God, you should see it. It's a bloody mansion, it is, and there's only an actual screening room where we're going to watch the match. Apparently Oliver's recording studio is next door to that, and there's a games room somewhere, Cullum said, with billiards and darts and all that boring bloke shite. His dad's obviously stinking rich."

"Are his parents there?"

"His mum's dead," Charlotte reminded her, "and I haven't seen his dad, but we only got here a few minutes ago. Listen, I have to ring off now, but I'll keep texting to let you know how everything's going, OK?"

When the first message came it said, *Tried speaking to Owen but he's avoiding me.*

The second, *Game's just kicked off so can't do it yet.*

The third, *Oliver sat on his own in great big chair for two, looking sad. Reckon he's missing you.*

Though Paige's heart had jumped at that, she'd known it couldn't be true. It was nice to think about it for a while, though, imagining him looking up as she walked in, putting his arm around her as she sat down.

Hello slag, how many dicks have you had today? Like the one I sent you earlier? Big enough for you?

Totally sickened, Paige was tempted to send a message back telling Kelly to drop dead, but in the end she managed to stop herself. If she responded, she'd only end up getting even more abuse, and she could definitely do without that.

"Paige! Are you all right in there?" her dad called out for what felt like the hundredth time.

"Yeah, I'm fine. I'll be down in a minute."

"You're missing the match."

"I said, I'll be down in a minute."

So what's it like being ugly? You know that's what everyone thinks, don't you?

Trying to tell herself it wasn't true, she deleted the text and clicked on to a new one from Charlotte.

Are you watching the game? You should, it's brilliant. Wales def going to win.

What's the score? she messaged back.

When she didn't receive a reply she wandered over to her laptop and sat down in front of it. There were a few emails in her inbox, all from school, and a private message on Facebook from Julie.

Hey, everything cool with you?

She messaged back saying, *Yeah, cool, how about you?* but there was no reply, so Julie was obviously no longer online. Deciding to try her on Pheed, she reached for her phone and opened the app just as another text came in from Kelly.

You know what I love about your face? The thought of punching it.

Why couldn't the girl just get lost? What was the matter with her that she had to keep doing this? Didn't she have a life, for God's sake?

Suddenly wanting to be close to her dad, she pulled a jumper on over her camisole and trackies, dug her feet into her slippers, and went downstairs, taking the phone with her in case Charlotte messaged again.

"Here she is." Her dad beamed, holding out an arm for her to come and snuggle in next to him. "We were beginning to think you were ignoring us, weren't we, Josh?"

"It's a brilliant game," Josh told her. "Wales are in the lead, seventeen to three. We've scored three tries and converted one, and the others have only scored one penalty."

"Sweet," she muttered.

"Sweet," Josh mimicked.

"Don't copy me," she snapped.

"Don't copy me."

"Dad, tell him, or I'm going to hit him."

"Dad, tell him—"

"All right, that's enough," Jack declared, holding up his hands. "Let's focus on the game, shall we?"

Still trying not to mind that she wasn't with her mates, Paige decided to text Hayley, seeing as Charlotte hadn't answered her yet. *How's it going over there? I hear Cullum's house is fantastic.*

Seconds later a reply came back. *Been before. Totally amazing. You should be here.*

Couldn't come because of Owen.

That's totally crap.

Yh, but what can I do?

We'll sort it.

Hoping they would, Paige hugged the phone to her chest and leaned in closer to her dad. Normally she loved rugby, but she was finding it hard to get into the game today even though Wales were winning.

"Feeling better now?" her dad asked after a while.

She bristled. "What do you mean? There was nothing wrong with me."

"Oh, sorry. Mum said you were upset about something."

Her mouth tightened. Grandma had obviously rung her mum, which she'd actually expected, but if Mum knew she was upset, why hadn't she rung herself to find out what the problem was? Because she was always too busy with Josh or the twins, that was why.

"You can always talk to me if something's bothering you," her dad told her, as if he were her best mate or the person she always turned to.

He was, sometimes.

"Yeah, right," she said. "Thanks."

"I mean it."

"Cool."

"I was your age once, remember?"

"Like a hundred years ago."

Laughing, he drew her in tighter. "Fancy something to eat? There are hamburgers."

She shook her head. "No thanks."

"Have you had anything today?"

She tried to think. Maybe she hadn't.

"You'll be wasting away," he chided. "Let me get you something."

"No, I'm not hungry. Where's Mum?"

"Taking the twins to get new shoes."

Should she ask her next question or not? It was making her insides churn up to think of it, but in the end she decided she would. "Are you two OK now?"

Sounding surprised, he said, "What do you mean, are we OK?"

"I heard you rowing last night."

Josh looked round worriedly. They all hated it when their parents fell out.

Jack laughed. "Would you believe, I was getting told off for leaving my dirty socks on the floor."

Paige screwed up her nose, pretending to be convinced—except her mother never went off about things like that. Still, if it was what he wanted her to think, she wasn't going to pry any further. In fact, given how late it had been, it might have been about sex, for God's sake. Just as long as they were all right now.

A few minutes later she was starting to drift to sleep against her dad's shoulder when his mobile brought her round. Being the closest, she went to pick it up from the coffee table, but he beat her to it.

"Who's Martha?" she asked as he clicked on.

Putting a finger to his lips, he said, "Hi, Martha. Working on a Saturday? How's the website coming along?"

Remembering who Martha was now, Paige lost interest, yawned, and closed her eyes again.

"Hang on, I'll go over to the office," he said. Unraveling himself from his children, he took off across the garden.

Five minutes later he was back, announcing, "Kids, I have to pop out for a bit. You'll be OK, won't you?"

Paige shrugged. "I guess we'll have to be."

"Don't worry, Dad, I'll look after Paige."

As Jack laughed, Paige shot her brother a look and followed it with a cushion.

She must have fallen asleep soon after that, because the next thing she knew the match was over, her mum was home, and Flora was tugging her awake to show off her new shoes.

"They've even got platforms," Flora was telling her, "but you can't see them because they're hidden, aren't they, Mum?"

"Where are Josh and Dad?" Jenna called through from the kitchen.

Paige was still stretching as she came round. "I don't know."

Jenna came to the door, hands on hips. "Paige!"

"OK, OK. Dad had to go out, and I expect Josh is upstairs in his room."

Not looking best pleased, her mother sent Wills to make sure Josh was in the house and said to Paige, "Did Dad tell you where he was going?"

Paige shook her head as she checked her phone.

"Paige!"

There were three texts from Charlotte.

The first: *OMG, don't know how to tell you this, but Lindsay French just turned up.*

The second: *They're definitely an item.*

The third: *Where are you, please text me back.*

"Paige, are you listening to me?" her mother snapped angrily. "Did Dad say where he was going?"

"Just out," Paige snapped back. Dodging Flora and her new shoes, she started upstairs to her room.

"I'm here, Mum," Josh shouted over the banister.

"Out where?" her mother called after her.

"I don't know, he didn't say." Closing the door behind her, she slid all the way down it. Crouching, she buried her head in her arms.

Lindsay French was at his house, and they were probably even kissing right now, while she was here all on her own like a waste of space, a filthy swot, a total loser, a piece of rubbish.

Chapter 6

"There's a woman over in Llanelli," Bena was reading from the paper, "who's only gone and left her body to medical science with the proviso that they use it to find a cure for cellulite. 'It's ruined my life,' she said. 'I want to stop others having to suffer the same way.'" She looked up to check that Jenna was listening. "I don't know whether to laugh or feel grateful," she commented dryly, "except it'll be too late for me by the time they get round to it. Speaking personally, I'd want my body to be used to kill off the redhead gene. It's a bloody pain in the neck being this color—all the teasing I had to go through at school, the deathly white skin, never being able to go in the sun. You're not listening to a word I'm saying, are you?"

There was a beat before Jenna connected with the question. "I am," she assured her, "and you've got lovely hair. Beautiful, in fact." She meant it, for Bena's cascade of golden waves was straight out of a Pre-Raphaelite painting. Her face was more Rubenesque, with prettily plump cheeks, large blue eyes, and a heart-shaped mouth, all of which combined to make her a strikingly attractive woman whom Jenna had grown very fond of.

Bena's head was tilted to one side. "Are you all right, lovely?"

she asked gently. "You don't seem yourself today. Something bothering you, is it?"

Jenna forced a smile. "I'm fine," she assured her. "Just a bit of a headache."

"Do you want me to get you something?"

"No, no, I'm sure it'll go in a minute. How are you getting on with the short stories?"

"Well, I've more or less finished the copy-edits, just a couple more to go. Are we still waiting for payment to come through before sending the script back for final approval?"

"Yes, I think so. Jack's more on top of that than I am."

"OK. Where is he today? I thought we were going to start transferring stuff onto the website."

"He's with the designers sorting out a few last-minute glitches. Something to do with the e-commerce side of things, apparently."

"Well, let's hope they're ready by the time we go live, or we're going to have a lot of angry and frustrated writers on our hands. They're getting impatient already, demanding to know when they're going to see a return on their investment, as they seem to be putting it."

Indeed, emails demanding an actual launch date were coming in all the time now, though Jenna was feeling less concerned about that this morning than about what was going on in her personal world. "Martha's confident we'll be able to start transferring by the end of the day," she commented, clicking to a new screen without quite knowing why.

"That's great. And Jack's finalized the deal with Amazon to use the Kindle?"

"He's seeing the lawyer today to sign off on it. The other e-readers are already in place."

She presumed this was true. She hadn't actually seen the contracts herself; however, since Martha was overseeing the business deals, she couldn't imagine they'd be going ahead without all the vital components in place.

Trying harder to bolster Jenna's spirits, Bena declared cheerily, "So when you go in front of the cameras to promote our launch you'll be able to announce to the world that we'll be trading—"

"Sorry, I'd better take this," Jenna interrupted as her mobile rang. "It's Jack." Connecting to him, she turned in her chair as she said, "Hi, how's it going?" There was little warmth in her voice, which she knew he wouldn't miss.

"All good," he replied coolly. "I'm just ringing to find out if you've sent any short stories yet. We haven't received anything this end and we're ready to run tests."

Remembering she was supposed to have asked Bena, she said, "We'll do it now. Were the twins and Josh all right when you dropped them off earlier?"

"I think so, no thanks to you."

Angered by the accusation, she snapped, "Don't you dare put all this on me."

"But you're the one getting worked up over nothing."

"I wouldn't exactly call the way you've been carrying on—" Remembering Bena, she cut herself off. "I'm not getting into this now," she told him. Clicking off the line, she put a hand to her head.

"Oh dear," Bena murmured. "That didn't sound good."

"It's not," Jenna admitted. "In fact, it's so bloody far from good I hardly know what it is."

Bena watched her worriedly. "I'm not going to pry, but if you want to talk . . ."

Jenna shook her head. "Thanks, but we've got a lot to do and I don't think talking's going to help much. He wants us to email some short stories. Can you do that? I think I'll go and get something for this headache."

A few minutes later she was standing in front of the bath-room mirror staring at her tired, pasty face and wishing she knew what the hell to do. Jack still hadn't told her where he'd had to "pop out" to on Saturday during the game. He wouldn't even engage in a conversation about it other than to say, "You're determined to think the worst, so you go right ahead and do that."

"Then tell me what I'm supposed to think," she'd demanded furiously.

"No way am I satisfying your paranoia by defending myself."

"If you've got nothing to hide, I don't understand why it's so difficult to tell me where you were."

"You're making it difficult. In fact, you're making it down-right impossible. Now, I'm through with this conversation. If you want to go on tormenting yourself with the stories you make up, that's up to you. Just don't lay them on me."

As he'd stormed out of the bedroom he'd almost fallen over Josh and the twins, who'd been pressed up against the door listening. The sight of their troubled faces had been enough to stop Jenna going after him, but luckily he hadn't left the house; he had simply gone downstairs and helped himself to a beer from the fridge.

For the rest of Saturday evening they'd managed to put on a front for the children, eating together, watching TV, reading bedtime stories, after which he'd gone over to the office to do some work while she'd helped Paige with her rehearsal of *Under Milk Wood*. At least that had been fun, making them laugh, and bringing them closer together than they'd seemed for a while. How proud her father would have been if he'd known Paige was playing First Voice. How proud she was.

Sunday had been no easier with Jack, although they'd seen little of each other, as he'd taken the boys to the leisure center for most of the day, while she and Flora had been in charge of a friend's jewelry stall at a local craft fair. Paige had gone to Charlotte's and stayed overnight, so Jenna hadn't actually seen her since Sunday morning. In a way it had been a relief not having her around while things were tense with Jack; fooling the younger children into thinking everything was OK wasn't nearly as hard as fooling Paige.

She'd blown it earlier, though, before he'd taken Josh and the twins to school. She simply hadn't been able to stand watching him laughing and joking with them as if nothing was wrong, when as far as she was concerned nothing was right.

"Are you planning on doing a disappearing act again today?" she'd demanded as he'd checked for his keys and phone.

His eyes had immediately turned flinty.

"Is that like a magician does?" Wills demanded excitedly. "I didn't know you could do that, Dad."

"It would appear that Mum thinks I do a lot of things I'm not actually capable of," Jack had responded, staring at her hard.

"Dad goes places without telling anyone where he is," Jenna had informed them. "I'd call that sneaky, not magic."

"For God's sake," he'd muttered.

"Don't 'for God's sake' me! I've had enough of your—"

"Mum! Don't shout," Flora cried, blocking her ears.

"It's all right," Jenna soothed, going to comfort her.

"Mum?" Josh whispered.

"Everything's fine," she assured him and an anxious-looking

Wills. "You're right, I shouldn't have raised my voice. I'm sorry," she said to Jack for their benefit, certainly not his.

"It's OK," he replied, "it's all better now," and after dishing out the lunch boxes they'd helped prepare, he told them to find their satchels and coats and be in the car by the time he'd counted to twenty.

He'd left without as much as a goodbye—no kiss, no *see you later* or *I'll call.* He'd just picked up his briefcase, gone for his coat, and walked out the door. Goddamn him, he was behaving as though she was in the wrong, and she couldn't be sure whether it was that or his continued refusal to explain himself that was making her angrier than ever.

After taking a couple of aspirin, she resisted the urge to call him again, and returned to the office.

"Feeling better?" Bena asked gently.

Jenna nodded, sighed, and shook her head. The words began tumbling out almost before she realized she was speaking them. "I think Jack's having an affair," she stated, and immediately regretted it. It was as though voicing her fear was lending it power, somehow turning it into a truth that she knew she wouldn't be able to bear.

Bena's eyes rounded with shock. "I'm sure you're wrong," she declared, sounding as certain as Jenna had hoped she might.

Their eyes met, and Jenna looked away.

"What's making you think it?" Bena probed gently.

Taking a shaky breath, Jenna told her about the lengthy phone calls, the disappearances, the refusal to say where he'd been on Saturday. The more she listened to herself the more convinced she was becoming. "It's been there, staring me in the face for I don't know how long," she said brokenly, "and because I trusted him, because I thought he loved me and that he'd never . . ." Dread cut off her words.

"He does love you," Bena assured her. "If I'm sure about anything, it's that."

Jenna regarded her helplessly. "You haven't suspected it?" she asked, desperate to hear Bena say that she hadn't.

Bena shook her head. "I mean, he's a flirt and a bit of a charmer, but everyone knows that and no one takes it seriously. It's just a harmless bit of fun—" She broke off as Jenna's eyes went down. "Who do you think he's having an affair with?" Bena ventured.

Jenna swallowed. "I—um . . . It could be Judy Ritch."

Bena's jaw dropped in astonishment.

"He admitted he was with her on Friday night, down at the pub," Jenna told her. "He came back reeking of perfume. He even admitted it was hers."

Bena was shaking her head.

"I understand that you want to defend him," Jenna said, "and I appreciate it, really I do, but it's hard to think anything else after the way he's behaved. He's angry with me now for catching him out, that's what's going on, although he thinks I can't see it."

"Sweetie, he's not seeing Judy Ritch," Bena told her carefully, "or let's say he certainly wasn't with her on Friday night, because I was at the pub myself and I didn't see him. She was there, but he wasn't."

Jenna's heart turned over as she looked at her friend. "But if he wasn't . . . Why would he say he was there when he knows I'd be bound to find out he wasn't?"

Bena had no answer for that.

"He wants me to find out," Jenna said shakily.

Looking almost as wretched as Jenna felt, Bena said, "Have you actually asked him if he's having an affair?"

"Not in so many words, but he knows it's what I'm thinking. He keeps saying I'm paranoid, or telling myself stories, but the one thing he's not doing is denying it."

"Then you have to ask him straight out. I know it won't be easy, but until you do you're going to keep putting yourself through this, and there might not be any need."

Though she could feel herself recoiling from the confrontation, Jenna knew Bena was right. She had to make herself face it, somehow deal with it if it was true, yet how was she going to do that if he was serious about whoever it was and wanted out of their marriage?

"Oh my God, oh my God," Charlotte was gasping excitedly as she checked her phone. "We're in! She can see us at five on Friday."

"No way," Paige cried, a bolt of nerves shooting like splinters through her own excitement.

"I swear, look." Charlotte passed over her mobile. *Appointment for 2 people confirmed for 5 pm on Friday. Thank you for your enquiry. Jasmina is looking forward to meeting you. Please see our website for further information and directions.*

They looked at each other, round-eyed with awe, and burst into girlish laughter. "We have to do it," Charlotte insisted.

"Definitely," Paige agreed. "I mean, she won't tell us anything bad, will she?"

"I don't think they're allowed to. My cousin said she was brilliant. Told her loads of things that were true that she couldn't possibly have known."

Hearing the bus doors hiss open, Paige led the way on board, choosing two seats close to the front. Kelly Durham and her gang would be bound to sit at the back, but they had to pass Paige on the way, so Paige kept her head averted and nudged Charlotte about the fortune-teller, trying to make it look as though she hadn't even noticed the Durmites were passing.

"It's going to be totally amazing," she whispered to Charlotte.

"I know, I know," Charlotte whispered back. "She might tell us if we're going to get married, how many babies we'll have, how many husbands even."

Kelly's voice cut across their giggles. "Oh my God, it's laughing. Please someone tell it not to—it only makes it look even uglier."

As the Durmites snorted and guffawed, Paige's cheeks flamed with embarrassment.

"Oh, get her with the filthy looks," Kelly mocked as Charlotte treated her to daggers. To Paige's relief she moved on through to the back.

"Well, we know now," Paige commented as Owen followed the Durmites without as much as a glance in her and Charlotte's direction, "who managed to convince him that it was me who put that post on Facebook."

Casting another of her vicious looks in Owen's direction, Charlotte said, "I should have realized on Saturday, when he told me he knew for a fact that you'd done it, that Kelly bloody Durham had got to him."

"You know what really gets me?" Paige declared, trying not to be upset. "It's that he could never stand her before."

"I know, and I'd love to see her face if she heard some of the things he said about her."

Paige would too, though she knew neither she nor Charlotte would ever repeat them. She didn't imagine Hayley, Courtenay, or Nicole would either, though not out of loyalty to her, but because they too seemed to be getting friendlier with Kelly lately. It was unnerving Paige considerably, the way the Durmites were drawing in all her friends, though she couldn't imagine they'd ever succeed with Charlotte. She and Charlotte were solid; nothing and no one was going to come between them.

Hearing a text ping into her phone, she decided not to read it. It would only be something vile from Kelly again, such as:

Faggot basher.

Homophobe.

Two-faced bitch.

Sad fucking loser.

Ugly fat cow.

These were only some of the names she'd been called by text or email over the past twenty-four hours, and not only by Kelly Durham but by Owen and others too. Though she was putting a brave face on it, determined that no one should think they were getting to her, each text that arrived upset her more than the last. Worst of all were the messages that said things like, *You're just a fucking nobody with no right to live, so why don't you do the world a favor and die?* Or *It's no wonder your family can't stand you, no one can.* Or *You make everyone feel totally sick the way you think you're so much better than everyone else. Filthy swot! Teacher's brown-noser.*

"Oh my God," Charlotte suddenly gasped as a text dropped into her phone. "I don't believe this. Please tell me I'm not dreaming."

Paige took her mobile and read the message. *Hey you, going to send me a Snapchat? Liam LOL.* ☺

Paige turned to look at her, envious and confused. "Why 'laugh out loud'?"

Charlotte shrugged. "Do you think he's taking the piss? Maybe it's not even him."

Paige looked at the text again.

"Shall I answer it?" Charlotte ventured.

Paige was trying to make up her mind. "I know," she decided, "ask him to send you one first."

Charlotte lit up. "Genius."

A few moments later, as Miss Kendrick, a stocky yet glamorous young woman, joined the bus, a shot of Liam blowing a kiss appeared on Charlotte's phone.

Charlotte looked like she might pass out. "Oh my God. It is him," she murmured. "I am so going to shag him."

"Phones away now," Miss Kendrick instructed, "and take out your copies of *Under Milk Wood*. We'll have a rehearsal during the journey."

"Oh no!" Charlotte panic-whispered. "I have to Snapchat him back."

"Do it when we get there," Paige advised. "We can go into the loo or something."

Since the alternative was having her phone confiscated, Charlotte managed a quick *In bad situation, more later Cxxx* before switching it to silent.

As Miss Kendrick gave the driver the go-ahead to start the fifteen-minute trip into Swansea, Paige stared fixedly out of the window, willing her teacher to pick on anyone but her to lead the rehearsal. She might as well have kept her telepathic energies to herself, because they'd gone no more than half a mile before the microphone was being thrust into her hand and

Miss Kendrick was saying, "Get us in the mood with the opening lines, Paige. Go up to 'Schooner House dreams of.' Then we'll have a little discussion on the syntax. I take it we all know what *syntax* means? Ruby, can you tell us?"

"Uh, it's kind of like grammar, miss."

Miss Kendrick sighed. "I suppose that'll do for now. Paige, off you go."

Trying not to think of the others pulling faces and gagging behind her, Paige steeled herself and started, very quietly, "To begin at the beginning: It is spring, moonless—"

"Speak up, we can't hear," someone shouted from the back.

"It's meant to be spoken softly," Miss Kendrick reminded them, "but perhaps you could give it a little more volume, Paige."

Wanting only to thrust the mic back at the teacher and tell her to get someone else to do it, Paige forced herself to start again. This time she got as far as "blind as Captain Cat," when a small chorus of voices began howling and meowing.

"That's enough," Miss Kendrick snapped. "Whoever's responsible, put your hand up."

No one did.

She waited, eyes shining with outrage. She adored Dylan Thomas—practically wet herself over him, Cullum had once said—so to treat his work to this kind of mockery would be seen as nothing short of a capital offense.

"I don't know who was making the noise, miss," Kelly Durham piped up sweetly, "but it's not the play that's the problem, it's Paige's voice. It's making people want to howl—you know, like dogs do when they hear music that's out of tune."

As the others laughed and Paige flushed to the roots of her

hair, Miss Kendrick said to Kelly, "For such an inane and un-pleasant remark, you have just earned yourself a report. Now kindly keep quiet, *everyone*, while Paige finishes the opening."

Somehow Paige got through it, mainly because she managed, by some miracle, to lose herself in the words, as though she were in the dawn hours of Llareggub rather than trapped amongst enemies on the school bus.

"Miss?" a boy's voice called out from just behind her. "Did you know that Llareggub, the name of the town, is 'bugger all' spelled backward?"

As everyone snickered, Miss Kendrick rolled her eyes. "Do you have to tell us that every time we read the play, Michael?"

Clearly proud to have got away with swearing again, Michael Preddy stood up and took a bow.

"I think Paige ought to carry on reading," Bethany Gates called out.

"Yeah, definitely," Kelly Durham agreed. "All the voices this time."

"Paige, Paige, Paige," the Durmites started to chant.

Knowing they were doing it to humiliate her, Paige looked imploringly at Miss Kendrick.

"Paige has done enough," Miss Kendrick shouted over the noise, "and as we're practically there, we'll delay our discussion until our visit is over."

Paige's eyes widened with alarm as she glanced at Charlotte.

"Miss," Charlotte cried, "I thought we were supposed to be making our own way home from the center."

"Indeed, I'd forgotten," Miss Kendrick admitted, "so we'll resume the reading at our next lesson, by which time I will expect every one of you to have rehearsed your role or roles thoroughly enough to convince me that you have a fuller understanding of the piece than you seem to have now. Part of that will come in the essays I will set for homework."

As everyone groaned, the bus came to a stop outside the elegant old building in the Maritime Quarter that had once been Swansea's guildhall but was now home to the Dylan Thomas Centre. With its exquisitely smooth Bath stone frontage, circular and arched windows, and neat little side garden, it was a place Paige knew quite well, due to several visits with her mum.

"Thank God for that," Charlotte muttered as they clambered down from the bus. "I thought for one horrible minute she'd changed her mind and was going to make us go back to school when this bloody trip is over."

Paige suddenly gasped. "I forgot to tell my dad not to pick us up." She opened up her phone. "I'd better call him."

Going through to his voicemail, she left a message saying, "No need to meet us at the Dylan Thomas Centre. Thanks anyway. Love you." After clicking off she rang her mother. "Hey, is Dad there?"

"No, he's out," Jenna answered. "Is everything all right?"

"Yeah, it's cool. He was going to pick us up later, but he doesn't need to now. Charlotte and I have decided to go over to Oxford Street and do some shopping. Is that OK?"

"I guess so. Do you have any money?"

"Some. We're not going to buy anything. It's just for a look round."

"What about homework?"

"I'll do it later. I've got to have some freedom, Mum."

"I understand that; I was just asking. Did you leave a message for Dad?"

"Yeah. Where is he?"

"I'm not sure at the moment. He had a meeting with Martha

and her team earlier, but he could be with the lawyer by now, which would be why he's not answering his phone."

"Right. Actually, that's who rang him before he went out on Saturday. Martha. I saw it come up on his phone."

There was a moment before her mother said, "Are you sure?"

"That's what I saw. Anyway, sorry, got to go. I'm not supposed to have my phone on."

As she rang off there was a sudden scuffle behind her, someone fell into her, and the next thing she knew her phone was being snatched from her hand.

"Hey!" she cried as Bethany Gates made off with it. "Give it back."

"Keep your mouth shut," Kelly Durham hissed in her ear, "or I'll shut it for you." Jamming an elbow into Paige's ribs, she took off after Bethany.

Paige turned to Charlotte, shock and fear darkening her eyes.

"They won't keep it," Charlotte told her. "They're just being stupid."

"What if they wipe everything, or send texts or emails making it look like they're from me?"

"Hey, Paige!" someone shouted.

Paige looked up, the camera went off, and all she could do was watch as Kelly, Bethany, Owen, and the others glanced at the shot and roared with laughter.

"What's going on?" Miss Kendrick demanded, coming up behind her. "Paige, are you all right? You're looking a little pale, dear."

"I'm fine, miss, thanks," Paige assured her. Clearly Miss Kendrick hadn't seen the phone being stolen or she'd have done something about it, and Paige was too scared of the consequences to tell her.

For the next interminable hour she tried to pay attention as Miss Kendrick and one of the center's organizers talked them through what was to happen and where they were to go on the evening of their special performance. Though Paige was excited about it, another part of her was starting to seriously wish that Miss Kendrick hadn't chosen year ten to perform for the centenary. It wasn't like most of the class was even familiar with the piece, and at least half of them probably never would be, the way they carried on.

"It's your fault," Cullum had grumbled when Miss Kendrick had first announced the honor she was bestowing upon the GCSE group. "You're the one who knows it, who can bloody recite from it, who loves it like she does, and now you've dropped the rest of us in it. Just don't go backing out, that's all I can say, because no way in the world am I getting up in front of anyone to play First Voice."

Since he was her understudy, he'd have to take part if something happened to her, but she'd assured him he needn't worry, because nothing would make her miss out on the role, even if she had to go onstage in a plaster cast or a wheelchair.

Famous last words?

At last the visit to the center was over, but no way was Paige leaving without her phone, so while Charlotte Snapchatted Liam she went to confront Bethany.

"Where is it?" she demanded, her heart thudding so fast she was sure everyone could hear it.

"Where's what?" Bethany answered snootily, while Kelly sniggered behind her.

"You know what I'm talking about. You took my phone and I want it back."

"I don't have your stupid phone," Bethany informed her.

"Yes you do."

"Are you calling me a liar?"

Flushing deeply, Paige said, "You know you have it, so please give it back."

Coming up beside her, Charlotte said, "Give it to her, Bethany."

Kelly's eyes widened. "I can't believe you're sticking up for her after what she said about you on Facebook."

"She didn't say it," Charlotte shot back.

Kelly sneered. "No, of course, someone hacked her account. Like as if."

"Owen," Paige said, appealing to him, "please make them give my phone back."

"Nothing to do with me," he retorted, turning away.

"Oh, looks like you dropped it," Bethany suddenly declared.

Paige turned round, and seeing a phone lying on the grass, she ran to it. It was hers, thank God, and grabbing it up, she hurried away to check it. Thankfully all her information still seemed to be there, but so too were several text messages sent during the past hour. A couple had gone to Kelly and Bethany with the photo they'd taken of her attached; the rest, she realized to her horror, had gone to Oliver.

How the hell did they know about Oliver?

With panic tearing through her she began to read.

Hi Oliver, I've just got to tell you how much I want you to shag me. Let me know if you want it too. Paige Moore.

Oliver, baby, I want your dick in my mouth.

I can't stop thinking about you. Come all over me.

She stopped reading. Sobs were tearing through her so hard that she could no longer see the words anyway.

Putting an arm round her, Charlotte took the phone and read the messages herself. "What's the fucking matter with them?" she hissed angrily. "They're sick, that's what they are. Sick and twisted."

"But how . . . how did they know I like Oliver?" Paige gasped. "I never told anyone apart from you."

Charlotte took a step back. "You don't think . . . Jesus Christ, Paige."

"No, I know you wouldn't have . . . I just . . . I mean . . ." She couldn't think what to say. She really hadn't told anyone else, so how had Kelly and Bethany found out?

"You've got to have told someone else," Charlotte insisted. "What about Julie the stalker? Did you tell her?"

Paige shook her head. "No way. She asked once if I had a boyfriend and I said no, because it's the truth. Oh God, Charlotte, what's he going to think? I have to text and let him know that someone stole my phone."

"Definitely," Charlotte agreed.

"What shall I say?"

Charlotte tried to think.

"What about if I say something like 'I'm really, really sorry you've received those vile messages. Some girls at school stole my phone and they thought it was funny to try and make me look stupid. Please ignore them. Sorry again'?"

"Yep. That sounds good," Charlotte agreed.

After tapping out the message, Paige said, "I want to know how they found out. It's like they've read my mind, for God's sake. . . . Are you sure nothing got said on Saturday?"

Charlotte was starting to color. "Actually, Hayley asked me if you fancied him."

Paige's face paled. "Why did she ask that? I've never mentioned anything to her."

"No idea. She just came out with it."

"And so you told her I did?"

"No, of course not. All I said was even if you did it was no one's business."

"So you more or less confirmed it?"

"No! I just tried to make light of it. Listen, I reckon Owen's behind it. He was with us when we went to watch Oliver playing rugby—it could be he noticed you looking at him, or overheard us saying something. I'm just guessing, but I can't think how else they'd know."

Paige couldn't either, and since she couldn't afford to be angry with the only friend she seemed to have left, she said, "They've got a photo of me. What do you think they're going to do with it?"

Charlotte regarded her uneasily. Though they both had a fair idea of what might happen, neither wanted to put it into words. "They've probably done it to scare you," she said lamely. "They won't actually do anything."

Wishing she could believe that, Paige stared down at her phone. At least it was only a head-and-shoulders shot of her looking surprised. There wouldn't be much they could do with that, apart from bombard Oliver with it, which was making her want to die just to think of it. Still, she'd let him know that her phone had been stolen, so at least he'd realize that any pictures he received would be a result of this.

"Do you still want to go shopping?" Charlotte asked dubiously.

Paige nodded. "Yes, I think we should." She was staring back along the street toward Salubrious Place, where a couple had just come out of Morgan's Hotel. "Dad!" she called out, starting toward him. "Dad!"

As he turned around she waved, hoping the Durmites had heard and were slithering away into the holes they belonged in, now that her dad was in the vicinity. No one would dare to say or do anything mean to her while he was around.

"Paige, sweetheart," Jack laughed, catching her in his arms as she reached him. "What are you doing here?"

"School trip," she told him. "What are *you* doing here?"

"I've just been in a meeting. You remember Martha, don't you?"

The cheerful-looking blond woman was regarding Paige with a kindly interest. "I don't think we've actually met, but you're helping with Mum and Dad's new business, aren't you?" Paige said to her.

"That's right." Martha smiled. "It's lovely to meet you. And this is your friend?"

"Oh yes. Charlotte, you know my dad, and this is Martha. Is there any chance you can give us a lift home after we've been shopping?" she asked her father. "Mum said it was all right to go. . . ."

"I'd love to, sweetheart," he told her, "but I'm on my way to another meeting now and I don't expect to be through until gone six. Tell you what, though, take this and treat yourselves to something nice, the two of you." Planting two 20-pound notes in her hand, he stroked her face and told her he'd see her at home later.

Chapter 7

"So how did everything go today?" Jenna asked stiffly as Jack came in the door just after seven.

"It was good," he replied, shrugging off his coat.

"Did you sign off with the lawyer?"

"More or less. There are a couple more things to straighten out. I have to go back tomorrow."

The way he was avoiding her eyes was making her insides churn with unease. Did he know that she'd guessed? Could he be steeling himself to tell her anyway?

Now would be a terrible time, with her mother due to bring the younger ones back from Rainbow Guides and Beaver Scouts at any minute.

She watched him go to the fridge and take out a beer. "I take it you got Paige's message that she didn't need picking up?" she said, going back to the peanut butter cookies she was making. They were Josh's favorites. Tomorrow she'd make strawberry jam tarts for the twins. Why was this feeling like part of another world? It was as though she was losing her grip when nothing had changed, at least on the surface.

Underneath there was a riptide trying to drag her to places she desperately didn't want to go.

"Yes, I did," he replied. "I ran into her, outside the Dylan Thomas Centre."

"Oh?"

"She was on a school trip. Is she home yet?"

"She went straight to Charlotte's. She should be back around eight."

Nodding, he downed half the beer and headed for the door.

Suddenly angry, she said, "Don't you have anything more to say to me?"

He stopped but didn't turn round. "What exactly do you want me to say?" he enquired tightly.

I'd like you to tell me this isn't happening, that you're sorry you've made me think the worst, that nothing's changing . . . "I'd like to know why you're behaving like this," she cried. "You're obviously hiding something."

"Exactly *what* do you think I'm hiding?" he growled, spinning round.

Flinching at his anger, she said, "Well, we both know you're hiding where you were on Saturday, and I'm told you weren't at the pub on Friday night either, when you said you were."

He gaped at her incredulously. "Have you been checking up on me?" he thundered.

"I wasn't checking up. Bena was there and she said you weren't."

Looking past her as the back door crashed open, he immediately set down his beer and opened his arms to catch the twins. "Are you home already?" he exclaimed, kissing them as they hugged him. "It only seems like an hour ago that I took you to school."

"We've been to Rainbow Guides and Beaver Scouts," Flora informed him, "and Wills got a medal—"

Wills immediately thumped her. "I wanted to tell him," he protested.

"You didn't have to hit me," she wailed. "He shouldn't have done that, should he, Dad?"

"He most definitely shouldn't have, but it wasn't hard, so I expect you'll survive. Where's Josh? Isn't he with you?"

"I'm here," Josh shouted, coming in the door behind a cardboard cut-out of some kind of alien. "Mum! Mr. Thacker, our leader, said I could have this to put in my bedroom. It's really cool, isn't it?"

"The coolest," she assured him.

"Oh wow! Are you making peanut butter cookies? Yum. They're my favorite. I'm going to eat them all."

"He has to save some for us, doesn't he, Mum?" Flora objected.

"I'm sure he will," Jenna replied, popping them in the oven. "Now everyone needs to go and get out of their uniforms and put on their pajamas. Flora, is that paint or mud on your cheeks?"

Appearing bemused, she wriggled out of her father's arms and ran off upstairs to check, with Josh and Wills close behind.

"I'm going to the office," Jack announced as Kay came in with the children's bags. "Are you OK?" he asked her. "Do you need a hand with anything?"

"This is the lot, thank you," she replied, setting them down.

Again avoiding Jenna's eyes, he left.

"I have letters from the school and from the Rainbows," Kay was saying as she dug into her own bag. "One is about an in-service day, the other a parents' evening. Oh, and I ran into Wendy Rivers; she wanted me to thank you again for looking after her stall on Sunday. She says takings were up by about fifteen percent."

Jenna was hardly listening. Her mind was all over the place, trying to cope with the shock of Jack being so cold, the disbelief that he didn't appear to be interested in making up. What further confirmation did she need for her worst fears?

"The cookies have to be in for ten minutes," she told her mother. "I need to go over to the office. If you can, stop the children from following me."

Aware of Kay watching her leave, she started across the garden, her eyes fixed on Jack, who was at his desk speaking to someone on the phone. When he spotted her coming he quickly rang off. As her temper rose she could feel the bottom dropping out of her world.

"Who was that?" she asked, closing the door behind her.

"What do you mean?" he countered.

"Who were you on the phone to?"

He sighed impatiently.

"I'd like an answer."

"Why does it matter who I was talking to?"

"Why won't you tell me?"

"Because you're trying to make something of it."

Going to him, she grabbed the phone and started to check.

"For God's sake," he growled, trying to wrest it from her.

"*What are you hiding?*" she shouted, trying to push him away.

"Give it to me," he demanded.

She could feel herself shaking. She wanted to smash the phone in his face, or beg him to stop—she hardly knew which.

"You're making a fool of yourself," he told her.

She stared at him, unable to understand what was happening, why this gulf was opening up between them and only getting wider. "How long has it been going on?" she heard herself ask.

He frowned irritably. "What are you talking about?"

"You know what I'm talking about. Your affair with Martha."

Whatever he'd been about to say died on his lips. He stood staring at her, rooted in shock, or maybe it was disbelief that she'd guessed.

Please God, let me be wrong. Please, please let him deny it now and show me that I really am making a fool of myself.

"I'm not having this conversation," he suddenly snapped. "You make things up, carry on like they're real, and expect me to go along with them. Well, it's not going to happen. Check the phone if you must. I'll even give you the password. You'll see I've spoken to Martha plenty of times, though how the hell I'm supposed to run the business without speaking to her I've no idea."

The phone was heavy in her hand, suspicion still dark in her heart, though doubt was starting to cast small, blessed slivers of hope across her fear. She wanted so desperately to be wrong that she knew she was in danger of backing down when she should probably stand firm.

He held out his hand. She looked at it, assuming he was asking for the phone, but then he was moving closer, taking her into his arms.

"I'm sorry," he whispered into her hair. "I don't know how we got into this, but it'll be my fault. Everything is, we know that."

She almost smiled. "So it's not true?" she whispered, gazing up into his eyes.

"It's not true," he murmured. Bringing her to him, he kissed her so lovingly that in those moments she no longer found it hard to believe him.

Over the next few days Jenna kept trying to convince herself that everything was back to normal, because on the surface it was. Jack was his usual, loving self, their closeness had returned on every level, and there were even moments when she was truly able to put her suspicions down to a fleeting aberration. The trouble was, the doubts just wouldn't go away. They were always there, hanging around like ghosts in a churchyard, unseen, unheard, but watching, looking out for any small sign to give their lingering presence some substance.

"You still don't believe him, do you?" Bena said on Thursday morning as she noticed Jenna watching him in the sitting room, head in hand, as he spoke to someone on the phone.

Jenna sighed. "I keep trying, because frankly it would be so much easier if I could, but then I see him like this . . . Who's he talking to? Why did he have to go over there to take the call? What's he saying that we're not supposed to hear?"

"Are you sure everything's all right with the business?" Bena ventured. "Perhaps there are problems that he doesn't want to tell you about."

Having already considered that, Jenna said, "He's insisting that the delay is no more than a technical hitch; something to do with copyright that has to be sorted out before we can launch."

Bena nodded. Since she'd helped compose the email to their contributors explaining the delay, this wasn't news to her.

"He didn't come home until eleven last night," Jenna murmured. She was still watching him, bound up in suspicion while willing him to catch her eye and make a gesture to show everything was all right.

"Did he say where he'd been?" Bena prompted.

"Apparently he had dinner with some marketing guys in Cardiff."

When Bena didn't respond, Jenna turned to look at her.

"You don't believe it," Bena stated.

"Do you?"

Bena shrugged. "You know there are other ways of getting answers," she said. "I'm not suggesting you should do it, but his credit card statements, phone records, they're all online . . . Do you have access to them?"

Jenna shook her head. "They're password-protected, and I can hardly ask what the passwords are when they're his personal accounts. He'd know right away that I'm checking up on him."

"What about looking at his phone while he's sleeping? Or going into his computer when he's not here?"

"Same problem: password-protected."

"Have you tried guessing the passwords?"

Jenna didn't want to admit it, but she had. "It always used to be our names combined, or Paige and Josh, or the twins, but he's obviously moved on to something else."

"You ought to have them in case of emergency," Bena pointed out.

Jenna nodded. It was true, she should. "We need to change the subject," she warned. "He's on his way back."

A few moments later, as he let himself into the office, she said casually, "Everything OK?"

"Just fine," he assured her, though she could see the strain in his eyes. "It's this bloody copyright issue dragging on. I need to go back to the lawyer. Can you or your mum pick Paige up from school? I said I would. What's the matter with her getting the bus?"

"I don't know. I'll ask Mum if she can go. If she can't, I will. What time should we expect you back?"

"I'm not sure. I'll call. By the way, Bena, thanks for all the files you prepared this morning. They're turning out to be even more helpful than I'd hoped."

"No problem," Bena said with a smile. "Hope it goes well with the lawyer."

He'd almost gone before he remembered to come and drop a kiss on Jenna's head. "Don't look so worried," he teased.

Waiting until the door had closed behind him, she sat back in her chair, drawing her hands over her face. "I need to call Mum," she said, reaching for the phone. "Actually, isn't she taking Josh and the twins to a birthday party after school? I'm sure it's today."

"It is," Bena confirmed. "Aiden's going too. If you like, I'll take Josh and the twins so your mum can fetch Paige. So how come Paige isn't getting the bus?"

Jenna threw out her hands. "She's suddenly decided she doesn't want to, and frankly it's easier to go along with her than it is to argue. She's turning into such a handful lately. Talk about moody."

"That's teenagers for you."

"Tell me about it. One minute she's all over us, full of affection, and the next we can't do anything right. You should have heard her laying into Josh this morning. Jack had to raise his voice to her in the end, which sent her into one of her mega-sulks. Then Flora turned up with a stomachache, which she blamed on Wills, and the next thing we knew they were fighting, with Josh egging them on and Paige screaming at them to grow up. Not a great start to the day. I can only hope it ends a bit better."

"Where's Charlotte?" Jenna asked as Paige got into the car.

"Gone to the dentist," Paige replied, checking her phone. "Where's Dad? I thought he was picking me up."

"He had to go to a meeting. Do you want to offer anyone else a lift before we leave?"

Paige gawped at her as though she were mad. "No! Why would I want to do that?"

"I was just suggesting it. No need to bite my head off." Putting the car into gear, she edged round one of the school buses to get back on the road.

Several minutes ticked by in silence. "So, this is nice, isn't it?" Jenna commented with a cheerfulness she was far from feeling.

"What is?" Paige didn't look up.

"Us, being on our own like this. We don't get much chance for a bit of a girlie chat these days."

"And that's, like, my fault?"

"No. I'm just saying, we're both busy."

"Anyway, Waffle's here, so we're not on our own."

"But he's hardly—"

"I just don't think you should leave him out."

"Which is why I brought him. I thought we could take him to the beach, if it's not raining by the time we get there."

Paige shrugged and carried on with her texting.

"Is everything all right?" Jenna ventured after a while.

"Yes. Why wouldn't it be?"

"I was just wondering. You've been a bit edgy lately, and—"

"Stop picking on me, will you?" Paige snapped. "Everyone's always bloody picking on me."

"Paige, I'm not."

"Yes you are."

"I'm merely saying if there's anything you'd like to talk about . . ."

"Like what?"

"I don't know. That's why I'm asking. Is everything all right at school?"

Paige didn't answer.

"How's the video project coming along? Are you still editing it?"

"Yes, and I don't want it being submitted to the Tourist Office. Will you contact Mr. Thomas and tell him that, please?"

"But why? If he thinks it's good enough . . ."

"I just don't want it to happen, OK? And while you're at it, will you please tell Miss Kendrick to stop my daffodil essay from going into the school magazine and that I don't want to be in her stupid production of *Under Milk Wood*?"

Jenna blinked in surprise. "But you—"

"Mum, will you just do it? I've tried telling them myself, but they won't listen. I don't want my video being treated as anything special, and I don't want to make a spectacle of myself in a play that no one gets."

Jenna tried to think what to say, but with Paige in such a prickly mood she could tell that pursuing anything now wouldn't get her anywhere. So, letting the subject drop, she drove on in silence, wishing she knew how to reach her daughter, or her husband. Either would do, though both would be better.

Maybe it was her. Perhaps she'd changed in a way she hadn't recognized, and now everyone was reacting to it without her even understanding what "it" was. Except, if there were something different about her, if she'd lost the plot without realizing, her mother wouldn't have been backward in telling her.

Nevertheless, she had to be to blame in some way; things didn't just start going wrong on their own. Maybe she was spreading herself too thin, taking on too many roles: wife, mother, businesswoman, writer-in-crisis . . . There was too much to think about, so much that she wasn't getting any of it straight.

"I'm sorry if I haven't been paying enough attention to you lately," she said gently.

Paige sighed.

"We used to be friends. . . ."

"Mum, you're just embarrassing yourself, so can we stop this, please?"

Trying not to be hurt, Jenna started as the phone rang. Seeing it was Martha, her heart gave a wrench of unease. Was this a call she wanted to take with Paige in the car? What reason could she give for ignoring it? "Hi," she said, clicking on with the hands-free. "How are you, Martha?"

"I'm fine, thank you," came the reply. "I was hoping we could get together in the next couple of days."

Jenna almost stammered as she said, "Yes, yes, of course."

Did she mean for the lunch they kept promising each other? Or was it about something else? "I'm quite flexible. When would suit you?"

"Tomorrow? Eleven o'clock. I can come to you."

Jenna's heart rose into her mouth. "That sounds fine," she responded.

"Great. I'll see you then." The line went dead.

Half expecting Paige to comment, Jenna waited, but it seemed Paige was too engrossed in her own texting—or chat room, or whatever she was currently connected to—to be bothered about a random call of her mother's.

They were heading across the Bryn now, and Jenna could feel herself becoming increasingly agitated, convinced that the reason Martha wanted to see her was to tell her about the affair she was having with Jack. Why else would she come to the house when there were no new computer systems to demonstrate? It was somewhere she could leave when she was done, and where Jenna wouldn't have to face the ordeal of getting home.

It wasn't Martha's place to tell her; it was Jack's.

"Mum! You nearly ran that pony over," Paige cried sharply.

"Did I? Sorry. I was miles away."

Paige turned to look at her. "What's the matter with you?" she challenged. "You've gone weird all of a sudden."

"What do you mean?"

"I don't know. Are you all right? Oh God, Mum, are you cry-ing?"

Jenna forced a laugh. "Of course not. I was just . . ." Just what? She didn't know what she was trying to say. "I was think-ing about Josh and the twins. They've gone to a birthday party at Pizza Express."

"And that's making you cry?"

Jenna laughed again. "I can get a bit emotional when I think about how much I love you children."

"Oh, puh-lease," Paige muttered.

Jenna's hands tightened on the wheel. "Why are you being so unkind to me?" she asked. "You can be very hurtful sometimes, did you know that?"

Paige colored as her face tightened defensively. A few seconds passed before she said, "Sorry, I don't mean to be."

Jenna glanced at her. "I'm sorry too."

"What for?"

"Getting on your nerves?"

Paige turned to look out of the window. "You wouldn't be a proper mother if you didn't do that."

Jenna laughed through a sob.

Paige turned back. "What's wrong?" she persisted.

"Nothing's wrong."

"Yes there is."

"No there isn't. Tell me about your day."

"Have you had a row with Dad?"

"No. Now stop trying to talk about me. I'm more interested in you."

"Because I'm *really* fascinating."

"You are to me."

"Did you know people used to be horrible to Grandma when she was young?"

"Yes, I did."

"She said it was because she was different."

"Like we always say, she's her own person."

"Do you think I'm like Grandma?"

Surprised, Jenna said, "No, not at all. Why? Is someone being horrible to you?"

When Paige didn't answer, Jenna turned to look at her. "I said, is someone—"

"It's just some stupid girls trying to look big."

"In what way?"

"It doesn't matter. They'll get over it. Dad's ringing."

Clicking on to answer, Jenna said, "Are you still with the lawyer?"

"Just finished. Where are you?"

"On the way home with Paige."

"OK. I should be there in about an hour. Are you all right?"

"Yes, I'm fine."

"She's not," Paige called out. "She was crying just now."

"I wasn't," Jenna objected. "I just got a bit emotional, that's all, the way I do sometimes."

"Yeah, like when you've had a row with Dad."

"I told you—"

A single tone suddenly came down the line.

Paige looked at her mother in shock. "Did he just hang up on us?" she demanded.

"No, of course not," Jenna replied, fearing that he might have. "We must have lost the connection. He'll ring back, I'm sure."

Several minutes ticked by as they drove through Reynoldston and on to Scurlage toward home. Jenna's heart was beating so fiercely it hurt. Surely to God he hadn't just cut them off. Would he really do that to Paige? Why would he do it at all?

Whatever the reason, it seemed he wasn't going to share it with them, because the phone remained resolutely silent until they pulled up at the house in the rain, and all Jenna could feel thankful for then was the fact that Paige appeared more interested in what she was texting than in whatever might be going on with her parents.

After getting out of the car Paige disappeared into the house and ran straight upstairs to her room. She was right in the middle of private-messaging with Julie, so she simply dumped her bag on the floor and sat cross-legged on the bed to carry on their chat. She still had no idea whether Julie was one of the Durmites, but just in case she was, Paige was using this chat to try to make them feel bad about what they were doing. With any luck it might persuade them to leave her alone.

So what happened after you saw the texts to Oliver? was Julie's last question.

I texted him myself to let him know my phone had been stolen. I don't know if he believed me, but I hope so, because it's not true that I fancy him. I hardly even know him, and anyway he's got a girlfriend who's really nice.

No one needed to know, apart from Charlotte, how devastated Paige really felt that Oliver had never responded to her friend request or to her text apologizing for the texts the Durmites had sent, or how torn up she felt every time she thought of him with the stunning Lindsay.

It just wasn't fair. Nothing was working out for her the way it was for Charlotte, who was sexting and Snapchatting all the time with Liam now. They still hadn't been on a date, but it was definitely going to happen, and Charlotte had already made up her mind that when it did, she was going all the way.

If you don't fancy Oliver you don't really need to worry about what he thinks, do you?

I suppose not, but if you'd seen the messages you'd realize why I wouldn't want him—or anyone—to think they were from me. They were really childish and disgusting.

I expect I can guess the sort of thing. Sorry you're having to go through it.

I'm thinking about telling someone, like my parents, or a teacher.

If she threatened that, maybe they'd think twice about bothering her anymore.

Are you sure it won't make things worse?

Like how?

When it happened to me I reported it and ended up wishing I hadn't. It got really bad then.

Paige swallowed dryly. *It happened to you?*

Yes, last year, before you started at The Landings. It's why I don't want to tell you who I really am. If they find out we're friends they'll probably turn on me again and I just couldn't handle it.

How did you get them to stop?

I didn't. I guess they just got bored with me and ended up leaving me alone. Then I saw them starting on you. That's why I got in touch, so you wouldn't feel so much on your own.

Paige wasn't sure what to say to that.

I know you think I might be one of them, but I promise you, I hate them every bit as much as you do.

Didn't you ever tell your parents? Paige asked.

Yes, but there's nothing anyone can do. They'll just say they're kidding around, and that you're taking things too seriously. Then they start getting at you in other ways. They beat me up once and threatened to kill me if I told anyone who did it.

Paige's head was spinning. It had never crossed her mind that it might get even worse, but obviously it could.

Another time they pushed my head down a toilet and made me drink the water.

Paige almost gagged just to think of it.

All that happened after I'd reported them. There was other stuff too, but I don't like thinking about it now.

They shouldn't be allowed to get away with it.

I know, but there's no law against it so they can carry on all they like. By the way, what made them think you fancy Oliver?

I'm not sure. I think Owen might have told them.

I see he's on their side now. I suppose I don't blame him. At least if he's with them they're less likely to pick on him.

Having figured that out for herself, Paige said, *I always thought he was a good friend.*

I'm sure he was, but it's a case of survival. Don't be surprised if they manage to get round your other friends too. It's what they did to me.

Do you have any friends now?

Some. Like you.

But we don't really know each other.

We can chat like this though. You said they took a photo of you. Have they done anything with it yet?

Paige's insides churned. *I don't think so. What do you reckon they'll do?*

Hard to say. Maybe they took it just to freak you out.

They'd definitely succeeded in that.

Sorry, I have to go. Will contact you later if I can.

As the connection was lost, Paige lowered her phone and stared with anxious eyes at her computer. It was making her feel sick to think of what might be waiting for her there: more lies, more abuse, more pretense of being her with crude and derogatory postings. She wasn't sure she had the courage to go online to find out, but at the same time, how could she not? She had to know what was being said. For all she knew someone had managed to hack her account again, or had even set up others in her name. They had her photo now and could do anything with it: use it as a profile, send it to perverts, even doctor it in ways she didn't want to think about.

Looking at her phone as it bleeped with a text, her heart turned over to see it was from Kelly.

Hey Daddy's bitch, big surprise waiting for you tomorrow. Think you're going to love it. LOL

Chapter 8

Jenna had decided to wait until the younger children were tucked up in bed and her mother had gone home before tackling Jack about ringing off on her earlier. This wasn't working out too well. It had been a difficult evening, most of which Jack hadn't been there for, with angry fights over nothing at all; delightful projectile vomiting from Wills, who'd eaten too much at the party; a tumble down the stairs from Flora, who'd screamed the place down more out of shock than injury; and the discovery of a leaked felt-tip pen all over Josh's carpet. All three had played up about going to bed, refusing to do so until Daddy came home, at which point, mercifully, Jack had walked in the door. Some order had then been restored, though not before Josh had managed to knock over and smash a lamp in the sitting room and Paige had wrenched open her door to yell, "I can't stand being in this family. You're all mental, and all you ever think about is yourselves."

She'd disappeared back into her room before anyone could respond, not that anyone seemed inclined to, apart from Jenna. However, the moment passed, and by the time all the going-to-bed rituals were over she'd completely forgotten the outburst. All she seemed able to think about now, as she started downstairs to pour herself a drink, was how wonderful it would be to snuggle up in Jack's arms and drift off to oblivion. It was just awful knowing it wasn't going to happen, not only because he wasn't inviting it, but because she wouldn't go there even if he were. There was far too much tension between them again, and though she desperately didn't want it to carry on like this, she wasn't sure she had it in her to confront it tonight.

You're just being cowardly, she told herself sharply as she walked into the kitchen. Seeing how clean and tidy it was, she melted with love for her mother. A beat later she was racked with guilt for not showing her appreciation more. It was hard with her mother, though; she was always uncomfortable with compliments, and whenever Jenna did try to thank her she'd simply say, "Well, if I didn't do it, I don't know who would."

The truth was Jenna didn't either, because bringing up four children wasn't easy. It was fun, of course, and wholly rewarding on levels she hadn't even known existed until she became a mother. But the day-to-day challenges, the constant anguish over whether she'd forgotten something vital, the lurking fear that something terrible was going to befall one of them, the worry over her ability to show them an equal amount of love—all of these things could sap her energy at times to a point where she almost couldn't take a step forward.

Was it any wonder she was unable to write?

Opening a bottle of wine, she filled two glasses.

Please don't let Jack walk in and say he's going out.

She wasn't sure where he was; maybe he'd already gone.

Seeing lights in the office, she breathed a little easier, until she realized he was on the phone. When was he ever not on the phone? Who, if it wasn't Martha, could he be speaking to so often and at such length?

If it was Martha . . .

Her heart twisted with the dread of it. She wondered if she should take his wine over to him, and decided not to. She didn't want to witness him abruptly ending the call when he saw her coming.

Finally he came back over to the house. Jenna was still in the kitchen packing lunch boxes with small cartons of pineapple chunks and Kit Kats. There was chicken and mayo for the twins' sandwiches, ham and pickle for Josh, plus the yogurts she mustn't forget to put in, making sure they all had their favorite flavors.

"Where's the dog?" he asked as he closed the door behind him.

"Upstairs with Paige," she replied. Was he planning another of his nighttime beach strolls? "I poured you some wine," she said.

He glanced at the glass and nodded. His face was taut, and he wasn't meeting her eyes. Suddenly she wanted to shout and rage or throw something at him.

Instead she carried on with what she was doing, waiting for him to break the silence.

Without taking a sip of his drink he went to close the kitchen doors. Since they were made of glass they could see through to the sitting room, so they would know if a child was coming. This was what they did if they needed privacy, unless they were in the bedroom.

"We need to talk," he said. He looked pale, almost haggard, and as if talking was the last thing he wanted to do.

As she watched him, her mind was darkening with the dread of what he was going to say. It would be about the business, she told herself quickly. Something had gone wrong. They'd lost all their money; they might have to move out of this house. If it was that, it might be a relief. Fighting back from bankruptcy and dealing with the loss of a dream were doable. Anything else wasn't.

"There's no easy way of saying this," he began roughly. "I've tried to think of one, but . . . I guess the only way is to come straight out with it."

She stood motionless, her head down as she waited for the blow.

"I'm leaving," he said quietly.

She could feel herself starting to sway. She knew she'd heard right, but she was unable to make herself take it in. If she did, her entire world would begin to fall apart.

"I'm sorry," he said. "I've . . . I didn't want this to happen. . . ."

"You have four children," she stated, as if he might have forgotten.

He flinched, but managed to keep his voice steady as he said, "I think it's best for them if I go."

Had he really just said that? Was he truly telling himself that leaving would be *best* for his children?

"I'd still see them," he went on. "All the time. I just—I just won't be living here anymore."

Her hand went to her head. This couldn't be happening. He wasn't really speaking these words and meaning them. It was all a terrible twist of her frightened mind. "Then exactly where would you be living?" she asked.

He swallowed dryly. "In Swansea. With Martha."

In spite of suspecting it, the name hit her with a sickening force.

She looked at him, finding herself unable to think of what to say or do. It was as though she'd become separated from her responses, paralyzed by the fear of going forward. She needed to push the words away, to render them meaningless or unspoken, or she might lose her mind. "So when I asked if you were having an affair," she said, "you lied."

He only looked at her.

"You've lied and you've cheated, and you've got the nerve to stand there now and tell me you're leaving."

He didn't defend himself.

"How does that work, Jack?" she cried brokenly. "Just tell me how it's so easy for you to walk out of here."

"It's not easy," he growled. "Christ, this is the hardest thing I've ever had to do, but I can't go on pretending."

"*Pretending!* All of this is a pretense for you? Me, our marriage, our children . . ."

"You know that's not what I mean."

"Then what do you mean?"

He took a breath but didn't answer. She saw tears in his eyes and wanted to hit him.

"*What do you mean?*" she raged.

"Please don't make me say things I'd rather not." His voice was ragged, shaky.

She felt herself backing away. He didn't have to say them; she could guess what they were and would almost rather die than hear them. "You've lied to us, betrayed us, and now, because *you* can't pretend, we'll be left here, trying to pick up the pieces, trying to work out where we went wrong, and all because you've got a hard-on for a woman—"

"It's more than that," he broke in quietly. "You surely can't think I'd do this if it wasn't."

She could only stare at him as everything inside her began breaking apart. He was serious about the woman; he was *in love* with her.

Panic was starting to take her over. She was shaking, tears were falling onto her cheeks, her breathing was labored. She suddenly realized there was a knife in her hand. She wanted to plunge it into him, to make him bleed and scream the way she was bleeding and screaming inside. "How long has it been going on?" she heard herself ask.

He dragged a hand over his mouth. "What does it matter?"

"*How* long?"

"Virtually since we arrived here."

More shock tore at her heart. How had it been possible for him to deceive her for an entire year without her suspecting sooner?

Because she'd always trusted him; that was how. She'd truly believed that she and the children meant as much to him as he did to them. She'd never imagined he'd do anything to jeopardize their happiness, to destroy everything they'd built together, and yet for the past year that was exactly what had been happening. How much worse could the betrayal get? "I don't know you," she told him, her voice threaded with pain and contempt. "You're not the man I married. You're not the father of my children."

He said nothing, simply stood there, tears rolling silently down his cheeks. Suddenly, without thinking, she picked up her wine and dashed it into his face.

For a long moment he only stared at her, the ruby liquid dripping onto his shirt.

"You're despicable," she told him brokenly. "You've been lying to me all this time—"

"Of course I lied," he cut in hoarsely. "I had to, to protect you."

"No! To protect *you*, and *her*. Tell me, the morning you disappeared on the beach, when you said you'd taken Irene Evans's dog home, where were you?"

His expression was impenetrable, his tone stiff, as he said, "I think you know the answer."

"So what happened? She rang when you were out walking with me and you . . . What did you do? Went running to her, we know that, but then what happened? Where did you go?"

"What difference does it make?"

"I want to know."

"OK. She picked me up in her car and we went . . . somewhere quiet."

She felt suddenly sick, dizzy, unable to stomach any more. The images he was creating of desperate lovemaking in the back of a car while she, sad little dupe that she was, continued to walk on the beach were too hard to bear.

"And the night you said you were at the pub?" she made herself ask.

His gaze remained steady. "I was with Martha."

Once again the name felt like a slap. "You'd seen her that day, but you couldn't wait to see her again?"

His failure to answer was answer enough.

"Did you go to see your mother? No, of course you didn't— more lies so you could spend two whole nights with your whore. Did you ever see anyone from the Arts Council? The email inviting you never found its way to my inbox. Do I even need to ask if it was where you went last Saturday when you decided to disappear?"

"I was with her," he confirmed.

She looked at the knife she'd dropped on the countertop, and for one insane moment she felt tempted to slash it across her own wrist. Real pain, something deep and physical, surely had to be easier than this.

"Why did she come here to talk me through the website?" she demanded, wondering why she was putting herself through this, yet unable to stop.

"What does it matter?"

"Why did she come?"

He took a breath, and she could see how hard he was finding this, but she couldn't care less. "I think a part of her wanted to be reminded of how much she likes you," he said.

"What?"

"She wanted her conscience to take over, to make her realize that she couldn't take me away, so that she would have to give me up."

Remembering how the woman had sat in this very kitchen, asking about her family, looking through pictures of the children and noticing that Jack wasn't in many, sent a bolt of outrage surging through her.

"And tomorrow? What's that supposed to be about?" she asked furiously.

"It won't happen now."

"Because you've already told me. Meaning she threatened to do it for you."

"It had to come out sometime, and dragging it on wasn't doing anyone any good."

It was all hurting so much that she hardly knew what to do with herself. She didn't understand how his mind could be so set on destroying his family. It wasn't making any sense, it wasn't who he was, and yet he was standing there telling her that Martha Gwynne meant so much to him that he couldn't give her up, not even for the sake of his children. "Does her husband know?" she asked.

He nodded and swallowed. "She moved out last week. We've rented an apartment in the Maritime Quarter."

Her eyes widened. *We've* rented an apartment. The word was like acid on an open wound. "When do you intend to go?" she said hoarsely.

"I hadn't—"

Suddenly losing it again, she stormed into the utility room and grabbed his coat. "You can go right now," she raged, thrusting it at him. "Here you are. Take it and get the hell out of here."

"Jenna, for heaven's sake . . ."

"*I said get out!*"

"You'll wake the children."

"What do you care about them?" she yelled. "You've already made the decision to abandon them, so as far as I'm concerned, you're not in their lives anymore."

"I'm not abandoning them, and I won't have you telling them that I am."

"Then what will you have me telling them? Better still, what will *you* tell them? After all, you're the one who's doing this, so you should be the one to explain that you've been fucking another woman who you've now decided to live with instead of them. Exactly how are you going to put that, Jack? What words have you?"

"You don't have to be crude."

"If what you're doing isn't crude, then I'm sure I don't know what is."

"I thought we could talk to the children together, explain that I won't be far away, that I'll still be picking them up from school, coming for tea, putting them to bed . . ."

"Are you out of your mind?" she cried hysterically. "Is that what you've been telling yourself, that you can carry on coming and going from this house as though nothing's changed? As if not living with their mother, not loving her anymore, counts for nothing?"

He stared at her helplessly.

"Well, is it? Is that what you've fooled yourself into believing? You seriously think you can carry on your relationship with them?"

"What do you want me to say?" he demanded.

"I want you to say that this isn't happening, that I'll wake up in a minute and find out it's a nightmare, that you aren't really standing there telling me that our marriage is over when I . . . when I . . ." She couldn't hold it together now, and as she started to break down he came to her. "No," she choked, pushing him back. "I don't want your pity. I just want . . . I just want you. Oh God, Jack, please don't do this, I beg you. I can't bear to lose you. We can work this out. Please say you'll give her up, that our lives can go on the way they are."

Pulling her to him, he stroked her hair as he said, "I swear I didn't set out to make this happen. The last thing in the world I ever wanted was to hurt you."

"Then don't do it. Think of everything we've meant to each other, of how much it would mean to the children if you were here to see them grow up . . ."

"But I will see them grow up. Swansea is only a few miles away, and like I said, I'll come every day."

"But you've got to see how impossible that would be for me. I can't let you do it, Jack, I just can't."

"I know it seems hard at the moment, but once things have calmed down—"

"It's never going to happen. You have to start believing that. If you leave here, you're out of our lives. It'll be over. You'll never see us again. Any of us."

The pain in his eyes was etched in his voice as he said, "You can't cut them off from me, and you know it."

"Paige would cut herself off."

"Maybe, if you told her to, but what good would that do her? I'm the only father she's ever known, nothing's ever going to change that, and I'll always be there for her, no matter—"

"No! You'll be at an apartment in Swansea with Martha Gwynne. That's not here. No, Jack, you can't have it all. You have to choose, Martha or us. We're not going to share you, even if she will."

Taking a breath, he said, "Now's not the right time to discuss this. We're both tired, emotional . . ."

"There's never going to be a right time."

"Maybe not, but I think we've said all we can for tonight. I don't want to hurt you any more; I just want you to know that I'd give anything for this never to have happened, but it has."

"Because you let it, and now you have to stop it."

His only answer was to pull her more tightly into his arms, and as he held her she'd never felt so helpless or afraid in her life.

In the end, she said, "Are you leaving tonight?"

"Not if you don't want me to."

"Had you intended to?"

"Not really."

"But she's waiting for you to call?"

"It doesn't matter."

Glad to think Martha might be worrying, fearing he'd changed his mind, perhaps even imagining him making love to his wife when he should have been leaving, she heard herself say, "Is she good in bed? Is that what it's really about?"

He didn't answer; simply closed his eyes and rested his head on hers.

"Is she better than me?" she asked brokenly.

"Jenna, don't do this."

"I want to know. Is it better with her than it is with me? I suppose it must be or you wouldn't be doing this. Who made the first move? Was it you or her?"

"I'm not getting into this."

"Do her staff know?"

"I don't think so."

She put a hand to her head as more tears welled in her eyes. "So she's taking my husband and my business. Is that the plan? You're going to leave me with nothing."

"The business is yours. We'll help you to run it, of course, but the profits, the success will be—"

"It's *ours*. We've built it together, like our family. It's a part of us, we're all a part of each other, you can't just . . ."

Sighing, he said, "Don't let's talk about it now."

She turned away, her heart raw with the pain of so much fear and betrayal. She could feel more panic rising, trying to steal her breath, to push her over the edge into a terrible, bottomless gulf of despair. She couldn't bear to think this was the end, that they'd already slept together for the last time, that she'd never again see him walking naked into the bathroom or simply going to open the curtains. There would be no laundry of his mixing with hers in the basket, no clothes hanging in his wardrobe or toothbrush next to hers in the mug. While she lived here alone, longing for him, unable to bear the loneliness, he'd be with Martha, loving her, laughing with her, and not even thinking about those he'd left behind.

As more sobs tore through her he held her close, murmuring softly, "I'm sorry, I'm sorry."

"Then don't do it," she pleaded. "Call her now and tell her you're not going through with it."

She heard him swallow and her heart tightened with a desperate hope as long, silent minutes ticked by. In the end he said, almost in a whisper, "I've tried to stop seeing her, lots of times, but what I feel for her . . . the way we are together . . . Oh God, Jen, I know how hard this is for you to hear, but if I say it, perhaps then you'll believe it. I love her, I want to be with her, and I'm prepared to leave our marriage so I can."

Her eyes were livid with pain, her heart was too big and raw for her chest. "Then you can leave our marriage right now," she told him. Not giving him the chance to protest, she thrust his coat at him again and left the room.

Moments later she heard his engine start, and it took every ounce of willpower she possessed not to run outside and beg him to stay.

Let him go for now, she told herself. *It's the only way he's going to find out this isn't what he wants, and then he'll come back.*

The instant Paige saw a large brown envelope stuck to the front of her locker with the school magazine behind it, she knew it

was going to be the surprise Kelly Durham had promised—
LOL.

As she opened it she had the sense of being watched, though
she couldn't actually see any of the Durmites; she was just con-
scious of them being around, camouflaged amongst all the
comings and goings of fellow students stuffing coats into lockers, grabbing their books, and scurrying or dawdling off to
their tutor groups. She had double maths this morning, a subject she'd always detested, but today she was actually looking
forward to it since Kelly and most of the morons were in a different group.

Charlotte was standing behind her. "What is it?" she whispered as Paige peered inside the envelope.

Paige couldn't tell at first, she was only able to see that it was
yellow, and there was an odd bitter-sweet smell coming from it.
Tentatively she put a hand inside, afraid of being bitten or stung
or covered in something revolting, but whatever it was felt soft
and cool, kind of like fabric, but not. She brought out a small
handful of something, and when she saw what it was her heart
gave a horrible thud.

The envelope was full of crushed daffodil heads. With them
was a note reading like a banner headline: *Mass Daffodil Suicide After Paige No Moore Tortures with Prose*.

As tears flooded her eyes, Charlotte quickly put an arm
around her.

"Come on," she urged, steering her toward the loos. "Don't
let them see they've got to you. They're just fuckwits who need
to fuck off and die," she added over her shoulder.

"Daffodils have a jaunty exuberance," Paige heard someone
shouting after them, and the quote was followed by loud groans
and gagging noises.

"It's OK, I'm fine," she told Charlotte as the door closed behind them. She couldn't be sure whether she was crying for the flowers or for herself; it was just that seeing them all mangled and discolored had felt so cruel and meaningless. She hated being the reason they'd been plucked from their stalks only to be crushed, but at least they couldn't feel anything, unlike her, because they were dead, unlike her.

Taking the envelope from her, Charlotte flushed the contents down a toilet. "That's what someone ought to do to them," she said savagely.

Only wishing she could, Paige tensed as the door opened. To her relief it wasn't any of the Durmites, so after drying her eyes and checking that her makeup wasn't ruined, she followed Charlotte back out to the corridor. Since the bell had sounded a couple of minutes ago, there were fewer people around now, but amongst those not yet in registration were Owen's sister and a couple of her friends, who were standing outside the sixth-form common room.

Without giving herself time to think, Paige hurried over to her. "I'm sorry to interrupt," she said awkwardly, "but if you don't mind, I need you to tell your brother that I didn't post anything about him on Facebook. Everyone's saying I did, but I swear my account was hacked and I thought . . . Well, if you told him it wasn't me, he might listen to you."

The coldness of the stare she received from her—the eyes, the face so like Owen's they could be twins—seemed to go right through her, and as she took a step back all three girls turned and walked away.

"We're going to be late," Charlotte said, putting a hand on her arm. "Have you got everything?"

Close to tears again, Paige managed to force them down as she nodded. She hadn't expected Owen's sister to cut her dead like that; then again, she wasn't sure what she'd expected. She was just an idiot for going up to her like that in the first place. It stood to reason she'd believe Owen, and even if she didn't she was friendly with Kelly Durham, so she probably despised Paige No Moore along with the rest of the world.

As she went into class, where Mrs. Haynes was already waiting, she kept her head up, reminding herself that she was over-emotional today because of the clash she'd had with her mum earlier over her clean shirt not being ironed. Ordinarily she'd have forgotten all about it by now, but she hadn't because, weirdly, her mum had just walked away and her dad had snapped at Paige for being rude. Of all the injustices! All she'd said was that in most people's homes their families came first. OK, it might have been a bit harsh, but her mother spent so much time on the business now that all sorts of things were getting forgotten. Anyway, she might have been better able to take the telling-off from her father if she hadn't felt so sure that he was the one who'd upset her mum in the first place.

Still, all that mattered right now was the fact that she wasn't having to suffer Kelly Durham for the rest of the morning. Equal bliss was that when lunchtime came round she and Charlotte didn't have to go to the canteen because they'd brought their own food today. Paige had had to make her sandwiches this morning, because neither of her parents had bothered to sort out anything for her, even though she'd texted from her bedroom last night to ask if they would.

She knew Charlotte's mother had made her lunch because the neat, triangle-shaped sandwiches were wrapped in foil with a ribbon around, and the slice of homemade carrot cake that Charlotte very generously shared had been carefully protected by a pretty pink serviette.

"By the way," Paige said as they sheltered from the wind in the art room's front porch, "I was chatting online with that Julie Morris again last night, and she said that Kelly Durham and the sickos used to pick on her. It's why she won't tell me who she is, because she doesn't want them turning on her again. Apparently it happened before I started, but you were here then, so you might know who she is."

Charlotte was wrinkling her nose as she thought. "That cow of a slapper has picked on so many people," she muttered. "She's been doing it ever since we were at St. Cenydd's primary, so it could be anyone. What else did *Julie* have to say?"

"That it got worse after she reported them."

Charlotte stifled a sneeze. "Yeah, well, I don't suppose that's a big surprise. I take it they're leaving her alone now."

"I think so."

"It's what'll happen with you. They'll get fed up in the end and move on to somebody else. I just hope it's not me, except they wouldn't now that I'm kind of official with Liam."

Though Paige knew it wasn't official at all, she let the delusion pass, since the last thing she wanted was to crush Charlotte's hopes. In fact, Charlotte and Liam still hadn't graduated beyond sexting and Snapchats, most of which made it pretty clear that he was only after one thing.

"And what's wrong with that?" Charlotte had laughed when Paige put it to her as gently as she could. "I don't want to be a virgin all my life, that's for sure."

"But wouldn't you rather be in a proper relationship before you go all the way?"

"What for? It's supposed to be fun, something you get a kick out of, not get all hung up about."

"So you want to be one of those fifteen-year-old mothers living on benefits who wheel their pushchairs up and down Oxford Street?"

"Stop! Who said anything about getting pregnant? We'll use condoms, or I'll go on the pill. I just want to have sex, Paige, not make a lifetime commitment, and I bet you'd give it up for Oliver if he asked."

Wondering if she would, Paige had simply sighed from the depths of her broken heart as she thought of him and Lindsay, and said, "Chance would be a fine thing."

She wasn't going to tell Charlotte that she was still listening to his music all the time, watching his video, and reading his Facebook page. She actually *felt* like a stalker when she was doing it, but as long as he had no idea she was behaving like someone obsessed, she couldn't see any harm in it. Admittedly, afterward she felt like a real saddo, and as big a loser as Kelly Durham kept saying she was.

Still, for all anyone knew, she and Oliver actually might end up together. No one could say what the future held other than people like Jasmina, the clairvoyant she and Charlotte were going to see later on today, and wouldn't it just be totally out there mega-awesome if she was told that Oliver Pryce was only waiting for her to be sixteen before asking her out?

Much later that afternoon Paige was sitting on a hand-shaped chair in Jasmina's New Age emporium, located in a back lane of Mumbles, trying to calm her nerves as she waited for Charlotte to come back through the beaded curtain she'd disappeared behind about half an hour ago. She couldn't hear anything going on through there, no voices or anything. There was only Indian-type music drifting and whining about the place, along with the tinkle of water fountains and smells of incense, herbs, and candle wax. There was a display case next to her full of crystals and charms and aromatherapy stuff, and the hundreds of books and CDs on the shelves were all about psychic development, meditation, and past lives. She wondered who or what she might have been in a past life, and if she was really interested to know. More pressing for her right now was finding out what might be about to happen in this one.

Her nerves went off like a set of wind chimes as the curtain suddenly parted and Charlotte, all glittery-eyed and flushed in the cheeks, practically floated back in.

"OMG," she mouthed, coming to perch on the rocking chair next to Paige's plastic hand. "She is totally amazing. She told me so much. . . . She even gave me a message from my gran."

Since Charlotte's gran had died six months ago, Paige was as spooked by that as she was awed. Would her grandpa come through and speak to her? She'd love it if he did, but she was sure it would terrify her too. "Did she tell you anything horrible?" she asked worriedly.

"No, nothing. It was all like totally amazeballs. She said she could see I was romantically involved with someone whose name begins either with *I* or *L*—they look a bit similar, so she couldn't quite tell. Anyway, it has to be Liam, obviously, because I don't know anyone whose name begins with *I*. And anyway she said he was very good-looking and likes sports and music, so it's definitely him. Oh yes, and she said it was up to me if I wanted the relationship to go any deeper."

Paige's eyes rounded.

"She saw you too," Charlotte went on excitedly. "She said a friend beginning with *P*—she does a lot of letters—was going through a difficult time right now and I should stand by you. Obviously that goes—"

They started at the gentle clatter of the curtain, and Paige felt her throat turning dry as the statuesque lady with silver wavy hair, eyes the same color as her aquamarine earrings and face as pale as the palest seashell, smiled warmly as she invited her in.

Minutes later Paige was seated across a small square table from the woman, her hands resting palms up on a black velvet tablecloth, her courage flitting about like an overstressed bird. She wasn't at all sure she wanted to go through with this now; on the other hand, nothing in the world could drag her away.

Cupping Paige's hands in her own, Jasmina closed her eyes and let several moments pass as she picked up the vibe, or communed with the future, or whatever she was doing. "I sense some disquiet," she said gently. She looked concerned. "You are not very happy at the moment."

Feeling instantly miserable, Paige said nothing.

"There are people around you who are a negative force," Jasmina continued. "I see the letters *B* and *D* and *M* . . . Yes, I'm definitely getting *M*. Does this mean anything to you?"

Paige shook her head.

Jasmina frowned. "It's someone . . . older, I think. A relative, maybe?"

Paige was still confused.

"She's stepping back now, but she's not going away. There's someone else here. . . . You have a friend . . . except she or he is not a friend. You should beware of this person. I'm getting the letter *J*. Is this making any sense to you?"

Certain she must be talking about Julie Morris, Paige said, "I think so. There's this girl who's contacted me online. . . ."

Jasmina considered it. "There's good and bad with the letter *J*," she decided. "A false friend, perhaps, and . . . What else does this letter mean to you?"

Only able to think of her parents and Josh, Paige told her their names.

Jasmina quietly absorbed the information. "Jenna is your mother," she repeated carefully. "I sense that she is very worried at the moment."

"She's always worried."

Jasmina smiled. "Like most mothers, mm? Her worry is very prominent here, but so is the *J* who means you harm. . . . Actually, I'm getting the letter *O*."

Paige's heart skipped a beat. "Oliver?" she whispered.

Jasmina's eyes closed again as she focused. "Who is this person?" she asked.

"He's just . . . someone I know."

"Have you had a falling-out with him? I can see a falling-out."

"But we haven't even . . . Oh, maybe it's Owen," she said flatly.

Jasmina neither confirmed nor denied it.

Paige waited, willing her to see Oliver. Surely he was there too—another *O* that had to be him.

"I'm getting this *M* back again," Jasmina eventually said. "She's quite forcefully pushing her way through. There is tension here. A lot of tension."

Paige could only look at her.

"Your mother is very upset about something. . . . It could be you. I'm sure it's you, but there's more. Something to do with this *M* . . . Ah, the *O* is back. You said it was Owen? Is he a boyfriend you've broken up with?"

"No. He's . . . Owen's gay."

Jasmina showed no response to that. "I see the false friend again. I can't tell if it's him, but it is clear that you shouldn't trust this person. She, or he, is telling you things you want to hear, but they aren't necessarily true."

Deciding to break all contact with Julie from now on, Paige said anxiously, "Am I ever going to have a boyfriend?"

Jasmina broke into a smile. "I think there is someone you like," she replied kindly. "Yes, there is. He's very handsome, a little older than you, I think, and he likes music?"

Paige's heart was on fire. "Is he going to be my boyfriend?" she whispered shyly.

"I'm not sure. He's certainly there, but . . . Does his name begin with *O*?"

"Yes, it does."

"Mm, then I would ask you to tread carefully, because there is certainly some negativity surrounding the letter *O*."

Paige's eyes stung. This wasn't what she wanted to hear. Why did Owen keep coming through and spoiling things?

More quiet minutes passed as Jasmina held Paige's hands steadily and murmured to herself. It wasn't possible to make out what she was saying, until finally the words became clearer. "There is someone here—your grandfather, he says. He wants you to know he's watching over you."

A tear dropped onto Paige's cheek. She couldn't bear that her grandfather was here but she couldn't see him.

"He's saying that you must trust your mother."

"I do," Paige whispered.

"Your grandmother too."

Paige didn't understand why he was saying that, because she definitely trusted them both.

Jasmina shook her head slowly. "The situation at school," she went on, "he's saying you must not let it get out of hand." Her eyes opened and came to rest on Paige's, so tenderly and with such intensity that Paige had to look away. "Can I ask what is troubling you at school?" she said softly.

Paige swallowed. "It's just girls. They're being mean to me, that's all."

Jasmina continued to regard her. "If it's worrying you, you need to tell someone. That is what your grandfather is saying."

Paige's eyes went down as her throat tightened. "It's all right," she mumbled. "I can handle it."

Closing her hands around Paige's, Jasmina said, "I think that's all for today, but if you want to talk again, at any time, you know where I am."

"Thank you," Paige murmured, trying not to be unnerved by the offer. What was the clairvoyant seeing that Paige might want to talk about in the future?

"Don't hide," Jasmina told her, "and don't listen to all the advice you get, especially when you know in your heart that it's wrong." She waited, as if making sure Paige had taken it in. "And look out for the false friend. She, *he*, is not someone you need in your life."

Minutes later Paige and Charlotte were walking away from the shop, down Newton Road toward the bay, oblivious to the world around them as they recounted everything they'd been told.

"Mine was awful," Paige wailed. "She's really freaked me out about everything, especially Oliver."

"But it's not Oliver, it's Owen you have to watch out for," Charlotte insisted. "And you knew that already."

"No I didn't. I mean, yes, we've had a falling-out, but she said there's some really negative stuff around him."

"So we just make sure we avoid him. And you've definitely got to tell that Julie Morris where to get off. I'll bet it's him."

"I'd think so too if she weren't being so friendly."

"Paige, for God's sake, you can't stick up for her, not after this."

"No, I know. I just . . . Oh God, that woman told me so much, it's going round and round in my head. . . . I can't remember it all now."

They turned onto the seafront, passing Patrick's, where her parents had taken her for dinner on her fifteenth birthday, and on toward the pier and Verdis, where her dad sometimes took Josh and the twins on Saturdays while she and her mum had special time at a beauty salon or roaming the farmers' market. She gazed out across the bay toward Swansea in the distance.

"She kept on about my mum being worried," she said, slowing to a stop, "and this *M* person pushing her way in. . . ." Her face suddenly paled as a terrible thought crashed into her mind. "Oh my God," she murmured shakily. "I said I didn't know anyone whose name begins with *M*, but I do." Her eyes went to Charlotte, wide and scared. "I have to get home," she said urgently. "I have to speak to my mum."

Chapter 9

Jenna was in the conservatory dining room, staring out at the dense, silvery sea mist rolling across the moor, closing in on the house, making everything disappear before her eyes.

It felt like a metaphor for her life.

Her cheeks were sallow, her eyes heavy with fatigue and pain. She felt drained, bewildered, the way she had after her father's death, as though she had somehow slipped from the real world and become caught in a place that had no sense or reality. The feeling of loss was overwhelming. She wanted Jack, but she wanted her dad too, so much she could almost cry out for him. He would know what to do, how she should cope with this crisis—and that was all it was, surely, a crisis that would eventually resolve itself, and life would go on as before.

Her mother was sitting at the table with Bena, empty cups of tea and plates of untouched biscuits in front of them. They were watching her and worrying, she could feel it, but she could think of no more to say. The past few hours had been spent talking things over and over, round and round in so many circles. Discussion was fruitless; everything depended on Jack changing his mind.

That wasn't going to happen.

"There's no point dragging it out," he'd said when they'd talked this morning, "it'll only make it harder. I'll take some things with me today, after I've collected Josh and the twins from school."

"So you won't stay for tea?" she'd asked, desperate for him to, while at the same time wanting to tell him to keep the hell away from her children.

"I thought I'd take them to McDonald's."

"What about Paige?"

He hadn't answered that, and she'd seen how anxious he was about breaking his news to his stepdaughter. Paige would know what betrayal was, would see his weakness and his failure to put his family first, would feel her mother's devastation.

He'd come back first thing this morning, not, as she'd told herself he would, to say he was making a terrible mistake, but to take Josh and the twins to school. Minutes after they'd gone she'd dumped his clothes on the drive and locked all the doors.

She couldn't remember now how he'd persuaded her to let him in when he'd come back. She'd watched him stuffing his clothes into the car, and then they were in the kitchen, talking, crying, holding each other tightly, as though neither of them could bear what was happening, though obviously he could. There had been bitterness and anger; she'd slapped his face, punched her fists into him, and collapsed on the floor in a hysterical state. He'd picked her up, carried her to the sofa, and brought her some tea.

Her head ached now. Her eyes were raw, and her stomach kept crying out for food she knew she couldn't eat. He'd told Bena and her mother himself when they'd turned up at their usual times. Bena's sadness and disappointment that Jenna's suspicions had proved right had brought yet more tears to Jenna's eyes.

"I'm going to be here for you," Bena had promised, in front of Jack. "I want you to know that no matter what, *I* won't let you down."

Whether Jack had caught the barb Jenna had no idea. He'd shown no sign of it and had only thanked Bena as though she were doing him the favor, not Jenna.

Her mother, who found it almost impossible to alter her schedule at any time, never mind at the last minute, had called the retirement home where she volunteered twice a week to tell them she wouldn't be in today. Because she didn't cry or shout or scream like other people, the terrible realization of what this was going to mean for her daughter and grandchildren was bottled up inside her. Watching her trying to cope was breaking Jenna's heart all over again. She might show little emotion on the surface, but she had feelings like anyone else, and Jack's betrayal, his desertion, was hurting her almost as much as it was Jenna.

"You're a married man," she'd told Jack with her typical frankness, "and the father of four, which means you have responsibilities. I don't understand how anything or anyone can be more important than that."

"Nothing is more important than them," he'd assured her. "That's why I'm doing this, because living a lie wouldn't be right."

"That's funny," Jenna had shot back acidly, "you seem to have managed it without any trouble for the past year—and please spare me the line that you're doing the right thing for us. What you're doing is for *you* and her. We don't matter anymore;

you're making that perfectly clear even if you're too cowardly to admit it."

Had he responded to that? If he had, she'd forgotten now what he'd said. She only remembered how beaten and sorry he'd managed to look throughout much of the day—though whether sorry for himself or for what he was doing, she guessed only he knew. Probably both. She'd told him to go, several times, but he hadn't listened, although the clothes she'd tossed into the drive remained in his car.

She watched the magpies and gulls, oystercatchers and curlews, weaving in and out of the mist, and felt exhausted by so many surges of emotion: anger, panic, utter despair. Each outburst was leaving her more depleted than the last, and yet there still seemed energy for more. She was aware that she wasn't handling things well, but she didn't know how else to be, and did she really care? Even the thought of the children was sapping her now. How was she going to cope when they raced through the door demanding food, drinks, her attention, her love? She was sure that if there were a way to avoid them, she'd take it—then she'd despise herself for being so weak. She'd despise Jack more, but how was that going to help anything?

"This is what hurts the most," she said, breaking the silence, "the fact that he's rejecting the children. I know he's choosing not to see it like that, but I can't see it any other way. He's going to shatter their world. They'll bear the scars of this for the rest of their lives, and I just don't know how he can do it."

Bena said, "Maybe he won't in the end. Maybe when what he's doing really starts to sink in he'll come to his senses."

Jenna wanted to believe it, so much that she could already

feel herself clinging to it. When Jack came back during the next hour he was going to say that of course it was her he loved, and this had been no more than some sort of midlife confusion.

"Is that Paige?" her mother said, getting up.

Jenna turned round as Paige threw open the kitchen door and dropped her school bag on the floor. Waffle instantly went to her, but she stood staring at her mother, her eyes too bright, her face too pale. Surely to God Jack hadn't already told her? If he had, he'd have done so on the phone, and that would be something Jenna would never forgive him for.

"Where's Dad?" Paige demanded.

"Gone to pick up the little ones," her grandmother answered. "Shall I make you a drink? Something to eat?"

Paige was still staring at her mother. Jenna held the gaze, feeling the strength of their bond tightening. "What's going on?" Paige asked. "I know something is, so don't—"

"Come and sit down," Jenna said, pulling out a chair.

Paige took a step back.

Realizing she needed to go to her, Jenna started forward, but Paige stopped her. "Is he . . . is he having an affair?" she choked out.

Jenna swallowed hard as her daughter's pain burned with her own.

"He is, isn't he?"

Jenna nodded.

"Oh God," Paige sobbed into her hands.

Going to her, Jenna held her close. "How do you know?" she asked softly.

Paige shook her head, too distraught to answer.

"Have you spoken to Dad?"

Again Paige shook her head. "I—I saw them," she stammered. "A few days ago. I didn't think anything of it at the time, but then I remembered she'd rung before he went out last Saturday. . . ."

"Where did you see them?"

"Near the Dylan Thomas Centre. He said they'd been to a meeting." Her frightened eyes came up to Jenna's. "Is he going to stop now you've found out?" she whispered.

Jenna's heart twisted so hard she had to close her eyes.

"Oh God, Mum, he is, isn't he? Please say he is."

Jenna could only shake her head. "He—he says he loves her."

Paige shook her head violently. "That is so *disgusting,*" she cried. "He can't love her. You're his wife."

"I know, but sometimes things happen this way, and there's nothing I can do to change it."

"But you have to. You can't just let him carry on seeing her. It's wrong. He's married, he's got children . . ."

Taking Paige's face between her hands, Jenna gazed into her eyes and almost couldn't bear what she was seeing. However, Paige was fifteen now, old enough to hear the truth—and what point would there have been in trying to hide it? "He's going to live with her," she said softly. "After he's brought Josh and the twins home this evening he's going to Martha's."

Paige's face turned so white that Jenna thought she might pass out. She felt like doing so herself, but she had to hold it together for Paige—and the others when they came in.

Where were they? They should have been back by now. She glanced at the clock, the worst possible scenarios spinning through her mind.

Picking up her mobile, she dialed his number.

"We're just coming up the lane," he told her, apparently guessing why she was ringing.

Remembering his plan to take the younger ones to McDonald's, she said, "Paige knows." Reaching for Paige's hand, she
pulled her in.

There was a silence before he asked, "How's she taking it?"

Resting her head on Paige's, Jenna said, "How do you think?
You're her father. You've betrayed her too."

"Is she there now?"

"Yes."

"And you're saying that in front of her?"

"It's the truth. Why should I hide it?"

Sighing, he said, "I'm just turning into the drive," and the
line went dead.

Moments later Josh burst through the door shouting, "Hi
Mum, got to go to the toilet." Dashing for the stairs, he went
thundering up to the bathroom.

"Mum! Mum! Guess what?" Flora cried, skipping in with
one pigtail bouncing, the other flopping around her ear. "We
had McDonald's and I had cheese with mine. Paige, can we play
dress-up after you've done your homework?"

"Flora," Kay called out, "did you remember to bring your PE
bag home?"

Flora clasped a hand to her mouth. "Oh no, I forgot."

"Don't worry, we'll pick it up tomorrow," Jenna told her.
"Wills, look at the state of you. Have you been in a fight?"

"Yes, with Josh in the back of the car," he cried, punching his
fists in the air, "and I won! Can we watch *Dexter* tonight, Mum?
Oh no, Abney and Teal are on. . . ."

"That's rubbish," Flora shouted. "Can we watch MTV?
That's really cool."

Gathering them up, Kay said, "Come on, we can argue it out
in the sitting room."

"Paige, can I sleep with you tonight?" Flora asked over her shoulder.

"No," Paige answered shortly.

Flora poked out her tongue and skipped on through the door.

"So where's Dad?" Paige wanted to know.

Jenna looked at Bena. "Probably on the phone to Martha," she replied.

"Do you want me to stay?" Bena asked.

As Jenna tried to decide, Jack came in, his mobile in one hand, the children's bags in the other. Jenna had never seen him looking so haggard, and she almost felt sorry for him as his eyes went to Paige.

"I don't know what your mother's told you," he began, "but I want—"

"She didn't tell me anything," Paige spat. "I worked it out for myself, and I think you're *disgusting*."

"Paige," Jenna chided.

"Don't stick up for him," Paige cried. "He's a lying, cheating hypocrite, and as far as I'm concerned he's not my father."

"Paige, please listen to me," he said roughly. "This doesn't have—"

"Shut up!" she shouted. "I don't want to hear anything you have to say, especially if it's about that bitch who ought—"

"Don't call her that."

"—to just fuck off and die."

"I understand you're angry," Jack said darkly, "but I don't want to hear that language coming from you again. Do you hear me?"

"You don't have the right to tell me off," she retorted. "You're nobody to me now, so just get out of here. Go on. Go! We don't need you. We can manage perfectly all right on our own. Can't we, Mum?"

Swallowing dryly, Jenna said, "Why don't you go on upstairs, sweetheart? I'll come and see you in a minute."

"Please don't tell me you're going to let him get away with this."

"Paige. You're not helping."

"Oh well, excuse me! I'll just pretend I don't matter, shall I? We all know I don't anyway, so I might just as well be dead." Grabbing her bag, she stormed off to her room.

Jenna looked at Jack. He was clearly badly shaken, but she refused to feel pity. "You deserved that," she told him.

His eyes closed. When he spoke, it was to Bena. "Is she deliberately turning Paige against me?" he asked.

"You shouldn't be bringing me into this," Bena objected, "but to answer your question, Paige already told you: she worked it out for herself."

"How?"

"Actually, she saw you together," Jenna informed him.

He eyed her harshly, and eventually started to nod. "Yes, she did," he confirmed. He started for the fridge, but Jenna slammed a hand against it. "You don't live here anymore," she reminded him.

He seemed about to argue, but then the fight went out of him as he dashed a hand through his hair.

"If you are going, don't you think you should say goodbye to Josh and the twins?" she threw at him. Now would be the time for him to say he wasn't going anywhere, that he was sorry for putting her through this and that he wanted to stay.

In the end, he said, "Don't you want help putting them to bed?"

"It's too early for them to go to bed," she heard herself retort, "and I'd rather you didn't hang around. So I think it would be best if you went now." She could hardly believe she was saying this, even sounding as though she meant it, when every single part of her was pleading with him to stay.

Looking at Bena, he said, "How long are you going to be here?"

"As long as I'm needed," she replied. "Al's taken Aiden to his parents' for the night."

Jack nodded, as though understanding that this arrangement had been made so she could be around for Jenna.

His eyes came to Jenna. "What do you want me to tell the children about why I'm going now?"

"What do you care?"

"You know I care. I don't want to make this any harder for them."

"You don't have to hurt them at all. Remember, it's your choice. You're the one who's putting her first. Paige already understands that, and in time the others will too."

He swallowed hard and glanced down at his phone as it rang. Whether it was Martha Jenna had no idea, because he didn't answer.

"Incidentally," she went on, "we're going to need the password for your computer."

His eyes stayed down as though he might not be connecting with the words. In the end he put it into a text and pressed send.

Though Jenna could almost have guessed what it was, seeing it made her feel sick to her soul. *JackMarthaXX.*

"Go now," she said tightly. "I can't stand to look at you anymore."

"I need to say goodbye to the children."

"What you need doesn't count for anything. You forfeited all rights the day you decided Martha Gwynne was going to take you from your family."

Clearly deciding not to argue anymore today, he said. "I'll call in the morning."

"Don't bother," she started to say, but the words were swallowed by a sob.

He stood where he was, seemingly unable to move, until eventually he turned for the door.

"Do you feel ashamed?" she asked him desperately. He stopped. "It's how you should feel, ashamed of what a spineless, selfish man you are to walk out on your family like this."

"What I feel," he said quietly, "is sorry that you're hurting so much, and sorrier still that I'm the cause." After ruffling the fur on Waffle's head he opened the door and left.

Paige's voice was choked with tears as she sat at her computer speaking to Charlotte on FaceTime. "I can't believe I was right," she protested. "How can he have a bloody affair? It's *sick*. I can't even bear to think of it. Ew! God, I so want to throw up."

"Is he still there?" Charlotte asked, looking both worried and intrigued.

"I don't think so. I heard his car just now. . . ." More tears overwhelmed her as she pictured him driving away, past the green, down the lane, and out to the main road, and her mum being left behind, all hurt and hardly knowing what to do. The mere thought of her mum suffering made her press a hand to her mouth to stop herself sobbing. She couldn't deal with that pain as well as her own; she just couldn't.

"So has he gone to this Martha woman?" Charlotte wondered gently.

Wanting to block it all out, pretend it wasn't happening, Paige said, "I don't know. I suppose so." Her head pounded with the horrendousness of it all. "Mum says he wants to live with her. . . . How can he bloody live with her when we're all here? It's like we don't count anymore. I hate him. I really, really hate him."

"Do the others know yet?" Charlotte asked. "I mean Josh and the twins."

"I don't know. I shouldn't think so. They wouldn't be *making all that noise*," she shouted over her shoulder, "if they did. Jesus! Why do they have to keep crashing into my bedroom door? I swear they're doing it on purpose." Getting up, she tore open the door. Wills shrieked and quickly shoved his bike into his room while Flora looked up at her with frightened eyes from her own bike.

Paige wanted to yell at her, to shake her even, but thinking of how terrible it was going to be for her when she realized her daddy had left, she started to cry instead.

"I'm sorry, I'm sorry," Flora hastily gulped. "I didn't mean to—"

"It's all right," Paige said, going down to her height and folding her in her arms. "I just don't want you to do that anymore, OK?"

"OK," Flora whispered, her own eyes filling with tears.

"What are you up to, Flora?" Grandma asked, coming up the stairs.

"We were just playing," Flora replied unsteadily. "I won't do it again," she promised Paige in a whisper.

"Good girl," Paige responded, giving her a kiss.

After watching Flora pedal into her bedroom, Kay turned to Paige. "Are you all right?" she enquired, her gray eyes blinking steadily.

Paige's throat was too tight to answer.

"You need to eat something," Kay told her.

Knowing she couldn't manage a crumb, Paige simply nodded and closed the door.

"This place is crazyville," she told Charlotte, returning to the computer. "Sometimes I don't think I can stand being here, and it's only going to get worse now this is happening."

"Do you really think he'll go for good?" Charlotte asked incredulously.

"He's already gone, unless he suddenly decides to come back. I haven't got a clue what anyone's doing. All I know is she shouldn't have let him go."

"You mean your mum? She can't make him stay if he doesn't want to."

Not needing to hear that, Paige pushed the thought away and picked up her mobile. No texts from Kelly Durham, thank God. With any luck she'd found someone else to torment. There was nothing from Oliver either—not that she'd expected it, but it would just make a nice change if something went right for once in her life.

"Do you want me to come over?" Charlotte offered.

Paige did, more than anything, but she ended up shaking her head. "I don't know what's going to happen here," she said. "If he does comes back . . . Even if he doesn't . . . *God, I hate him,*" she seethed.

Charlotte murmured in sympathy.

Paige forced herself to go on. "I expect Mum will want to talk to me," she said. "I wish I knew how to get out of that, but even if I did, I'd feel mean turning my back on her." Merely to think it set her crying again. Her mum's pain definitely felt worse than her own, and if her dad didn't come back it was never going to get any better.

Clicking on to her Pheed account, she said, "I've got a message from that Julie Morris."

"Dump her!" Charlotte instructed hotly.

"I will. I just haven't had time yet."

"So what's she saying?"

"She wants to know how we got on at the fortune-teller's."

Charlotte gasped. "You told her we were going!"

Paige nodded miserably. "I just mentioned it, like no big deal."

"Like no big deal? You've got no idea who she is, yet you tell her all your business and the next thing we know it'll be all over Facebook that you've been to see a psychic."

"I wasn't planning on telling her what was said."

"Actually, what you should tell her is that you were warned about a false friend *who can only be her.*"

Paige sighed and put her phone down. She was on the verge of tears again, of doing something drastic even, she just didn't know what.

"I'd better go," Charlotte said. "I'm supposed to be Snapchatting Liam." Her eyes danced. "He only wants me to do it topless, cheeky bugger, so I was thinking I might take a picture of my bare back in the mirror and send that. I mean, he didn't say it had to be the front."

Paige managed a smile. "What are you going to do if he takes a screenshot and sends it to everyone?"

Charlotte shrugged. "Why would I care if anyone sees my back?"

"I bet you'll send one of your front if he asks."

"I might. Then again, I might not. You know, if I didn't include my head no one would know it was me."

"Apart from the fact it's come from your phone."

"True, but I could have taken it of someone else."

"Just as long as no one thinks it's me."

"Don't worry—given the difference in our sizes, they won't. Anyway, I haven't even decided if I'm going to do it yet. If I do, I'll make it disappear in three seconds, so he won't have time to screenshot. So, let me know how you get on with *Julie* if you message her back. Personally, I don't think you should, unless it's to tell her to eff off."

After ending the call Paige walked over to her bed and slumped down on the edge of it. She wished her mum would come up to see her, but at the same time she hoped she never did. She just wanted everything to be normal again, the way it had been before the Durmites had started picking on her and her dad had got involved with this Martha cow. She hardly knew which was worse; it was all so horrible. At least when her dad was here she could go to him for help, but he wouldn't be interested now. Obviously all that mattered to him was being with this woman; he didn't care what it was doing to her mum, or how the young ones—*his real children*—were going to feel, and he definitely wouldn't care about her. No one ever did. She needed Grandpa to be around. He would understand everything. He'd know how to protect her from the bullies the way he'd protected Grandma, and he'd know what to do to help Mum and Dad stay together.

She could hear everyone banging and crashing about as usual, the twins shouting something about a sleepover, Josh insisting he'd had a bath two days ago so he didn't need another.

She listened for her mother's voice but couldn't hear it. Grandma seemed to be in charge, which meant her mum was probably still in the kitchen with Bena. She was glad her mum had a best friend. Bena was so lovely, really kind and down to earth and always ready for a laugh. Nothing to laugh at tonight, but it was still good that Bena was there so her mum didn't have to be on her own.

She hoped Charlotte FaceTimed back tonight. She felt better when she had someone to talk to, even if Charlotte was really more interested in Liam. She wished things would work out for her the way they did for Charlotte, the only child, whose parents were really cool and faithful to each other, and who had a boyfriend whom she Snapchatted and sexted, and who wasn't being picked on at school or online.

She considered going on Facebook to check what was happening with the rest of her friends, not that she really had any left, but she still wanted to know what was going on. The trouble was she was afraid of finding her account had been hacked again. She supposed someone would have warned her by now if it had, but there was still the friend request to Oliver that had never been answered, and she was too afraid of posting anything herself in case one of the Durmites picked up on it.

At least Julie never said anything bad. She was always sweet and tried to be helpful, so it was hard to think of her being a false friend. The more Paige considered it, the more certain she felt that the false friend was Owen. He hadn't even given her the benefit of the doubt of that horrible posting. He had never been prepared to listen, and he had even told people he knew for a fact she'd done it herself. Why would he do that if he didn't mean her some kind of harm? For all she knew he'd posted it himself and made it look like her, so everyone would turn on her instead of him. Of all the people she knew, he and Harry Adcock were the only ones able to hack into someone else's account. They were brilliant on the computer, both of them, top of the class, the ones everyone went to when they had problems.

Feeling in sore need of talking to someone, she picked up her phone again and clicked on to answer Julie's message. *It was OK, don't think I'd go again though. Have you ever been?*

Long minutes ticked by as she waited for an answer, meaning Julie wasn't online. She began trawling through other websites and chat rooms, watching stuff on YouTube, and checking to see if Oliver was on Pheed. He wasn't, but Julie was now because an answer to her message had just come up.

No, never been, but have always wanted to. What sorts of things did she tell you?

Paige hesitated, having to think about how to answer that. In the end, she said, *Boring stuff, mostly about my mum and dad. She said I had a false friend and I thought it might be you.*

OMG! Why do you think that?

Because you won't tell me who you are.

I thought you understood that.

I suppose I do. I just couldn't think who else it might be. Apart from Owen.

When there was no immediate response she started to tense, aware she could have just accused Owen himself, or at least someone who knew him.

You know, I've been thinking about it, Julie finally replied, *and I reckon you could be right about Owen. He definitely turned against you after the posting. Do you know yet who did that?*

No, but I thought it might be him.

What, you think he outed himself and made it look like you so you got the blame? Awesome. But why would he do that?

Because everyone would turn on me then, instead of him.

Pretty genius if it's true, because it worked. No one's taken much notice of him being gay, it's all about you and what you did.

Except I didn't do it.

Point taken. Are the Durmites still hassling you?

They did this morning, but haven't seen much of them since.

Best to keep away from them if possible. I heard about the daffodils. Totally sick. BTW thought it was a great piece myself. Can see why Miss Kendrick put it in the mag.

Thanks. Thought it was pretty lame myself, but you know what Miss K is like when she fixates on something. Are you in her class?

Sometimes. Depends. Tell me more about the fortune-teller. Did she say anything about boyfriends?

Not really, just that there's someone I like who she described pretty accurately.

No way! Who is it?

No one you know.

I might.

Even if you did it wouldn't make a difference, he's not interested in me.

How do you know?

I just do. To be honest life's pretty f'd up at the moment. Nothing's going right.

Sorry to hear that. Anything I can do?

Shouldn't think so, but thanks for asking. Do you have a boyfriend?

No. Like you, there's someone I'm interested in, but he's going out with someone else.

Does he go to our school?

No. He's at college.

Paige's heart jarred. It couldn't possibly be Oliver; it was insane even to think it. *What's his name?*

Brad.

Breathing again, Paige said, *Have you ever spoken to him?*

Not really. I just look at him and he looks right through me.

Paige had to smile. *Sorry to hear that. Know how you feel.*

I heard him call me butterhead once.

What does that mean?

Everything about her's fit, but-her-head.

Paige's heart contracted with pity. *That's terrible. What a tosser. Bet you were really upset.*

Just a bit. I'll get over it. Couple of saddos, us? Not really.

Feeling like it at the moment. She paused, but only for a moment. *My dad's just left home.* As she stared at the words she could hardly believe they were true, or that she was telling someone she didn't know.

OMG. That really sucks. No wonder you feel bad. Between us, I keep wishing mine would go, but I suppose it's different when it happens.

Definitely. Can't get my head round it. Only found out tonight that he's having an affair.

Ew! How did your mum take it?

Badly, I think. Haven't really spoken to her yet.

It probably won't last and he'll come home again.

That's what I'm hoping. If he doesn't will never want to speak to him again.

I can understand that.

Anyway, he's my stepdad, not my real dad. Saying that felt like a punishment; she knew it would hurt him and it was meant to.

Hearing a knock on her door, she quickly typed, *Sorry, got to go* and cut the connection. "Who is it?" she called out.

"Just me," her mother answered. "Can I come in?"

Paige desperately wanted to say no, but knowing how much it would upset her mother if she did, she said grudgingly, "If you must."

As Jenna pushed the door open she was saying to the twins, "Please do as Grandma tells you for now. . . . Yes, we can go and see the lambs tomorrow. . . . Just clean your teeth, I'll be in to see you in a minute."

"Mum!" Josh roared across the landing.

"Josh, I'm only here. What is it?"

"There's a spider in my room. Where's Dad? He has to come and kill it."

"I'll sort it out in—"

"No! You can't. When's Dad coming home?"

"I know how to deal with spiders," Grandma informed him, marching across the landing. "Come and show me where it is."

Rolling her eyes as she closed Paige's door behind her, Jenna attempted a smile. "Are you OK?" she asked tenderly.

"Not really," Paige answered.

Going to sit next to her on the bed, Jenna slipped an arm around her and rested her head on hers. "I'm sorry this is happening," she whispered. "I wish it wasn't."

"I hate him."

Jenna sighed softly. "I know you think you do at the moment."

"Don't you?"

"I'm angry, obviously, and upset. . . . The truth is, I hardly know how I'm feeling."

"How did you find out?"

"Like you, I worked it out for myself. I didn't want to believe it, but then he told me."

"When?"

"Last night."

Last night, when I was sitting here thinking about Oliver and feeling sorry for myself about everything. Paige didn't want to think about it, but how could she not? "Does he really mean it?" she said huskily. "Is he actually going to live with her?"

Jenna swallowed hard. "I think so. It's where he—he's gone tonight." As she started to cry Paige wrapped her arms around her.

"It'll be all right, Mum, honest," she promised, crying too. "We'll get through it. We can manage without him if we have to."

Jenna sat up and smoothed Paige's hair silently for a few moments. "You told Charlotte he'd gone?" she asked after a while.

Paige stiffened. "Yes," she admitted. "She's my best friend. . . . How do you know?"

"Because her mother just rang asking if there was anything she could do to help."

Paige regarded her mother with guilty, helpless eyes. Sweet and kind though Lucy Griffiths could be, everyone knew she was one of the biggest gossips on the Gower. "I'm sorry," she whispered brokenly. "I didn't think. . . ."

"It's OK. I understand you needed to talk to your friend, and it'll have to come out sometime. I suppose I just hadn't imagined it would be quite so soon."

Chapter 10

Three dreadful days had passed since Jack had left, and the nights had been even worse. There were moments when Jenna felt she might be losing her mind. How could something that wasn't even physical hurt so much? The ache of it, the sheer torment of what her own thoughts were doing to her, never mind what Jack was doing, was such agony at times that she almost wanted to die rather than endure any more.

Somehow she'd forced herself through the weekend, mainly thanks to her mother and Bena, and yesterday morning she'd managed to get Josh and the twins ready for school and had arranged their lunches, pickups, and social extras without them seeming to notice anything was wrong. She had told them that their father had gone to stay with Grandma Moore for a few days, and Jack had accepted that, apparently understanding that she wasn't yet ready to tackle what his departure was going to mean to them. It was true, she wasn't, though she couldn't deny that a part of her reason for delaying was to give him time to change his mind.

So far he'd shown no sign of it, had hardly even been in touch since he'd gone, but as Bena kept reminding her, it was still early days. "The real proof of whether he can go through with it will come when he realizes how much he's missing you all."

It was hard to imagine him missing them. Much easier was picturing him with Martha, running his hands through her curls, gazing adoringly into her eyes, making love to her at any time of the day. Merely thinking of Martha could enrage her to the point of violence—when it wasn't making her feel dowdy and worthless. If she wasn't those things, then why had he left? Each time she looked in the mirror she saw a woman who meant nothing, a woman who had lost her center, her purpose, her understanding of the world. She was so used to being Jack's wife, his lover, his friend, that it was how she identified herself now, and she didn't want it to change. She needed him more than she'd ever realized: emotionally, physically, in every possible way. Only now was she coming to see how much she'd taken him for granted, how deeply she'd trusted that he'd always be there.

How could he have been having an affair for so long without her suspecting? It hardly seemed possible, and yet apparently it was true.

It must have been an instant attraction between them, a *coup de foudre* with a chemistry so powerful, so irresistible that neither could fight it. She wondered who had made the first move, where it had happened, how guilty or exhilarated or desperate for more he'd felt afterward. And what had Jenna herself been doing at the time? Nothing more than going about her life, bringing up his children, and sucking up all the lies. She thought back to the long, hot days they'd spent at the beach last summer with his brother's family, surfing, body-boarding, sailing, building sandcastles, exploring rock pools, tucking into picnics. He'd been there for all of it, challenging, praising, laughing, mopping up tears, making everything wonderful and right. How often had he sneaked away to speak to Martha on the phone? How many times had he actually disappeared to snatch a few moments with her? Jenna had no idea, nor would she ask.

She recalled the twins starting school in September, and how proud he'd made them feel of their uniforms and satchels—how insistent he'd been that he take them and pick them up on their very first day. She was sure he hadn't come home in between, had said he was going to some meeting or other, and now she realized he'd probably spent the time with Martha. A perfect father at the beginning and end of the day, a cheating husband for the rest of it, while she, fool that she was, had felt so lucky and happy to be his wife.

Over the weekend, during quiet moments when Josh and the twins were cycling or scootering around the village and Paige was in her room or over at Charlotte's, she'd written him a letter. Long, tender passages reminding him of the special happiness they'd felt when the three younger children were born; their heartache when she'd miscarried two babies before Josh came along, the way he'd supported her through that grief while quietly coping with his own. She'd reminded him of the cancer scare he'd had several years ago that had turned out to be a false alarm, but not before it had frightened them half to death. They'd been close before, but facing his mortality had brought them even closer together. She'd gone on to describe various Christmases and birthdays, Bonfire Nights and Easter egg hunts. They celebrated everything as a family, with Jack always there making it so much fun that the children's friends begged to come to their house for special occasions. She'd ended with the reminder of how excited they'd been to move here, how thrilled to own such a beautiful home, how optimistic for the future of their fledgling business.

She'd shed so many tears while writing the letter that by the end she'd had to go upstairs and lie down. She had so little energy; her mind, her entire body, was like a leaden cloud caught in the eye of a storm. Every now and again a violent rage would overtake her, or a stultifying despair, or a longing so fierce, so consuming that she had to scream or she might go mad. Though she was careful never to let the children hear her, she could tell that her mother always knew when the suffering was becoming unendurable. She didn't say anything, but she was always there, close at hand to help in every way that she could.

As for Paige, Jenna wasn't sure how she was coping. Abandoned first by her real father, now by Jack. Was that how Paige was seeing it? How could she not? The only time they'd talked properly was the night Jack had left, when they'd held each other and cried together. Since then Paige had seemed to withdraw from her. She didn't want to talk, she said, she only wanted to be left alone.

"No, I haven't tried to call him," she'd cried when Jenna had asked last night, "and I'm not going to."

"Has he called you?"

"Only like about fifty times, but as far as I'm concerned he can fuck off and die."

Though Jenna had winced at the language, she hadn't remonstrated—after all, Paige needed to vent her emotions, and if swearing was helping, that was fine. She just thanked God for Charlotte. It was at times like this that girls really needed their best friends, and it was clear from how much time they were spending together that Charlotte wasn't letting Paige down. She might wish she could hear what they were saying, but perhaps it was best that she didn't. She could sense an anger in Paige that wasn't only directed at Jack but was directed at her too, and she wasn't sure how to handle it. She didn't even know if she had it in her to try.

She'd returned a few minutes ago from taking Josh and the twins to school. They'd been full of their father picking them up later—Jack had told them on the phone first thing that he would.

"Can we go to the King for tea?" Josh had demanded excitedly. "We usually do when Dad comes back after he's been away."

"I want nachos if we go," Flora informed them. "I don't like anything else."

"I like sausages, the same as Dad," Wills reminded them. "I'm going to do him a painting in school today."

"Me too!" Flora cried. "Mine's going to be of daffodils to go with what Paige wrote."

"That was my idea!" Josh protested.

"No it wasn't. It was mine."

"It was mine, wasn't it Mum? Tell her to stop copying me. Anyway, I'm going to make a pot for his pens because we're doing pottery today. And I've got my new PlayStation game that Grandma bought yesterday. Dad will definitely want to play that, won't he, Mum?"

"He's going to play with us too, isn't he, Wills?" Flora pouted.

"Definitely with me," Wills told her, "but you've only got stupid dolls and stuff. He won't want to play with them."

"He always plays with my dolls," Flora shouted. "He even made my cot and my pushchair."

"He didn't make them, did he, Mum? He bought them, stupid," Josh retorted.

"You're stupid!"

"*You* are."

"No, *you* are, and I'm going to tell Dad what you said. He'll make you go to bed without any tea."

"If it's not raining," Wills said, "can me and Dad take Waffle for a walk before tea?"

"I want to come too," Flora piped up.

"You can't."

"Yes I can. He's my dad, and he's my dog."

"He's Paige's dog."

And so it had gone on, arguing, planning, getting increasingly excited in a way that had put more and more fractures in Jenna's heart and left her with nothing to say. They had no idea that Jack was coming to tell them he wouldn't be living with them anymore; how could they know that when they believed with all their hearts that he would always be there?

Hearing a car pull into the drive, she immediately tensed. Bena was already in the office and her mother was at her yoga class, so unless it was Jack she couldn't think who it might be.

Glancing at her mobile as it bleeped with a text, she quickly texted Paige back to say yes, she'd speak to Mr. Thomas about the video if she was sure it was what she wanted, and went to answer the door.

"Hanna?" she gasped, stunned to see her sister in the porch.

"I set off at dawn," Hanna told her, pulling her into a hearty embrace. "I wondered why I couldn't get hold of you on Sunday. You should have rung as soon as it happened. You know I'd have come right away."

"Mum told you," Jenna said flatly.

"Of course. Oh, Jen, I'm so sorry. I feel so responsible. If I hadn't introduced you to that woman . . ."

"It's not your fault," Jenna insisted, turning back inside. "You couldn't have known."

"I realize that, but I swear, when I recommended her I never dreamt anything like this would happen. She's always seemed so . . . I don't know . . ."

"His type?"

"That's not what I'm saying."

"But she is."

"That might be what you're telling yourself, but you're wrong. Anyway, don't worry, I'm going to see her myself. I need to make her understand that she can't just break up your family."

"It takes two," Jenna pointed out. "And she has a family too."

"Not in quite the same way."

"I'm sure she cares about them just as much."

"Which would be why she shipped the kids off to boarding school and why her husband is almost never at home."

Jenna let it go at that and watched as Hanna cast an eye round the kitchen, reminding her of how like their mother she could be at times. She showed more emotion, that was for sure, and wasn't quite as compulsive or literal, but her need for order and her way of speaking her mind were vintage Kay. "Would you like a coffee?" Jenna offered.

"I'll make it," Hanna insisted, putting down her bag and starting to clear a worktop. "Are you here on your own?"

"Bena's in the office."

Hanna stopped what she was doing and looked up. "The office," she repeated. "What are you going to do about that? OK, I realize it's early days and you probably haven't worked it all out yet, but if he's known for a while that he's going to leave, he's surely come up with some sort of plan."

"He has," Jenna replied. "Apparently he's going to let me have Celticulture, but they'll help me to run it."

Hanna's jaw dropped. "By 'they' I take it you mean him and Martha?"

Jenna nodded.

"And you're in agreement with that?"

"No."

"So what are you going to do?"

"I've hardly had time to decide, but I suppose, if it comes to it, I'll throw it back in his face."

Coming to her, Hanna said, "I'm sorry you're going through this."

They looked up as the door opened and Bena let herself in.

"Hanna?" Bena said in surprise. "I had no idea. . . . When did you get here?"

"About five minutes ago," Hanna replied, going to hug her. "Mum's told me how wonderful you're being. I can't thank you enough. Coping with all this is hard enough, and when you factor in four children on top of it . . . How are they?" she asked Jenna. "Mum says Paige is the only one who knows. How's she taken it?"

"Hard," Jenna told her, "but she's internalizing at the moment. Or she's hiding it from me, anyway. I think a part of her might even blame me."

"No! That can't be true," Hanna protested. She glanced at Bena for support, but Bena merely shrugged. "She's got to know that it's not your fault her father had an affair."

"Maybe she thinks I wasn't a good enough wife. Maybe she's right."

"I'm not listening to any more of this," Hanna declared.

"There are only two people to blame here, and one of them is definitely not you."

Jenna didn't bother to argue.

Sighing, Hanna said, "Men can be so bloody weak at times, and everyone knows Martha's marriage has been dead for years. Her children aren't living at home, so she hardly ever sees them, and I'm not entirely sure she has any proper friends."

"She has plenty," Jenna assured her. "They were at the party Jack and I went to last year." She wondered if the pair of them had managed to snatch some time together while everyone was milling about the terrace sipping cocktails and making small talk, if they'd got a kick out of the risk, if it was something they did often. Her eyes closed as the thought of it seared through her.

What are they doing now?

"I have to pop over to the post office to pick up some parcels," Bena told them. "Is there anything you need?"

Hanna shook her head as Jenna said, "Why don't I go? I'm sure you two are dying to talk, and I need to take the dog out."

"It's you I've come to see," Hanna reminded her briskly.

"I know, and I appreciate it, I really do, but it's probably best if Bena fills you in on everything. I don't want to go through it again."

A few minutes later she was in the car with Waffle happily filling up the rear compartment and her hands-free turned on in case Jack rang. If he did, there was a good chance she'd end up losing her temper, but she was going to try not to because all this shouting, ranting, and raging were never going to get her anywhere.

Maybe her letter would make him understand how she felt.

It was in her bag ready to be mailed at the post office, first class to make sure it reached him tomorrow, even though she'd see him later when he brought the children home. Maybe she should hang on to it, wait and see what happened when he broke his news to them; she might want to say something different after that.

Suddenly needing to speak to him right now, she connected to his number and listened to the ringtone, imagining him trying to decide whether to take her call or let her go through to messages.

"Hi, are you OK?" he said when he answered.

"Not really, but I doubt you expected me to be."

Sounding irritated, he said, "What can I do for you?"

What can I do for you? As if she were some nuisance client he needed to be rid of, rather than a wife of fourteen years. "Josh and the twins are excited about you coming home tonight. They want to go to the King."

He sighed audibly. "Did you tell them we would?"

"I didn't say anything, but I think you should break your news to them at home."

"Of course. Are you going to be there?"

"Where else would you expect me to be? They're my children. They're in for a horrible shock, so they're going to need me there."

He said nothing, leaving her to imagine his anger, or guilt, or whatever the heck he was feeling. It was impossible for her to guess, because he was no longer the man she knew.

When he still didn't speak she said, "Are you really going to do it? Can you actually bring yourself to shatter their world the way you have mine and Paige's?"

"I've said I'm sorry."

"You think that's all it takes? To say you're sorry?"

He didn't answer. Unable to hold back the tears, she pulled into the drive of Scurlage Rugby Club to rest her head on the steering wheel.

"Where are you?" he asked.

She couldn't answer; she was fighting too hard to stop herself crying.

"Jenna, are you still there?"

Deciding she didn't want to be, she clicked off the line and started to sob.

A few minutes later her phone rang. Hoping it was him, she looked at the screen, but it was a number she didn't recognize at first, until she realized it was Paige's school.

"Hello?" she answered, clearing her throat.

"Mrs. Moore? It's Eddie Thomas here, Paige's ICT teacher."

Remembering she was supposed to have called him, Jenna said, "Oh yes. Is everything all right?"

"I'm not sure," he replied. "Paige is refusing to carry on with the edit of her tourist video, and she won't say why. It's not like her to pull out of a project, especially one that's showing so much promise. I was wondering if you could throw any light on things."

Realizing Paige could be rejecting the video because she'd shot it with Jack, Jenna said, "I'm afraid we've been having a few problems at home lately. Would you mind bearing with her for a while?"

"No, of course not. I'm sorry to hear that. Please let us know if there's anything the school can do to help."

"Thank you, I will." Wondering when she'd ever felt so helpless or hopeless, she quickly ended the call before she could break down again.

*   *   *

Bena was in the office with Hanna showing her what she'd found on Jack's computer, needing Hanna's advice on how and when she should pass it on to Jenna.

"I wanted you to see this in case there's something I'm not understanding," Bena said as the phone rang.

Hanna's attention was totally focused on the screen as she continued to read.

Seeing it was Jenna calling, Bena picked up. "Hello, lovely," she greeted her. "Is everything all right?"

"Yes, it's fine," Jenna replied, sounding as though it was anything but. "I'm just going to be a bit longer than I thought."

Frowning, Bena said, "OK. So what time do you think you'll be back?"

"I'm not sure. I'll call when I'm on my way. Tell Hanna not to worry, and don't you either."

Bena glanced worriedly at Hanna. "Do you want to tell me where you're going?" she prompted.

"I'll tell you when I get back. I have to go now." The line went dead.

"What was that about?" Hanna asked as Bena rang off.

"I'm not sure, but apparently she's going to be out for longer than we thought."

Hanna was clearly as concerned by that as Bena was, but she replied, "I guess it's no bad thing in the circumstances. It'll give us more time to go through this."

Bena nodded and returned to Hanna's side so that they were looking at Jack's computer screen together.

As Hanna resumed scrolling through page after page of the company's accounts, she said, "Are you sure Jenna's never seen this?"

"I'd stake my life on it," Bena replied.

Hanna nodded. "Mm. So would I." She looked up at Bena's anxious face. "She can't cope with this right now," she said decisively. "I mean, obviously she has to know at some point, but we need to give it to Mum first. She's brilliant with figures. It's what she used to do when she was working; in fact, she ran a whole team of bookkeepers. She'll be able to give us the bottom line so we'll know what we're dealing with."

Bena nodded her agreement. "What about Jack? Do you think we should contact him?"

Hanna didn't ponder it for long. "Not yet," she decided. "He's got to know this is going to come out now that he's handed over the business. . . ." She broke off, still trying to get her head round the potential catastrophe in front of her.

"You have to wonder if he was ever planning to tell her," Bena remarked, going back to her desk.

"He'd have had to sooner or later. What's amazing is that he's managed to keep it from her for so long."

"She trusted him," Bena reminded her.

Hanna's arch expression showed what she thought of that.

"Do you think the other one knows? Martha?" Bena asked.

"It's hard to imagine that she doesn't, given that she's been *advising* them." Hanna shook her head in disbelief. "I hardly know what to say," she murmured, "but I certainly know what I'd like to do."

"You and me both," Bena retorted, checking the caller ID as the phone rang again. "Hi, Paige. Everything all right, sweetie?" she answered.

"Yeah, cool," Paige replied, sounding far too nasal for that to be true. "Is Mum there? She's not answering her mobile."

Careful to hide her alarm, Bena said, "She's just popped out to the post office and to walk the dog, so she could be out of range. Is there anything I can do?"

"No, it's OK, thanks." Before Bena could tell her that her auntie Hanna was there, the line went dead.

Tucking her mobile back into her bag, Paige kept on walking, not sure where she was going, just knowing that she couldn't go to the gym, no matter what anyone said or did to try to make her. She was due there now for her next lesson and they might already be looking for her, but she wasn't anywhere close by. She was at the other side of the school grounds, heading past the science block and art rooms, keeping her head down as she made for the back lane, where she could hide out for a while, or maybe even escape.

She'd called Charlotte just now, but she was at home with a really bad cold, so there was nothing she could do, and Julie, who'd texted her the warning of what was going to happen if she went to the gym, had done all she could to help.

Just heard they're planning to steal your clothes and push you outside or into boys' changing rooms with nothing on. Jxx

Wanting to believe that Cullum or Matt would stop it from happening, Paige had texted them to ask if they'd heard what Kelly was planning. Neither boy had texted back, which didn't necessarily mean they were ignoring her, but it might mean that; after all, they hadn't done anything to help her when the Durmites had snatched her bag last night, swinging it round and round, slamming it into her, and making sure everything, including her Tampax, fell out on the floor. They'd just walked away, leaving her and Charlotte to pick it all up, while the Durmites carried on sniggering and jeering.

Now, climbing over a gnarled obstacle of tree roots, Paige jumped down onto the lane and began walking toward the main road. She didn't have her iPod plugged into her ears, too nervous about someone coming up behind her to take the risk.

If she'd been able to get hold of her mother, she would have said she was sick and asked her to come and pick her up, but she couldn't, and no way in the world was she going to ring her dad.

Thinking of him brought hot, angry tears to her eyes, making it hard to see where she was going, but she pressed on, stumbling over random rocks and catching her hair in low-hanging branches. He'd come, she was sure of it, but he wasn't going to get the chance.

When the rain started she didn't bother putting up her hood. She let it fall onto her hair and face, so it smudged her makeup and mingled with her tears. Who cared what she looked like, how wet she got, or how cold? Since it didn't matter to anyone else, why should it to her?

Just before reaching the main road she came to a stop and took out her phone again. Still no answer from her mother, so she tried her grandma instead.

Kay answered on the second ring. "Shouldn't you be in lessons?" she asked straightaway.

"I'm not feeling very well," Paige told her, "and I can't get hold of Mum. Would you be able to come and get me?"

"Of course. Where shall I meet you?"

"At the school bus stop?"

"I should be there in ten minutes."

"Ten minutes?"

"I'm just leaving my yoga class," Kay explained. "It's only down the road."

When Paige got into the car nine minutes later, Kay asked, "What's wrong with you? Do we need to see a doctor?"

"No, I'm all right really. I mean, I've got a stomachache and I feel a bit sick."

"Temperature?"

"Maybe. I think so."

"Then we should get you to bed. Have you managed to get hold of Mum yet?"

"No, but I left a message letting her know what's happening."

"Good girl. Pull the blanket over from the back and wrap yourself up. You shouldn't have allowed yourself to get so wet."

Doing as she was told, Paige huddled down into the seat and closed her eyes. The trouble was that didn't stop the tears from coming, and then suddenly she was sobbing and her grandma was pulling over to the side of the road.

"Here," Kay said, passing her a tissue. "Something's happened at school?"

Paige tried to swallow as she nodded.

Kay waited.

"It's nothing," Paige told her. "I'll be all right in a minute."

"It can't be nothing if it's making you cry. Now tell me what it is."

"I just had a row with some girls."

"What about?"

"Nothing."

Kay waited again.

"They're being a bit mean to me," Paige finally confessed, "and I don't know how to make them stop."

"Then we shall find a way."

"No, you can't. It'll just make it worse."

Kay didn't look convinced.

"I can handle it, I promise, they're just being stupid, and now with Dad going and everything . . ."

As she dissolved into yet more tears Kay passed her another tissue. "It's a very bad thing your father's doing," she declared. "I can't make excuses for him, so I'm not going to try."

Glad of it, Paige almost managed a smile. "Mum doesn't want me to fall out with him, or she says she doesn't, but I'd want me to if I were her."

Kay didn't comment on that. She simply said, "He's been a good father up to now."

"So you're saying I *should* cut him some slack?"

"What I'm saying is we've no idea what will happen in the future, but I understand why you're angry with him, because I'm angry myself."

"So you don't blame me for not wanting to see him?"

"No. I don't want to see him either, but I don't expect we'll have much choice in the matter. Are you ready to carry on now?"

Though Paige was desperate to spill out everything that was happening at school, she didn't feel it was fair to load any more on her grandma when Kay already had so much to be dealing with. Everyone was leaning on her, especially Josh and the twins, and of course her mum too, which was only right when they were mother and daughter. Paige's problems didn't mean anything in comparison to everything else that was going on, so, keeping them to herself, she simply watched her funny little grandma turn around in her seat, put the car into gear, and steer them back onto the road. To hell with the Durmites and her father; they were nobodies who meant nothing, and she wasn't going to let them get the better of her.

Chapter 11

Jenna was sitting in her car with Waffle asleep in the back and the radio turned off. She was staring at the building opposite with its smoky glass facade, revolving doors, and ornamental trees outside. It wasn't possible to see through the windows, but she knew Martha's offices were on the third floor with gold lettering on the door saying *Gwynne & Associates* and a pretty receptionist to welcome visitors.

She wasn't intending to go up; she'd probably never get past ground-floor security anyway. She was here waiting for Martha to come down.

"I'm outside in the car," she'd told her on the phone a few minutes ago. "I want to talk to you."

After a pause, Martha had said, "I don't think that's a good idea."

"I'm in the car park opposite, and I'm not going anywhere until you come down here and face me."

There was every chance Jack would come instead, or maybe Martha would sneak out of the building by a back door. There was nothing Jenna could do to prevent either eventuality; she was only able to wait in a place where she knew they could see her, so they'd know she wasn't going away.

More minutes ticked by. She wondered what they were saying to each other, what sort of plan they were making, whether they were even considering calling the police. It made her feel so terrible, so sick of herself, and yet how could she not have come? She needed to fight for her marriage, to do something other than yell at Jack and torment herself with how empty and awful life was going to be without him.

She checked her messages, and after listening to Paige's she rang her back. "Where are you?" she asked, keeping her eyes trained on the revolving doors.

"We've just got home," Paige replied. "Grandma's making me something hot to drink, then I'm going to bed. Auntie Hanna's here."

"I know. I shouldn't be long. Do you think you've picked up Charlotte's cold?"

"Maybe."

"I spoke to Mr. Thomas. Actually, he called me."

"What did he say?"

"He wanted to know why you're not interested in editing your video."

"So you said . . . ?"

"That I'd talk to you about it. I'm guessing it's because you shot it with Dad."

"Something like that."

"You shouldn't allow this to—"

"I don't want to do it, OK? And I don't want to have a discussion about it either."

Sighing, Jenna said, "It's your decision, but I think it's a shame when it's showing so much promise."

Silence.

"Are you still there?"

"Yes, but my drink's ready."

"OK. Sorry I'm not there."

More silence.

"Bye then. I love you."

"Yeah, right."

As she rang off Jenna was watching Martha coming toward her. Her heart was starting to thud with so many emotions they were making her nauseous. The hardest part of this was that she could understand what Jack saw in the woman. What man wouldn't be attracted to such a luscious figure and come-to-bed eyes? Martha oozed sex appeal, fun, daring, and excitement—and she was rich.

Thankfully, Jack wasn't with her, but Jenna felt sure he was watching from a window, and would probably come down after a set amount of time to rescue his lover. Five minutes? Ten? How was it possible to know? How had she even come to be in this position where she was the enemy and he cared more about somebody else than about her?

Pulling open the passenger door, Martha got in, and Jenna instantly recognized her perfume.

As they sat there, neither of them speaking for the moment, Jenna could feel the demons at work, conjuring images of Jack's hands on this woman, his mouth seeking hers, his passion as he sated himself on her.

"You don't have to do this," Jenna said in the end. "No one is forcing you to. You can let him go and we can all get on with our lives."

Martha didn't answer. She simply kept her eyes straight

ahead, as though only half listening, though of course she'd heard every word.

"He has four children," Jenna pointed out. "Don't you at least care about that?"

Martha swallowed and pressed her hands together. "Of course I care," she replied quietly. "Believe me, none of this has been easy. We didn't want it to happen. We've done everything we can to fight it, but we can't . . . we can't help the way we feel."

Almost flinching from the words, Jenna said, "So the way you feel is more important than the way anyone else feels, including his children?"

"That's not what I'm saying."

"That's what it sounds like."

At last Martha turned to look at her. Her face was strained; her eyes seemed clouded and tired. "Look, I understand what you're going through—"

"*No* you don't. Your husband hasn't left you or abandoned your children."

"Jack hasn't abandoned his."

"Yes he has. I know you want to put a different spin on it, tell yourselves a sweet little story about how he's going to pick them up from school every day, always be there for their birthdays and Christmas, take them out for weekends, actually anytime they want, but it's not going to happen, and shall I tell you why? Because I'm going to take them away from here. I'm going to take them so far he'll never get to see them, if they even want to see him. Is that what you want for him? To separate him from his children?"

Martha's eyes went down. "Jenna, I—"

"I'm appealing to you as one woman to another," Jenna

broke in harshly, "as one mother to another. You can't really want to do this. Your place is with your own family, not in some . . . *love nest* with *my* husband."

Martha took a breath. "I'm with him," she said, "because it's where he wants to be, where *we both* want to be. You have to know he'd never have left you unless he was sure."

Forcing herself to speak over the pain, while grabbing at anything she could think of to shatter this woman's belief, Jenna said, "You think you know him, but you don't. You don't have the first idea what makes him tick, so take it from me, you'll end up destroying him. He can't live without his children, but he'll have to if you don't let him go."

"I understand what you're doing. . . ."

"You're nothing special, Martha. I know he's making you think you are, but believe me, he'll drop you the minute he realizes you're going to cost him his children."

For a long time Martha simply stared down at her hands, letting Jenna's words hang in the air, absorbing their damage.

"Do you want all your clients to know what kind of woman you really are?" Jenna said in the end. "I'd be duty bound to tell them."

"Jenna . . ."

"Tell him to come home," Jenna continued through her teeth. "Do it now before you lose your business and reputation."

"I only came out here—"

"He's going to leave you anyway," Jenna shouted over her, "so spare yourself."

"Listen, whatever you say, whatever you're telling yourself, I know how he feels about me and I know what it's costing him to do this. It's not that he doesn't love you anymore, because he does; he's just not *in* love with you, and that's what makes the difference."

Jenna could feel the words whipping her into a fury. "That's what he's telling you," she cried, "but he'll end up coming back to me, and shall I tell you what? It'll be too late. I won't want him by then, and he won't want you, so what will you have achieved, Martha? What good is this going to do anyone?"

Martha was shaking her head. "I'm sorry, Jenna, I really am. I hate to see you hurting like this. . . ."

Jenna tried to cling to her temper, but everything was falling apart; her resolve, her hope, her dignity were rapidly deserting her. She was so close to breaking down, to begging and pleading, that she hardly trusted herself to speak. In the end she managed to say, "And your husband? What does he think of it all?"

Martha took a breath. "We haven't been close for a while. In fact, it's quite possible that he already has someone else."

"So rather than be left on your own," Jenna sneered, "you've found yourself another man who happens to be someone else's husband, and father to someone else's children? How proud you must feel of yourself."

"What happened between me and Jack . . . I swear I didn't expect it, but since knowing him I've come to realize that I've . . . I've never actually been in love before."

Jenna's voice was choked by the misery in her throat as she retorted, "And I suppose he's saying he hasn't either?"

"No, he's simply saying that it's different with me." Her eyes flicked briefly to Jenna. "I don't think we need to go into any more detail than that."

Unable to bear the thought of them discussing her, their love, or the life they were planning together, Jenna said, "You can go now."

Martha's hand went to the door. "Will you be all right?" she asked.

Jenna's eyes darkened with outrage. "Don't you dare ask me that," she seethed. "Just get out of my car before I end up doing something we'll both regret."

Martha opened the door, but she still didn't leave. "The more you try to hurt him," she said, "the more you're going to hurt yourself and the children."

Before she could stop herself Jenna was grabbing the blond curls, twisting them ruthlessly, yanking Martha's head back so violently that hair was coming loose in her hands. "Don't you ever tell me what to do again," she hissed furiously. "Do you hear me? *Don't ever tell me how to live my life.*"

"Let me go," Martha cried. "I'm sorry, I was only trying . . . Jenna, please . . ."

"I could kill you, do you know that?" Jenna raged over Waffle's barking. "That's what happens in situations like this. People end up dead." Thrusting Martha away, she started the engine and barely waited for the door to close before driving off.

Minutes later Jack was on the phone. "What the hell got into you?" he snapped. "I saw what you did."

"Get off this line," she sobbed. "One of my children might be trying to get through."

"Jenna, listen—"

"No, *you* listen. I'm going to see a lawyer. I want a divorce and I'm going to do everything in my power to stop you ever seeing—"

"You shouldn't be driving," he shouted over her. "You're too upset. Pull over."

"*Don't tell me what to do.* And don't pretend you care, because we know it's not true."

"Where are you going?"

"Home. Where I have responsibilities, children . . ."

"I'll see you there when I bring Josh and the twins. Does Paige need picking up?"

"No. And don't take the others out for tea. It wouldn't be fair to let them think everything is normal when *it's anything but.*" And before he could say any more, she cut the connection.

When Jenna walked in the door an hour later, dumping groceries and parcels on the floor and finding a treat for Waffle, Bena, Hanna, and her mother were all in the kitchen looking so serious that she felt sure Jack must have been in touch.

Before they could start remonstrating she cut them off with, "How's Paige?"

"She was asleep the last time I went up," her mother replied. "I think she's having problems at school."

Jenna frowned. "What sort of problems?"

"She said some girls are being mean to her."

Sighing, Jenna started to unpack the shopping. "You know what teenagers are like. They're always falling in and out of friendships."

Her mother didn't argue; she simply continued to look concerned as Hanna said gravely, "We have something to tell you."

Jenna looked at her and felt her heart turn inside out. "Please, not one of the children," she implored desperately. "I couldn't—"

"The children are fine," Hanna quickly assured her. "It's not about them. It's about Jack and the new company."

Jenna looked from her, to Bena, to her mother.

"You need to come and sit down," Hanna told her. "Mum's already made some tea. . . ."

"What I need is for you to tell me what this is about," Jenna almost shouted.

Hanna took a breath as she glanced at Bena. "Jack has been charging the contributors to put their submissions on the website."

Jenna shook her head. "That's not right. The whole point of the—"

"I know what the point was," Hanna interrupted, "and frankly I was always skeptical about how it was going to work, but I'm afraid it's gone even further than charging them to upload their material. They've been invited to take part in a quite costly marketing plan, and it would appear that more than a few have done so."

Jenna started to speak but didn't know what to say. This was going against everything she and Jack had intended, everything they'd believed in.

"Mum's been through the figures," Hanna went on, "and over the past few months the company has taken in over twenty-five thousand pounds."

"That's right. From the Welsh Arts Council."

Hanna shook her head. "There's no grant," she told her. "Or not that we can find."

Jenna's head started to spin.

"The twenty-five thousand in deposits," Hanna continued, "has come from contributors, and the entire amount, plus a further five thousand, has gradually been transferred out of the company into Jack's personal account. Right now there is just over one thousand pounds in the business."

Jenna's mouth opened and closed again.

"I'm sorry to say it gets worse," Hanna pressed on. "During the past several weeks he's received a good number of emails from writers demanding action or their money back. Some are quite threatening, particularly the more recent ones. I take it you haven't received any?"

Jenna shook her head. "No one's even mentioned it," she replied. "I mean, they've been badgering me about a launch date, naturally, and they've wanted to know when they're going to see a return for their . . ." Her eyes widened with alarm. "Investment," she finished. "I took it to be a euphemism for their work, but . . . Oh my God, this can't be true. There must be some sort of mistake."

"I've created a document for you to look at," her mother told her. "It shows the funds that have come in, when they've gone out, and how much the company now owes to the contributors unless the company is launched—"

"Which it can't be," Hanna cut in, "because I'm afraid the business model simply isn't viable."

Jenna reeled. The company was in *debt,* with only a thousand pounds to its name? The business model wasn't *viable*? "But Martha oversaw it," she pointed out.

"I've no idea how much Martha knows about the accounting," Hanna replied. "All I can tell you for certain right now is that these people will have to be paid back or you could find yourself facing criminal charges. I'm no expert, but I'd imagine it would be fraud."

Jenna's throat was dry. Her disbelief was so great she was suddenly finding it difficult to stand. "I need to get this straight," she said. "What you're saying is that Jack has knowingly, purposefully stolen money from the people who trusted us?"

"We've gone over and over it," Hanna assured her, "but there's no other way of seeing it, especially when you factor in the transfers to his personal account."

Jenna didn't want to accept it. She put up her hands, almost as though she could push it away. "But he's not . . . He would never . . ." She stopped, silenced by the realization that until a week ago she'd never have believed he'd cheat on her. Now it seemed he'd cheated their writers too. "I don't know what to say," she murmured. "This isn't . . . I can't . . . How has he managed to hide it?"

"He takes care of the business side of things," Bena reminded her. "We're the creatives."

"Who aren't supposed to worry our pretty heads about such things as how it's all going to work, because 'It will, trust me, it's going to be a sensation.' That's what he said, and I believed him. I allowed myself to be distracted by everything else, to put the children first, but of course I would, I'm their mother. . . . He kept encouraging me to write. . . . Dear God, I should have realized what was happening. How could I have been so blind?" She looked at her sister, then her mother. "Who have I been married to all this time? What kind of a man is he?"

"He can be very convincing when he wants to be," Hanna said lamely.

"Let's go back to Martha Gwynne," Bena put in. "She's surely got to have known what was going on; for all we know, she's the architect behind it all."

Hanna said, "As much as I'd like to believe that, I have to point out that Martha runs a very successful company with a great reputation. I can't see her putting it in jeopardy for this sort of scam, which, in the grand scheme of things, hasn't actually brought in that much money. My guess is, Jack started it, she found out, and now she's very likely doing what she can to troubleshoot."

"Or," Bena suggested, "she could be using it to blackmail him into leaving you to live with her."

This was too much for Jenna. She needed to sit down now. More than that, she needed a drink.

After downing half the Scotch Hanna passed her, she said, "If he didn't want to be with her, he'd have found a way to tell me about this, not let himself be blackmailed into it." As the next natural conclusion hit her, she suddenly felt as though the entire world had gone mad. "They're planning to put the company in my name," she reminded them. "He said, 'The business will be yours.'" Her eyes were glassy with disbelief as she looked at them. "Are they intending to make me responsible for the debt?" she whispered incredulously.

"You will be if you accept the company," her mother assured her.

"I could go to prison for what he's done, and he . . . he would end up with the children."

Hanna came in quickly. "We're getting ahead of ourselves here. Nothing like that is going to happen, but you do need to find yourself a lawyer. Bena's already contacted someone."

"He's a senior partner at one of the big firms in Swansea," Bena told her. "He's also married to Al's stepsister, which kind of makes him family. Well, he *was* married to her; unfortunately she died a couple of years ago from cancer."

Jenna could only look at her.

"He specializes in criminal law," Bena explained.

"But how will I pay him?" Jenna pointed out.

"Hanna and I will take care of that," her mother informed her.

"All you need to worry about for now," Hanna said, "is what you're going to say to Jack when you next see him."

"Which will be in about an hour. He's picking the children up from school."

"So you need to have decided by then whether you're going to come clean with what you know, or whether you're going to speak to the lawyer first."

Paige was lying on the bed listening to one of her favorite singers, Natalie Imbruglia, through her earpods. The song was "Torn," which had lyrics that really resonated with her, about a fortune-teller being right and about not having faith anymore. It was like Natalie had been through all the same things she was going through now, except she probably hadn't, but it didn't matter; it just made her feel a bit better to think someone might understand.

She'd heard her mum come back just after she'd woken up, but she still hadn't been down to see her, nor had Jenna come to check if she was all right. She probably wouldn't bother. She had so much on her mind with all that was happening she might even have forgotten her elder daughter was at home, sick.

She wondered what Oliver was doing now, whether he was at college or somewhere else today. He might be with Lindsay, or Liam . . . Charlotte had Snapchatted a topless picture of herself last night, full frontal, and made it disappear in three seconds so he wouldn't have time to freeze it with a screenshot. It made Paige feel weirdly light-headed to think of doing something like that, then violently sick at the thought of the Durmites getting hold of it.

Kelly had texted her at least half a dozen times since she'd skipped gym.

Where are you, bitch?

Getting fed up now.

Just heard you went home sick. Hope you die.

Are you dead yet?

Better off dead than having to live with such an ugly face.

What songs would you like at your funeral, troll?

It was the last question that had made Paige reach for her iPod to start searching through her tunes to find out which ones she'd choose, if she had to. She'd selected four so far: the one she was listening to now; "Kiss You," by One Direction, because she and Charlotte loved dancing to it; "Moves Like Jagger," because her mum liked it; and Oliver's song, "Every Time You Smile." It was probably a bit creepy that she'd managed to download that one to her iPod, but only if anyone found out, and even if they did, she could always say she thought it was totally brilliant, which it was, so why wouldn't she want to listen to it? He might find it a bit weird that she wanted it played at her funeral, though.

Realizing her door was opening, she yanked out one of the earpods, ready to shout at a small child to go away, but when she saw it was her mum she relaxed. Jenna hadn't forgotten her after all.

"I thought you must be asleep," Jenna said. "Didn't you hear me knock?"

Paige shook her head. "I was listening to music."

"How are you feeling now?"

Paige shrugged.

Coming to sit on the edge of the bed, Jenna put a hand on

her forehead to test her temperature. "I think you'll live," she teased.

Funny, that, when she'd just been thinking about her funeral.

"Do you feel like something to eat?"

"No thanks. Where were you earlier when you weren't answering your phone?"

As her mother's eyes dulled Paige immediately wished she hadn't asked.

"I went to see Martha," Jenna told her.

Paige waited, feeling her mother's heartache going all the way through her. "Why?" she said in the end.

Jenna's gaze drifted. "I thought I might be able to talk her out of taking Dad away."

Hating how everything was, Paige said, "So what happened?"

Jenna tried to smile. "She doesn't want to give him up, and other things have come to light since that . . . Well, it's all a bit complicated really, but I expect we'll manage to sort it out."

"Have you seen Dad today?"

"No, but he should be here any minute with Josh and the twins. He's going to tell them tonight that he won't be living here anymore."

Paige turned away, wishing she could be anywhere but here, belong to any family but this one. "I don't want to see him," she muttered.

"It's OK, no one will force you to, but remember, whatever else he's done, he still loves you very much."

"Yeah, he's got a great way of showing it."

"Maybe you should give him a chance."

"Like he's given us a chance? No way am I having anything to do with him."

Using her fingers to wipe the tears from Paige's cheeks, Jenna said, "Do you want to talk about what happened in school today? Grandma said some girls were being mean to you."

Paige could feel her face becoming pinched. Though she desperately wanted to tell her mother everything, she didn't dare in case Jenna went to the school and reported it. "It's nothing," she replied, keeping her eyes averted. "Just some stupid stuff, really childish. They need to grow up, that's all."

Hearing a car pull into the drive, Jenna turned to the window. "I expect that's Dad."

Seeing how anxious she was, Paige reached for her hand and gave it a squeeze. "We've always got each other," she reminded her mother.

Jenna sobbed on a laugh as she hugged her. "And don't you forget it."

As soon as she was alone again Paige got up from the bed and went to turn on her computer. She had a lot to prepare for the school eco project she was involved in, and since there was a double period of geography tomorrow, she needed to get started. First though, she checked her emails and various accounts in case Julie had been in touch again.

There was one message that had arrived a couple of hours ago.

Good that you didn't make gym. Bitches in right bad mood!

Immediately nervous about what they might do to her tomorrow, Paige messaged back saying, *Thanks for the warning.*

For several minutes she sat staring at the screen, caught in the dilemma of whether she should try to skip school again the next day or just face up to it. She hated to think of them getting the better of her, but on the other hand, the things they said and did were so horrible she really didn't want to go through any more.

Maybe she should just run away and never come back.

Chapter  12

"Dad's got something important to tell us," Josh was informing Jenna as she came into the dining room, where he and the twins were sitting at the table trying to be on their best behavior. "Do you know what it is?"

"I do," she replied, deliberately not sounding as though it were a big, wonderful secret that was going to thrill them all to bits, which it seemed Jack had led them to believe. Would the twins even begin to comprehend what any of it was going to mean?

Maybe it would be easier if they didn't.

"Important things are important," Wills declared.

"Of course they are, silly," Flora piped up, "that's why they're called important. Where's Dad? Can I have something to eat?"

"You've just had the buns Grandma bought," Jenna reminded her.

"Can we go down to Grandma's later to see Auntie Hanna again?" Josh asked.

"Auntie Hanna will be coming back here to read you a bedtime story."

"Oh, cool! *Please* can we have some crisps?"

Leaving them to wriggle around on their chairs, Jenna went into the kitchen to rustle up a snack. They could have the pizzas she'd picked up at the supermarket once all this was over—presuming they'd want to eat, which they might not. For now she simply chopped up some carrots and set them on a plate with a bowl of hummus. An easy way of disguising one of their five servings of vegetables a day—or seven, as it was now supposed to be, or even ten if they could manage it. What planet did these nutritionists live on? Clearly one without children.

Stiffening as Jack came in the door, she said, "Did you really have to speak to your mistress now? The children are waiting—"

"It wasn't her," he interrupted.

Turning away, she carried the plate through to the table, where it was immediately pounced upon. She stood watching them munch away noisily, kicking their feet and grinning up at her, and felt her heart breaking as she thought of how their excitement over hearing something important was very probably going to turn to confusion, tears, even fear once the secret was out. They shouldn't have to be suffering this. They were too young. Their father was supposed to protect them, stop them from being hurt, but here he was about to devastate them.

For the second time that day she asked herself what kind of man she had married, and felt herself even more distanced from an answer. Never, in her wildest imaginings, had she seen him as a home-wrecker, much less someone who'd steal other people's money and try to pin the crime on her. Of course, she still didn't know for certain if that was his intention, but even if it weren't, the fact still remained that he had gone behind her back to extract payments from the writers, which he'd then transferred to his personal account. Whether it was still there, had been spent, or had been moved again, she had no idea, nor was she going to ask. Not yet, anyway. She'd decided to speak to the lawyer first for advice on how to handle this.

I am consulting a lawyer about Jack. It hardly seemed credible, made her head throb merely to think it.

"OK, everyone," Jack began brightly, rubbing his hands as though he was about to deliver a special treat or perform a conjuring trick, "are you ready to hear my important news?"

"Yes," they chorused, mouths full, fists in the air.

"I've got some important news too," Flora told him.

"Really? Then shall we hear yours first?"

"I did forty-four skips without being out today," she announced, "so I nearly made fifty. That's how many we have to do for charity."

"That's amazing," he cried, slapping his hands on the table. "Let's hear it for Flora."

As the others dutifully cheered, Jenna watched dumbfounded. How was it in any way possible for him to be so upbeat in the face of what he was about to do? Did he have no understanding or conscience over this? Was it actually mattering to him at all?

"OK, is everyone paying attention?" he asked.

"Yes," they shouted together.

"Good. So this is what I have to say. From now on I won't be living here anymore . . ."

Jenna watched their faces start to fall.

". . . but other than that nothing's going to be any different. I shall still be picking you up from school, even coming to get you up in the mornings when I can. We'll have tea together lots of times at Ben & Jerry's, or the King, or TGI Fridays, and we'll do all the things together we've always done."

"Where are you going to live?" Wills wanted to know.

"I shan't be far away, just over in Swansea."

"Why are you going to live there?" Flora asked, a forgotten carrot still in her fist.

"Because I have to."

"Why?"

"Well . . ." He glanced awkwardly at Jenna. "Mummy and Daddy have decided—"

"No," Jenna cut in quickly, and warned him with her eyes that he was not to include her in this decision.

"Sorry, *I* have decided that it's best for me and Mummy, actually for all of us, if I don't live here anymore."

"Why is it best for us?" Wills demanded, his eyes as troubled as Flora's and Josh's.

"Is it because we've been naughty?" Flora asked worriedly.

"No, no, it's nothing to do with that," Jack reassured her. "It's not your fault at all. It's mine. I've met . . . Well, I . . ." As his words dried, Jenna realized he was finally catching up with how much harder this was going to be than he'd apparently expected.

The children's eyes remained glued to him; no one moved as they waited for him to continue. Jenna tried to imagine how she'd have felt if her father had ever done this to her and Hanna. It wasn't possible, for the simple reason he never would have.

"Sometimes," Jack pressed on, "mummies and daddies stop living together and one of them goes to live with somebody else."

"Why?" Wills asked.

Jack swallowed, clearly floundering badly now. "Well, because . . . they've . . . they've fallen in love with somebody else.

It happens to lots of people. I don't expect all your friends' parents live together, do they?"

If they didn't, it was evident that Josh and the twins had no idea of it.

"So, that's my important news," Jack declared, sitting back in his chair, as if it were all done and dusted and they could move on to other things now.

All three children looked at Jenna, their eyes round with confusion, their need for her to explain as clear as the fear that they were understanding correctly. She tried to think of something to say that might help to make this better in some way, but there was nothing, unless she wanted them to think she was happy about their father's decision, and she couldn't bring herself to do that.

"You're still going to live here, aren't you, Mummy?" Flora asked, going to her.

"Yes, I'll still be here," Jenna promised. "I'll never leave you."

She could feel Jack's eyes boring into her, but he'd deserved that, and no way was she taking it back.

"I don't want you to go," Wills told his father.

"Nor me," Flora added. "We want you to stay here with us, because you're our daddy and daddies should live with their children."

"I know, sweetheart," he sighed, "but like I said just now, sometimes it doesn't happen that way."

"But I want it to."

"You can't go," Wills told him, "because we won't let you."

"No, we're definitely not going to let you," Flora echoed.

Though Jack's smile was unsteady, Jenna felt no pity for him, only the beginnings of contempt. He'd brought this on himself, so it was his to deal with—until he'd gone, when she'd be left to pick up the pieces. What was concerning her much more for the moment was the fact that Josh hadn't yet spoken. He'd simply sat there watching his father, thinking his own eight-year-old's thoughts, feeling whatever was going on in his young heart and keeping it all to himself.

"I'm not going yet," Jack was telling them. "I shall stay for tea and then we'll play some games until it's time for bed."

"I don't want to play any games," Flora pouted.

"Nor me," Wills snapped.

Jack looked at Josh. "What about you? What would you like to play?"

Without uttering a word Josh slid down from the table and walked out of the room.

"Josh," Jenna said, following him.

He kept going, all the way up the stairs to the landing, where Paige was standing. From the tautness of her face it was clear she'd been listening, but she didn't look at her mother, simply went to Josh and put her arms around him. He didn't hug her back; he simply stood with his head resting against her as though not entirely sure if this was a safe place to be.

Jenna couldn't tell if he was crying; she only knew that she was struggling with her own emotions as she left Paige to comfort her brother and returned to the twins, who were shouting at their father.

"Is he all right?" Jack asked as she came in.

"What do you think?" she replied.

Sighing, he dashed a hand through his hair and started to stand up.

"No! No! Don't go," Wills yelled, running to him.

"I'm not, son," Jack promised, settling him on one knee. "I already told you, I'll be here until bedtime."

"Then I'm not going to bed."

"Nor me," Flora declared, plonking herself on his other knee.

"Now that's just daft, isn't it?" he teased. "Everyone has to go to bed, and you've got school in the morning."

"If you stay here, like you always do," Flora said, gazing up through her pink-rimmed glasses, "then you can take us to school."

"I can take you anyway, if that's what you want."

"No, only if you stay here. I won't be your friend anymore if you don't."

"Well, I'll always be yours."

"I don't care." She turned to Jenna. "You don't want him to go, do you, Mummy?"

Jenna started to answer and stopped, as she realized that actually she didn't want him to stay. Not now, tonight. She wanted him gone, out of the way so she could tend to her children and think more clearly.

"Daddy knows I don't want him to go," she heard herself answering, "but he's decided it's what he has to do because he's fallen in love with another woman. Her name is Martha and I expect he'll want you to meet her one of these days."

"I don't want to meet her," Wills protested angrily. "She's not our mummy, you are."

Jack was glaring at her.

Ignoring him, she said, "Of course, and I always will be, but if she's going to be in Daddy's life that means she'll be in yours too."

"No!" he shouted.

"Wills," Jack said gently, "try to understand that—"

"I don't want to understand," Wills seethed, throwing his arms round Jack's neck. "I just want you to stay."

Clinging on too, and starting to sob, Flora said, "You're being horrible to us, and it's not fair. We haven't done anything wrong and it's mean of you to say you're going to live somewhere else."

Deciding to let him carry on alone, Jenna ran upstairs to check on Josh and Paige.

"Is he still with you?" she asked when Paige opened her door.

"No, he's gone to his room."

"Did he say anything?"

"Not really. He just asked if I already knew and I said I did."

Jenna was regarding her closely. "Are you all right?" she asked.

Paige shrugged as she looked away.

"He's still downstairs if you want to speak to him."

"No way," Paige snapped, and she slammed the door.

Going to Josh's room, Jenna knocked gently and put her head in. Her heart immediately turned over to see him sitting on the edge of the bed, feet dangling, head bowed.

Going to him, she put an arm around his shoulders so he was leaning in to her. "Do you want to ask me anything?" she said softly.

She felt him shake his head, and she tightened her hold.

"Everyone's going to think he doesn't love us anymore," he whispered after a while.

"Oh no they won't," she assured him. "They know how much he loves you."

"So why does he want to live somewhere else?"

"Because he's decided he doesn't want to live with me. It has nothing to do with not wanting to be with you."

"So can I go and live with him?"

Feeling the words cutting through her, Jenna said, "Is that what you want?"

He tilted his face to look up at her and shook his head. "I want to live here with you and Paige and the twins, but I want Daddy to live here too."

"I know you do, sweetheart, and if I could make it happen I would, but his mind is made up and I don't think we're going to change it."

As two large tears rolled onto his cheeks Jenna caught them with her fingers and blinked back her own. "We'll be fine," she promised hoarsely.

"No we won't. It's not going to be the same anymore."

"But you heard what Daddy said—he'll be seeing you all the time."

"It's not the same," he growled.

Since he was right, she didn't argue.

After a while his stricken blue eyes came pleadingly to hers. "Can you make him stay, Mummy, please?"

"I've already tried my best," she assured him, "but that doesn't mean we have to give up. We just have to be patient and see what happens. Can you do that, be patient with me?"

After a while he nodded and, sliding his arms around her, buried his face in her chest.

You need to check out Kelly Durham's FB page, Julie had messaged a few minutes ago, so Paige had, and what she'd found was so beyond terrible and humiliating that she just didn't know what to do. It didn't matter that the whole photograph couldn't possibly be of her; anyone who looked at her could see that no way did she have massive boobs like the ones on the body her photo had been attached to. What mattered was that the face was hers; even worse was that it had been shared to twenty other pages already, and one of them was Oliver's.

My name is Paige Moore and that's what I want, More and More and More, someone had captioned underneath.

The other comments were so crude, so vile, that she couldn't bring herself to read any further. All she could do was add her own, saying, *This is a sick joke played by Kelly Durham and her friends.*

Within seconds a return post hit the screen.

You're the sicko for taking this selfie in the first place.

I didn't take it. You stole my camera and now you've Photoshopped the picture you took with it.

A boy from year eleven posted, *I'll give you more anytime. When shall we meet?*

Another boy said, *Now that's what I call tits. Give 'em to me baby.*

Kelly wrote, *It's a selfie and everyone knows it, bitch.*

Deciding it would do no good to continue this, Paige closed down her laptop and grabbed her iPad to FaceTime Charlotte. "Have you seen what's on Facebook?" she asked when a bleary-eyed Charlotte came on the screen.

"No, haven't been on today," Charlotte answered, sounding so bunged up she was hardly getting the words out.

Paige winced as screaming started downstairs. It was obviously the twins, but her parents were shouting too, and she felt as though she was in the middle of a nightmare.

"So what does it say?" Charlotte asked.

"You need to see it. Go to Kelly Durham's page. The photo she took of me the other day? She's used it."

"Oh crap," Charlotte muttered. "I was hoping she'd forgotten about that."

"Me too, but she hasn't. She's even posted it on Oliver's page."

"What is the matter with her? She's *such* a bitch."

Hearing voices outside on the drive, Paige said, "Hang on." Running to the window, she peered out to see her dad talking to Auntie Hanna. Actually, it seemed more like they were rowing, which was no surprise, but whatever they were saying she couldn't hear, so she went back to her iPad.

"Have you heard from Liam today?" she asked, feeling she couldn't make everything about her all the time.

Charlotte immediately perked up. "Only four times," she replied, "and I think I'm seeing him on Saturday. We haven't actually arranged it yet, but he asked if I was doing anything and I said no, so we'll see what he says when he comes back. How about you? What's going on with your parents?"

Paige almost sobbed. "Don't ask. It's all terrible, and I swear if I could leave home I would. Except my dad's already done that and now he's about to do it again."

"You mean he's there?"

"He was. I've just heard his car pulling away. Thank God Auntie Hanna's turned up. I don't know how I'd cope with my mum on my own."

"I feel really bad for you. It totally sucks, all this crap you're going through."

"I know. I wish I knew how to make it stop."

"I reckon you should tell your mum about Kelly Durham."

"I keep wanting to, but she's dealing with so much right now, and anyway what can she do? Even if she goes to the school, which would be a total catastrophe, she won't be able to make her stop, because no one can. I've been reading about it online. There are no laws against what she's doing."

"Yeah, but we've had talks about bullying, and that's what this is."

"Big-time."

"Exactly, so you're supposed to tell someone about it. A parent, or a teacher. Why don't you talk to Miss Kendrick? She's cool and she really likes you."

"If I do, it'll just get worse. Julie's already warned me about that, and from what I've read on other people's blogs who've experienced it, it went quiet for a while after they told, then it got worse for them too."

"So what are you going to do?"

"*I don't know.* I keep trying to think of something, but there isn't anything."

Charlotte regarded her helplessly.

In the end Paige simply shrugged. She wasn't sure about running away yet, mainly because of how much it would upset her mum. So there was nothing left to say unless they wanted to talk about Liam again, and since Charlotte was definitely up for that, it was what they did.

It was close to midnight by now, and Josh and the twins had only just dropped off to sleep—all three in Jenna's room— tucked up with their favorite bears and fluffy rabbits, and Waffle keeping vigil at the foot of the bed. Since Jack had gone, several hours ago, there had been so many tears and tantrums that Jenna's exhaustion had reached a point where she'd lost track of what was being said or done. If it weren't for Hanna and her mother, she was sure, she'd have stuffed the children in the car, driven them to Jack's little love nest, and told him to sort them out. She was still thinking about it, though of course she never would. It would scare them half to death if she were to dump them somewhere they'd never been before, then drive off and leave them, and that was the last thing she wanted.

What she actually wanted was to know that Jack was suffering for what he was doing; that his conscience was destroying every minute of his time with Martha; that his heart was in as many pieces as hers.

"Of course it isn't making me happy to do this," he'd shouted at Hanna before he'd left, "but I'm not prepared to carry on living a lie."

"You sanctimonious bastard," Hanna had shouted back. "*You* don't want to live a lie, so your family has to carry on without you while you go have yourself some fun. It makes you feel better to do that than to man up to the responsibilities of fatherhood? To honor your marriage vows? To prove that you're a worthwhile human being?"

"I'm not arguing about this any more tonight," he'd shot back. "We're just going round in circles. The children are getting more distressed by the second, and me being here is making it worse."

"So that's what you're telling yourself, is it? That's the out you've given yourself, that being here is making things worse? Jesus Christ, it's making me sick just to look at you. You're a liar, a cheat, a spineless bastard, and a bloody con man into the bargain. How could we have been taken in by you? What fools you've made of us all."

It was at this point that Jenna had come out to drag her sister inside. "He's right," she'd said, "it's not helping to have him here, so let him go." She'd closed the door then without a single glance in his direction. Though it had hurt her badly to do it, she'd wanted him to feel shut out, unwelcome, an outsider who'd never belong here again. She wondered if it had worked, how wretched he'd felt during his drive to his new home, if it had all melted away the instant he'd seen Martha, or if he was awake even now, tortured by guilt and fearing that he'd made the wrong decision.

"Thanks," she sighed as Kay brought a tray of snacks into the dining room. She really didn't want any food, and wasn't sure she could stomach the wine either, but she probably ought to try something. "Is Paige still awake?" she asked.

"Her light wasn't on when I checked just now," Hanna answered, pouring the wine.

Jenna looked at the cheesy biscuits her mother was offering. Taking one, she put it on the plate in front of her and sipped the wine. "She's probably got the right idea, locking herself away," she commented. "It's too hard trying to deal with something like this, so probably best to pretend it isn't happening."

"She'll have a different way of dealing with it than the others," Hanna decided, "but we should keep an eye on her, because internalizing problems is never a good thing."

Jenna didn't disagree, though right now she had neither the energy nor the inclination to go and check on Paige. It would have to wait. Jack would still be gone tomorrow and the next day and the day after that . . . "How long are you staying?" she asked Hanna.

"I can be here till next Wednesday," Hanna replied, "at which point I have to be in London to prep for a presentation on Friday."

"But you'll come to the lawyer's with me?"

"Of course."

Jenna's eyes went to her mother. As usual, Kay's expression was showing little, but Jenna knew that she was finding this as hard as the rest of them. Maybe for someone like Kay, who couldn't let her emotions go, it was even harder. "Are you all right?" she asked softly.

"Yes, I'm fine," Kay responded. "You need to eat."

Knowing it would mean a lot to her mother if she made the effort, she picked up the biscuit and bit into it. Chewing and swallowing felt strange, like old skills she couldn't quite remember how to use. She realized it was probably tiredness playing tricks on her mind, but everything was starting to feel strange, as though this house were no longer hers, nor the children, not even her life. For bewildering moments she felt as though she was watching herself from a distance, wondering what she might do next, if she was going to hear what was being said or be able to carry out what was expected of her.

"... or shall I?" her mother asked.

Jenna looked at her in confusion.

"The phone's ringing," Kay told her. "Would you like me to go?"

"I will," Hanna declared. Getting to her feet, she went into the kitchen. As she answered she turned to look at Jenna. "Yes, Jack, we're still awake," she said. "What can I do for you?"

Jenna shook her head.

"Well, I'm afraid she doesn't want to speak to you. . . . No, I won't try to persuade her. . . . Yes, fortunately the children are asleep at last. It's been a difficult evening all round, but please don't let it bother you. We'd hate for anything to get in the way of your fun. . . . I have no idea why Paige isn't answering her mobile, but I'm guessing it's because she doesn't want to speak to you either. . . . Actually, Jack, no one's talked to Paige about your desertion. . . . Oh, what would you rather I call it? I could try betrayal, adultery, duplicity . . . I see. Well, do let me know when you've come up with something honest and repeatable that we can use to describe your—" Sighing and holding the phone from her ear, she allowed him to rant for a while before saying, "Jack, if you're not happy with the way things are, and you certainly don't sound it to me, then it's up to you to do something about it. . . . No, I will not pass you to Jenna. . . . Yes, she's sitting right here, she can hear every word I'm saying, and she's perfectly sure she doesn't want to speak to you. . . . I've no idea if she'll have changed her mind by tomorrow. Where do you want to take the children? . . . OK, I'll discuss it with Jenna and let you know. Goodbye, and please don't ring again to-night."

Watching her sister coming back into the dining room, Jenna could feel herself shrinking from the awful truth of where she was, the nightmare that shouldn't have been real but was, the changes already taking place in her life that she couldn't stop.

"He wants to take the children out for the day tomorrow," Hanna told her. "He didn't say where, but at least it shows he's not trying to cut himself off."

"Maybe it would be easier if he did," Jenna replied, thinking of how it would be when he brought them back.

"He should come here if he wants to see them," Kay stated. "They won't want to be separated from you."

"But maybe she could do with some time on her own," Hanna suggested.

"Then I'll take them out."

Hanna looked at Jenna. "Why don't you decide in the morn-ing?" she said gently.

Jenna nodded and looked down at her glass. After a while she spoke quietly, almost to herself. "He's never coming back. He can't now, even if he wanted to."

"Why do you say that?" her mother asked.

"Because what we had, what we shared, it's just not possible for us to get it back. He's ruined it."

"Things can be rebuilt, if it's what you want to happen," Hanna pointed out.

Jenna shook her head and looked up. To her surprise Paige was standing in the doorway. "Are you all right?" she asked softly.

Hanna and Kay turned around as Paige shrugged. "I wanted a drink," she said.

"Let me," Hanna offered, getting up.

Paige was still looking at her mother.

"Why don't you come and sit with us?" Jenna suggested.

Paige shrugged dismissively.

Not knowing what else to say, Jenna let her eyes drift away.

"I'll make you a fresh hot-water bottle," Kay decided, starting into the kitchen.

"Mum?"

Jenna looked at Paige again.

For a long time Paige simply stared back, looking as though she wanted to say something, until, taking the lemonade Hanna passed her, she turned around and went back upstairs.

"What was that about?" Hanna wondered.

"I'm not sure," Jenna replied, "but you're right, we do need to keep an eye on her, because she's obviously taking this hard, and the one thing we know for certain is that it's going to get a lot harder yet."

Chapter 13

"Thanks very much for seeing us at such short notice," Hanna was saying to the lawyer as he showed them into his office. "We realize how busy you are, so we do appreciate you squeezing us in."

"It's no problem, really," he insisted, directing her and Jenna to a plush cream leather sofa while he took one of the matching armchairs opposite. "Bena explained, when she rang, that it was urgent."

"She also told you what it was about?" Hanna prompted.

As the lawyer nodded he glanced at Jenna. His name was Richard Pryce, she kept reminding herself, senior partner of Denwell Pryce and Associates. He was younger than she'd expected, mid-forties maybe, certainly not the grandfatherly figure her imagination had for some reason conjured. In fact, he was quite a good-looking man in an understated, rather elegant sort of way, with thick, graying hair and astute blue eyes. His smile, though naturally polite, seemed genuine and relaxed, his demeanor that of a man both confident and in control. Though she sensed he was someone to be trusted, she felt loath to trust anyone at the moment, least of all herself.

"Will you have some coffee?" he offered, gesturing toward the pot on the table. "Or we can manage tea if you prefer."

Jenna cleared her throat. "Coffee's fine, thank you," she replied. She was suddenly embarrassed about being here. Though she'd done nothing wrong herself, she still felt responsible, foolish, and afraid that this man was never going to believe that she truly hadn't known what was going on in the company she part-owned. If he accepted this fact, he'd presumably consider her very stupid indeed, or at best naive.

After pouring three coffees Richard Pryce sat back in his chair and crossed one long leg over the other. "I've received your emails and attachments," he told them, "so I've had a quick look through, but it would be helpful to hear what you're thinking."

Immediately taking the lead, Hanna began explaining the initial premise of the company, how it had been agreed that Jack would run the business side of things—marketing, publicity, sales, et cetera—while Jenna concentrated solely on the creative content, as well as running a home, organizing four children, and attempting to write a book of her own.

As she listened, Jenna watched Richard Pryce taking everything in, his face inscrutable. She couldn't stop wondering what Jack would do if he knew she was here. As far as she was aware he still had no idea that she'd found out about the payments he'd extracted from the writers; he certainly hadn't broached the subject during the disastrous occasions he'd visited over the weekend. She couldn't think about those ugly scenes now, as it would do no good, especially when she was dangerously close to the edge already.

Obviously, with the children around and so much else to sort out, it hadn't been the right time to discuss business, but maybe she should have called him this morning and given him the chance to explain before coming here to seek legal advice. Not that she was feeling any loyalty toward him; why would she after he'd torn their family apart and cheated innocent people out of their precious savings? She was still finding it hard to accept that he'd do something so dishonest, even cruel. Even if he had, did she want the father of her children to face prosecution, particularly when it could very easily take her down too?

What the hell would happen to the children if both their parents ended up in prison?

Suddenly panicked by how little thought she'd given to this, how she'd allowed bitterness and anger to rush her to a course of action she was very likely going to regret, she quickly tried to think of a way to pull back. But how could she when the lawyer had already seen the outline Kay had prepared, had probably already formed an opinion on whether a criminal act had taken place? What could she possibly say that wasn't going to make her look guilty or ridiculous?

As Hanna stopped speaking, Richard Pryce's watchful blue eyes moved to Jenna. "Is there anything you'd like to add?" he invited.

"Uh, well, I . . . Perhaps we're being a bit hasty," she managed, and tried to ignore the way Hanna's head spun round to look at her. "We haven't actually discussed anything with my husband yet," she went on. "It could be there's a perfectly good explanation for why he suddenly started to charge our clients for their submissions."

"And what exactly do you think that reason could be?" Hanna demanded. "More to the point, why didn't he tell you, and where's the money now?"

Jenna looked awkwardly at Richard Pryce. "I know it doesn't

look good," she admitted, "but I'm afraid that if he has committed a crime, I'll be implicated in some way."

Nodding his understanding, the lawyer put his cup back on
the table and kept his eyes on hers as he said, "It's clear that
funds have come into the company that were subsequently
transferred to your husband's personal account. What we need
to find out, from him, is where the money is now and what he
intends to do with it. If he has a legitimate, workable plan for
your clients, then there should be nothing to worry about.
However, the fact that he has removed the money from the
company, ostensibly for his personal use, does give cause for
concern."

Hearing it put like that, Jenna realized she really did need his
advice. "So what do you suggest we do?" she asked.

"The choice is yours. You can either confront your husband
with what you know and ask for an explanation, or, if you prefer, I can do it for you."

Without hesitation Hanna said, "I think it should come
from you."

Richard was looking at Jenna, but she couldn't think clearly
enough to make a decision.

"He needs to understand," Hanna pressed on, "that we aren't
going to sit back and let him get away with whatever he's planning."

"Do you have any idea, Mrs. Moore, what your husband
might be intending to do with the money?"

Jenna started to speak but stopped. Had Bena told him that
Jack had left her for another woman? If she hadn't and Jenna
admitted it now, he might be even less inclined to believe in her
innocence and think this was all about revenge.

Having no such qualms, Hanna said, "My brother-in-law

recently walked out on Jenna and the children to go and live with another woman. This woman is, I believe, relevant to our case, because she's been advising him on setting up the business. My guess is he's using the money to set up a home with her."

Feeling ludicrously ashamed, Jenna watched Richard's shrewd eyes returning to hers. "Do you have any reason to think this woman might be involved in these charges for your clients?" he asked carefully.

Jenna shook her head. "I've no idea, but she's very hands-on with the business, so I'd be surprised if she doesn't know about them."

"Much more hands-on than Jenna is," Hanna added, "which is suspicious in itself, don't you think?"

Richard didn't comment on that. "The woman's name?" he enquired.

"Martha Gwynne," Jenna replied.

His eyebrows rose. "The business consultant?"

She nodded. "Do you know her?"

"I know of her, yes."

"I introduced her to my sister and brother-in-law," Hanna explained. "She did some work for us a couple of years ago—my husband and I have a PR company in London—and her services were faultless. Obviously, or I'd never have recommended her to anyone, least of all someone in my family."

"She does have a good reputation," Richard agreed, "but we still need to find out exactly what kind of role, if any, she's played in these recent developments. So, would you like me to draft a letter, or would you rather speak to your husband yourself?"

"I'd like you to do it," Jenna replied decisively. If she took it on herself, it would only turn into yet another ugly showdown, with the probability of not much being resolved at the end of it. However, if he knew for a fact that she'd already spoken to a lawyer, he'd have to come up with some answers.

"If you're sure about this, you need to let me have a current address for him."

"I don't have one," Jenna replied helplessly. "He hasn't told me where he's living, only that it's in the Maritime Quarter."

"I see. Well, I would strongly suggest that you do find out where he is, for your children's sake, if not for your own."

"Of course," she replied, feeling useless for not having done it sooner.

"When do you think you'll send the letter?" Hanna asked.

"It'll probably go in tomorrow evening's mail, first class," he replied. "This will give you some time to think it over in case you'd like to change your mind," he explained to Jenna. "If you do, you simply have to call me. Now, there's one more thing before you go. I would suggest you order a more thorough audit of the company, so we can be sure there is nothing else to be concerned about."

Jenna looked at Hanna.

"Do you have someone you can recommend?" Hanna asked him.

"Yes, I do. He's done a lot of work for us in the past, so I can assure you he's discreet, thorough, and fast. My secretary will give you his number as you leave, but I'll call myself to let him know that you'll be getting in touch."

"Thank you," Jenna murmured as he got to his feet. "You've been very helpful."

"Yes, very helpful," Hanna added, shaking his hand. "I have

to go back to London tomorrow, so it's a big relief to know I'm leaving my sister in your capable hands."

Richard's smile was ironic as he said to Jenna, "You have my number. If you are uncertain about something, or if you need more advice, don't be afraid to use it."

Once outside and in the car on the way home, Hanna said, "I think that went well, don't you?"

"I guess so, in the circumstances," Jenna responded.

Hanna glanced at her. "You're worried this isn't going to do anything to help repair your marriage," she stated.

Jenna turned to look out of the window. Yes, she was worried about that, but more worrying still was the fear that they were already past the point of repair.

"Are you going to call this auditor?" Hanna prompted.

Feeling she had no choice, Jenna said, "I'll give Richard the chance to call first. Maybe I'll do it this afternoon."

"Richard?" Hanna teased.

Surprised, Jenna said, "It's what Bena calls him."

"Of course, and it's his name, so why not? I liked him, did you?"

Jenna nodded and continued to stare out of the window. She was wondering again where Jack was now and what he might be doing. Wherever and whatever it was, she guessed he was with Martha. Was she planning to give him a job with her company, something to release him from the delusional ambitions of the Internet enterprise he'd dreamed up with his naively trusting wife? Had he used the money he'd taken from their clients to buy his way into Martha's firm? Or had it gone toward their new apartment?

Remembering that she needed to get an address from him,

she took out her mobile and pressed in his number. She wasn't surprised, only annoyed when she found herself going straight to voicemail. "I realize you're screening my calls," she said evenly, "so if you don't want to speak to me, perhaps you can text me the address of your new apartment. Don't worry, I won't be paying you a visit. This is purely in case of emergency."

After ringing off she stared down at the phone, as though expecting a text to arrive straightaway. It didn't, but a call came in a few minutes later from Miss Kendrick at Paige's school.

"Mrs. Moore, I hope I haven't caught you at a bad time?"

"No, now is fine," Jenna assured her. "Is everything all right?"

"I hope so. I'm just a little concerned about Paige. Is she still unwell?"

It took Jenna a moment to remember that her mother had collected Paige from school last Friday. "Oh, yes, she seems fine now," Jenna assured her. "Thank you for asking."

"So she'll be returning to school tomorrow?"

Jenna frowned. Unless she was imagining things, Paige had left home at her usual time that morning to get the bus. Waffle had gone with her and returned about ten minutes later, as he always did. "Are you saying . . . I'm sorry, but isn't Paige there now?" she asked.

"I'm afraid not," Miss Kendrick replied. "Mrs. Haynes tells me she attended registration first thing, but she didn't turn up for maths straight after, nor for my class after that. I was hoping she'd changed her mind about withdrawing from her part in *Under Milk Wood* for the centenary celebrations."

Stunned to learn that Paige had actually pulled out, Jenna said, "I'm sorry about the confusion. She must have felt unwell

again, and I expect my mother has come to the rescue. I'll find
out what's going on and call you back."

After ringing off she immediately rang Paige, but once again
found herself going to voicemail. "Paige, where are you?" she
asked. "I've just had a call from Miss Kendrick and I'd like to
know what's going on. Please ring me as soon as you get this
message."

Paige was curled up in a corner of a sofa in Charlotte's bedroom
listening to her mother's message, while Charlotte, still suffering with the flu, lay tucked up and fast asleep in bed. Paige was
desperate to catch the bug too, so she'd have a legitimate excuse
to be off school, but so far, in spite of spending most of the
weekend here, she hadn't produced as much as a sneeze.

Now, with Charlotte's mother at work all day, she could
stay as long as she liked and no one would even know she was
here. The trouble was she couldn't just ignore her mother's
message, or Jenna would end up calling the police or something equally as random, and that was the last thing either of
them needed.

They'd had the worst weekend ever. It had made Paige rage
inside every time she saw her mum crying, or shouting at her
dad, or trying to pry the twins off him. It was like they'd all
gone mad, and she despised the way her dad had started shouting into her mother's face as if he could beat her down with the
sheer force of his words. She wanted her mum to stick up for
herself and win, but no matter how hard Jenna fought back she
never seemed to get the better of him.

Paige didn't understand it. They'd always been such a close

family, but she was coming to learn that things could change
with no warning, like her dad going off with another woman—
and like people who'd never paid her any attention before, or
who didn't even know her, suddenly making her the butt of
their jokes or the focus of their cruelty.

Your face makes me want to smash it up.

Didn't you know that no one likes an arse-licker?

I think of you, bitch, and I vomit.

Come into school on Monday and get killed.

Oliver Pryce wants you to back off.

Stop bugging people who can't stand you.

The texts and posts and IMs were coming from loads of different people now, numbers and names she didn't even recognize. It was like everyone was jumping on board and no one,
apart from Charlotte, was sticking up for her. At least Julie was
tipping her off when she heard what the Durmites were planning, though she never tackled anyone publicly, which Paige
didn't blame her for, given that she'd been through it before.
She definitely wouldn't want to run the risk of having to endure
it all again.

How long did it go on for? she'd asked Julie over the weekend.

About six months, came the reply. *It was the worst time of my
entire life.*

Paige didn't doubt it, because this was definitely the worst
time of hers, and the thought that it could go on for so many
more months before they gave up was making her more afraid
than ever.

So far today there hadn't been any texts or posts, though she
didn't believe for a minute that it was all over. They'd gone
quiet for long periods over the weekend, but then they'd come

back with just as much bad stuff as before. She'd thought about trying to block them, but as much as she hated reading the messages she needed to know what was being said. It was the only way she could stay on top of it.

Looking at her phone as her mum rang again, she felt a sudden flash of resentment and frustration that Jenna hadn't realized for herself what was happening to her daughter. No one had. They were so wrapped up in what was going on with that bloody woman Martha that they weren't sparing a thought for anyone else. Not that she wanted their help; they'd only end up making things worse, or confiscating her phone and computer. It was just that they ought to remember that they had children who might need their attention.

"Yes?" she said shortly as she clicked on the line.

"Where are you?" her mother demanded. "Why aren't you at school?"

"I didn't feel well so I came back to Charlotte's, all right?"

"No, Paige, it isn't all right. You can't just disappear."

"I didn't disappear. You know where I am now, so why are you making such a fuss?"

"Because it's not acceptable for you to walk out of school without telling someone where you're going. Things are tough enough at the moment, I really don't need you adding to them."

"And I don't need you getting on my case when I'm not very well."

"What's the matter with you?"

"I think I've got the same as Charlotte."

"You don't sound ill."

"Oh, so now I'm a liar?"

"Paige . . ."

"No, it's OK. I get that everyone thinks I'm a waste of space and ought to go away somewhere and die."

"Don't be ridiculous. Would you like me to come and get you?"

"What for? I'll only be in the way at home."

"Paige, why are you doing this? You know what's happening with Dad; I don't want you turning against me too."

"He's not my dad, and it's you who's turning against me."

"I don't understand why you think that."

"You just are. You never listen to anything I'm saying, you're not interested in anything I'm doing . . ."

"You know that's not true. OK, I'm preoccupied at the moment, but you're fifteen, Paige, you understand what's going on, so why on earth are you telling yourself I'm turning against you when you know it's not true?"

"No I don't."

"Yes you do. And why have you pulled out of *Under Milk Wood*? I thought you were mad keen to do it."

"I told you I didn't want to be in it, but you weren't listening. And I don't want to go on the ski trip at the end of the month either."

There was a short silence before her mother said, "I'd forgotten about that trip. Why don't you want to go?"

"Because I don't."

"Is Charlotte backing out too?"

"I don't know. What does it matter? I don't want to go, end of story."

"Has Dad already paid for it?"

"Not yet, no."

"OK. We need to talk."

"I'm not changing my mind."

"I'm not saying you have to, but something's obviously bothering you."

"Nothing's bothering me. I'm just telling you—"

"Paige, stop shouting at me."

"I'm not shouting."

"Yes you are."

"I'm ringing off now and *don't* come and get me. I'm going to stay here, where I know I'm wanted." Clicking off the line, she took herself off to the bathroom so Charlotte wouldn't hear her sobbing.

Everything was such a nightmare. Her whole life was falling apart and nothing she did was making it right. She hated herself for being so weak, for not standing up to the Durmites, for picking on her mother, for detesting her father, for wanting to hit Josh and the twins just to shut them up. Her grandma was the only one who really understood, but she wasn't very easy to talk to, and anyway she had enough on her plate, taking care of everyone now that her dad had gone.

"Paige, I heard you on the phone," Charlotte said from outside the door. "Don't cry. It'll be all right."

Grabbing a handful of loo roll, Paige dried her eyes as she slid back the bolt to let her in. "Sorry I woke you up," she said hoarsely. "My stupid mother was having a go. It's like it's my fault my dad has left her. How can it be my fault when it has nothing to do with me?"

"Is that what she said?" Charlotte asked worriedly.

Paige shook her head. "Not really. I mean, I don't know what she's saying half the time. I'm not sure she does either." She inhaled shakily and blew her nose. "I'm dreading Auntie Hanna going back to London," she confessed. "It'll all be down to me then, and it's not fair. I don't want to be caught in the middle, sticking up for my mum, having a go at my dad . . . He's the one who's turned our lives inside out, so he's the one who ought to be putting it right."

"Why don't you tell him that?" Charlotte suggested.

Paige regarded her warily.

"Ring him up—or text him—and tell him you've got your own life to lead, so you don't need to be dealing with his shit. No, no, this is what you should do. You should tell him what's going on at school and say it's up to him to sort it out."

Paige looked uneasy. "I don't want to talk to him," she said, "and definitely not about that."

"But you have to talk to someone, Paige, because it's totally stressing you out."

Paige stiffened. "Wouldn't you be the same if it was happening to you?"

"Of course, but I'm pretty sure I'd tell my mum."

"Even if you knew it was going to make it worse, or that she might take your phone and computer away?"

Charlotte shuddered. "She'd never do that," she responded, clearly appalled at the mere idea. "No way would I let her."

"I wouldn't want to let my mum either, but she'd end up finding a way."

"So what are you going to do? Just carry on letting them get away with it? That photo was obscene, and remember Julie said it went on for about six months with her. Are you seriously going to let that happen to you?"

"No. I don't know." Her eyes were full of helplessness as she looked at Charlotte. "I haven't heard anything today," she said. "Maybe they're fed up already and have moved on to someone else."

Charlotte shrugged. "Let's hope you're right, because you

can't stay away from school forever, and my mum's saying I probably ought to go back tomorrow."

"It won't be as bad if you're there. I just didn't want to face it on my own today, I'm scared stiff they're going to start beating me up."

"They haven't done anything physical yet," Charlotte pointed out. "I mean not seriously physical, so I don't expect they'd dare. Look at it this way—if you had bruises and stuff, your mum and the teachers would want to know how you got them."

Paige nodded distractedly. She was thinking of her grandpa and how easy he'd always been to talk to. She wished he were still here so she could ask him what to do.

"I know what I'm going to do," Charlotte declared importantly. "If I see Liam at the weekend, and I reckon I will, I'm going to tell him what's happening. At least he'll be able to convince Oliver you're not behind any of it."

Paige didn't like the idea at all. "And I'll end up looking like a miserable victim who can't stand up for herself," she retorted. "Great."

"Well someone has to stand up for you if you're not going to."

"I will," Paige snapped back. "I'll talk to someone, just not yet, OK? Let's wait and see if they've stopped first, because for all we know they might have."

"Mrs. Moore? It's Richard Pryce speaking. Is this a good time?"

"Yes, yes, it's fine," Jenna assured him, wishing she didn't know him, yet relieved that she did.

"A couple of things. I've spoken to Sean Burrows, the auditor

I mentioned when you were here yesterday, and he's happy to work with you."

"Yes, I called him about an hour ago. We've arranged for him to come here at ten o'clock tomorrow."

"That's good. Hopefully it won't take long, and once we have a complete picture of what's happening in the company, we'll have a better idea of how to proceed."

"Of course." Why did this man make her feel so ashamed, so pathetic, for not having realized a long time ago what her husband was up to? She was sure he didn't mean to, but it was how she felt every time she thought of him, never mind when they spoke.

"Second thing," he continued, "have you had time to read the letter we drafted to your husband? We attached it to an email earlier today."

She swallowed dryly. "Yes, I've read it," she replied.

"And how are you feeling about sending it?"

"I think you should." God only knew how Jack was going to react, though it wouldn't be well, she was sure of that. However, she couldn't handle him on her own, not without Hanna here as backup, so he needed to know that she had support from elsewhere.

"OK, I see we've received the address, so it'll go in the mail tonight. I'm very hopeful we can resolve this without going to court."

"Thank you," she murmured. "You're being . . ." She wanted to say "very kind," but the words became lodged in her throat.

"I'll let you know if he contacts me," he told her, "and perhaps you could do the same if he contacts you."

After assuring him she would, she put the phone down and looked at Bena.

"Richard?" Bena asked.

Jenna nodded.

"He's a good person to have on your side."

Sure of it, but wishing there didn't have to be sides, Jenna said, "You know I can't go on paying you—"

"Don't even mention it," Bena interrupted. "I'm here for you, and that's that. Between friends it's not about money."

Smiling past the lump in her throat, Jenna whispered, "Thank you." After taking a breath she said, "Jack obviously wanted us to find out what he's been doing, or he wouldn't have given us the password to his computer."

Bena didn't disagree.

"He's probably even wondering why we haven't brought it up."

"Or he thinks we haven't bothered to look at his files yet."

"Whichever, it clearly doesn't seem as though he's planning to tell me himself. He's left me to find out on my own and made me a gift of the company into the bargain."

Bena's expression showed her disgust.

Getting to her feet to let Waffle into the office, Jenna said, "I know it sounds daft because Richard's much younger than my dad, but he reminded me of him in a way."

"I wish I'd met your dad. I can tell by the things you've told me that he was very special."

Jenna had to swallow. "I'm missing him so much at the moment," she confessed. "I think we all are, me, Mum, and Hanna. He was our rock. He always knew what to do in a crisis. It's very hard to have to cope on your own when you're so used to having someone like him in your life."

"But you're managing very well, and you'll get through this, I promise. OK, it probably won't be easy at times, but we'll all be here for you, and you're much stronger than you think."

Jenna's smile was faint. "I'd like to believe that, but I'm not so sure. Sunday was just awful, the way Jack laid into me. It was as though he hated me and was blaming me for everything that's happening, and now I'm even questioning myself. What did I do wrong? Why didn't I see we were in trouble?"

"You're not to blame," Bena said forcefully. "This is all down to him, every last bit of it, and it's typical of someone who knows he's in the wrong to twist things round to make someone else the guilty party. The only good part of that is it shows he has a conscience, though it makes me sick to think of how he's using it to hurt you even more."

Sighing, Jenna picked up her mobile to text Paige. *How are you feeling?*

She wasn't expecting a reply anytime soon. Paige would be in class, and she didn't always turn her phone on between lessons either.

"I know all this business with Dad is upsetting you," Jenna had said to her last night, "but I'm worried that there's more you're not telling me."

"I don't want you to worry about me, all right?" Paige had snapped. "I'm fine. I just don't want to listen to you shouting at him on the phone, or him trying to pretend that everything's normal when it isn't. You should stop him from coming. It's not helping anyone, least of all you. And just in case you didn't know, Josh wet the bed last night."

"Yes, I know," Jenna had said softly. "And it's not the first time since Dad went."

"So stop him from coming. He's the cause of it, and so are you because you let Josh see how upset you are."

Those words were still resonating painfully through Jenna's mind. She knew she had to pull herself together and get on top of what was happening or they were all going to fall apart, and she just couldn't let that happen.

Paige's text arrived.

Today is total shit. Hate this school. Wish we'd never come here.

Though she loved the Gower herself, Jenna knew she'd wish the same if it would mean Jack had never met Martha. *Tell me what I can do to make things better,* she texted back.

She waited and waited but Paige didn't respond, and by the time Kay brought Josh and the twins in from school Jenna's concerns for her elder daughter had slipped to the back of her mind.

"I thought Dad was picking us up," Wills cried angrily. "He said he would today, but when we came out he wasn't there."

Jenna looked at her mother.

"He texted me about an hour ago to ask if I could do it," Kay told her.

"And you didn't tell me?"

"I assumed he had."

"Did he give a reason for not going?"

"Not to me. Flora, you've left your coat in the car."

"I don't care," Flora pouted. "I don't want it."

"Go and get it," Jenna told her.

"No!"

"Do it now or you're going straight to bed."

"I hate you," Flora cried, starting back to the car, and quickly returning with her coat.

"Josh, sweetheart," Jenna said, "how did you get on in school today?"

He simply shrugged and trudged into the sitting room.

"Did he say anything on the way home?" she asked her mother.

"He kept telling us to shut up," Wills answered.

"So what did you do?" Kay prompted.

Wills looked sheepish. "He was asking for it," he protested.

"So you hit him?" Jenna queried.

"Because he was asking for it."

"Go and apologize."

"Oh, Mum!"

"Now!"

"Can I have something to eat first?"

"I bought some chocolate eclairs on the way back," Kay told her. "Is Bena still in the office? I brought one for her too."

"I'm sure she'd love one," Jenna replied. "Pop over and get her, Wills."

"I thought I was supposed to apologize to Josh."

"Yes, do that, and Flora, you can go and get Bena."

"Why wasn't Dad there when we came out of school?" Flora demanded.

"That's what I'm about to find out," Jenna told her, reaching for the phone.

To her surprise Jack answered on the second ring.

"The children want to know why you didn't pick them up," she informed him.

"I got held up in a meeting," he retorted.

"What kind of meeting? Do you have a new job now?"

"What are you talking about?"

"Well, you're not running our company anymore, so what are you having meetings about?"

"I don't have to answer that."

"Maybe not, but you do have to explain to the children why you weren't there when you said."

"I was going to call them later."

"Really?"

"Yes, really. I suppose you've already told them that it's because I put Martha ahead of them."

"Actually, I've said no such thing, but it is what you've done."

With an exasperated sigh he said, "Why don't I speak to them now?"

"Are you sure you have the time?"

"Put one of them on, will you?"

"Before I do, have you been in touch with Paige?"

"I've texted her, but she hasn't texted back."

"Well, for your information, she hates school and wishes we'd never come here. I wonder how big a part you're playing in that." Handing the phone to Wills, she said, "Here's your hero, sweetheart. The daddy you love and look up to."

It was after seven by the time she heard from Paige again. *I suppose you haven't even noticed I'm not home yet. Am at Charlotte's and staying the night. Please bring clean underwear.*

No *P* for Paige, or *x* for a kiss.

And nowhere to turn with all the panic she could feel building inside.

Chapter 14

The following afternoon Jenna was in the kitchen when she heard Jack's car practically skidding to a halt in the drive outside. The slam of the driver's door and determined crunch of his footsteps on the gravel was followed by the throwing open of the utility room door and an explosive entrance into the kitchen.

"What the hell is this?" he demanded, waving Richard Pryce's letter in her face. "What in God's name do you think you're doing?"

"If you've read it, you know what I'm doing," she managed to say smoothly, inwardly quailing at such aggression.

"This is asking me to explain things that are no one else's bloody business," he shouted. "What the hell's the matter with you? Didn't it occur to you to talk to me before consulting a lawyer? And what's going on in your head that you think you even need one?"

"I'd like to know what's going on in yours that you suddenly started charging people—"

"That sister of yours is behind this."

"—*without telling me.* And you can blame Hanna all you

like. In fact, why don't you blame everyone except yourself, because you've never done anything underhanded or wrong or duplicitous, have you, Jack?"

His expression was so murderous she almost took a step back. "Exactly what do you expect to gain from this?" he growled. "Exactly what—"

"The letter makes it perfectly clear," she cut in angrily. "I want to know where the money is that you tricked out of the writers."

"What do you mean, *tricked*?"

"What I said. You haven't given them anything for it, so you've taken it under false pretenses. That's called fraud, in case you didn't know."

"There are all kinds of marketing opportunities being put into place," he shouted. "That's what they're paying for. I'm offering worldwide exposure."

"Since when? And if it's true, why have you never discussed it with me?"

"I've been trying to put it together."

"How? With whom? And once again, why don't I know about it? I haven't found anything on your computer to back this up."

"You won't if you're not looking in the right places. And why am I standing here justifying this as if I'm some sort of criminal?"

"Because I'm very much afraid that's what you are. As far as I can see, you've taken money from people and given them promises you can't keep."

"For Christ's sake . . ."

"If it was honest, had real integrity and genuine possibility, you'd have told me about it. So where is their money, Jack?

What have you done with their savings, their dreams, their trust? You know it was never our intention to charge them."

"Correction! It was never *your* intention, and if it had been even remotely possible to set up a company without charging the authors, you might have had your way. But it wasn't. So I did what I had to do to make things work."

"Like lying about a grant from the Arts Council."

He flushed. "I was sure it would come through."

"And exactly how is anything going to *work for the company* when the money's gone into your personal account? Is it still there?"

"Of course it's not there. What the hell do you think we've been living on all this time?"

Her heart gave a horrible thump. "Are you saying . . . ?" She didn't want to believe this, she really didn't. "What's happened to our savings, your severance pay, my inheritance?" she asked quietly.

"What do you think?" he cried furiously. "It ran out months ago, so I had to think of something to keep us going."

"And that something was to *cheat* other people out of money that's probably even more hard-earned than ours? Jesus Christ, what's the matter with you, Jack? Surely you can see how wrong that is."

"And it would be right to stop paying our bills, feeding our children, giving them what other kids have?"

"But they never needed smart TVs, iPads, iPods, or whatever the hell else you decided they should have. Oh God, Jack, I can't believe you've done this. If you'd told me we were in trouble, I could have cut back."

"It's a bit late to be telling me that now."

"You never gave me the chance."

"You didn't want to hear it."

"Did you even try?"

"Plenty of times, you just weren't listening."

Knowing he was lying, she tried to bring her focus back to the real issue they were facing. "You need to pay that money back to the writers," she told him forcefully. "If you don't, you could go to prison. Have you thought about that?"

"Of course I've thought about it. And like it or not, the real truth is we both could, which is why it was the stupidest thing you ever did, going to a lawyer before you'd even spoken to me."

She took a moment to absorb the fact that he'd just admitted to committing a crime. "And what were you going to say to me that would make it all right?" she asked cuttingly. "What quick fix do you have up your sleeve for fraud or embezzlement or whatever the hell it is? Because from where I'm sitting there's not a single sign of a mitigating circumstance anywhere close to a horizon. You're talking about marketing packages that don't exist."

"That are in the process of being set up."

"Which means they didn't exist when you offered them. You've taken over twenty thousand pounds from our contributors, which you've just admitted to using for our personal expenses, so I want to know what you're going to do about paying it back. What plans do you have for returning what is rightfully theirs before letters start arriving threatening to sue us? Maybe you've already had some. Have you?"

"What I have," he growled defensively, "is a stack of bills that need paying and nothing to pay them with, unless we carry on charging."

"Are you out of your mind?" she raged. "We can't steal any more of their money."

"Then you'd better come up with another way of making it."

"And I need to do that on my own?"

"What do you think I've been doing all this time?"

"I'll tell you what you've been doing," she shot back. "You've been stealing, cheating, living a double life, screwing another woman while I had no idea."

"Because you didn't want to know. You never do. You just carry on as though everything is perfect in the world, Jack will provide, Jack will make everything wonderful, even if it's shit. Well, it's time to wake up and find out what's really going on around you, because this is your problem every bit as much as it's mine, and the only way we're going to solve it is for you to use what you've got left from your advance—or deliver another damned book."

Jenna's eyes widened with shock. "Whatever I might have left," she cried angrily, "belongs to me and the children. It is *not* going to be used to get you out of this mess. You put yourself there—now you can get yourself out."

"The company belongs to both of us," he reminded her tightly.

Her mouth fell open. She could hardly believe he'd just said that, much less what it actually meant. "Are you seriously telling me," she demanded, "that you're intending to let me, the mother of your children, an innocent party in all this, take the blame for something you know that you did?"

"I did it so we could live," he shouted. "If you want to see it any other way, that's up to you."

She could hardly think straight anymore. In the end she forced herself to look him in the eye. What she saw was a man she couldn't imagine loving, a man whose morals and integrity were as absent as any sign of regret or compassion. "What changed you?" she asked hoarsely. "What, *who*, turned you into this person?"

He stared at her hard, but she could sense a powerful guilt cracking through his conscience.

"You've got to sort this out," she told him gravely. "You know that, don't you?"

"Of course I know it, and we need to start by getting this lawyer off our backs."

She was shaking her head. "As far as I can see, I need him more now than ever. You stole that money, Jack, and you need to pay it back, or there are going to be some dire consequences."

This time he didn't answer, merely stared down at the letter as if he was no longer quite so sure of himself.

"Was she a part of it?" she asked. "Martha? Did she know what you were doing?"

Though he flinched, he sounded credible as he said, "She had nothing to do with it."

"But she knows about it?"

"She does now."

"And she still wants to be with you knowing that you're a thief and a liar, a man who would put his wife, his whole family in jeopardy?"

"No one's been trying to put you in jeopardy, for God's sake. My intention is to transfer the company to your name so—if we can get it going—you'll reap all the profits. I swear I've never intended to take anything for myself."

"Because there's nothing *to* take," she pointed out shrilly. "You already have it, in your account."

"Which is all but empty. Once again, you're the one who's been spending it, Jenna."

"And you know damned well that I had no idea where it had

come from. If you'd told me we were in such dire straits, I could have got a job."

"Where? You're not qualified to do anything around here even if there were jobs to be had, and there aren't. All you can do is write, and you're not even doing that anymore."

Stung by the cruelty of that, she said, "I think you should go. I've got no more to say to you. The next time you hear from me will be through the lawyer."

Thumping a hand on the countertop, he said, "Don't be ridiculous. He's not going to help you; he'll only make things worse. We have to find a way of working this out together."

"No! *You* have to find a way, because *you're* the one who did it. I need what little money I have to keep my family fed and clothed, and for all I know my publisher will be asking for it back any day now anyway. What's going to happen then, Jack? How are you going to provide for your children if what little I have is taken away?"

"If you're really afraid of that," he responded, "then you should transfer it to me. That way you won't have it even if they do ask for it back."

It had started again. Not as soon as Paige and Charlotte had returned to school; in fact, their first day back had almost allowed Paige to believe it might be over at last. She'd received no spiteful texts or emails, no snide remarks as she'd passed the Durmites in the corridors, nor had there been any cruel or bogus postings online. It was as though everything had gone back to normal. She'd even started to wonder if it would be OK to tell Miss Kendrick that she'd do *Under Milk Wood* after all, although she was still nervous about putting herself forward in case it goaded the Durmites into targeting her again.

In the end they hadn't needed any help from her: they returned to it anyway, starting in the corridor outside the history room that morning when someone had deliberately tripped her up and made sure she'd hit the floor hard. She'd been careful not to show how much it hurt or let them know how foolish they'd made her feel; she'd simply picked herself up, collected her books, and carried on along the corridor.

Fortunately, she hadn't been in the same lessons as them for the rest of the morning so nothing else had happened, and she felt reasonably safe here in the study center with Charlotte as they researched Alexander Fleming as part of their GCSE coursework. Everyone else was either in the canteen having lunch or milling about the grounds, but Mrs. Dyer had allowed them to come inside to carry on with their project.

However, Paige was finding it hard to focus. Her mind kept wandering off to places where she didn't really want it to go at all, but she couldn't seem to make it stop. Mostly it was focusing on her dad. Twice now he'd said he'd pick Josh and the twins up from school and take them to athletics or Cubs or Rainbows or wherever they were supposed to be going, and both times he'd got Grandma to do it instead. He wasn't anything like the dad she used to know. He'd become selfish and mean, putting himself first in a way he never had before. He wasn't even interested in her tourist video anymore. She knew that because he hadn't mentioned it once since he'd gone. But that was OK. The last thing she wanted was it being singled out as something special; she'd only be ridiculed and punished for it if it were.

"Oh, wow! It's from Liam," Charlotte suddenly squealed as a text beeped into her phone. "Oh my God, oh my God," she gasped after reading it. "Listen to this: 'Hope you're still free Saturday to come to game and party after at Oliver's.'" She was grinning wickedly as she turned to Paige. "A party," she repeated. "How amazing is that? I've got to get something to wear. Or I know—can I borrow that blue dress you got in New Look?"

"I haven't worn it yet," Paige complained.

"Oh right. Well, will you come into town with me to find something? We can go tomorrow, after school . . . Oh shit, I'm sorry," she said with a gulp, abruptly realizing her mistake. "I wasn't thinking. It's at Cullum and Oliver's, and you . . . I know, I'll find out if I can invite a friend."

"No, no," Paige protested. "Honestly, don't. I'd only feel embarrassed after all the texts and Facebook stuff."

Charlotte appeared undecided.

Forcing a smile, Paige said, "It's brilliant that Liam wants to take you."

Charlotte's eyes sparkled. "You know what it means, don't you?" she whispered excitedly.

Paige frowned.

"It means we might do it." She clapped her hands to her face. "Oh my God. Can you believe it? I might not be a virgin anymore after Saturday. That will be so amazing, just as long as no one starts calling me slag or slapper or anything like that."

"It's what they call me and I haven't even done anything," Paige reminded her.

"Yeah, but everyone knows it's not true about you."

"Do they?"

"Course they do. Hang on, I need to text him back." She

spoke the message aloud as she tapped it in. *Def still free would love to come. Is party an all-nighter?* "If it is," she said to Paige, "can I say I'm staying at yours?"

"Sure," Paige agreed miserably.

A minute later Charlotte received a reply. *Yes, all-nighter, but don't bother with pajamas.* ☺

Charlotte was beaming as she turned to Paige. "Do you think I should get some condoms or leave it to him?" she whispered.

"I think you should take some, just in case," Paige replied. "You don't want to end up pregnant or with some horrible STD."

Charlotte's smile vanished. "He won't have an STD," she protested. "What made you even think it?"

Paige shrugged awkwardly. "I was just saying, that's all. I mean, you don't know who he's been with before, and Mrs. Mars keeps banging on about it in PHSE. 'You've got more chance of catching an STD than becoming pregnant, and it could ruin your chances of ever getting pregnant.'"

Having to concede that this was indeed what their Physical Health and Social Education teacher kept drumming into them, Charlotte said, "We'll have to get some tomorrow while we're in town, where no one knows us. If I went to the local pharmacy, it would get back to my mum quicker than you could get your knickers off."

Relieved that the tricky moment seemed to be over, Paige laughed and checked her own mobile as it vibrated. *Heard what happened this morning. Hope you didn't get hurt. Jx*

Paige messaged back: *I'm cool. Thanks for asking. Px*

Speak later?

Sure.

Deciding to tell Charlotte it was her mum rather than give her a reason to have a go about Julie again, Paige tucked her phone away and tried to return to her project. It was hard not to think about the party, though, and how upset she was at not being invited. However, she was determined not to let it show, as it would only make Charlotte feel bad, and what was the point of that? It was going to be horrible being at home on Saturday on her own, really vile and lonely imagining everyone having a brilliant time dancing and getting wasted or stoned, neither of which she'd ever done before. She'd really like to now, if only to prove to herself and to Charlotte that she was up for it. She wasn't sure she'd go as far as having sex, unless it was with Oliver, but that was never going to happen, so she might just as well put it out of her mind.

What was wrong with her that nothing ever went right?

It was much later that day, just after she'd arrived home to find an empty house, that she received an email from Hayley telling her to check out the Happy Landings chat room. This was the school chat room, generally only used by years seven to nine, so she was surprised to get the message, and immediately suspicious. It wasn't that Hayley had gone over to the Durmites altogether, but like so many, she'd been giving Paige a wide berth lately in case the Durmites started picking on her too. It was as if Paige was contaminated.

She was even starting to hate herself.

Hearing her mum's car pulling up outside, she was about to open the website when a message came through from Julie. *Don't go on the HL chat room. They're a bunch of losers and you don't need to read what they're saying.*

Someone knocked on her bedroom door. She shouted for

whoever it was to go away, and clicked through to the chat room.

"Paige," Josh called out. "Please, can I come in?"

"No! Go away!" she seethed. She really couldn't deal with her baby siblings right now.

"He was put on the black bench today," Flora shouted. "I told him me and Wills are always on the black bench, so it's nothing to worry about."

Though she didn't want to remember how sensitive Josh could be at times, or realize what a big deal it would be for him to find himself on the naughty side of the classroom, Paige found herself getting angrily up from her chair and tearing open the door. "It's not the end of the world," she snapped at Josh. "You have to toughen up and deal with things."

"That's what I said," Flora informed her.

"But I don't know what I did wrong," Josh protested. "The teacher never told me."

"Then you have to ask her, not me," Paige retorted. "I wasn't there, was I?"

As his eyes flooded with tears she threw out her hands in frustration. "It's not my fault you got put on the black bench," she cried.

"I never said it was."

"You shouldn't be mean to him when he's upset," Flora scolded.

"Well, what do you want me to do?"

"Come on," Flora said, trying to put an arm round Josh's shoulders, "let's go away from her. She's just horrible."

"And so are you," Paige called after them before slamming the door and returning to her computer. She'd make it up to them later, somehow; she just couldn't deal with them right now.

Minutes later, after finding the worst imaginable exchange on the HL chat room, she was staring at the screen as though the whole world had shifted to a place she couldn't even begin to understand.

You can't blame her dad for leaving, who'd want to live with her?

Wonder if she knows he left because he can't stand her?

Do you think someone should tell her?

Is it true she's got an STD?

She's bound to have, amount of blokes she goes with.

She meets them online and goes on dates with them.

Apparently her dad found out and fixed her up with one of his mates. You know he's not her real dad, don't you?

Even if he's not, that's still sick.

Bet it's not true.

I heard she has threesomes with her dad included. That's why he left, because her mum caught them.

Paige was shaking with disgust and horror. How could anyone say something so revolting? It was beyond anything she could imagine herself; it was the worst thing she'd ever heard in her life.

Like she'd ever sleep with her dad.

She wanted to be sick, tear out her hair, or do something really terrible, like beat herself up or throw herself out of a window.

She snatched up her phone as Charlotte came through on FaceTime.

"Please tell me," Charlotte cried desperately, "that you haven't been on the HL chat room."

"I'm looking at it now," Paige choked out. "How did you know about it?"

"I got an email from Hayley. Jesus Christ, what are they thinking? They're a bunch of fucking perverts. And they're such cowards—not one of them has used a real identity."

"The whole school is going to see it. Even those who never use the chat room will hear about it and go on to have a look."

Charlotte couldn't deny it.

"What shall I do?" Paige whispered through her tears.

"We're going to tell someone," Charlotte answered decisively. "I'll come with you tomorrow to see Miss Kendrick. Or maybe we ought to go straight to Mr. Charles?"

Shuddering at the very thought of involving the headmaster, Paige said, "What if they're right and he did leave because of me?"

"Just no way did that happen," Charlotte insisted, "and you can't let them get away with the other stuff they said. It is totally *disgusting*. We are going to see Miss Kendrick tomorrow, and if you don't want to come with me, I'll go on my own."

Jenna looked up as Paige wandered into the kitchen, wearing her slouchy pajamas and a depressingly sullen expression. "Are you OK?" she asked, peering at her closely. "Have you been crying?"

"No," Paige retorted. "Why would I be crying?"

Jenna's eyebrows rose.

"I haven't been crying, all right? But you have—your eyes are all red and your face is puffy."

Jenna's smile was wry. "I was about to make myself an omelette," she said. "Would you like to share it with me?"

Paige shrugged and went to perch on one of the bar stools.

"I'll take that to be a yes," Jenna decided, and turned to the fridge for more eggs. "Cheese, ham, mushrooms, tomatoes, or all of the above?" she offered.

"Whatever."

"Then we'll have it all. Would you like a glass of wine to go with it?"

Paige looked up in surprise. It wasn't that her parents never allowed her wine with a meal, but she usually had to ask for it. "If you like," she responded.

After pouring them half a glass each, Jenna returned to the hob. "So how are things at school?" she asked.

"Same old," Paige mumbled.

"Do you feel you're on top of things?"

"I suppose so."

Jenna opened a bag of grated cheese and added it to the eggs. She could feel her daughter's tension as if it were tightening the air, trying to strangle her, and because of it she found herself struggling for something to say.

"Have you seen Dad?" Paige suddenly asked.

"Not since yesterday," Jenna replied. "He came here. We had a few things to sort out."

"Did you row?"

"I'm afraid so."

"What about?"

Since she didn't want Paige knowing anything about the company issues, Jenna said, "Nothing really. I mean, silly things."

"Was it about me?"

Jenna's eyes rounded. "Why would you think that?"

Paige's face was pinched as she shrugged.

"No, we didn't row about you," Jenna told her.

Several minutes ticked by with lots of thundering about upstairs, an unwatched TV blaring from the sitting room, and Wills shouting at Josh to "come and look." Jenna poured the omelette mixture into a pan and picked up the phone as it rang. After speaking to another mother about a birthday party after school next Thursday, she rang off. Moments later it rang again. This time it was Bena. The call was short and left Jenna feeling wearier than ever.

"Apparently Aiden's got nits," she told Paige. "That means we'll have to check Josh and the twins tonight."

"What do you mean, *we*? That's Dad's job, get him to do it."

"Dad's not here, is he, and it has to be done."

"But it's not up to me . . ."

"I need your help. Will you get that, please?" she added as the phone rang again.

Paige picked it up, listened to the person at the other end, and said, "No, we don't need new windows, but if you're any good at finding nits . . ."

As she hung up Jenna smiled. "That's one way of dealing with them," she commented.

Paige didn't smile back; she simply sat staring at the wine she hadn't touched, her face as pale as Jenna had ever seen it, her young heart clearly badly troubled.

"Did Dad leave because of me?" she suddenly blurted out.

Jenna stopped what she was doing and turned to her. "No, of course not," she replied. "It had nothing to do with you. Why do you even think that?"

Paige didn't seem comforted.

"I know this might come as a shock," Jenna pressed on, trying to put a tease in her voice, "but not *everything's* about you."

Paige's surly expression told what she thought of that little joke.

"It really isn't," Jenna insisted, "and I can promise you—"

"All right, it isn't about me," Paige cut in irritably.

"Paige . . ."

"So let's make it about Josh. He's really upset about what's happening. I can hear him crying at night, even if you can't."

"Mummy! Mummy!" Flora screamed. "Wills is scribbling on my walls."

"She scribbled on mine first," Wills yelled.

"Mum, he's hitting me."

"She hit me first."

"Go and sort them out," Jenna sighed. "Tell them no stories if they don't brush their teeth and get into bed by the time I come up."

Looking about as thrilled to play mother as she was to be in the house at all, Paige took herself off upstairs, leaving Jenna to gulp down her wine and refresh the glass.

Seconds later the phone rang again. This time it was Hanna.

"How are you?" she asked. "Have you heard from Jack today?"

"No," Jenna replied. "He's supposed to be calling the children this evening, but no word from him yet. Maybe he'll ring Josh's mobile to try and avoid me."

"Where did that yellow streak come from?" Hanna muttered. "So what's happened about the auditor?"

"He's been here for most of the day, and I'm due to see Richard Pryce on Friday to go over the findings."

"I take it you've told Richard about the conversation you had with Jack yesterday?"

"Yes, we spoke on the phone earlier."

"And he said?"

"Not much really."

"No, lawyers never do, but he must have been mightily impressed by Jack's suggestion that you transfer your money to him."

"In order to cheat my publisher of it. You know, I don't think he even sees it that way."

"Whether he does or doesn't, I wouldn't trust him with a dime of my hard-earned money after all this. Tell me how you're feeling."

"If you really want to know, terrible. It's like it's all starting to crowd in on me now, getting bigger and heavier and darker . . . I keep reminding myself I should hate him, but that doesn't help, because I don't actually want to hate him. I just want to go back to the way things were. OK, I know it's not going to happen, but you can't just wipe out fourteen years of your life as if they meant nothing. . . ." She took a breath. "I keep wondering if it was losing his job that changed him, or if it was something I did."

"Losing his job was hard," Hanna agreed, "we know that from the depression he sank into, and looking back I'd say he's been quite . . . *extreme* since then. You know, the way he suddenly bounced you all off to the Gower without much of a discussion. Then he was launching a new business, joining every society and club going . . . Maybe we shouldn't even get into all the money he's spent on cars and gadgets and heaven only knows what else. It's as though he's lost his brakes, or his off switch, or his reality checks, and this affair with Martha is another example. He can't just have an affair, as if that's not bad enough; he has to abandon his family and go and live with her. I mean, how extreme is that?"

Though these same thoughts had been going round in Jenna's head for days now, it was the first time she'd heard them spoken out loud, and while in a way they were giving her hope that there might be a cure for Jack's excessiveness, in another way she felt horribly flattened by them. "Even if he is experiencing some sort of backlash from losing his job, which is what I guess you're saying," she responded, "I'd never get him to admit it, much less to see anyone about it."

"No, I don't suppose you would, but I think it's something worth mentioning to Richard when you see him, because if this does end up in court it could help your case no end if it turns out your husband has a mental condition."

Jenna flinched. Jack with a mental condition? It just didn't seem feasible, much less anywhere she wanted to go. What would it mean for their three youngest children? "Maybe it's a midlife crisis," she suggested, realizing even as she said it that this new label wasn't really making anything better.

"Whatever it is, it has the potential for getting you into a lot of trouble, and it has to be sorted out."

Since there was no arguing with that, Jenna said, "How's the prep for the presentation going?"

"Just fine, thanks. We're on target, so I'm hopeful we'll get it through. How are the children?"

"Up and down. It doesn't help that their father's breaking promises all over the place."

"You should keep a note of it; you never know when it might be useful."

"You mean if we end up in a custody battle?"

"I'm sorry—I know it's not what you want to hear."

"But it's practical advice, so I'll take it."

"Good. What time are you seeing Richard on Friday?"

"Five o'clock. I can't get into Swansea because I have to collect the children from school—Mum's got bell-ringing practice
and she's giving up enough of her time already. So he suggested
coming here on his way home."

"That's kind of him. Does he live nearby?"

"Not really. Bena says he's in Caswell."

"That's the posh part, isn't it, close to Mumbles?"

"You could see it that way."

"If he's a successful lawyer, and we know he is, he'll be in one
of the big houses overlooking the bay. Did Bena also tell you
he's a widower?"

"Yes, she did. Hanna, I know you've never been overly fond
of Jack, but if you're—"

"Don't worry, I'm not trying to suggest anything—obviously
it's far too early days for that. But whatever happens over the
coming weeks and months, you can't deny Richard could be a
good friend to have."

Too tired to think how to respond to that, Jenna was about
to change the subject when Josh appeared in the doorway.
"What's up?" she asked, noting his stricken face. "You don't
have to keep worrying about being put on the black bench. I'm
sure it was a mistake. We'll sort it out with the teacher tomorrow."

"Dad says he can't make it for our special time on Saturday,"
he told her brokenly.

Jenna's anger immediately flared. "Hanna, I'll call you back,"
she said into the phone, and after ringing off she dialed Jack's
mobile.

"*You,*" she said to the voicemail, "are the one who told them
nothing would change, that you'd still be picking them up from
school and doing all the same things with them you always

have. Now, after letting them down three times already this week, Josh tells me you can't make his special time on Saturday. I don't know what's going on with you, and frankly I don't care, but I'm not going to have you treating the children this way. So as of now you can consider yourself banned from this family." Slamming down the phone, she went to pull Josh into her arms.

"I'm sorry," she whispered, already regretting exploding in front of him, "but I had to say something to make him realize that his behavior is wrong. We can't have him messing around with us, letting us down, and making us upset all the time, can we?"

"No," Josh murmured.

Hugging him tight, she said, "We'll find something else to do."

He nodded.

"Where's Paige?"

"In her room."

Feeling a sudden intense anger with her daughter for having abandoned the young ones to their nits and misery to go and indulge in her chat rooms or self-pity or whatever the hell she was doing, Jenna grabbed the omelette pan, emptied it into the bin, and sent a text to Paige letting her know that if she wanted to eat she could damned well make it herself.

Chapter 15

"This is monstrous behavior," Miss Kendrick declared, her steely gray eyes fixed harshly on Kelly Durham, her slim, ring-less fingers resting on the computer printouts in front of her. It was the end of the school day and almost everyone else had gone home—even the buses had left—but Miss Kendrick wasn't allowing Kelly Durham or Paige Moore to go anywhere until she'd sorted this out. "I'm appalled that you could even think anything like this," she continued, directing her wrath at Kelly, "never mind write it in a public forum. And please don't tell me it wasn't you."

"It wasn't, miss," Kelly protested, her large oval face flushed with innocence. "Where's my name? There's nothing there to say—"

"It's been traced back to you," Miss Kendrick interrupted forcefully. "You wouldn't be sitting here if it hadn't, and you have to admit, Kelly, this isn't the first time we've had this sort of trouble with you."

"Because people keep hacking into my account," Kelly cried. "It's not my fault if they know how to do it and I don't know how to stop them."

Miss Kendrick's eyes flitted to Paige.

"Frankly, miss," Kelly continued, "anyone could have done this, so I don't think you should pick on me." She should have stopped there, but didn't. "If I tell my granddad, he'll be really upset, and that's not a good way to treat someone who's made so many donations to the school."

Miss Kendrick's eyes flashed. "Many of these remarks came from *your* school account," she reminded Kelly, "and Mr. Thomas assures me there is no evidence of hacking."

Kelly threw out her immaculately manicured hands. "So someone got my password! It's happening all the time."

Miss Kendrick's expression showed how unimpressed she was.

Kelly's face tightened. "I'm telling the truth," she cried tearfully, "but I can see you'd rather believe her, because she's your favorite and everyone knows it."

Miss Kendrick still wasn't regarding her kindly. "The comments about Paige's father . . ."

"Had nothing to do with me. I don't even know him. You need to ask the person who posted it."

"Maybe you can tell me who it was."

"I swear I would if I could, but I've got no idea."

Miss Kendrick's eyes moved to Paige.

Though Paige was in no doubt that Kelly was behind it, and that she could easily use all the other abuse she'd suffered at Kelly's hands to back up her claim, she remained silent. It was bad enough that they were here at all without her doing anything to make it worse.

"I'm of two minds whether to take this to Mr. Charles," Miss Kendrick stated.

"No, please," Paige and Kelly said together.

Miss Kendrick regarded them worriedly.

Paige knew she should never have allowed Charlotte to talk to Miss Kendrick. She'd tried telling her a hundred times that it would only make things worse, but Charlotte had refused to listen, and now here they were with everything running out of control.

"I know you've got it in for me," Kelly suddenly erupted. "You always have had, just because I don't like your stupid lessons and can't stand the way you—"

"Stop it, Kelly. Stop right now."

"I will," Kelly sobbed, "but my granddad—"

"You really don't have to keep reminding me that he's a generous benefactor," Miss Kendrick interrupted. "I just need to know that you girls are friends before you leave here."

Clenching her hands tightly, Paige said, "I probably jumped to conclusions, miss."

Miss Kendrick was still staring at Kelly.

"Please, let's just forget it," Paige implored. "I didn't want to come here. . . ."

"You did the right thing."

"No, honestly. I believe Kelly's account was hacked, because it's happened to mine too."

Miss Kendrick's eyes moved between them. "Kelly," she said in the end, "do you understand that what's written here isn't only highly offensive, it could be very damaging?"

"Of course I do, miss, but I swear it wasn't me."

Miss Kendrick really didn't look like she believed her, and for several heart-stopping moments Paige was sure Kelly was going to tell Miss Kendrick to eff off, or something equally terrible. In the end nothing at all was said.

Paige reached the door first but stood aside as Kelly trod on her foot to go through ahead of her. If Miss Kendrick saw, she didn't comment, nor did Paige look back. She just wanted to get out of here and as far away from Kelly Durham as possible.

Charlotte was waiting at the end of the corridor, as were a couple of the Durmites. To Paige's surprise Charlotte seemed to be talking to them, but broke away as soon as she spotted Paige coming.

"How did it go?" she whispered, linking her arm with Paige's as they walked off toward the stairs.

"Oi, bitch," Kelly Durham hissed after them.

Paige came to a stop, hunching her shoulders.

"Don't think this is the end of it," Kelly warned.

Paige turned round. "I told her I didn't think you did it," she reminded her.

"Yeah, right, and we all believe that, don't we?"

"Why did you do it?" Charlotte demanded fiercely.

Kelly seemed about to retort when Bethany whispered something in her ear. Kelly's eyebrows rose as she looked at Charlotte again. "You've got weird taste in friends," she told her, and turning her back, she and the Durmites went off in the opposite direction.

"Why did you say you didn't think she did it?" Charlotte asked crossly as they continued down the stairs.

"Because I could tell that just being there was making things worse," Paige cried. "I told you it would."

"You had to do something."

"Well, I have now, and you heard what she just said—it's still not over."

"She only said it to save face. She won't dare to do anything like it again. You wait and see."

Not in any way convinced, Paige stopped at her locker and

took out her bag and coat. "So what were you and the others talking about while we were in there?" she asked, trying to sound casual in spite of how worried she was feeling.

Charlotte merely shrugged. "Nothing, really," she replied.

Sensing there was more, Paige insisted, "It must have been something."

Charlotte turned to look at her. "Actually, I didn't want to tell you this," she said, making Paige's heart turn over, "but you'll find out soon enough anyway. Apparently they're going to the party on Saturday. They were trying to find out if you were too."

Paige's eyes filled with misery as it spread all the way through her. "So everyone's invited except me?"

"Not everyone, just them, and you wouldn't want to go with them there anyway."

It was true, she wouldn't, but it was still a terrible feeling knowing she was excluded. "I might try and see if I can get Julie to meet up with me at the weekend," she said, more to remind herself and Charlotte that she had another friend than because she actually meant it.

Though Charlotte didn't seem to approve, all she said was, "If she will, at least you'll know then who she really is."

Paige was suddenly struggling with tears. "Actually, if she's Owen or Kelly or Bethany, as you seem to think, she'll be at the party with you," she told Charlotte, walking away.

Charlotte hurried after her. "Don't be upset," she urged, trying to put an arm around her.

Pulling away, Paige said, "It's all right for you—they never pick on you. You don't know what it's like always being made to feel small or horrible or like you're nobody."

"I know, but—"

"I don't know how you can even speak to them when they're being so mean to me."

"All I said was that I'm going to the party on Saturday."

"I bet it was more than that. I bet you know what they're going to be wearing, and you told them you're borrowing my blue dress, except no way would you tell them it's mine."

"Paige, that's not—"

"Why don't they ever have a go at you, Charlotte? You say whatever you like to them, but they never turn on you the way they turn on me, and I don't even say anything."

"Then maybe you should."

"And what? Get myself beaten up for my trouble? They're never going to leave me alone, and I can tell you're going to be friends with them from now on, so you might as well go and be with them now."

"Paige!" Charlotte called after her. "Paige, stop."

Paige ran even faster, clutching her book bag to her chest, trying to catch her breath as she sobbed. She'd give anything in the world for her mum or dad to be waiting at the gates now, or her grandma, or Auntie Hanna, but the only person there was Lucy, Charlotte's mum, who would just keep asking her about what was happening with her parents all the way home, and she really didn't want to talk about them or anything else right now. So she just kept on running, along the street and down the side lane where no one could see her, and where she could hide until Charlotte and her mum had gone home.

The house was the tidiest Jenna had seen it in a long time, mostly thanks to her mother, who had spent the best part of the day clearing away toys, repacking DVDs, and turning up long-lost shoes, shirts, hairbands, and missing pieces of jigsaws. While all this was going on Jenna had been in town with Bena, picking up groceries, dry cleaning, and assorted presents for upcoming birthdays—and doing her best not to torment herself with what was really going on in her life. She'd also, because Bena had accompanied her to the door to make sure it happened, luxuriated in a neck and shoulder massage at a salon she hadn't visited in too long, and ended up being talked into a manicure as well.

She'd known, of course, that Hanna was behind the double makeover of her and the house, not only to try to cheer her up a little but also to get them looking their best for Richard when he came at five.

No, I am not trying to do any matchmaking, Hanna had hotly responded to Jenna's exasperated text. *I just want you to feel good about yourself so you're in the right mood to deal with whatever Richard has to say. Will call later when presentation is over. Remember you're beautiful and I love you very much. Hxxx*

Jenna wasn't feeling very beautiful or loved as she pulled up outside the house and dashed inside to avoid the rain. In fact, now that she was home and the little perks of the day were over, she was starting to wish she'd gone to collect the children from school, as originally planned. If she had, she'd be too preoccupied now even to think of how she looked or felt. As it was, she was sinking into an awful place of loneliness as she pictured Jack scooping them up as they ran out of school before taking them off somewhere for tea.

"I'm not having you banning me from seeing them just because I've had to cry off a couple of times," he'd informed Jenna tersely earlier in the day. "I'll go this afternoon, it'll be a nice surprise. And I'll have them home by six."

She hadn't argued, mainly because it would mean a quiet house while Richard was there. Otherwise she'd almost certainly have put her foot down and told him that he didn't get to pick and choose when it worked for him, as if she had no life, no commitments, nothing outside his and the children's needs. Never mind that it might be true; she simply wasn't prepared to have him bursting in and out of their schedules as though he were the only one who mattered.

"Waffle!" she called as she began unpacking the shopping. "Where are you, sweetie?"

Expecting to hear him thump down off someone's bed, or trot in from one of the sofas, it took a moment for her to realize it hadn't happened. Curious, she stopped what she was doing and went to call him again.

"He's up here with me," Paige shouted from her room.

Surprised that Paige was home, Jenna shouted back, "I thought you were having tea at Charlotte's."

Paige came to open her door. "I texted to tell you my plans had changed but obviously you didn't bother to read it."

Remembering a message had arrived while she was driving, Jenna said, "Is everything all right with you and Charlotte?"

Paige gave a surly sort of shrug.

Sighing, Jenna caught Waffle by the collar as he bounded down the stairs to greet her. "What did you fall out about?"

"I never said we fell out," Paige snapped. "Oh, and by the way, someone's been in my room tidying up. I've told you a thousand times . . ."

"Grandma can't help herself, you know that, and she's not the type to pry, so don't worry—your secrets are safe."

"Who says I've got secrets?"

Jenna merely looked at her.

"What?"

"I wish I knew," Jenna sighed. "I'm expecting a visitor at five. We'll go over to the office, so—"

"Who is it?"

"Nobody you know."

"So why can't you tell me who it is?"

Biting back a sharp retort, Jenna said, "If you must know, he's a lawyer."

As Paige's eyes widened, Jenna felt her panicked suspicion. "So you're getting a divorce?"

"No, that's not what it's about."

"So what is it about?"

"Some things to do with the company."

"Does that mean Dad's coming?"

"No. He's taking Josh and the twins out for tea."

"So you're letting him see them again."

"I never really stopped it. Are you going out later?"

"Like where?"

"Like anywhere."

"What difference does it make?"

Reminding herself that these conversations never led anywhere useful, Jenna simply shook her head and turned back to the kitchen.

A few minutes later Paige was standing in the doorway.

"If you're here to try and pick an argument . . . ," Jenna said.

"I'm not. I was just thinking . . . Is Dad coming in when he brings the others home?"

"I don't know. Why? Do you want to see him?"

"Not really."

"So why are you asking?"

Paige shrugged, watching as Jenna put things away in cupboards. "Do you reckon," she said eventually, "you two will ever get back together?"

Jenna's heart thumped. "You probably won't want to hear this," she replied, not wanting to hear it herself, "but I really don't think it's what Dad wants."

"Have you asked him?"

"No."

"Maybe you should."

"It's not as simple as that."

"I don't see why not. If he knows you want him . . ."

"He knows. He's always known, but it didn't stop him getting involved with Martha." Turning to her daughter curiously, she said, "Are you having some boyfriend issues? Is that what this is really about?"

Paige drew back. "No! What makes you say that?"

"I just wondered. You know, if there is anything, I'm always here."

"Like when you're not searching for nits, or cooking someone's tea, or brushing their hair, or looking for their shoes, or giving them a bath, or rowing with Dad . . ."

"What's this about?" Jenna demanded. "Are you saying I'm neglecting you?"

"I'm just saying, you're always busy, so even if I wanted to talk, which I don't—"

"I think you do."

Paige's eyes flashed. "OK. So when are we supposed to be having our next special time?" she challenged. "I don't expect you've even thought about that, have you?"

Jenna sighed. "The honest answer is no, I haven't, but not because I don't want it. It's just with everything else that's happening . . . We'll work something out, I promise, and you should ask Dad when you're next having special time with him."

"I know when that's meant to be, but he's bound to have forgotten."

"I'm sure he hasn't."

"Even if he hasn't, I'm not going. Anyway, he'll just let me down the way he has Josh this weekend."

"Which reminds me, we should do something to try and make up for it. In fact, why don't you give Flora some special time—you know how much she'd love that—and I'll do something with Josh and Wills?"

"Great. Just what I want, to spend my Saturday babysitting a five-year-old while everyone else is at the match or going to a party."

"If you have a party to go to . . ."

"I don't, so it's cool. I'll do something with Flora. Happy now?"

Jenna put a hand to her head. "Paige, I don't know what you want me to say."

"You don't have to say anything. I get how much I matter round here."

"Stop that right now," Jenna snapped. "Don't you think this is hard enough without you constantly getting at me? Why don't you try to be helpful, or sympathetic, or a *grown-up* for once in your life?"

"Because I'm not a bloody grown-up," Paige shouted back. "I'm fifteen, and you're expecting me to behave like I'm thirty. And you're not the only one he's gone off and left. He left us too, but no one cares about that."

"Everyone cares about it, including him," Jenna cried, "but right now there's nothing I can do to change it. You need to speak to him. Ask him to explain—" She broke off at the sound of the doorbell. "That'll be the lawyer," she said tiredly. "We'll continue this later."

Without answering, Paige stood sulkily aside so Jenna could go to the front door.

"Richard," she said warmly, inviting him in from the porch. "Did you get my message? I could have come to you."

"It's no problem," he assured her, ruffling the fur of an enthusiastic Waffle. "I was happy to get away from the office. And who are you?" he asked the dog.

"This is Waffle," Jenna said with a smile. "As you can see, he doesn't like to be ignored."

"Which makes him just like my own retriever," he chuckled, "and if I had my walking coat on, I could probably produce a treat."

"Don't worry, he doesn't go short," Jenna assured him. "Please, come in. Can I get you some tea or coffee?"

"Only if you're having something," he responded, breaking into a smile as he spotted Paige.

"This is my elder daughter, Paige," Jenna told him. "Paige, this is—"

"Richard," he interrupted, holding out a hand to shake. "It's lovely to meet you."

"And to meet you," she replied politely. "Mum says you're a lawyer."

His eyes turned playfully wary. "I hope that doesn't paint me in a bad light."

She almost smiled. "I suppose that depends whose side you're on."

He laughed. "Well, today it's definitely yours. Am I allowed to ask what school you go to?"

"The Landings."

He seemed pleased. "I have a son who goes there," he said. "Perhaps you know him."

To Jenna's surprise Paige's face flushed crimson, though it was doubtful Richard noticed, as his phone rang at that moment.

"I'm sorry, will you excuse me?" he said. "This is my other son, who's ringing to let me know how he got on in an exam today. It won't take a moment."

As he turned away to take the call, Jenna said to Paige, "Are you all right?"

Still flushed, Paige muttered, "Of course, why wouldn't I be? And you don't have to go over to the office on my account. I'm going back upstairs."

"Do you want a drink?"

"I had one when I came in. Oh, by the way, I've got a new art project. We're supposed to make a Venetian-style mask."

Jenna regarded her steadily. "Are you going to ask Dad to help you?"

Paige shook her head as she glanced at Richard. "I thought you might, if you can find the time."

Though Jenna was pleased to be asked, she couldn't help the wrenching sadness inside. Jack had always helped with the art projects. "We'll make a start over the weekend," she promised as Richard finished his call.

Saying no more, Paige took herself back to her room.

A while later Jenna and Richard were seated either end of the kitchen sofa, with two mugs of tea and a detailed copy of the auditor's report between them.

"Basically, what it's telling us," Richard was saying, "is that the sums obtained from your contributors remain the biggest and most immediate problem. The good part of that is there were no hidden issues waiting to bite us. The not-so-good part is that the actual amount is a little more than initially thought, but luckily not significantly so. I know your husband claims that various marketing packages were being offered in return for the payments, but there doesn't seem to be any evidence of these packages actually existing. Certainly there are enquiries, proposals, and estimates that would suggest some efforts have been made in this direction, but as far as Sean could ascertain, no contracts have been signed with a supplier, so there is no product, as such, for your company to provide in return for the writers' investments."

Jenna's throat was dry; she felt overwhelmed by disappointment and humiliation. "So he really has cheated them," she said quietly.

Richard's eyes were gentle. "I'm afraid that is how it's looking," he agreed.

She tried to swallow. "So what happens next?"

He gave it a moment, apparently waiting until he was sure of her complete attention. "You have a couple of options," he replied in a tone that held no hint of foreboding. "You can report it to the police, which is actually what should happen now that you know a crime has been committed, unless you want to find yourself facing a charge of conspiring to pervert the cause of justice, and I'm sure you don't."

Jenna felt the blood chilling in her veins. "So I will be held accountable?" she said.

"It's certainly possible, unless we can prove that you knew nothing about it."

"I didn't," she assured him. "I know that sounds unlikely, but I swear I had absolutely no idea."

"I'm not doubting you, but if this does go any further, there's every chance the Crown Prosecution Service will hold you and your husband jointly responsible. Unless, of course, your husband is prepared to admit that he went behind your back to obtain the money. Do you think he would?"

Jenna's sigh caught in her heart. "The honest answer is that I don't know," she replied. "Until all this happened—" She cut herself off, not wanting to get into some excruciating self-pitying diatribe about how he wasn't the man she'd married and how betrayed she was feeling. "My biggest fear," she said, "is that he's trying to get me sent to prison so he'll get custody of the children."

Richard's eyes narrowed. "Has he said as much?"

Jenna shook her head. "No, but if he could land it all on me—"

"Let me stop you there. He really won't be able to do that. There is far too much incriminating evidence in his own files and emails for him to escape prosecution. But before we go any further down that road, let's take a look at a second option."

Relieved to know there was one, though still anxious over what it might be, she waited for him to continue.

"We can be fairly certain," he began, "that none of your contributors has gone to the police themselves yet. If they had, someone from the Fraud Squad would already have been in touch. I take it no one has?"

She shook her head. "Unless they've spoken to Jack and he hasn't told me."

"I think that's unlikely, because if there had been contact they'd have taken your computers by now. So for the moment it would appear that the writers are still prepared to believe that the marketing strategies they've been promised will go into action as soon as the site goes live. However, as we know from recent emails, some are already beginning to harbor suspicions, and the longer the site launch is delayed the greater the probability becomes that someone will contact the police. So what I'm proposing, or asking, actually, is how possible would it be to repay the money, preferably within the next couple of weeks?"

Jenna's insides jarred as her hopes fell into despair. "Not possible at all," she admitted. "I have just over fifteen thousand pounds in my personal account, which doesn't cover it, and anyway I'm going to need it for the children and me to live on until I can find some sort of job."

"And what about your husband? Could he find the money?"

A fleeting image of Jack's wealthy girlfriend flashed in her mind, but she wasn't going to bring her up now, when Richard was watching her so closely. How pathetic he must be finding her, how stupid and naive to have got herself into this position. Not that it should matter what he thought, but for some reason it seemed to. "He's claiming not to have any," she replied. "He says everything he transferred from the company has gone, spent by me. On the family, of course, not me personally."

Nodding his understanding, he said, "If necessary we'll ask him to provide proof of his finances, but first I think we need to establish if there is a way to avoid a prosecution by refunding the money. Do you have a mortgage on this house?"

She shook her head. "We bought it outright from . . ." Her eyes went to his. "I don't think we do," she corrected, "but for all I know he might have taken one out without me knowing." *Please God, don't let that be the case.* If they owed money on the house on top of everything else, they were never going to survive this. They'd lose their home and their liberty, the children would be taken into care . . .

As though sensing her rising panic, he said quite firmly, "It's highly unlikely he'd have been able to obtain a mortgage without your knowledge."

"But not impossible?"

Instead of answering, he said, "We need to take one step at a time. First we must fully ascertain what chance there is of satisfying the contributors."

"But even if we could do that, how can we be sure it would stop them going to the police? I'm thinking of how crushed their hopes are going to be, and how angry, or vengeful, that might make some of them."

"It's true, you might well have to contend with some mighty Welsh wrath, but if we can show that they've been completely reimbursed, with an accompanying letter of profound and sincere apology, I doubt the CPS will want to use up valuable resources to take it any further."

"But first we have to find a way of repaying it."

Since it wasn't a question, he didn't answer, but simply sat quietly watching her with an expression she found hard to read, although nothing in his manner suggested he was thinking the worst of her or considering what he himself could suggest.

"If there isn't already a mortgage on the house," she said, "then that would be one way of raising . . . Except neither of us has an income, so no one's going to lend us any money."

Acknowledging that with a nod, he said, "Is there a relative who might be willing to help out?"

She felt her hands clenching together as she thought of her mother, but there was no way in the world she could turn to

SUSAN LEWIS

her. She'd done so much for them already, and it wasn't even as if she had very much. Hanna did, of course, but she was afraid Hanna might rather see Jack in prison than offer a single cent to save his skin. Besides, she and Kay were already covering the cost of the lawyer, and Jenna still had no idea how she was going to pay them back for that. Once her fifteen thousand pounds ran out, which would be in a matter of months, perhaps a year if she was careful, she was too afraid even to think of what she and the children were going to do—or where Jack might be by then.

"My husband has a brother," she said hoarsely. "Maybe he could speak to him." She looked at Richard again and this time felt only relief that he was there, quietly supporting, advising, and not appearing in any way overly anxious. "I'm sure you must have a very dim view of my husband by now," she commented.

Though he didn't deny it, what he said was, "It's very easy to make mistakes, but not always so easy to put them right."

Wasn't that the truth? "My sister thinks his extreme behavior, as she puts it, is evidence of some sort of personality disorder."

His eyebrows rose. "And what do you think?"

With a certain wryness she replied, "I've seen enough friends go through this kind of breakup to know that saying your husband's off his head or experiencing some kind of midlife crisis is pretty standard. I suppose it provides something to hold on to, a kind of hope that allows you to think he'll get over it or seek some sort of help that'll guide him back to the fold. The only trouble is that if a man actually leaves his wife for another woman, he almost never comes back."

Realizing how close she suddenly was to tears, she quickly got up to spare them both the embarrassment. "I'm sorry," she said, glancing at the clock, "I didn't realize how late it was. He should be here any minute with the children."

"In which case," he said, getting to his feet, "I should be going."

She was glad he didn't add that Jack finding him here would be awkward all round. They both knew that, anyway.

"Thank you for everything," she said, walking him to the door. "You've made the situation very clear, so all I have to decide now is what I'm going to do next."

"Call me when you're ready," he replied, "but you probably shouldn't leave it too long."

"Who was that I just saw driving out of here?" Jack asked as he came in the door a few minutes later.

Jenna didn't look up from washing Wills's face. "His name's Richard Pryce," she replied evenly. "You received a letter from him."

"You mean the lawyer you . . . So what was he doing here?"

"Outlining my options. Wills, hold still."

"But you're hurting me."

"Well, if you will get ink all over you . . ."

"Josh did it, not me."

"Dad! Dad!" Flora cried, bursting into the kitchen. "We've got to make Mother's Day cards for Mummy at school and Miss Saunders said we need to take in some glue and sparkles."

"You're not supposed to ask him in front of Mummy," Wills exclaimed. "You've spoiled the surprise now."

Flora's eyes rounded with concern.

Jenna smiled. "Don't worry, I knew it was coming up," she told her, "and I'm sure Grandma will take you to buy everything you need."

"It's OK, I'll take them," Jack interjected brusquely.

Not arguing, Jenna reached for a towel and treated Wills to a giant smackeroo as she dried him.

"You're so sloppy," Wills complained. "Girls are really sloppy, aren't they, Dad?"

Grabbing Flora, Jack said, "Yes, but we wouldn't have them any other way, would we?"

"Stop, stop!" Flora protested. "You're scratching me. Daddy! You need a shave."

Setting her down, he watched her and Wills rush off to their video games, or TV programs, or whatever they had planned before bathtime. Then, closing the door, he turned back to Jenna.

Before he could say anything, she said, "Paige has a new art project. I think you should offer to help with it."

"I would if I thought she'd let me."

"You can at least try asking."

"Is she here?"

"In her room, as usual."

"Then I'll go up when we've finished here."

Jenna was picking up discarded boots, bags, and coats. She had no desire to discuss anything with him right now, but as Richard had reminded her when he was leaving, time wasn't on their side. So, coming straight to the point, she said, "The only way we're going to avoid prosecution is if we repay every last penny that you charged for services you had no intention of providing."

His face immediately darkened. "What the hell is that supposed to mean? I told you there are marketing strategies—"

"That don't actually exist. The auditor's been through your computer and found no evidence of a package of any sort that you could provide in return for the writers' investments. That's fraud, Jack, plain and simple."

"Just because the information isn't on my computer doesn't mean it doesn't exist."

"Then where is it?"

"On the computers in Martha's office. Her team have been drawing up—"

"I'm not listening to this. You've played me for a fool for far too long, and it's going to stop. If those packages existed, if they were legitimate or even viable, they would have been sent to the writers by now."

"And how do you know they haven't?"

"Because you're being bombarded with emails asking when they can see a finalized version of the bullshit you sent them in the first place. What the hell were you thinking? 'National media coverage, newspaper serialization, worldwide exposure . . .' I can only wonder that they were stupid enough to believe it, but then again, I of all people know how convincing you can be. Well, you're going to have to be pretty convincing now if you don't want to end up in court."

"It's not going to happen."

"No, it won't, as long as we pay the money back. I don't have the funds to cover it, and you're saying you don't either, so you'll have to borrow it. Please tell me you haven't already mortgaged the house."

"I'm not dignifying that with an answer."

Her blood ran cold. "Jack, have you . . . ?"

"No! I have not mortgaged the house."

Needing to believe him, at least for now, she said, "Then there's a chance you could—"

"I've just told you, the marketing plans are in place."

"Then show me. Get them up on the computer right now and let me see what you're offering for an investment of up to seven thousand pounds that's ready to go live on the website."

"They're still finalizing things."

"And you're still stalling. Face it, Jack, you've created a situation you don't know how to get out of, so I'm trying to do it for you, but you have to help me. We need close to thirty thousand pounds within the next couple of weeks or the police are going to be knocking at this door. For all I know they'll end up coming anyway, but Richard, the lawyer, is doing his best to prevent that from happening."

"By getting us to pay back money we don't have. Great plan! And there's no point talking about a mortgage, because I've already tried and got turned down."

Torn between relief and outrage that he'd gone behind her back, she said, "Then we—*you*—have to find another way to come up with it."

He glared at her furiously.

"You're the one who got us into this," she pointed out.

"Maybe your mother would like—"

"Stop right there," she seethed. "Hell will freeze over before you'll get me to ask for her help. This is your problem, Jack. You created it, and it's up to you to get yourself out of it. Maybe you can talk to your brother, or perhaps your girlfriend won't see thirty grand as too high a price to pay for keeping her lover in her bed."

Clearly bursting with rage, he snatched his keys from the

worktop and leaned in toward her menacingly. "I can see there's no reasoning with you. You've got all this crap stuck in your head."

"Prove to me it's crap and we might get somewhere."

He turned away. "You just keep telling yourself your little stories, and with any luck you might find one good enough to send in to your publisher."

Grabbing the nearest thing to hand, she flung it at him, and watched a blackcurrant juice carton explode all over his face. "I'll tell the children you had urgent business," she spat. "Now get the hell out of here before I end up doing something I actually regret."

Chapter 16

Paige grunted as her head hit the wall so hard she saw stars.

She was in the girls' toilets being held by her hair and arms as Kelly Durham, Bethany Gates, and Matilda Watts took turns to slap her face and punch her. She was crying and begging them to stop, but they were having far too much fun to break off anytime soon.

"I served a fucking detention for you," Kelly snarled. "Now say you're sorry and lick my shoes."

"Please leave me alone," Paige sobbed. "I'm sorry about the detention . . ."

"Lick my fucking shoes," Kelly barked.

Matilda jabbed her head toward Kelly's feet.

"I know, let's stick her head down the bog," Bethany suggested excitedly.

"Brilliant," Kelly declared.

"Yeah, but one of us ought to pee first," Matilda piped up.

Kelly snickered. "Let that be me," she decided, and disappeared into a cubicle.

Minutes later Paige was gagging and choking as they forced

her to drink from the bottom of the bowl. Someone pulled the flush and water gushed over her head.

"Please, please, no more," she gasped, struggling for air.

"Shut the fuck up," Kelly spat. "We don't want to hear your whining."

"We ought to drown her," Matilda cried eagerly.

"Ssh, someone's coming," Bethany hissed.

Charlotte appeared in the doorway, and when she saw what was happening her face turned white with shock. "What the hell are you doing?" she exclaimed, rushing to Paige. "Get away from her. Get away now or I'm going straight to Mr. Charles." As she pulled Paige back from the loo the Durmites began melting away, muttering a warning to Charlotte that she'd get the same treatment if she didn't start minding her own business.

"Are you all right?" Charlotte asked anxiously, helping Paige to her feet. "I was looking for you, and someone said they saw you come in here. They are such fucking bitches. I want to kill every one of them."

Paige was still gagging and panting as she splashed clean water over her face, not caring about her makeup, just desperate to get the stench of urine out of her mouth and nose. "I didn't realize they were in here," she sobbed. "As soon as I did I tried to get out again, but they grabbed me and they . . . and they . . ."

"It's all right," Charlotte said, trying to soothe her. She tugged paper towels from the holder to help dry her hair. "You're OK now, and we're going straight back to Miss—"

"No!" Paige pleaded. "That's why they did this, to punish me for going to her in the first place."

Charlotte regarded her helplessly. She couldn't argue, because Paige was right: going to Miss Kendrick had definitely made things worse. They'd never attacked Paige physically before, and the messages she was receiving now were so gross and hateful it was no wonder Paige was getting into such a state over them. At least Charlotte and Paige were friends again after that stupid falling-out over Charlotte speaking to the Durmites, or Paige would have no one.

"Here," she said gently, passing Paige more paper towels. "It'll be all right, I promise."

Paige didn't respond. Why bother pointing out that nothing ever would be all right again when Charlotte didn't understand what it was like to be Kelly Durham's victim or to have her dad walk out and her mum fall apart? Charlotte's life was so totally different, with her together parents, her boyfriend, her freedom to move about the school any way she wanted to, that Paige could only imagine how lovely it was to be her.

"Come on, we're already late," Charlotte said, looking anxiously at Paige's hair. "Do you have a scrunchie or something to tie it up with?"

Paige shook her head.

Charlotte didn't have one either. "You'll have to plait it," she decided.

"We don't have time."

"Do it as we go."

A few minutes later they crept quietly into their geography class, where Mrs. Spinetti was already handing out last week's homework. "You're late," she barked. "You know I don't tolerate . . . Paige, why is your hair wet? It's not raining."

Paige's heart hammered as she tried to think what to say. She could feel everyone's eyes on her, especially Kelly Durham's, daring her to cough out the truth. "I—um, I spilled something on it," she mumbled. "Some paint, so I had to wash it out."

"Actually, miss—" Charlotte began.

The teacher wasn't listening. "Well, we can't have you sitting here dripping all over the place. Go and see the nurse, get yourself sorted out."

Leaving the class, Paige returned to the girls' toilets, where she carried on drying her hair with paper towels before going to her locker and taking out her coat. She felt sick to her very core, so wretched, ugly, and hated that she wished she could just disappear and never have to see herself or anyone else ever again.

A letter fell from her locker, and she stooped to pick it up. Seeing her name in cut-out newsprint letters on the front, she felt herself choking with misery again, and she stuffed the letter in her pocket.

They were never going to leave her alone. This was never going to end, and she couldn't stand it.

She wasn't really sure where she was going now; she just had to get away from here. And if she ended up being run over by a bus somewhere out on the Bryn, or murdered by some pervert who might be hanging around in his creepy van, she really wouldn't care one bit.

Jenna was pulling into the drive with Josh and the twins in the back of the car when her mobile rang. Seeing it was Charlotte, she turned off the engine and clicked on.

"Mrs. Moore? Jenna?" Charlotte said urgently. "Is Paige with you? I've been trying to get hold of her."

"No, I don't think she's home yet," Jenna replied. "I guess you've tried ringing her?"

"Yes, but her phone must be out of battery. Never mind, I'll try Hayley to see if she's with her."

Not sure if she should be worried, Jenna rang off and opened the back doors for the children to spill out and run into the house. They'd have to go out again in a quarter of an hour to get Josh to athletics, Wills to rugby, and Flora to dance. However, there should be enough time for them to wolf down some cereal and dash to the toilet while she sorted out the various kits and leotards they needed to change into.

To her relief, when she followed them into the kitchen she saw that her mother had dropped off a pile of ironing. However, to her dismay not a single item that she needed right now was amongst it, which probably meant it was either in the wash, on a floor somewhere, or stuffed in the bottom of a bag.

Leaving them to help themselves to Cheerios, she set off in search of whatever she could find, and came to a sudden stop when she realized Waffle hadn't leapt all over them as they'd come in. She was about to call him when she heard the thump of his tail on the landing.

She found him lying outside Paige's door, looking pleased to see her but apparently not inclined to move.

"Hello, sweetie," she whispered, going to smooth him. "Is she in there?"

His mouth parted in a sort of grin as he wagged his tail again.

"Paige?" she called out, knocking on the door.

No reply.

"Paige? Can I come in?"

When there was still no answer she gingerly pushed open the door and peered inside. Paige was lying on her bed facing the wall with her coat and boots still on.

"Are you asleep?" she whispered, going to her.

It seemed she was, because she didn't move as Jenna sat on

the bed and reached round to feel her forehead. She didn't seem to have a temperature, but she'd been working hard lately, so she was probably just exhausted.

After fetching a small duvet from the linen cupboard to cover her, Jenna said, "I'll be back by six. There's plenty in the fridge if you want something to eat, or Grandma should be home by five if you want to go and see her."

She waited, but there was still no response. Since she had no choice but to leave her if she was going to get the others ready in time, she tiptoed out again and ran downstairs to break up a fight.

In the end they were late for everything, with everyone in a terrible mood. Wills was furious at having to wear a pair of Josh's shorts with a safety pin in the waistband to hold them up, Josh was complaining at having to wear the wrong-color kit, and Flora was shouting that she hated her mother for forcing her to wear a Care Bears pajama top and the lime-green tights they'd bought specially for her appearance as a leek at last year's harvest festival.

As soon as she was back in the car, Jenna tried calling Paige. Finding herself going to voicemail, she rang Charlotte instead to let her know that Paige was at home and to ask if Paige had been ill during the day. However, Charlotte wasn't answering either, which wasn't a surprise once Jenna remembered that tonight was the first tennis coaching session of the season. Paige should have been there too, and since she loved tennis above most other sports and had been vowing to beat her mother by the summer without, as she'd put it, being allowed to win, Jenna wondered again if she might be coming down with something.

As she toyed with the idea of asking her mother to pop in to check on her, her mobile rang. Seeing it was Jack, she braced herself and clicked on.

"What can I do for you?" she asked shortly.

"I have a couple of things I need to tell you," he responded, "and I thought . . . I was hoping now might be a good time."

Tensing around the flare of hope that everything was falling apart with Martha, she gave him no encouragement to continue.

"First up," he said, "I don't want you to worry about repaying anything the company owes. Martha has offered to take care of it."

Jenna's eyes closed as the enormousness of the gesture seemed to drown her. "Lucky you to have a rich girlfriend," she murmured. "She must love you very much to be turning a blind eye to the fact that you cheated all those innocent people out of their money."

Not rising to it, he said, "Perhaps you could tell your lawyer."

She didn't bother to reply.

"The other thing," he continued, "is I thought I ought to let you know that I'm going to be away for a few weeks."

As the words registered she sat very still, as though not moving could stop this from going any further.

"Are you still there?" he asked.

"Yes, I'm here. Where are you going?"

"To the States. Martha and I have some business in Boston and Seattle, and we thought, as it's going to be close to Easter by the time we're done, that we'd fly her children out for a holiday after."

Jenna's mind reeled, and she tried to breathe but found she couldn't. *He* and Martha had business; Martha had children who he was going to spend Easter with, in the States, where his own children had never been but would love to go.

What could she say to that? What words existed in the English language that could even begin to express how she felt right now? Since she could find none she simply ended the call.

A while later Jenna was sitting in the dining room, staring out of the window, barely registering what was going on around her, though she'd heard Paige come downstairs a moment ago and start talking to Josh.

Was Paige all right? Hadn't she been in bed earlier, with her coat on?

Where were the twins?

Remembering they were down at her mother's, she tried to stir herself, but her limbs felt so heavy she could barely move. Maybe she'd taken the wrong dosage of Valium, but she'd needed to take something to keep herself breathing.

"What *is* that?" she heard Paige demanding.

"Peanut butter and noodles," Josh answered through a mouthful.

"You're kidding! Mum! Do you know what he's eating?"

Jenna didn't answer.

"Mum!" Paige shouted, going into the dining room. "What's the matter with you? He's eating peanut butter with his noodles, for God's sake."

Jenna turned round.

"Josh is eating—"

"Yes, I heard you, and you shouldn't be eating that, Josh. It's not good for you."

"I don't care, it's my favorite, and you said I could have anything I wanted with my noodles."

"Then I guess we're lucky you didn't choose jam or cottage cheese."

"Ugh! Yuk! Yuk! I hate cottage cheese."

Jenna felt Paige's eyes on her as she got up and went to take a bottle of wine from the fridge.

"Would you like a glass?" she offered Paige.

"No, I wouldn't," Paige retorted, "and I don't think you should either."

Jenna's eyebrows rose. "Why ever not?"

"Because . . ."

Jenna waited.

Paige colored with anger and frustration. "Because you're like you are," she cried, "and wine won't help."

"Then what will?"

"I don't know. Dad coming back, I suppose, but—"

"But we know that's not going to happen, so I'll have a glass of wine instead."

Taking the bottle from her, Paige pushed her onto a bar stool and said, "When did you last eat?"

Jenna blinked with amusement.

"I said—"

"Paige, why don't you make something for yourself and stop worrying about me?"

"Do you think I want to worry about you?" Paige exclaimed heatedly. "Hasn't it crossed your mind I might have better things to do? And I don't want to be worrying about him and the twins either, but someone has to or our whole family's going to fall apart."

"Don't cry."

"I'm not."

"We'll be fine."

"Have you seen Dad today? Is that why you're like this?"

"We spoke on the phone," Jenna told her.

"Did you row?"

"No, we didn't."

Paige looked at Josh again. Grabbing his bowl, she carried it to the bin and emptied it.

"Mum! Mum! Did you see what she did?" Josh cried angrily. "She stole my tea."

"Yes, I saw," Jenna replied. "You shouldn't have done that, Paige. He was hungry."

"I'll make you some proper food," Paige snapped at Josh. "What do you want?"

"Peanut butter and noodles."

"Don't be stupid. What about pasta and—"

"I don't want pasta."

"Egg on toast?"

"No! I want—"

"You're not having it, so *shut up.* I'll make some nachos. You like them."

Slightly appeased, since nachos were his next favorite to peanut butter, Josh watched as she took out a bag of tortilla chips and scattered them over a baking sheet.

"Do you want some?" she asked her mother as her phone bleeped with a text.

Jenna shook her head. "There's some guacamole in the fridge," she said, wandering through to the sitting room.

Finding it next to the salsa, Paige took out both cartons and reached for her phone. Seeing the message was from Kelly, she tried not to open it, but couldn't stop herself.

No words, just a photo—the same shot they'd used of her before, but this time it was attached to a totally naked body striking the kind of pose that belonged on an Internet porn site.

"What's the matter?" Josh asked as she struggled not to cry.

"Nothing," she mumbled, closing her phone down. The last thing she wanted to do now was make nachos, but Josh was waiting and her mum was on another planet and so all she could do was carry on spreading the salsa, grating the cheese, and adding some chile flakes.

"Dad!" she seethed into her phone half an hour later. She was in her bathroom with both doors firmly closed so no one could hear. "What happened when you spoke to Mum today?"

"Ah, so you're talking to me at last," he responded. "I knew it—"

"I said *what happened to Mum*?" she broke in furiously.

"Nothing happened. Why?"

"She's acting really weird. I don't know what to do."

"Tell me what's wrong with her."

"I don't know. She's strange, like she's not really here, but she is."

"Where is she now?"

"Lying down. The twins'll be back soon, and I don't want to be the one to put them to bed."

"Then ask Grandma to help."

"Mum should be doing it. I want *her* to do it, because I want everything to be normal, but it never will be now, thanks to you." Cutting the line dead, she slid to the floor and buried her face in her hands.

A moment later he rang back. "Paige, listen to me . . ."

"No! You listen to me. You haven't got the first idea of what I'm going through. You don't even care."

"Sweetheart, calm down, please. I know you're upset, and that things are difficult right now, but we can work through it. Let me meet you at school tomorrow."

"No! As long as you're living with that witch, I don't want you to come anywhere near me."

"Please don't call her that."

"Witch! Witch! Witch!" she shouted. Ringing off again, she closed the phone down completely and squeezed herself into the tightest little ball she could manage, as though it might keep everything and everyone in the whole horrible nightmare of her life from getting to her ever again.

"What's going on?" Jack demanded down the phone to Jenna. "Paige has just rung me in a terrible state saying there's something wrong with you."

"There's nothing wrong with me," Jenna informed him, "and I don't want to speak to you, so kindly get off the line."

"Not until you tell me—"

"I don't have to tell you anything. You're not running this house, or me, or the children, so mind your own business and get on with your own life."

"Jenna, you're sounding strange even to me, so what's going on? Have you taken something?"

Sighing, she said, "I got some tranquilizers from the doctor. . . ."

"Why? What kind of tranquilizers?"

"They're helping to take the edge off things, and I don't need to explain myself to you, so just do as I ask and get off the line."

"Where are the children? I hope you're not going to be driving anywhere—"

"I'm not," she said, and rang off.

A few minutes later he sent a text. *Make sure Paige is all right and don't freak her out any more than you already have.*

Letting her head fall back against the pillows, Jenna closed her eyes. She'd go to see Paige in a minute; she just needed to have a little nap first and then everything would be all right.

Chapter 17

It was the night of Cullum and Oliver's party. Paige was in her room waiting for Julie to come back online so they could carry on chatting. It had been a really terrible week at school, one of the worst so far, but at least the Durmites hadn't shoved her head down the toilet again. Instead they were doing stuff like creeping up behind her and pulling her hair so hard it made her scream, or tripping her up with a push that made sure she went down, or snatching her bag and emptying it on the ground, sometimes in puddles, before sauntering off. The texts and postings were every bit as bad—morning, noon, and night, they hardly stopped—and the whole world had seen the fake nude picture of her now. It was making her want to stay curled up in her room and never come out rather than have to face the way people were smirking and wolf-whistling as she went past, as if the photo were real when everyone surely knew it wasn't.

The ugliness had continued throughout today, in spite of it being Saturday, with the Durmites posting how relieved they were that she wasn't going to be at the party stinking the place out and spreading her STDs.

She takes getting pissed to a whole new level, one of them had commented. *She actually drinks the real stuff. Ask her, she can't deny it.*

So loads of people had asked, but she hadn't answered. She'd simply watched it all unfold and kept wondering why they wouldn't just leave her alone.

"Paige, do you want to come and watch a film with us?" her mother called through the door.

"No thanks," Paige replied.

"What are you doing in there?"

"Reviewing."

"We've hardly seen you today."

"I've got a lot to do."

"You should take a break."

"I will, tomorrow."

As she heard Jenna walking away she went to open the door. "Are you all right?" she asked when her mother turned round. She wasn't, that much was plain just from looking at her.

"I'm fine," Jenna replied. "Are you?"

Paige nodded. "I might come down in a minute," she said. "I've got to finish something first."

Jenna smiled hesitantly.

Back in her room Paige tried not to think about the way her mother was falling apart. She kept telling herself that this bad spell wouldn't last, she'd pull out of it soon, but it didn't seem to be happening. She just thanked God Grandma was around to keep an eye on things, so it wasn't all being left to her, although it didn't seem very fair on Grandma either, when she was going to be seventy next year.

Deciding she had to do her best to help out more with Josh and the twins and be a bit nicer to her mum than she had been lately, she returned to her laptop to find a message from Julie.

Are you still there?

Still here.

Sorry I had to duck out. Anyway, I was saying before, I think it's totally gross all the stuff they were saying about your dad. Everyone does. They definitely went too far this time. You were right to go to Miss K.

Paige hated even thinking about those posts. She still felt so repulsed by them that she never wanted to see her dad again. *Let's change the subject.*

Sure. Sorry.

You said it got worse after you reported them. That's definitely happening to me.

Yes, I heard what they did in the girls' toilets the other day. It's what they did to me.

What happened after that?

I can't really remember now. I don't like thinking about it.

It would just be good to know what to expect.

I wouldn't worry about it, it'll probably be different for you, anyway. Where are you now?

At home in my room.

Were you invited to the party at Cullum's?

No, not really. Were you?

Yes, but I couldn't go.

Why?

Long story—my dad's a bit of a control freak and he doesn't really believe in parties. How are things with your dad?

Terrible. My mum's taking it really hard now, I hardly know what to say to her.

So sad. Really sorry to hear that.

Thank you. I wish we could meet up.

We definitely will. Once the Durmites have moved on and left you alone. Sorry to be a wimp about it, but I just don't want to remind them I'm around. So, do you think your parents will get back together?

I don't know. I wish they would.

If you had a dad like mine you'd be glad he was gone.

Is he really that bad?

Sometimes.

Not wanting to stay on the subject of dads, Paige said, *Do you wish you were at the party?*

Definitely. Do you?

Sort of. I mean, yes, but you saw the stuff they posted on Cullum's brother's wall, you know, the photos of me and everything. I wouldn't want to face him.

Oh yeah, I'd forgotten about that. BTW I can see why you like him.

I don't.

It's OK, you don't have to hide it from me. I mean, who wouldn't fancy someone like him? He's totally drop-dead. No way is that Lindsay French good enough for him, but don't tell anyone I said that.

She's very pretty.

Not as pretty as you. That's why the Durmites are always picking on you, because they're jealous of your looks and how brainy you are.

No way am I either of those things. Is it why they picked on you, because you're brainy and pretty?

Ha ha! They just saw me as a typical victim, which I suppose I am in a way. I'm only brave when I'm behind a computer, in case you hadn't noticed. ☺

I think that's sad.

So do I, but you have to admit it's a lot easier to say things like this than it is face-to-face.

I guess, sometimes.

Checking her phone as it bleeped with a text, Paige saw it was from Charlotte and quickly clicked on. *Amazing news! Sit down before you read! Oliver and Lindsay about to break up! Liam told me, so def true! Reckon your luck is changing. Cxxx*

Feeling a rush of elation, Paige quickly sent a message back. *How's it going with Liam?*

Will tell you everything tomorrow, but reckon it's def going to happen tonight!☺xxx

Have you gone? Julie was asking.

Paige was about to say she hadn't, but then suddenly decided that she'd had enough for tonight. She only wanted to think about Oliver now, and she was going to do that downstairs, cuddled up in front of a movie with her mum and the others.

Hearing Paige going downstairs, Jenna tried to force herself up from the bed, but decided to rest for a few more minutes. Although she'd stopped taking the tranquilizers after her first unsuccessful trial, the only time she seemed able to summon any energy lately was when she argued with Jack. It was as though flames came out of her then, huge angry bursts of bitterness and frustration, but that was happening less and less as time passed, mainly because he'd stopped coming in when he brought the children home.

The writers' investments were being refunded, so that problem at least was going away. True to her word, Martha had advanced the money, and Bena was working closely with Richard to make sure that every last penny of the fraudulent charges was returned to the victims. Bena had even drafted the letter of apology to accompany the checks, which Richard had approved and Jenna had signed. Jack wasn't involving himself in the resolution at all, only in transferring the funds, though Richard was sending him copies of everything and Bena was taking much delight in forwarding disgruntled and even threatening emails to his new account.

"Let him deal with the blowback," she declared, pushing send triumphantly as she forwarded yet another email. "If this mightily pissed-off Taffy with his marvelous gift for invective doesn't spoil his day, then I'm sure we'll be able to follow it up with an even more devastating tirade from someone who can."

Jack and Martha were a couple about town now, having been photographed coming and going from two different functions this week, though the local press weren't kind to them. No one, it seemed, had respect for a man who'd abandon a wife and four children, nor did they approve of the woman who'd lured him away. Whether the negative publicity was having any effect on them or on Martha's business, only they knew, but it had elicited a great deal of sympathy for Jenna. She was receiving no end of phone calls from people she hardly knew asking if they could do anything to help, or inviting her for coffee, or lunch, or simply a walk on the beach if she felt like getting out for a while.

In fact, she only went out now to ferry the children around or to exercise Waffle. With spring under way, part of the beach at Port Eynon had been closed to dogs, so she'd taken to driving him over to Oxwich, where she was less likely to run into someone she knew. However, Waffle was much given to making friends, which he promptly did with another retriever, who turned out to be Richard's dog, Jasper. Apparently the beach over at Caswell was also a dog-free zone until after the summer, so Richard too had taken to driving to Oxwich—though Jenna had to admit to being surprised to find him there at ten-thirty on a Thursday morning. It was, he'd explained, the anniversary of his wife's death, so he'd decided not to go into the office that day.

They'd ended up walking together as the dogs chased each other in and out of the waves and the wind swept gently over the dunes. He'd talked openly and tenderly about the woman he still missed every day, and her struggle with the cancer that had finally claimed her. He'd told her about his sons and how proud he was of them, when he wasn't exasperated or worried or wondering what the heck one or the other of them would get up to next. For Jenna it was a relief not to have to talk about anything; she simply listened to the details of someone else's life and felt for his loss while admiring how he was getting through it. Though she wasn't proud of it, she couldn't stop herself wishing Jack had died; at least then her memories would be intact and she wouldn't constantly have to be dealing with the engulfing cruelty of rejection. There were even times, usually during the darkest, bleakest hours of the night, when she fantasized about killing him, or Martha, or both. It happened in these situations—the courts were full of such cases—and she could completely understand why.

The next time she ran into Richard walking his dog had been this morning, and they'd ended up wandering off the beach into the Oxwich Bay Hotel for a coffee. The staff there clearly knew him, and offered as warm a welcome to Waffle and Jasper as they did to their human guests. It was a place full of memories for them both. Jack had brought Jenna here on

their last anniversary, and Paige had chosen it for her most recent special time with both parents. Apparently Richard and
his wife had stayed here on several occasions over the years as
well, using it as a romantic getaway when pressures of time
wouldn't allow them to travel far.

Though they'd made an arrangement to meet up again next
Sunday, Jenna had rung him earlier after receiving a call from
the police. Apparently one of the contributors had decided that
a full refund and apology just didn't hack it when it came to the
decimation of her dreams. She'd truly believed in Celticulture's
promises to publish and market her on a national, even global
scale, and now she wanted to make sure that they suffered the
consequences of their deceit.

"Don't worry," Richard had responded calmly. "Just tell me
who you spoke to and I'll take it from here."

After passing on the officer's name, she'd said, "I'm really
sorry. I guess it was naive to think it would all just go away and
get forgotten."

"There's nothing wrong with hoping it might, but you know
what Congreve said about hell having no fury like a woman
scorned, and this woman's Welsh, remember, so it's quite possible she makes a career out of proving Congreve right."

Jenna had smiled. "That doesn't sound like any of the Welsh
women I know."

"Take it from someone whose grandmothers, mother, aunts,
sisters, and female cousins are all Welsh—they're not someone
you'd want to be on the wrong side of. Anyway, I'll call one of
my friendlier contacts at police HQ in Bridgend. I don't think
there'll be too much trouble making this disappear, given the
full reimbursement and apology. There just isn't the time or

manpower to follow up on something that's essentially been resolved."

"Should I tell Jack about it?" she asked. "Actually, I think I will. In fact, before you make that call, why don't we give the perpetrator of this crime the opportunity to do something for the wronged woman himself?"

With a smile in his voice, Richard said, "It's your decision, but if I were you I'd want to know it was sorted out."

"I do, but I still think Jack has got away with too much already."

"Indeed he has, but in my opinion you don't need this hanging over you any longer than it has to."

Accepting that he was right, she agreed to let him make the call to his contact while she rang Jack. When he didn't pick up she left a message on his voicemail saying that she hoped it wouldn't affect his upcoming trip to the States, but the police had been in touch and she'd given them his number, so he probably ought to be prepared for further enquiries.

"Why did you give them my number?" he demanded when he rang straight back. "What are you trying to do?"

"I'm not trying to *do* anything. I was simply pointing the police in the direction of the person who committed the fraud."

"And that's what you said, was it? That I committed the fraud?"

"Not in those exact words, but we both know it was you, so we don't have to pretend with each other."

After a short, furious pause, he said, "You need to get over it."

Her temper instantly flared. "What I need is for you to own up to what you really are: a liar, a cheat, an adulterer, a fraudster. I just wish to God you weren't the father of my children, because they really don't deserve someone as lowdown and worthless as you."

The line had gone dead at that point and he hadn't rung back, although he had texted to ask for the police officer's name. She hadn't replied yet and she probably wouldn't bother. Let him sweat, let him suffer, let him get worked up into a state of abject panic over what his future might be, the way she did over hers.

If only revenge made her feel better, provided even some momentary relief, but it rarely did. Indeed, it could end up making her feel worse.

Was anything *ever* going to make her feel better?

It was Sunday morning, and Charlotte was shouting angrily at Paige over FaceTime. "Yes, I've seen the posts this morning. They're horrible! Sick! Which is why you have to tell your mum. If you don't, I'll tell mine."

"Don't you dare."

"So you want this to carry on?"

"My mum's not in a good place."

"I get that, but it's not your fault."

"I'm not saying it is, but if you tell your mum what's happening to me I'll tell her what you did with Liam last night."

Charlotte's face turned white. "You bitch," she hissed. "I told you that in confidence."

"If you want your mum to know you're not a virgin anymore . . ."

Charlotte gasped. "What the hell's the matter with you?"

"I might ask you the same question. You said you saw the

posts this morning, and you're the only one who knows about Julie. I've never told anyone else."

"So it's obvious, isn't it? She posted them herself."

"She says she didn't."

"And you believe her rather than me? Jesus Christ, Paige, I thought I was supposed to be your best friend."

"So did I, but I'm not so sure anymore."

"In that case, you can just fuck off. No way am I standing up for you in the future. You're on your own with the Durmites. And perhaps they're right about you—you are a loser and maybe your dad did leave home because of you."

As the screen went blank Paige jabbed off her own connection and clasped her hands to her face. Julie wasn't online now; she'd had to break off a few minutes ago, but she'd promised to come back as soon as she could. She'd been as shocked as Paige when the latest posts had gone up, and Paige really couldn't see that she'd have written them herself.

Paige No Moore is a lezzie who drinks piss and has sex with her father. She hangs round girls' loos drinking from the bowl if they don't flush. She's especially into her friend Julie's piss who . . .

Paige couldn't read any more. It had been bad enough the first time; looking at it again would only make it worse, if it could actually get any worse, and she was finding that hard to imagine. She desperately wanted to deny it, to say what had really happened in the girls' loos that day, but knew that if she did they'd manage to twist everything she said into meaning something else. Or they'd bring up about her dad again, or the letter someone had stuffed in her locker that she'd forgotten about until last night.

She still had it, even though she knew she should have thrown it away as soon as she'd realized what it was. In case she'd been in any doubt they'd put a note in with it: *This razor blade is for you. You know what to do with it.*

The reason she hadn't got rid of it was because she was starting to think that maybe this was the only way she could make it stop. Everything was so horrible in her life that there seemed no point to it anymore. The Durmites were just going to go on and on bullying her, her dad was never coming back, her mum was too sad and too busy with the younger ones even to notice what was happening to her. And now Charlotte had told someone about Julie, which went to show that Charlotte had probably never been on her side anyway. She'd just pretended to be so she could get information out of her to pass on to the Durmites. The only person she could really trust was Julie, who'd been through this herself, but look how she was living now, behind an alias, too scared to let anyone know who she was or what she was doing in case the Durmites picked on her again.

I know how you're feeling, Julie wrote when she came back online. *It's just the worst. I wanted to kill myself too. Still do if I'm being honest.*

Did they send you a razor blade?

Yes. I've still got it even, not that I'm going to use it. I thought I'd jump off a cliff, or just walk out into the sea.

What stops you?

I'm not sure really. I suppose I don't have the courage.

Paige wondered if she herself did and decided probably not, though she wished she did.

There are some websites you can go on that tell you all the different ways to do it, Julie continued. *I can send you some links if you like.*

OK.

You won't do anything without telling me, though, will you?

No, of course not. Is it going to make it seem like they've won?

They always win. That's the trouble. No one can stop them, not even the police. Did they put a note in with your razor blade?

Yes.

What did it say?

Paige typed it in.

That's what they said to me. Do you realize if they're ever questioned about it they'll just say they were telling you to shave your legs or under your arms?

Seeing how that would get them off the hook, Paige replied with, *I expect they've got answers for everything.*

Definitely. That's why I said they always win. I can't have a proper life anymore, and it's all because of them. You end up living in the shadows, afraid to talk to anyone, or to be yourself.

That's how I feel.

I'll send you those links.

Chapter  18

The safety net should have been around the trampoline. Jack had promised to do it the last time he'd come, but had ended up forgetting, and Jenna hadn't reminded him.

The first she knew of the accident was when all three younger children started to scream from the garden. She hadn't even realized they were out there, had thought they were upstairs cleaning their teeth before school, but somehow they'd slipped past her, and now disaster had struck.

While her mother whisked the twins off to school, Jenna gathered Josh up and drove like a maniac to the emergency room.

After a two-hour wait it turned out he'd broken his arm, which actually seemed to delight him, since the instant he was back in the car he'd got Jenna to take a photo of him and his cast to send to Paige and to Bena's son, Aiden.

Jenna hadn't called Jack to tell him to come to the hospital because he was already in the States. He and Martha had left on Thursday and weren't due back until after the Easter holidays. Jenna bitterly regretted not making him tell the children himself that he was going. If he had, he'd have seen their faces for himself, and would surely never have been able to enjoy his time away.

"Why can't we go too?" Flora had asked, looking as hurt and confused as the other two.

"He promised us we could one day," Wills reminded her.

"He said we'd go to Disneyland and the Harry Potter park," Josh said brokenly.

"He's mean not taking us."

"He shouldn't break promises."

"Shall we ring him up and make sure he doesn't want us to come?"

It had been a horribly difficult evening that had ended up with them all sleeping in her bed as a special treat.

What Paige thought of her dad going to America for almost a month only Paige knew, because she'd simply walked off when she'd heard the news, and Jenna hadn't had an opportunity to talk to her since.

Reaching for her mobile as it rang, she saw it was Hanna and clicked on.

"Hi, how are you?" Hanna asked. "More to the point, how's the wounded soldier?"

"He seems fine, apart from the fact that he's not thrilled about me having to do just about everything for him, and I can't say I'm particularly thrilled about it either."

"As if you don't have enough to cope with. Where is he now?"

"Upstairs trying to play left-handed on his computer. He wanted to go to school until I reminded him that he'd need help going to the loo."

"Poor thing. Get him to Skype me later so I can see his cast."

"He'll like that."

"So when are you next walking with Richard?"

"We don't have an arrangement. Hanna, I hope you're not making something—"

"I promise I'm not. I'm just happy that you're getting out once in a while *without* the children, and with someone who can help take your mind off Jack."

"I've walked with him a grand total of four times now, and OK, I'll admit I don't think about Jack as much when I'm with him."

"I'll live with that. So any word from the fraudster?"

"Not yet. It was Paige's turn to have special time with him this evening, but I'm pretty sure he's forgotten—not that he can do anything about it now."

"He's such a bastard. I'll give her a call. Do you think she might like to come up to London for a few days during the holidays?"

Jenna's heart warmed with love for her sister. "I'm sure she'd jump at it. She keeps talking about getting away from here. I think she's still having problems at school, on top of all this business with Jack, and I have to be honest, I wouldn't mind having one less to worry about for a while."

"I'm sure you wouldn't, and if my lovely niece needs some cheering up, she can leave it to her auntie Hanna to lay on a few treats. I'm just wondering if she'll be parted from you."

"I don't think we'll have a problem with that, but if we do I'll drive her there myself."

Sighing, Hanna said, "You sound tired. I think you're the one who really needs a break."

"I'm fine, so please don't start worrying. I'll email you the date Paige's break starts so you can book the time off."

After ending the call Jenna went to check on Josh, who was

doing quite well with his favorite game, Skylanders, so she sat down to watch. Thank God he was all right; if anything more serious had happened to him . . . She couldn't even bear to think of it, so she had to put it out of her mind.

"Your phone's ringing, Mum," he told her.

Realizing it was, she saw it was Paige and clicked on. "Hi, is everything all right?"

"Yeah, I just saw Josh's picture. Is it broken? How did he do it?"

"On the trampoline, and yes, it's broken. Do you want to speak to him?"

"In a minute. Have you told Dad about it?"

"Not yet."

"So you haven't spoken to him today?"

"No. Why? Have you?"

"No way. And of course he's forgotten about tonight. We knew he would, and even if he remembered he wouldn't be able to do anything about it, seeing as he's in *America*."

"He could apologize and make another arrangement," Jenna retorted.

"Except I'm not interested."

Aching for her, Jenna said, "Where are you?"

"At school, where do you think?"

"I thought I could hear traffic. Would you like me to come and pick you up later so we—"

"No, it's OK. I'll get the bus home. I have to go now." And before Jenna could say any more, the line went dead.

Texting her, Jenna said, *Why don't we go to the King tonight, just the two of us? I'm sure Grandma will babysit.* Was that going to be a good thing for Josh? He would need help eating, but her mother was perfectly capable.

She waited for an answer, but none came, and by the time she thought of it again they were all sitting down for tea, apart from Paige, who'd taken a poached egg on toast up to her room.

Over a week had gone by since Julie had started sending links to special websites, and Paige's eyes were starting to feel swollen and raw. She'd hardly slept for the past few nights; in fact, the most sleep she was getting was during the day when she dozed off while riding buses around Swansea and even over to Cardiff. It was the only thing she could think of to escape the Durmites. Going into school wasn't an option any longer, especially now that she and Charlotte weren't speaking, so she was forging sick notes from her mother. It ripped her apart to be ignored by her best friend, and she couldn't take any more of the physical abuse, simply couldn't handle it on her own, although there was nothing she could do to stop it coming through her phone and over the Internet. She was no longer sure how much of it was from Kelly, since anonymous messages were coming from all over now, swamping her inboxes, filling her phone, all of them taunting and tormenting her, telling her what a waste of space, a troll, a saddo, or a loser she was. A lot said even worse than that, really disgusting stuff that made her feel so ashamed that she couldn't bring herself to look in the mirror.

She didn't understand why people felt the need to be so obscene and cruel, or what made them attack someone they didn't even know, using their venom, their evil, as if twisting and turning knives.

The only place she could go for proper understanding and advice was these websites. There were quite a few, with hundreds, maybe thousands of contributors from all over the world, many suffering in the same way she was. A lot had become self-harmers who wrote about the relief they achieved through cutting themselves with razor blades, hacksaws, pieces of plastic, even the corners of toothpaste tubes. Though she hadn't yet done the same, she was being encouraged to all the time. It would make her feel better, she was told. She'd be taking control, ensuring she was the one who caused herself harm rather than leaving it to someone else. Some had posted videos of themselves bleeding from wounds so deep that they surely needed stitches, but as far as she could make out no one ever went to a hospital. It was like a challenge they set themselves: who could cause the most damage to their arms, legs, faces, or even bones without anyone noticing? One girl liked to burn herself; she loved the smell, she said. Another scraped the skin from her legs with a peeler.

Paige usually chatted with her new friends in the dead of night, when darkness seemed to acquire so many more depths that she wondered where they might end. Down and down she would go, like the White Rabbit in *Alice in Wonderland*, to a place where perspective felt different, and everything was deathly quiet and still. The only sounds were the tapping of her keys and the gentle hum of the computer. She could imagine the others in their own pockets of light, dotted around the world like small, lonely stars in a vast night sky. Several were suicidal, or so they claimed, but she didn't know of anyone who'd actually gone through with it yet. They were always talking about it, all the different ways they'd explored, and why one might be more effective, less painful, easier to achieve than another. Hanging, wrist-slitting, ODing, leaping from a bridge into the path of a lorry . . . She'd followed some of the links through to step-by-step guides of how to prepare, what not to do, and what was recommended when the time came.

As she read the posts she could feel her friends' loneliness as deeply as she felt her own. It was an invisible yet powerful connection between them that held them together, made them feel less lonely for a while, and even gave them a sense of belonging. This was where they could exist without fear of their persecutors finding them.

Though Paige never offered advice the way some did, she was always ready with sympathy when she felt it was needed. And she received plenty too. They understood her in a way no one had before, apart from Julie, who was constantly sending her links to new blogs or sites and meeting up with her in chat rooms where suicide was the main theme.

I want to do it so badly, Julie confessed in their private messaging one night, *and I think I'm getting there. How about you?*

I think I am too. I read on one of the sites the other day that dying might be painful, but after death there is no pain, or abuse, or anything that can hurt you again. That makes so much sense.

Yes, it does. Have you thought about how you'd do it?

I think the same way as you, either off a cliff or I'd walk into the sea.

I reckon that would be the most painless. Sometimes when I think about it I feel I'd be flying like a bird or an angel as I jumped, and as soon as I hit the rocks below I'd leave my body and be flying again.

I get what you mean. It sounds lovely. Do you think you'll do it?

I want to. I guess we'll see. Maybe I'm like all the others, just talk. I reckon you've got more courage than me.

Sometimes I want to do it so badly that I go to the cliffs and stand looking down at the sea. I'm not sure what stops me.

You're just not ready yet, but I think you will be. Did you notice that Karina hasn't been online since she posted her goodbye note? That was over a week ago.

Paige had noticed, but she was still waiting for Karina to turn up again. It wasn't her real name, of course; everyone used an alias—Paige's was Giselle, Beyoncé's middle name. She hadn't found anything in any of the news websites about a teenage girl killing herself, but it could have happened in Australia or Singapore or anywhere in the world and just not got through to them.

Has your mum found out yet that you're not going to school?

No, but she's bound to soon. Someone'll ring her up or Charlotte will tell.

I think it really sucks that you and Charlotte aren't friends anymore. Just goes to show you never know who you can trust.

Paige hadn't responded to that. She didn't like to talk about Charlotte much, or even to think about her really. After what she'd said about her dad, Paige didn't want any more to do with her. She was never going to forgive her for that, not ever.

Earlier today she'd taken a risk by riding the bus from Swansea to Llanrhidian. Usually she didn't come onto the Gower for her truancy journeys, or not very far onto it anyway, but when she'd been at the station trying to decide which bus to take she'd spotted one of the rangers who helped tourists heading her way. Afraid he was going to ask why she wasn't at school, she avoided him by jumping onto the nearest bus, which had turned out to be heading for Llanrhidian. At least it was the opposite side of the peninsula from where she lived, so the chance of someone getting on who knew her wasn't as likely as if she'd found herself on her way to Oxwich or Port Eynon.

She was at home now, safe in her room, except it wasn't safe, because they still got to her here through her phone and computer. Amongst all the horrible stuff today she'd had a sweet Snapchat from someone called Petra telling her to be brave, everyone was with her. The photo was of a kitten, so she had no idea what Petra looked like, if she was even a girl. It didn't matter. All that did matter was that in amongst the blizzard of abuse she had people to communicate with who cared, and though she often chatted with them during the day she always felt the best times were at night. She knew she was entering the darkest part of the dark side when she connected with them then—she even felt as though she was being swallowed right up in the shadows—but it was getting so that she could hardly wait to be there. It was the only place that seemed to make any sense, the only time she could express herself in ways that would have been impossible elsewhere.

Flora was with her now, sitting on the bed playing with the stuffed animals that Paige had had since she was a baby.

"Can I take Little Kanga to sleep with me tonight?" Flora asked, cuddling the downy toy to her cheek.

"If you like," Paige answered, keeping her back turned and eyes on the chat room. She wasn't taking part, just reading, absorbing, and fretting.

"He's my favorite. He's yours too, isn't he?"

Paige didn't bother to respond.

"I like Sally the rag doll as well, and Hippo, and Teddy, and

Penguin, and everything you have, because you've got all the best stuff and I don't have very much."

Paige wasn't listening. Someone new was in the chat room saying that Karina was definitely gone and that she wanted to thank all her friends for their messages of love and support that had helped her to find the courage to take the only way out. *She's free now. She's happy and with the people she loves.*

Paige felt suddenly horribly light-headed and scared.

Someone she had chatted with had actually taken her own life.

If Paige did the same, she would be with Grandpa. There would be no more texts or emails, tweets or postings; she'd be beyond it all, no longer a loser, or ugly, or someone whose father had left home because of her. She wouldn't have to read any more nastiness about her "weird grandma" or her "wimpy brother Josh" or the "four-eyed twins." Her mother wouldn't be the whore who'd taught her all she knew, her father wouldn't be a rapist, and the perverts who'd joined in would have no one to send their revolting videos to. She wouldn't feel as though she was being watched all the time and hated and despised. There would no longer be any shame in being her, because she really would be Paige No Moore.

"Please, Paige, please, please, please," Flora was begging.

"Please what?" Paige muttered.

"Put some makeup on me, make me look pretty like you."

Paige turned round. "I'm not pretty, OK?" she snapped. "There's nothing pretty about me, so don't ever say it again."

Flora's eyes grew huge behind the frames of her glasses.

"You have to go now," Paige told her. "I don't want you in here anymore."

Climbing off the bed with Little Kanga clutched to her chest,

Flora walked to the door with her head bowed. "I'm sorry," she whispered, "I didn't mean to make you cross."

"I'm not cross, I'm just . . . I've got private stuff going on, so you need to go."

Minutes after the door closed behind Flora, Julie came online.

Did you read about Karina?

Yes. Lucky her, she's already done it.

I think I might be ready to.

Me too.

I've been thinking. How about we do it together?

Paige's heart leapt. She'd been thinking the same thing. *That's a good idea.*

When?

Paige hesitated, not sure what to say.

I'll be ready when you are. Just let me know. There's a place we can go. I'll give you directions.

Paige felt her head starting to spin. It was coming closer now. It wouldn't be long before it was all over.

You should write down everything that's happened to you, make sure the Durmites get the blame they deserve.

Paige was definitely up for that. *Do you know anyone who's already on the other side? I mean someone in your family.*

My mother.

Paige blinked in surprise. Julie had never mentioned that before. *How long ago did she die?*

Ages. I never really think about her. Is there someone there for you?

My grandpa. I know he'll take care of me.

Then you'll be all right.

Your mum will take care of you.

I have to go now. Don't forget to let me know when you're ready. I can't wait much longer.

Do you realize we'll get to meet? I'll know who you are. Do I already know you?

Not really. We'll have plenty of time to get to know each other on the other side.

As the contact was lost Paige felt a numbing bleakness stealing over her, like a dense gray mist rolling in from the sea. She thought of her mother, her father, Josh and the twins, her grandma, and Auntie Hanna. Tears began spilling from her eyes; sobs were trying to choke her. Then she remembered what she'd been told. *You will only be thinking about yourself when the time comes. No one else will matter or even exist. If they do, then it means you're not ready to go.*

"Why the hell are you only telling me this now?" Jack was shouting into the phone.

Jenna held it away from her ear. She didn't want to shout back; she had neither the will nor the time for it.

"My son breaks his arm and *you* don't think it's important enough to pick up the phone?"

"I dealt with it, OK?" she cut in sharply.

"That's not the point. Did you stop Josh from telling me himself?"

Incensed, she snapped, "No one stopped him. He just didn't ask to call you, and this is the first time you've found a minute to call us."

Grinding out the words, he said, "You can't resist it, can you?"

"Do you know what, Jack, I really don't need this. I'm trying to get them ready for school, which you'd know if you'd bothered to check the time difference before you rang. What the hell time is it there?"

"Just after midnight."

"So why are you calling now?"

"Because I knew they'd all be at home."

"Great! Everything has to happen on your schedule, doesn't it, Jack? Let's make sure we all fit in around you. Never mind that we're up to our eyes here, already running late, can't find our shoes, don't want to brush our teeth, have to finish watching a program or playing a game . . ."

"I'll call back another time," he said, and the line went dead.

Hanging up her end, Jenna stood over the phone, afraid to move, to think, to do anything that might end up pushing her that final step over the edge. She was so close, so dangerously and calamitously close, that even breathing felt like an unsafe thing to do.

She counted to ten and tried to will herself to carry on with the morning. All she had to do was clear up the spilled cereal, rescue crayons floating in milk, pick up the Legos before Waffle chewed one of them, brush Flora's hair, make sure everyone had the right books in their bags after checking them to make sure there were no notes they'd forgotten to give her, find out who had PE . . .

She'd been arrested for shoplifting yesterday. A security guard had stopped her on the way out of Tesco and marched her to the manager's office. She'd had two bags full of groceries she hadn't paid for. She hadn't even realized that until they'd pointed it out. All she'd been able to think about at the time was Paige and the call she'd just received from The Landings. Paige hadn't been to school for over a fortnight, and they were worried; they wanted to know what was wrong with her, how things were at home, and if there was anything they could do to help.

"I can explain," she'd told the supermarket manager, but she hadn't been able to because she hadn't wanted to admit to being such a terrible mother that she'd had no idea her daughter wasn't going to school.

They'd let her go in the end, but not until the police had been called and she'd contacted Richard to ask for his help. He'd come straightaway and sorted it out somehow, had probably even paid for the shopping, because she'd had it when she got home.

He'd rung last night to find out how she was, and she'd told him she was fine.

"A stupid aberration," she'd tried to joke. "I've never done anything like it before."

"You've got a lot on your mind."

"Not a very good excuse, but it's the only one I have."

"You need a break, some time for yourself, but I know it isn't easy when you have children."

"Or when your husband is in the States with another woman, so he can't help out."

"What about your mother and sister?"

"Yes, they'll help, definitely. Easter's coming and the children will be on holiday, so it won't be as stressful."

"You'll let me know if there's anything I can do?"

"Of course, and thank you for today. I'm horribly embarrassed, and I'm not sure I want to know what you said to them."

"It doesn't matter. What does is that they realized it was a mistake and now you're home in one piece."

Except she wasn't in one piece. She was in so many pieces that she had no idea how to pull herself together.

"Shall we walk on Sunday?" he suggested.

"That would be lovely. Thank you."

A walk on Sunday with Richard and the dogs. Just think of that, Jenna. It'll keep you calm, help you to stay focused, give you something to look forward to.

She registered feet thundering down the stairs. Music blaring from someone's TV. Voices from the radio. Sunlight blazing across the kitchen.

Paige had refused to open her door last night.

She had to speak to her.

"Mum! Can I take my boxing gloves to school?"

"Mum! Josh can't brush his teeth."

"I can. I already did it."

"Mum! Wills has broken his glasses again."

"Mum! Can I have a piece of toast?"

"Mum! I can't find any socks."

"Mum! I dropped my reading book in Waffle's water."

"Mum! Have you seen my ruler?"

"Mum! Is Dad going to ring again?"

Mum, Mum, Mum, Mum . . .

"Mum, why are you banging your head on the wall?"

"Stop, Mum, you'll make yourself bleed."

"Please, Mum, stop . . ."

"For God's sake," Paige exclaimed, grabbing her mother's shoulders. "What the hell are you doing? You're scaring everyone."

"And everyone's scaring me." Jenna's voice was hysterical. "Especially you! I don't know what's happening to you, what you're doing on that bloody computer, where you're going when you're supposed to be at school."

"I'm not going anywhere."

"Stop it!" Wills cried, clasping his hands to his ears.

"I want some answers," Jenna shouted as Paige made to walk off. "Don't you dare . . ."

"Just leave me alone," Paige yelled back at her. "I'm sick of this place."

"And I'm sick of you shutting yourself up in that room, never letting anyone in, being unpleasant to your sister, ignoring your brothers . . . You put yourself first all the time, never thinking about how things are for them."

"They're not my children. They're yours. I didn't ask you to have them, so stop trying to make them my responsibility."

Jenna glared at her menacingly. "I'll never forget you said that," she seethed. "Now get out of my sight and don't show me your face again until you're ready to apologize."

"That's never going to happen," Paige threw over her shoulder. "I've got nothing to apologize for, and you're going to seriously regret all the horrible things you've said to me. You just wait and see."

Ignoring her, Jenna turned on the others. "I want you ready to get in the car by the time I come down again. That means teeth and hair brushed, shoelaces tied, bags packed, and Wills, your glasses in their case ready for the repairer." Leaving their worried faces staring after her, she ran upstairs, slamming the bedroom door behind her.

Since she had no time for anything else, she simply splashed cold water on her face, scrunched up her hair, and dragged a sweater over her jeans.

Minutes later she was on the landing. "Paige, I don't want you to leave this house before I get back," she called out. "If you do, there's going to be serious trouble."

Paige was sitting on the edge of her bed, her face as white as the blossom floating past her window, her hand shaking from clutching her phone so hard.

I'm definitely ready, she'd just messaged to Julie. *I need directions. Please send as soon as you get this and will meet you there.*

Chapter 19

By the time Jenna returned from a nightmare of a school run, trying to calm the little ones down and assure them she was fine, there was no sign of Paige. Though she wasn't surprised, she was angry and worried, and half ready to start banging her head against the wall again. It had been a dreadful start to the day, one of the worst, but she had to get a grip. She couldn't allow herself to lose it like that again, or God only knew what kind of mess they were going to end up in.

I'm sorry about earlier, she texted to Paige. *I know I expect too much of you. Please call or text when you get this and I'll come and get you.*

If she was at school, it would have to wait until later. *Please God, let her be at school.*

She spent the next hour clearing up the kitchen, bundling clothes into the wash, scrubbing felt-pen drawings off windows, and trying to find cases for DVDs. Every few minutes she checked her phone, but there was nothing from Paige, and as time passed her guilt and worry escalated sharply. She tried ringing, over and over, but kept going to voicemail. "Paige, please call me," she said the first time. "Darling, I'm sorry, I didn't mean to upset you," she said the next time, "please let's talk." In the third message she said, "Paige, this isn't fair. You know how much you mean to me, and you know I'll be thinking the worst, so please either text or call so we can sort things out."

By lunchtime there was still no word, so she rang the school.

A terrible fear came over her when she was told that Paige wasn't there.

"I don't mean to pry," Mrs. Haynes, the form tutor, said, "but I've heard there are difficulties at home. If we can help in any way—"

"I need to find her," Jenna broke in shrilly. "We had a row this morning. Is Charlotte Griffiths there? She'll know where she is."

"I'll track her down and make sure she calls you."

Only as she rang off did it dawn on Jenna that she hadn't seen Charlotte in a while. Those two were never out of each other's pockets, were constantly texting or FaceTiming if they weren't actually together, so what had happened to make them fall out? If they had fallen out . . .

Though she guessed Charlotte's mother, Lucy, would be at work, she tried calling anyway and was about to leave a message when her line signaled an incoming call. "Hello?" she said, quickly switching over.

"Hi, it's Charlotte. Mrs. Haynes told me to call you."

Jenna's heart was thudding. "Do you know where Paige is?" she asked, trying to sound calm.

"No, I haven't seen her," Charlotte replied.

Oh God no. "Since when?"

"I don't know. A couple of weeks, I guess. She hasn't been

coming to school. I thought she was . . . you know, sick or something."

"No, she's not. Do you have any idea where she might be going?"

"No, sorry. She doesn't speak to me anymore."

"Why? What happened?"

"We kind of had this bust-up. She thought I was . . . She accused me of telling people stuff about her."

"What kind of stuff?"

"Just stuff."

"Charlotte, please. I'm very worried. We had a row this morning and I think I've really upset her. I need to find out where she is."

"I'm sorry, but I honestly don't know."

"Does she have any other friends who might know?"

Charlotte fell silent.

"Are you still there?" Jenna urged.

"Yes, I'm here, I'm just trying to think . . . I mean, there's this friend she has online . . . I don't know her name, or not her real name, anyway. She says it's Julie, but to be honest, I don't even know if it's a girl."

Jenna tried desperately not to overreact. "Do you think she could be with this friend now?"

Charlotte sounded wary. "I suppose it's possible, but this Julie person never wanted anyone to know who she was."

Reading everything terrible into that, Jenna said, "Is there a chance anyone else might know who this Julie is?"

"I shouldn't think so. As far as I know, Paige is the only one she chats with."

"You mean online?"

"Yeah. They private-message on Facebook and some other sites as well, I think. I don't really know, because I was never invited to join in."

Jenna's mind was racing. "Will you ask around, try to find out if anyone knows who this Julie might be?"

"I've already done that and no one does. I did it so I could show Paige she was trusting the wrong person."

"Why did you think that?"

"Because this Julie would never say who she was. In my book, if you're a real friend you don't have to hide who you are."

Jenna couldn't think of a good reason for it either. "OK. Promise me you'll call if you see her, or if you hear anything that might tell us where she is."

"Promise."

As she rang off her mother came in the door. "Paige is missing," Jenna blurted out, and found herself close to panic simply on hearing the words.

Kay's eyes were wide with alarm.

"I mean, not missing," Jenna stumbled. "Yes, missing . . . I don't know where she is. Apparently she hasn't been going to school . . . Oh, Mum, I shouted at her this morning . . . I said things—"

"There's no point going over that now," Kay interrupted sharply. "If she's gone off in a temper, she'll cool down soon enough. What we need to know is why she hasn't been going to school."

"Because someone called Julie has got to her. Don't ask me who this person is. Even Charlotte's not sure, and if Charlotte doesn't know . . ." Jenna put a hand to her head. "It'll be some godawful pervert who's befriended her, lured her out of school to do things with her—"

"Before you go any further with that," Kay cut in, "she's been coming home every night, and—"

"And acting very strangely. You must have noticed that she hardly speaks to us anymore. She's not interested in anything we have to say, never wants to do anything with us. I keep putting it down to her age and to Jack leaving, but now that I know about this . . ." Jenna's eyes were heavy with foreboding. "Mum, what am I going to do? I can't just sit here. She's out there somewhere, and I don't know what she's doing, who she's with . . . I have to call the police."

Kay didn't disagree. "I have Euan's number," she said, taking out her mobile. "I'm sure he'll come right away."

Not at all sure the local bobby was going to be up to this, Jenna said, "Maybe we should ring 999. She's only fifteen. She's not at school . . ."

"If we do that, we'll go through to some central switchboard and they'll end up sending Euan anyway. Let me call him."

"OK. I'll go up and see what I can find on her computer."

Minutes later she was staring at Paige's laptop screen in helpless frustration. The machine was password-protected and none of her attempts so far had cracked it.

"Euan's on his way," her mother declared, coming to the door. "So's Bena."

"You rang Bena?"

"She rang me, and I told her what was happening."

Remembering how dependable Bena could be in a crisis, Jenna nodded. "Do you have any idea what password Paige might use?"

"I'm sure my guesses would be the same as yours: the dog, the children, her school, you and Jack, me and Grandpa, favorite bands . . ."

Jenna looked around the walls and typed in every name she could spot, but none of those worked either. Going downstairs for her mobile, she rang Charlotte.

"It's Jenna. Can you call me as soon as you're free?" she said into the voicemail. "Or text me if you know the password to Paige's computer." Clicking off, she tried Paige again, but still no reply.

"She has to be somewhere," she muttered as Kay came down the stairs. "Can you think of anywhere?"

Kay's expression was intense as she thought, but neither of them could come up with anything that seemed to make sense.

"I'm going to search the garden," Kay announced. "Sometimes, when I was young and felt things getting on top of me, I used to hide in the shed."

Just after her mother had gone, the back door opened and Bena came in.

"Any news?" she asked, the sight of her worried face making Jenna feel even worse.

Jenna shook her head. "I can't get into her computer. I thought that might tell us something."

"Euan's just pulled up."

Hating the thought of the police being involved, though relieved he'd arrived so quickly, Jenna went to open the front door.

Euan was already getting out of his car; he was a large man with florid cheeks, sandy hair, and kindly blue eyes. "So what's all this about young Paige doing a moonlight?" he asked as he came in, making it sound like a load of old nonsense. "She's a sensible girl, so I can't see she'll have gone far. Just forgot to tell you, I expect."

Appreciating his efforts to calm her, while not feeling calmed at all, Jenna said, "We've been having some problems. . . . Jack's left home. . . . I'm not sure that has anything to do with where she is now, I'm . . . She's . . . I found out yesterday that she hasn't been to school for a fortnight, and now Charlotte . . . You know Charlotte?"

"Griffiths?"

She nodded. "She told me this morning that Paige has been communicating with someone online. Apparently this person calls herself Julie, but Charlotte's not even sure if it's a girl."

Euan was looking more concerned now. "So when did you last see her?" he asked, taking out his notebook.

"This morning. We had words, and I said some things—we both did. She was still here when I left to take the younger ones to school, but by the time I got back she'd gone."

He nodded thoughtfully as he noted this down. "Has she taken anything with her?"

Jenna went blank. "Uh, I . . . I didn't check."

"Then it's worth having a scout round her room to see if anything's missing."

They looked up as Kay came in.

"She's not out there," Kay informed them.

Starting for the stairs, Jenna said, "Mum, can you check the cupboard in the hall to see if any backpacks have gone? She wouldn't have been able to get into the attic for anything bigger."

Moments later Euan followed her into Paige's room.

"Her computer's still here," she said, "but I can't get into it."

"Nothing appears to be out of place," he commented, surveying the room. "She's quite tidy for a teenager. Can you check her wardrobe and drawers?"

Jenna found herself shaking as she pushed aside underwear and socks, containers of costume jewelry, nail polishes and hair slides. "It's hard remembering everything she has," she said, "but nothing seems to be missing from the drawers."

As she checked the wardrobe Euan went around the other bedrooms opening doors and cupboards to see if Paige had squirreled herself away there.

"She hasn't taken her toothbrush or toothpaste," Jenna announced, coming out of Paige's bathroom. She felt almost weak with relief, as though she needed to sit down and take a few breaths, but she wouldn't be able to until they were certain Paige was safe.

"So on the face of it," Euan said, "we don't have any reason to think she's not planning to come home?"

Jenna shook her head. "Unless this Julie person is providing everything she needs." Why had she just said that? She'd frightened herself again, just when she was starting to think it might be all right.

Euan was frowning pensively. "I'm going to call this in," he decided. "It probably won't be given a high priority, with it looking more like a truancy than anything else, but it won't do any harm for her picture to be circulated so the beat officers can keep an eye out for her."

"I'm worried about this Julie character," Jenna persisted. "What if it's a man, someone who's been grooming her?"

"Jenna, it's Charlotte for you," Bena announced, bringing Jenna's mobile into the room.

Grabbing it, Jenna said, "Charlotte, thanks for calling back. We need to get into Paige's computer. Do you have any idea what the password might be?"

"I'm not sure. . . . I mean, she might have changed it. . . ."

"Please, just tell me what you think it is."

"I don't know that she'd want me to."

"Charlotte, the police are here. If she's been communicating with someone who won't give their real identity . . . You have to understand how serious that could be."

Still sounding reluctant, Charlotte said, "OK, you can try Oliver18."

Having no idea of the relevance of that, or even caring, Jenna turned on the laptop and typed it in. The machine unlocked. "That's it," she cried, her voice heavy with relief. "Thank you, Charlotte. And her Facebook account? Would that be the same password?"

"You can try, but she kept changing it because of all the crap she was getting."

"What sort of crap?"

"You'll see if you can get on. She's been using other sites as well, like AskFM and Pheed and Tumblr, though they'll be mostly on her phone."

"What kind of sites are they?"

"Social media, same as Facebook, but it's easier to be anonymous on some of them."

Jenna was trying to log in but couldn't manage to open any of the accounts. She looked at Euan, not sure what to do.

Holding a hand out for the phone, he said, "Charlotte, it's Euan Matthews here. Are you at school? If you are, I'm going to come by and see you. I'll call Mr. Charles myself to let him know I'm on my way."

Taking the phone back from him, Jenna clicked off as she said, "What are we going to do about the computer? Is there a way of getting into her accounts?"

Moving it around so he could see the screen himself, Euan

checked the Internet search history and found all the websites Charlotte had mentioned and more. "The last time she used it was just after three this morning," he said, "but I'm not technical enough to find out who she might have contacted or what kind of exchange there might have been." Closing the laptop down and unplugging it, he went on, "I'll have our tech guys take a look at it. Meantime, you need to sit tight here and let me know right away if you hear from her."

Five hours or more had passed since Jenna had returned to the house and found Paige gone. There was still no word from her. Jenna was beside herself, hardly knowing what to do from one minute to the next. She'd left more messages, sent her mother to search the beaches and coastal paths with Waffle, and asked Bena to drive around the countryside and villages trying to spot her. All reports back were negative, but she'd told them to keep going until just after three o'clock, when Euan rang to let her know that there had been some developments.

With her heart in her mouth she listened as he said, "First of all, a couple of CID officers are on their way to see you."

Panic instantly flared. "Why? What's happened?" she cried.

"Nothing's actually happened," he replied, "but my conversation with Charlotte has raised some concerns. It seems Paige has been the victim of some pretty unpleasant bullying at school."

Jenna was suddenly struggling to think straight. This wasn't what she'd expected to hear, and yet . . . "She tried to tell me," she gasped, "but . . . I didn't think . . . I didn't realize . . . What have they been doing to her?"

"Mostly bombarding her with hate mail in an effort to make

her feel small and disliked, sending lots of spiteful messages on Facebook, ridiculing her, doctoring explicit photographs to try and make it seem they're of her. Apparently it's turned more physical lately, punching, slapping, sticking her head down a toilet and making her drink urine . . ."

Jenna could hardly believe it. "Who's been doing all this?" she demanded furiously.

"The culprits are being rounded up as we speak, but it isn't the source of our biggest concern. Mr. Thomas, the technology master here, has taken a look at her computer, and the contact she's been having with this Julie Morris is of a very grave nature."

Jenna couldn't breathe. She desperately wanted the world to stop so that none of this could go any further.

"In the last few days she's been visiting suicide sites," Euan told her gently.

Jenna sobbed a scream. "No! No! She would never do that. Please, you have to believe me. . . . Oh my God, Paige. My baby. What are we going to do?"

"We've already raised the alarm," he assured her. "This is high priority now, and we've alerted all local and national media outlets. Everything's going to be done to find her, Jenna, I can promise you that."

"But what if . . . what if she's . . . ?" She couldn't say it. *Oh dear God, dear God, Paige! Paige! Paige!*

"The CID officers should be with you shortly," Euan continued. "You need to tell them everything you know about Paige's friends, her movements, anything you can think of, even if it doesn't seem relevant. They'll talk you through it, and they'll want to search the house for any journals or letters that might give them a clue as to where she might be."

This wasn't real. It was a nightmare, and she was going to wake up any minute. Paige would be walking in the door, or coming down the stairs, or standing right here in the kitchen making toast.

"A detective's already talking to Charlotte," Euan went on, "and we should know more once the police experts have their hands on the computer. It's on its way to Bridgend now, and hopefully it won't take long for them to come back with some answers."

Jenna spun round as someone opened the back door. *Please God, let it be Paige.*

It was her mother, looking glazed with shock as she was followed in by two strangers who Jenna realized must be the CID officers. "Your colleagues are here," Jenna said to Euan.

"OK. Charlotte wants to come and see you as soon as they've finished with her."

"Yes, please tell her to do that." Ringing off, she tried to explain to her mother what was happening, but found herself starting to break down. She wanted to run, scream, tear down everything that stood between her and Paige, if only she knew what that was. In the end she managed to say, "Paige has been visiting suicide websites."

Kay looked as though she'd been struck. Her mouth opened, closed, and opened again. She turned to the officer closer to her, a short, plump woman with wispy dark hair and several moles on her cheeks. "Has my granddaughter . . . ?"

"We don't know anything yet," the officer told her in a tone that was neither friendly nor hostile. To Jenna she said, "I take it you're Mrs. Moore, Paige's mother?"

Jenna nodded as she tried to pull herself together. *Suicide websites. Why would she visit them unless the thought was in her mind?* Jenna could feel herself backing away as though physically recoiling, her hands coming up to stave off the terrible threat of the words.

"I'm DS Lesley Mariner," the female detective was informing her. "This is DC Rob Fuller. Is there a Mr. Moore?"

Jenna took a breath and dashed back her hair. "He's in the States, on business," she replied.

"Is there any chance your daughter might have gone to join him?"

Jenna blinked in shock. The thought hadn't even occurred to her. "I don't think so," she said. "They haven't been getting along. He's there with his . . . with another woman and her children."

"I see." The officer looked around. "Is there somewhere we could sit down?"

"Yes, yes, of course. Mum, would you . . ."

"I'll make some tea," Kay told her. "Bena's going to pick up the children. I'll ask her to take them to her place for now."

Jenna was barely listening. She was shaking so hard it hurt. All she could think about was her baby, her precious, beautiful firstborn who was out there somewhere. *Please God, let her still be out there. It can't be too late. I'll never survive if it is.*

"We need to talk about what happened prior to Paige leaving," Lesley Mariner began once they were in the sitting room with the connecting doors closed. "I believe that was around nine this morning."

"That's right. I don't know the exact time, because I wasn't here. I was taking my other children to school."

"What ages are your other children?"

"Josh is eight, and the twins are five. Is this relevant? How's it going to help find Paige?"

"We're trying to establish whether one of her siblings might know where she is. Maybe she talked to one of them."

"She's hardly been talking to any of us lately. She's been in her own world . . . I thought it was about her dad leaving . . . I mean, I knew she was having problems at school; I just never realized they were so serious."

"So she spoke to you about the bullying?"

Bullying! How could someone be bullying her daughter without her knowing? "She said some girls were picking on her and being mean. I should have paid more attention, but she never made a big deal of it. It's my fault, though. If I'd listened properly . . . I know her so well, I'd have realized . . . If it weren't for everything else that was happening, I would have known . . ."

"Everything else?"

"My husband leaving. It's shaken us all." She gasped for breath. "I—I haven't handled it well."

"When did your husband leave, exactly?"

"About six weeks ago."

"And they were close, he and Paige?"

"Yes, very. He's her stepdad, actually, but she's taken it hard."

DS Mariner glanced at her colleague, apparently his cue to take over.

Sitting forward, Rob Fuller fixed her with his pale gray eyes, his freckly hands gnarled together like tree roots. "Are you aware of anything inappropriate ever taking place between your husband and daughter?" he asked evenly.

Jenna stared at him speechlessly. Surely to God he didn't mean . . . *"No!"* she cried angrily. "How can you even suggest it? My husband would never—" She broke off, remembering that she'd never thought he'd leave. But not this. No. Never this.

"I realize you haven't seen any of the social media postings as yet," Fuller continued, "but it's being suggested, actually more than suggested in some, that your husband left home because you discovered he was having sexual relations with your daughter."

Jenna felt as though she was losing her mind. She stared at the detectives wide-eyed with horror, unable to believe what they were saying, that they would even be thinking this way when Paige was missing. "I swear to you," she said brokenly, "that isn't true. He left home to be with another woman. Her name is Martha Gwynne. I can give you his phone number. . . . Nothing like that happened between him and Paige. If it had, I would know."

Lesley Mariner was watching her closely.

"You have to believe me," Jenna insisted. "My husband is a lot of things, but he'd never, *never* do anything like that. You need to find out who's been saying these things and ask *them* what grounds they have for such terrible accusations."

"It is being looked into," Fuller assured her, "but please try to understand that we'd be failing in our duty if we didn't take the allegations seriously."

"She was being bullied," Jenna almost shouted. "Isn't that the sort of thing bullies say?"

"It has certainly been known. It's also, on occasion, turned out to be true."

"Well, not on this occasion. I know my daughter—she'd never allow anything like that to happen to her. She has a strong mind, she isn't afraid to speak up for herself, and she's never, *ever* shown any fear of her father."

"Have you informed your husband yet that she's missing?"

Jenna blinked. Then, realizing what they were driving at, she said, "The only reason I haven't is because Euan only just told me, right before you walked in the door, that Paige has . . . that she's been visiting suicide . . ." Her voice failed as the horror of it swamped her again.

Mariner started to respond, but Jenna cut her off.

"Listen, I realize you have to do your job, but how is this helping to find my daughter? She's not with her father. If you like, I'll call him right now to establish that. Or I can get her passport to show you. She wouldn't have been able to leave the country without it."

"It would be helpful to know if it's still here," Mariner conceded. "And to speak to her father."

Running upstairs to her bedroom, Jenna took out the passports, her hands shaking so badly she could hardly hold them. Paige's had to be there. *Please God, it has to be.*

It was, and she almost unraveled with relief as she ran back down to the sitting room and shoved it at Mariner. By then her mother had brought in the tea, and Jenna could only pray that Kay hadn't heard what had been going on so far.

"I'll call Jack," she said, picking up the landline.

Aware of their scrutiny as they sipped their tea, Jenna scrolled to his number and pressed to connect. On the second ring she went through to voicemail and had to stop herself screaming in frustration. "You have to call me back right away," she told him. "There's a problem with Paige. We don't know where she is. The police are here and they want to speak to you."

After ringing off she wrote down his number and handed it to Mariner. "In case you want to call him yourself."

Taking it, Mariner said, "Tell us about your own relations with Paige since her stepfather left. What have they been like?"

Jenna glanced at her mother as she replied, "The same as

"What the hell's going on?" Jack demanded. "Where's Paige? What's happened to her?"

"That's what we're trying to find out," Jenna told him, trying to sound calm. "She left this morning, and the police wondered if she'd come to join you."

"*What?* Why would they think that? And why are they involved?"

Taking a breath, she said, "Apparently Paige has been the victim of bullying at school—so badly, it would seem, that she's started looking at suicide websites."

Jenna felt the word hit her like a blow again, and knew it would be the same for him.

"Please tell me you're not serious," he managed at last.

"You know I wouldn't joke about something like this."

She heard him swallow. "Don't you have any idea where she might be?"

"None. The police are talking to Charlotte and trying to track down a friend she's made on the Internet called Julie Morris. Does the name mean anything to you?"

"No. Is she the person who's been doing the bullying?"

"I don't know yet; I'm still waiting to find out more. It only came to light this afternoon when Euan went to the school."

"Jesus Christ, I can't believe this is happening. How could you not have known she was being bullied?"

Jenna was about to rage back when she stopped herself. The last thing they needed was to reduce this to a ludicrous show-down between them. "The police want to talk to you," she informed him, "but before I pass you over, I want to know if you're coming back."

"Of course I'm coming back. I'll be on the next damned plane if you haven't found her by the time it leaves."

"And if we have found her? You'll stay there?"

"Just put the police on."

Handing the phone over, Jenna walked into the kitchen, not wanting to hear the conversation, not wanting to do anything at all apart from find her daughter. "Where is she, Waffle?" she asked tearfully as she stooped to stroke the dog. "We have to find out where she is before it's too late, or we just won't be able to carry on."

The police questioning went on and on, as did the search of the house. Their computers were confiscated. Though Jenna knew that parents were almost always the first suspects when something happened to a child, the fact that they might actually think that she or another member of the family was this Julie Morris beggared belief. However, she didn't argue; there was no point, as it hardly mattered what they did with the computers or anything else, just as long as they found Paige.

It was just after six when Euan turned up with Charlotte and her mother, Lucy. By then the detectives had left with an assurance that the search for Paige would continue through the night and they'd be in touch the instant there was any news.

"I'm your Family Liaison Officer," Euan informed Jenna as she hugged Charlotte tightly. "I'll be with you until they've found her."

"I'm so sorry about this," Lucy cried, clearly distraught. "If I'd known . . . I still don't understand why you didn't tell me," she said angrily to Charlotte.

"Paige didn't want me to," Charlotte retorted stroppily. The she turned to Jenna. "She was worried about you," she told

Jenna. "She didn't want to load any more on you, but I said she should."

Directing Charlotte to the kitchen sofa while Euan and Lucy sat on the bar stools, Jenna encouraged Charlotte to tell her everything she knew. "Please don't hold anything back," she urged. "No matter how bad it is, I need to know."

"That Kelly Durham has been a bully all her life," Lucy jumped in forcefully. "I can't tell you how many kids she's picked on over the years, and she always bloody gets away with it. And do you know why? Because her grandfather makes donations to the schools. It's like he buys her a free ride to do whatever the hell she wants and there's never any price to pay. She's a nasty piece of work, always has been, always will be— just like her mother."

Jenna's eyes moved to Charlotte as Charlotte said, "It's not like she never gets into trouble or anything, but she puts on this act when she's questioned by the teachers, crying and pretending not to know what they're talking about. She makes out like other people have hacked into her computer, or that she was just having a joke and it got taken the wrong way. Then when she comes out she gets all threatening again, only worse."

Torn between anger and frustration, Jenna forced herself to remain calm as she said, "Tell me what happened with Paige."

As Charlotte went through it all, constantly breaking down, Jenna couldn't stop herself crying either.

"I just can't bear to think of it," she said when Charlotte had finished. "How can people be so cruel? Why on earth did this dreadful girl pick on her? What's Paige ever done to her?"

"She's clever and pretty and everyone likes her," Charlotte replied.

"But not enough to stand up for her and make them stop?"

"I tried, all the time, I promise, but she'd never let me tell anyone, apart from once when we went to Miss Kendrick. Paige didn't want to, but when they started saying stuff about her dad I said I'd go myself if she didn't."

Grateful to Charlotte for that, Jenna said, "And what did Miss Kendrick do?"

"She called Kelly in, but like she always does, Kelly denied it, then twisted things round to try and make it look like she was as much a victim as Paige."

"Didn't Miss Kendrick investigate?" Lucy wanted to know.

"Not really, but to be fair, I don't think she realized how bad it actually was. Paige didn't tell her because she was really worried about how much worse it might get if she reported it, and she was right to be worried, because it did."

"That was when they pushed her head down the toilet?" Jenna asked.

Charlotte nodded miserably. "It was disgusting. They ought to be arrested for doing stuff like that."

Or made to suffer the same thing, Jenna thought bitterly, and she'd happily be the one to do it. "So tell me more about this Julie."

"That's just it—I don't know anything. It was only ever Paige that she contacted, and the weird thing was she always seemed to know what was going on. Or she'd tip Paige off to warn her not to be somewhere, or tell her to look at a certain website . . . It was dead spooky if you ask me, but Paige never seemed to see it like that. She believed this person when they said they'd been bullied too, and that was why they wouldn't let on who they were, because they didn't want anyone coming after them again."

Jenna looked at Euan, who shook his head, clearly as baffled as they were.

"Everyone in our year is being questioned," Charlotte told her, taking another tissue to dab her eyes, "and Kelly Durham's mother was called to the school this afternoon. I don't know what happened, but everyone's saying Kelly's going to be expelled—unless her granddad pays them off again."

"But she wasn't doing it alone?" Jenna pointed out.

"No, there's a gang of them, but Kelly's definitely the ringleader. Like Mum said, Paige isn't her first victim either; she's been doing it ever since she was in primary school. It's like she gets off on it or something."

Jenna looked at her mobile as it rang, but before she could answer Euan stopped her. "Is it a number you recognize?" he asked.

She shook her head. Her heart was thudding with urgency. Maybe Paige was calling from someone else's mobile.

"Let me," he advised, taking it. "It could be someone from the press and I don't think you want to be dealing with them just now." Clicking on, he said, "Hello, can I help you?"

Jenna's eyes were fixed on his face as he listened, her hands, her heart, her whole self bound so tightly with hope she couldn't even breathe.

"I don't know how you got this number," Euan said, giving her a rueful glance, "but please don't call it again. If you want information, there are the official channels. . . . OK, thank you," he said, and rang off.

Crushed that it wasn't Paige, and having to fight down yet more panic, Jenna turned back to Charlotte.

"I really thought it was going to be her," Charlotte confessed weepily.

"So did I," Jenna sighed.

"Everyone's saying they're going to join in the search if she hasn't come home by tomorrow," Charlotte told her. "I think they all feel really bad now that they didn't stand up for her."

And so they should. Cowards, every one of them. "Tell me about her password," she said. "Is Oliver a singer or an actor or something?"

Charlotte colored slightly. "No, he's a boy she really likes. He doesn't go to our school or anything. He's at college doing his A levels."

Confused, Jenna said, "But how does she know him?"

"He's the brother of someone in our year. We went to watch him play rugby a couple of times and she . . . you know . . ."

"No, I don't know."

"Well, she just liked him, but he had a girlfriend, so he wasn't really interested."

Jenna looked at Euan, wondering if he was thinking the same thing she was. "Is there any chance," she asked Charlotte, "that this boy, or his girlfriend, might be masquerading as Julie Morris?"

Charlotte drew back in amazement. "I wouldn't have thought so," she replied. "I mean, why would they?"

"I don't know."

Euan held up her mobile as it rang again. Recognizing the name of Richard's firm, her heart contracted as she nodded and took the phone.

"I'm sorry, I've been in court all afternoon," he told her. "I called as soon as I heard. Is there any more news?"

"No," Jenna replied, only just pushing the word through the tightness in her throat. "Apparently they're going to keep the search going all night, if need be. Jack's on his way back." Was this really happening? It felt so surreal, so distant from where reality should be, that she could hardly get a grip on it—until it came back to hit her with all its terrible force.

"Is there anything I can do?" he offered.

"I don't think so, but thanks for asking."

"You know I'm at the end of the phone."

"Thanks," she said again.

"Call anytime, day or night. Promise?"

"I promise."

Moments after the call ended Hanna came through the door and went straight to Jenna. "I don't know what to say," she said in a choked voice, hugging her. "When Mum rang me I didn't even pack, I just had to get here. . . . Oh God, Jen, to think of what she's been going through and none of us knew."

"She's too brave for her own good," Jenna said brokenly. "She's always put other people ahead of herself, and now she's done it with me and look what it's costing her." Her eyes went imploringly to her sister's. "She won't do anything stupid, will she?" she sobbed desperately. "Please tell me she won't."

"Of course she won't," Hanna replied firmly. "Not our girl. She's brave, like you said, and resilient, and too full of love for life and her family and everyone else to try anything like that. She just needs to have some time to herself for a while, that's all, get away from all those ghastly bullies. I'm sure she'll call any minute now and say she's sorry for causing so much fuss."

Chapter 20

At around eight that evening Euan took a call from DS Mariner. When he'd finished he signaled to Jenna to come into the kitchen, where they couldn't be overheard by the little ones. Bena had brought them home, and bless them, they were trying to be good in the belief it would bring Paige home.

"A bus driver's been in touch," he told her, glancing up as Hanna joined them. "He's saying that he thinks Paige was on his bus this morning."

Jenna's heart was in her mouth. "Does he remember where she got off?" she asked.

"If it was her, he dropped her over at Rhossili. Is there anyone you know over that way she might have gone to see?"

Jenna tried to think. "There are only a couple of my mother's friends," she replied, "and I'm not sure if Paige has even met them."

"OK, well, give it some more thought, see if anything comes to you. Meantime, they're going to start focusing the search around that area."

Only able to picture cliffs, rough seas, and bleak, dark moorland, Jenna wanted to leap into the car and race over there now.

If Paige heard her calling, if she realized how deeply she was loved and needed, maybe she would come out of hiding and allow herself to be brought home.

"Leave it to the police search-and-rescue team," Euan gently advised. "They know what they're doing, and we don't want you going out there and getting lost or injuring yourself."

"But if she knew I was there . . ."

"The driver isn't a hundred percent certain it was her. He says the girl he saw was wearing a navy school uniform and a coat of the same color, but she had the hood up, so he didn't get a good look at her face."

Jenna was desperate to do something. "Can I talk to the driver?" she pressed.

"I'm sure it'll be possible at some point, but he's still helping the police for now."

"Do you know what time he dropped her off?" Hanna asked.

"Just after ten, apparently. There's a bus from here to Rhossili that would get her in around then if she left home after nine, which is why he's being seen as a credible witness."

"But if she got off the bus at that time, what's she been doing since?" Jenna asked. She needed to know. "Do you think someone was waiting for her? Someone with a car, maybe?"

"Anything's possible. They should know more once they've carried out the house-to-house enquiries. Hopefully someone will remember seeing her after she left the bus."

After that there was no more news, though Jenna got Euan to call several times to make sure.

In the end she stayed up throughout the long night, barely sleeping, agitated and worrying, sometimes driving herself into a near frenzy of fear or despair. Had someone preyed on Paige's vulnerability, using it to lure her into a situation she'd never dreamt was waiting for her? She could be anywhere now, with anyone taking advantage of her in ways too horrifying to imagine, except Jenna couldn't stop imagining them.

In calmer moments she managed to convince herself that she would *know* if Paige was dead. Something in her would change; the bond they shared would slip, unravel, or do something else to warn her. The essence that was Paige, that she felt as constantly as if it were her own life force, would fade or disappear or perhaps become explosive at the last, and it had done none of those things. She was as strongly *there* as she'd always been, with no echo of a cry as she left this world for the next, no fleeting scent of her as she passed on her way to the angels.

She had *not* committed suicide.

She was still alive.

Hanna and her mother sat up with her; so did the children, though they slept for most of the time in corners of the sofa or on Jenna's or Hanna's lap. Jenna could see what a toll this was taking on her mother and longed to be able to hold her, though she knew that would be more for her comfort than for Kay's.

It was at times like this that she missed her father the most, when she needed someone to cling to, someone who could bring calm to her panic, who knew the right thing to say and the right thing to do.

Tell me what it is, Dad, she whispered desperately. *Please let me know that she isn't with you.*

Jack's plane was due to land at ten-thirty, three hours from now. Apparently Martha and her children were continuing their holiday without him. If—*when*—they found Paige alive and well, Jenna imagined, Jack would fly back to join them. If they didn't find Paige . . . She couldn't allow her mind to go there. It wasn't going to happen, so she wasn't going to torment herself with how she'd cope if it did.

Realizing she was only breathing into the top of her lungs, as though taking in any more air would somehow inflate the nightmare, she forced herself up from the sofa and went upstairs. She needed to shower and dress before the others were awake. She was going to join in the search today, no matter what anyone said. She couldn't carry on sitting here doing nothing. If Paige rang she'd call Jenna's mobile, and the police were monitoring the landline, so someone would pick up. She had to find her girl, even if it meant combing every inch of this peninsula herself. This was presuming Paige was still on the Gower, and so far the only actual evidence of that was from the bus driver who'd seen her almost twenty-four hours ago. Her heart thumped at the horror of so much time passing; Paige had been gone all night, and she could be almost anywhere by now. However, Rhossili was in the far southwestern corner of the Gower, so why head in the complete opposite direction to the mainland if she was planning to go elsewhere?

Realizing there was no logic to any of it, much less any source of comfort, she showered and dressed before going back downstairs to find her mother pottering about the kitchen.

"There you are," Kay said as Jenna came in. "The others are still asleep. Euan's outside in his car."

"Has he heard anything this morning?"

"He says not. You need to eat something."

Accepting this was true, Jenna agreed to a bowl of cornflakes and managed part of a slice of toast. "It's Saturday," she told her mother as Kay started setting out the cereal boxes. "The children are allowed Coco Pops on Saturdays."

Kay knew this, so Jenna had no idea why she'd mentioned it. Perhaps it was a grasp for normality, the need to know that something, no matter how small, was going to be as it should be today.

"Any news?" Hanna asked, coming to join them.

Jenna shook her head. "I'm going to—" Her mobile rang, and she made a grab for it.

"Is it someone you know?" Hanna cautioned.

Jenna nodded and clicked on. "Charlotte," she gasped, daring to hope Paige had turned up at her house during the night. "Have you heard from her?"

"No, I'm sorry, I haven't," came the teary reply. "I was hoping you might have."

Feeling an irrational surge of anger, as though it were somehow Charlotte's fault that Paige hadn't been in touch, Jenna quickly stifled it. "No, nothing yet," she said, "but a bus driver thinks he might have dropped her off in Rhossili. Does she know anyone over there?"

"The police have already asked me, and I told them I can't think of anyone."

Why couldn't she? There had to be some reason Paige had gone to Rhossili, if it had been Paige, and Jenna wasn't sure if she wanted it to be or not.

"I thought you'd like to know," Charlotte was saying, "that a whole gang of us are going to help with the search today. We're just waiting to hear from the police where we should go."

Hating hearing this as much as she hated the fact it was happening, Jenna said, "That's very kind of you all. I'm going to join in myself."

"Cool."

"I'll see you there then."

"Yes, see you there."

Over the next hour the phone continued to ring with more and more people offering to come and help. At nine Richard called to say that he and his boys would be there.

"Do you know where they want us?" he asked.

"No, but as soon as I do I'll text you," she promised. "I'm going myself."

"Would you like me to drive you?"

She was about to refuse when she realized it might be a good idea. "Thank you," she said. "My sister will almost certainly want to come too. Will there be enough room for us both?"

"Plenty. What time would you like me to collect you?"

"I'm not sure yet. Can I let you know when I've heard from the police?"

"Of course. Has Jack arrived?"

"He's due in at ten-thirty. I haven't checked to see if his plane is on time, but even if it is he won't get here until two at the earliest."

"By which time we'll hopefully have found her."

"Of course."

After a pause he said, "Call me when you're ready."

As she rang off Jenna looked into the sitting room, where the children were watching TV and eating their second bowls of Coco Pops. They were unusually quiet this morning as their tender little hearts tried to cope with the worry over Paige and where she might be. "They'll want to come with me," she said softly to Kay and Hanna, "but I'm not sure they should."

Hanna said to her mother, "How would you feel about taking them somewhere to do their own search?"

"If you think that's a good idea," Kay responded, looking at Jenna.

Deciding it would be, Jenna nodded and went to start getting them ready. In truth she didn't want them out of her sight for a single minute, but they'd be safe with her mother, and she wouldn't want them nearby if the search at Rhossili didn't end the way it simply had to.

By the time Richard and his sons turned up at ten Kay had already taken the children to search Port Eynon, and Jenna and Hanna, with their backpacks, were ready to go.

"My sons, Oliver and Cullum," Richard said, introducing them as Jenna left Hanna to lock up.

As she shook their hands she thought fleetingly of Paige's password, but it couldn't be the same Oliver. It would be too much of a coincidence—except hadn't Charlotte said that he was the brother of someone at school? And Cullum was in their year.

"Do you know Paige?" Jenna asked him, thinking how handsome he was with his shock of dark wavy hair, aqua blue eyes, and trendy stubble. He was as tall as his father, though not quite as filled out, and if he was the one Paige had fallen for, Jenna could understand why.

"Not exactly," Oliver replied, coloring slightly. "We met a couple of times. My brother knows her."

Turning to Cullum, Jenna said, "Did you know what was happening to her?"

Cullum nodded miserably. "I kept wanting to make them stop, but I . . ." He shrugged. "I should have. I feel really bad about it now."

How many kids had simply stood by and let it carry on?

Were they as much to blame as those who'd joined in? "Do you know who Julie Morris is?" she asked him.

He shook his head. "No one does." His eyes came to hers. "I'm really sorry I didn't stick up for her. I mean, I did a couple of times, but I don't think she knew and it didn't have any effect anyway."

Not knowing what else to say, Jenna looked at Richard.

"I'm sorry," he said gravely. "Obviously, if I'd known—"

"It's not your fault," she interrupted. "It's mine. I wasn't paying attention."

Putting an arm around her, Hanna stepped forward. "Hi, you might remember me," she said to Richard, holding out a hand to shake. "I was with Jenna the first time she came to see you."

"Of course," he responded, "Hanna. It's good to see you again, though I could wish for better circumstances."

"Indeed," she agreed. "Thank you for driving us. I'm not sure either of us would be safe behind a wheel right now."

"I'm glad to be of help." He opened the rear door for her and Jenna to climb in with Cullum.

"It's OK, I'll go in the back," Oliver offered.

"No, no, you're far taller than us," Jenna protested. "You stay in the front."

Minutes later they were driving out of the village with a dozen or more cars falling in behind them: friends and neighbors coming to join in the search, maybe some reporters amongst them. Jenna was so tense, so horrified that her family had somehow turned into the kind of story they only ever saw on the news, that she had to close her eyes and try to pretend she was somewhere else. She felt Hanna's hand slip into hers, and she rested her head on her sister's shoulder. How lucky she was to have her, and their mother, and everyone else who cared, though right now she'd give up every single one of them just to know her child was safe.

She's been out all night and no one has heard from her. That can't be good. How could it possibly be anything but bad?

She had to stop the images that kept tormenting her. If she didn't, she would lose her mind.

By the time they arrived at the car park in Rhossili it was so jammed with the vehicles of yet more volunteers that the police directed them to park in a specially cordoned-off area a few yards away. Euan, having traveled behind them in the convoy, was quick to jump out of his car to make sure his fellow officers were fully aware of who Jenna was.

She was treated as kindly by the police and those who recognized her as the weather was treating the stunning landscape around them. There was no wind, no rain, no dull leaden clouds, only sunshine and early spring warmth. She could sense people staring at her, feeling pity—and relief that they weren't in her shoes. She didn't look back at them.

The search was already under way, with many volunteers split into groups spreading out over the downs, the beach, and the cliffs, wherever they'd been sent. Jenna's party was assigned a section of moorland close to the village.

So far three more people had confirmed seeing a teenage girl getting off the bus around ten yesterday morning. As yet no one seemed to know where she'd gone from there, apart from one person who was sure they'd spotted her in the churchyard.

"They've given you this area close to the village," Euan told her, "so you won't have a problem getting to the car if you need to leave."

Jenna turned to look out at the Worm's Head, stretching its rocky self out into the sun-spangled sea. She was trying to recall the poem Paige had whispered over her misty shots of the landmark, but her mind had gone blank. "She might have got cut off by the tide," she said to no one in particular. "Has anyone checked out there?"

"Yes, we have," she was told by one of the officers in her group. "No sign of her. Would you like to make a start now?"

The answer was no, because it shouldn't be happening, but she obediently followed him and the others along a footpath she'd trodden many times on family walks out onto the moor. Every step felt wrong; she was desperate to turn back, to run from the reality of what she was doing because it was making no sense, but how could she trust her instinct that Paige wasn't here when her instinct had let her down so badly till now?

Hours passed as the volunteers combed every inch of the territory, spreading out for miles, digging into ditches, tearing at bracken, lowering themselves into caves, and even trying to tune in to the prehistoric stone circles and burial chambers to connect with Paige on another level.

Nothing was found: not a single trace of a teenage girl having spent the night in the open, or something she might have dropped on her way to who knew where.

It was just after two when Jack rang to let Jenna know he was in the car park.

Hanna walked back with her, holding her arm and trying in her touching, steadfast way to transmit some moral support into her heart.

They found Jack talking to DS Mariner. His face was ashen, his eyes tired and bleak. Jenna wondered if he'd already been questioned about his relationship with Paige. If he had, this would surely have taken place on the phone before now, not here with so many people around.

"I was asking your husband how you'd feel about broadcasting an appeal," Mariner told her.

A bolt of cruel reality crashed through Jenna as she looked at Jack. "What did you say?" she asked him.

"That I'd be guided by you," he replied, showing no trace of hostility.

Jenna turned back to Mariner. "How's it going to help?" she wanted to know. "It can't unless she has access to the news."

"Which she might have," Mariner pointed out. "She has her phone."

"Has she turned it on?"

Mariner shook her head. "If she's staying with someone . . ."

"You mean this Julie?" *Whoever this Julie might be.*

Mariner drew them aside so they'd be out of earshot. Sensing they were about to be told something bad, Jenna almost turned away. But what good would it do Paige if she was too afraid to hear the truth?

"What is it?" she asked, feeling the awful shaking starting again. "Have you found something?"

"Not here," Mariner answered. "On her computer. It seems she and Julie had a suicide pact. . . ."

"Oh my God!" Jenna sobbed.

Hanna slipped an arm around her, while Jack stared glassy-eyed at the detective.

"You have to find this Julie," Jenna cried. "Do you know who she is yet?"

Mariner said, "I'm hoping to have some answers very soon. Are you sure she's never mentioned her?"

"Of course I'm sure. I'd have told you if she had."

Mariner looked at Jack. "I've no idea," Jack said.

The detective nodded. "Are you ready to come to the station?" she asked him.

As he assented, Jenna could almost feel the depth of his fear and exhaustion. He was clearly jet-lagged, probably hadn't slept all night, and had then driven all the way from Heathrow to join the search, only now to be hauled in by the police to be interrogated in a way that was going to tear him apart. She wished there was something she could say to help him, but she'd done all she could yesterday when they were questioning her. She truly didn't believe he'd ever laid a finger on Paige in the way they were suggesting, but the only person who could persuade them of that was Paige herself.

After Jack had gone Jenna and Hanna rejoined their group, more to feel they were doing something than because they believed they were going to find her. Reports were starting to come in of sightings in Swansea and Cardiff, even as far afield as Newport, and Jenna could feel her hopes draining away with each one.

It was five o'clock by the time Richard took them back to the house. They were all tired and hungry, and Jenna was more afraid than ever. *Please God, don't let there be another night without us knowing where she is.* Why hadn't the computer experts found this Julie yet? What was proving so difficult? Surely identities couldn't be that hard to uncover.

"Mummy! Mummy!" Josh and the twins cried as she walked in the door. "Did you find her?"

Catching them as they ran to her, Jenna had to say, "Not yet."

"Nor did we," Josh confessed solemnly.

"We looked everywhere," Flora told her. "All along the beach and the dunes, in the Salt House, even in the churchyard where the big sailor is."

"He's a lifeboatman," Josh reminded her.

"Oh yes."

"And when we told people what we were doing they joined in," Wills added.

"That was nice of them," Jenna sighed as Richard followed her inside. "This is Mr. Pryce," she told the children, "and these are his sons, Oliver and Cullum."

Flora and Wills had such a long way to look up at Oliver and his father, and were so cute in their circular glasses as they did so, that Jenna's heart folded with love. "Hello," they said in unison.

"Hello," Richard replied, going down to their height. "I'm guessing you're Flora and you're Wills, which means you must be Josh?"

Josh nodded and leaned into his mother.

"We can't find our sister," Flora whispered. "She's got lost somewhere and we don't know where she is."

"I know," Richard replied gently, "but we'll find her, don't you worry about that."

Flora looked up at Jenna as though needing her to confirm it.

"We will," Jenna insisted, needing to hear herself say it.

"Grandma bought hot cross buns," Wills told them. "She's put them in the oven to warm up."

Since they'd rung ahead to let Kay know they were on their way, the tea was already made, so while Richard and Oliver joined Jenna, Hanna, and their mother in the kitchen, Cullum went off to be impressed by the children's gadgets and toys.

"Any word from Jack yet?" Kay asked. "Is he still with the police?"

Jenna checked her mobile and shook her head. What could be taking so long?

"He might have gone home to get some sleep," Hanna suggested. "Why don't you try him?"

When Jenna pressed in his number she went straight to voicemail. "No news," she told him, "but you probably already know that. Are you still with the police? Call when you get this." Turning back to the others, she said to Richard, "Do you think a televised appeal is a good idea?"

"Actually, I do," he replied. "If she's hiding out somewhere and sees it and realizes how worried you are, it could make all the difference."

Jenna nodded and took the tea her mother was passing. Of course it made sense to try to communicate with Paige in any way she could; she just didn't want to become one of the tragic mothers she'd watched so many times on the news. It wasn't who they were. Things like this didn't happen to their family, and yet it was happening, right here and now, and she had to drag herself out of this need to deny it or she was going to be of no help at all.

"Would you like me to go?" Oliver offered as someone knocked on the front door.

"Please," Jenna responded. "If it's someone from the press, say I'm not here, and if it's one of the neighbors, tell them I'm having a lie-down."

As they waited for him to come back Jenna was tempted to tell Richard about Paige's crush on his son, but before she could decide whether it might be breaking Paige's confidence the sound of raised voices reached them.

Putting their cups down, they hurried to the front door, where a stocky blond woman with a furious red face was shouting at Oliver. It wasn't clear at first why she was so angry. When Jenna understood the reason, she turned cold to her core.

"Get her out of here," she said to Richard. "Please. Do whatever it takes."

Moving past his son, Richard said to the woman, "Mrs. Durham, you shouldn't be here."

"And she shouldn't be accusing my girl of things she hasn't done. It's not my Kelly's fault your daughter has gone and run off."

"Yes, it is her fault," Cullum shouted from behind them. "I saw what she did to Paige. I know what she's like, everyone does."

Mrs. Durham's face twitched.

"It's time to go," Richard told her. "Please leave."

"It was others that put her up to it," Mrs. Durham cried as she got into her car. "My Kelly can't take all the blame. The way everyone's turning on her . . ."

"It's what she deserves, the way she turned everyone against Paige," Cullum called after her. "The messages my brother got, we know they came from her."

"Ssh, that's enough," his father cautioned.

"I'm telling you this," the woman shouted through her car window, "if my girl gets thrown out of school I won't be the only one coming after you."

As Jenna turned back inside she saw the younger ones watching from the stairs, round-eyed with fright. "It's OK," she told them gently. "It was someone who . . ." Someone who what? What could she tell them?

"It was someone who should know better than to go round shouting at other people," Richard provided. "Between us, I think she was a bit drunk and didn't realize she'd got the wrong house, so don't you worry about her anymore. She's gone now and she won't be coming back."

"She'd better not," Hanna muttered as they returned to the kitchen. "If that's the kind of family the girl comes from, it's no wonder she's like she is."

Shaking his head, Richard said, "I'm gathering from this that the chief bully in the case is Kelly Durham, daughter of Wendy, who just graced us with a visit?"

"Do you know them?" Jenna asked.

"I've had occasion to represent various members of the family," he admitted. "The father's a car dealer, currently in prison for tax evasion. His brother's about to be prosecuted for the same. And one of the mother's sisters is on a suspended sentence for aggravated assault. She attacked the manager of a store who apprehended her for shoplifting."

Jenna could hardly believe it. "And it's someone from that family who's been picking on Paige? Dear God, is it any wonder no one wants to stand up for her?"

"I think you ought to tell the police she's been here," Hanna stated.

Jenna nodded. "I will when Euan turns up."

"Where is he? I thought he was following us."

"He popped home to see his family for a while. Jack's rung," she added after checking her mobile. Quickly connecting to him, she took the phone into the dining room to speak more privately.

"Sorry, I was asleep when you rang," he said. "I take it there's still no news."

"No. Where are you?"

"At home."

At home? Isn't this his home? "What did the police have to say?" she asked.

"Are you pretending not to know, or do you really not know?"

Moving past the belligerence, she said, "I told them it was nonsense. I know nothing like that ever happened."

"Of course it didn't, and I'd like to get my hands on the kids who tried to make out it did. Can you imagine how it must have made her feel? It's no wonder she didn't want to talk to me. She probably couldn't even stand to look at me without thinking of what they were saying."

Realizing that was probably true, Jenna told him, "We've just had a visit from the bully's mother. If you'd seen her . . . heard her . . . Our lovely girl must have been terrified out of her mind, and what were we doing all that time? Thinking about ourselves, not sparing—"

"Just a minute," he interrupted. "I hope you're not about to start blaming me for any of this."

Stunned, Jenna retorted, "You can't seriously think you bear no responsibility at all. If you hadn't gone off in pursuit of your own—"

"Jenna, I really don't need this."

"Nor do I," she cried furiously, "but for me there's no escaping it. She's missing, no one seems to have the first idea where she is or who she's with, and if we end up not being able to find her then let me tell you, I won't only be holding you responsible, I'll be making sure the rest of the world does too."

As she ended the call she was so incensed by his words and disbelieving of his attitude that she had to give herself a moment before she could return to the kitchen. When she did,

Jack rang again. She couldn't answer. She was too wound up to be able to deal with whatever else he had to say. So she sent him a text.

I know you care about Paige and want to find her as much as I do, so we have to try to support each other, not keep attacking, she wrote. *The children need you. They're scared and I hardly know what to tell them. It would help if you were here, but only if you can control the way you're speaking to me.*

It wasn't until after Richard and his sons had gone home and she was getting the children ready for bed that he texted back. *I'm sorry for what I said. After the things I've been accused of today I guess I wasn't thinking straight. I want to help with the children, please let me. I want to be there for you too.*

Deciding to call him, she went into her bedroom and closed the door. "If you want to come and spend the night here you can," she told him. "I can't imagine either of us will get any sleep, but I know I wouldn't want to be on my own right now, so there's no reason why you should be."

"Are you sure?" he asked.

"Yes, I'm sure."

"Then I'll be there within the hour."

It was just after seven-thirty the following morning that the police rang to speak to Jenna. She was already awake, though huddled under a blanket on the sofa, while Jack slept in Josh's room. The children were spread out around her, with Hanna and her mother dozing in the armchairs until the phone roused them.

Torn between hope and dread, Jenna clicked on the line and waited for the person at the other end to speak.

"Mrs. Moore? It's Lesley Mariner."

"Have you found her?" Jenna asked faintly.

"I'm afraid not, but a dog walker's just called in . . ."

Jenna didn't hear any more. It was always dog walkers who found bodies. "No!" she sobbed wretchedly. "Please, please no."

Hanna rushed to her.

"I don't think you heard me," Mariner was saying. "Are you still there, Mrs. Moore?"

"Yes, I'm here," Jenna whispered, stilling Hanna.

"This person is claiming to have seen a teenage girl on Whiteford Sands about half an hour ago," Mariner told her.

Jenna was trying to make sense of it. A teenage girl on the beach a few miles away, at this hour . . . "Was . . . was it her?" she asked.

"We don't know, but she fits the description, so the search-and-rescue team is on its way. I thought you'd like to know."

"Of course. Thank you. I . . ." She was trying to think. She needed to go over there, and she needed to go now. "There's been a sighting at Whiteford Sands," she told the others. "They don't know if it's her, but it was a teenage girl who fits the description."

Dashing upstairs, she roused Jack and ran back down again, not even taking the time to splash water on her face or comb her hair. It was going to be Paige. It had to be, and if it was, she needed to get to her as fast as she possibly could.

Minutes later she, Jack, and Hanna were in the car with Waffle in the back. "He'll find her," Jenna declared, brimming with confidence. "He's her dog. He'll know where she is. We should have taken him yesterday. Why didn't I think of it? She wasn't there, though, was she, so he couldn't have found her then. But he will this morning, won't you, sweetie? You're going to find Paige, and then we'll bring her home."

Jack glanced at her worriedly, while Hanna put a hand on Jenna's shoulder as though to calm her.

"It'll be her," Jenna insisted, her eyes swimming in tears. "I know it. I swear, it's going to be her."

By the time they drove into the quaint little hamlet of Cwm Ivy, heading for the wooded hillsides around Whiteford Sands, the place was already teeming with police cars. Recognizing Jenna, a uniformed officer waved them through, and directed Jack to pull up at the side of the track.

Leaping out, Jenna ran to the back of the car for Waffle. "Go find Paige," she instructed urgently. "Go find her, there's a good boy."

Obediently Waffle bounded off down the track, sniffing and swerving, kicking up dust as he went and barely pausing to query a scent.

Jenna, Jack, and Hanna ran after him, but there was no way they could keep up.

"He knows where she is," Jenna cried excitedly. "I can tell. He knows where he's going."

She received no contradiction; the others were too full of hope themselves to try to rationalize hers.

Waffle was at least fifty yards ahead, almost at the end of the track, ready to run up into the dunes. In the distance they could see the beach, swarming with police and tracker dogs. It was a beautiful morning: sunlight was sparkling over the sea, the sky was blue, and the sands were as softly golden as the sun itself. It was like being in a dream. Everything seemed so perfect that nothing could go wrong now.

She was here. Jenna could feel it. Her baby was close now, and at any minute she'd be holding her in her arms.

Please God, don't let me be fooling myself. I have to be right about this.

All of a sudden Waffle turned off the main track and started along another, where he came to an abrupt halt in front of a five-bar gate. He sniffed around it, frantically trying to find a way past. In the end he squeezed through a tiny gap at the side and charged on.

"Waffle, wait!" Jenna called. "We're going to lose you."

The dog wasn't listening. He bounded on, past a small bungalow tucked into the trees, around a bend in the trail, and disappeared into the woods.

"Waffle!" Jack shouted as they climbed the gate. "Waffle, wait, boy!"

By the time they reached the bend, breathless, hearts pounding with exertion and hope, there was no longer any sign of the dog, only a fork in the track that left them not knowing which way to go.

There was a part in the book *The Lovely Bones* when the girl who was dead realized her dog could see her, which meant he was dead too. It had always made Paige cry. This was what she thought of when Waffle bounded in through the door of her shelter and jumped on her in slobbery glee.

We're both dead, she was thinking as she hugged him, and though she was happier than she'd ever been in her life to see him, she was devastated too. Waffle was dead. She didn't want him to die, ever.

"Hello," she whispered, squeezing him with all her might.

He licked the tears from her cheeks and wagged his tail so hard his back legs lifted.

Waffle was here for her. He'd come because he didn't want to let her down the way everyone else had. Especially Julie, who had directed her to this place that was a shack, but like someone's home with sofas and chairs, a kitchen and fireplace. There were even beds in other rooms and a bathroom.

But Julie hadn't come.

Paige had waited and waited out here in the woods, all alone, terrified, and confused, desperate to find the courage to act alone—until finally she'd walked into the waves, never to come back.

So now she was dead. She didn't exist anymore, but like the girl in *The Lovely Bones* she could see and hear everyone else, even though they couldn't see or hear her.

Her mother was shouting for Waffle. "Where are you, boy? Waffle, come back."

"Waffle!" Auntie Hanna called. "Here, boy."

"They want you," she told him, "but you're here now, we're together, and I won't let you go."

A shadow filled the sunlit doorway.

Paige kept her face buried in Waffle.

"Oh my God. Oh my God," she heard her mother sob. "Paige . . ."

"No!" Paige cried, leaping to her feet and backing away. "Don't touch me! Don't come near me."

Her mother stopped.

"It's your fault," Paige sobbed wildly. "I could have done it if it weren't for you."

Her mother's arms were outstretched, and so were Paige's, blocking her from coming any further.

"I don't understand," Jenna whispered. "Please . . ."

"They said I'm not supposed to think about anyone else, or care about them, or do anything except think about me, then it would be all right, I'd be ready to do it, but I kept thinking about *you*! I couldn't stop thinking about *you*. You were here in my head all the time, you wouldn't stop, wouldn't let me go, and I have to because I can't take any more."

"Paige, listen to me," Jenna implored. "It's going to be all right . . ."

"No! *No!* It's never going to be all right because I love you too much and if I didn't I could have made everything stop. . . ." Tears were streaming down her cheeks, and her whole body was jerking with violent sobs.

Jenna tried going forward, but Paige backed further away.

"Darling, we're going to work it out," Jenna told her. "The bullies are already being dealt with, and Dad's here. . . . We know what they said about you and him, and we know it wasn't true. Everyone does."

"Then why did they say it?"

"Because they're mean and spiteful and they don't have dads who love them anywhere near as much."

"So why did he leave?"

"Paige," Jack said, stepping into the room, "I swear it had nothing to do with you. I love you more—"

"No! You're with *her* now. You don't care about us."

"That isn't true. Please try to understand how sorry I am that I've done this to you. If I hadn't, I know you'd have talked to me and Mum about what was happening."

Paige's eyes shot to the door as a police officer appeared.

"It's OK," Jenna told him. "She's fine, we all are. If you could give us a minute . . ."

As he stepped back Jenna moved closer to Paige. "Can we take you home now?" she asked softly.

Paige started to shake her head, but there was nothing she could do to stop herself falling into Jenna's arms, whispering, "Mummy, Mummy, Mummy."

Chapter 21

Paige was taken by ambulance from the ecologist's bunkhouse at Whiteford Sands to Morriston Hospital in Swansea. Jenna traveled with her, while Jack, Hanna, and Waffle followed in the car and Kay drove across from Port Eynon with Josh and the twins.

After the doctor finished checking Paige over, the children were allowed to see her. The reunion was boisterous and tearful, and did much to endear them to the staff. However, Paige was apparently still suffering from a mild delirium caused by exposure to the elements, emotional trauma, and a two-day fast, so the young ones weren't allowed to stay long.

She fell asleep almost as soon as they'd gone, and slept deeply until late afternoon, at which point the doctor said, "I'd like to keep her for further observation, but under the circumstances, perhaps being back in the bosom of her family is where she really needs to be."

"I think so," Jenna agreed. "And don't worry, we understand about the psychiatric assessment. We'll make sure it happens."

"I'm sure you realize that working through something like this can be a long process," he cautioned, "so it's important that she's fully recharged physically before she begins. Were you given the number to call?"

After assuring him she had been, Jenna took Paige the fresh clothes Kay had brought in, and Jack went to fetch the car. It was while they were waiting for him to come back that DS Mariner rang.

"How is she?" the detective asked.

"She's doing well," Jenna said with a smile, slipping an arm round Paige's shoulders. "We're about to go home."

"That's good. I'm glad it turned out this way."

"Thank you."

"We'll need to speak to her at some point."

"I realize that, but not yet."

"No, of course not. I thought you'd want to know that we've identified Julie Morris."

Yes, Jenna did want to know, but not with Paige sitting right next to her; there would be time later for her daughter to deal with whatever else was to come. So leaving her texting Charlotte, she walked outside. "Who is it?" she asked.

"Her real name is Olivia Masters. She's at the same school, a year above Paige."

Jenna was frowning as she tried to recall the name. "Does she have a brother called Owen?" she asked.

"Yes, she does. She was rushed to the emergency room last night after taking an overdose."

Stunned, Jenna said, "Is she . . . did she . . . ?"

"She was at home when it happened, so I'm guessing Paige knows nothing about it."

"Is she going to be all right?"

"I believe so."

Glad of that, though confused about her feelings for the girl herself, Jenna asked, "Do you know why . . . ?" She shook her head. "There are so many whys. Why Paige? Why change her name? Why try to kill herself?"

"All questions we need answers to, and hopefully we'll get them when she's ready to talk. Meantime, if anything should come to light that you think might be helpful, you have my number; please be in touch."

Paige was at home now in her own bed, surrounded by her siblings, who couldn't do enough for her, and her dog, the hero of the hour. Jenna thought she still looked tired and anxious, but at least she was managing to put on a show for the children. Her old self was still in there somewhere; it was just going to need some time to find its confidence again.

"She's always had a strong personality," Hanna declared when they were in the sitting room later, with everyone asleep upstairs. "It's what'll get her through this—and her mother, of course."

Jenna looked at Jack. He seemed so lost, so beaten, even, that she could only wonder what was going through his mind. "How long are you staying?" she asked him.

"You mean tonight?" he replied.

"Yes, and after that. Will you be booking a flight back to the States once we've seen the psychiatrist? Or perhaps you'd rather not stay around for that."

His eyes went down. "I'm getting the impression she'd rather I wasn't here," he said. "She's barely spoken to me since we found her."

Irritated by the self-pity, Jenna said, "You know she's not in a good place, and frankly I don't think disappearing again is going to help things between you. This is presuming, of course, that you want there to be a relationship between you."

His eyes showed his pain. "I'm surprised you can even ask it."

Before Jenna could respond, Hanna said, "I'm guessing she won't be going back to school for the rest of this term."

Jenna shook her head. "They break for Easter on Thursday, so I don't think anyone will be expecting her to. I'll call Mr. Charles in the morning."

"Did you see that he rang while you were at the hospital?" Hanna asked. "He wanted to say how relieved everyone was that Paige had been found, and he wants you to call to discuss what's happened when you're ready."

"Did he mention anything about Kelly Durham and what's going to happen to her?"

"No, but I don't suppose he would to me. It was about Paige today. As far as I'm concerned, it's always about Paige."

"Have you told her about this Olivia girl yet?" Jack wanted to know.

Jenna shook her head. "She's had enough for one day."

"Do you know the parents?" Hanna asked.

"I've seen them, but I've never met them. They always seem . . . how shall I put it . . . a bit reclusive, stand-offish even, but like I say, I don't actually know them. She's a gifted musician, Olivia. Paige has often talked about her. Apparently she plays in assembly sometimes."

"So why did she need an alias to make friends? And what on earth drove her to forge a friendship with Paige that ended in a suicide pact?"

"I've no idea yet. Just thank God she stood Paige up and acted alone—although, of course, it's tragic that she did. It seems she's going to pull through." She looked around. "Where's Mum? I don't think I've seen her since the children went to bed."

"She was going to do some ironing," Hanna answered, peering through to the kitchen. "Doesn't look like she's there, though."

Going to check, Jenna found her mother in the dining room, standing in the darkness staring out at the starry night sky. "Are you OK?" she asked softly. "I wondered where you'd got to."

When Kay didn't answer, Jenna went to stand in front of her. "Mum?"

Kay still said nothing, but as she turned her head Jenna caught the glint of tears on her cheeks.

"Oh, Mum, what is it?" she urged. She couldn't remember ever seeing her mother cry before, not even when her father died.

"It's my fault," Kay stated. "I should have taken it more seriously. She told me—she said people were being mean to her. And because I did nothing we nearly lost her."

"You can't blame yourself, Mum," Jenna protested. "She told me too."

"But I've been through it. I know what it's like to be bullied."

"Which doesn't mean you would automatically understand what was happening, or that you could have stopped it. You were there for her when she needed you, that's what counts."

Kay's face remained strained with grief. "I've never been a good enough parent, or grandma," she said bluntly. "I keep trying, but I know you need more. . . ."

"How can you say that when we'd never manage without you? You're our rock, Mum. You're always there for us, and always have been."

"But not in the way your father was."

"In other ways. Oh, Mum, please don't do this to yourself.

We love you so much, all of us, and we know you love us too. You're still crying. . . . I'm sorry, but I have to do this. I know you don't like it, but I'm going to."

Kay stood very still as Jenna folded her into her arms and rested her head against hers. Though she didn't hug her back, she didn't try to break away either, and after a while she gave her a hesitant little pat.

Jenna smiled through her own tears. "That was lovely," she whispered.

Kay's eyes came to hers. "Perhaps if I got some counseling?" she suggested.

"I think we all need it," Jenna told her. "You, me, and Paige."

"But she's our priority."

"Of course."

Kay's eyes drifted back to the garden. "I had some once," she admitted, "but it didn't do me much good."

"Times have changed; therapies are different, more effective. Even so, we love you just the way you are."

Kay nodded. "What's happened here, with Paige," she said, "will change a lot of things for a lot of people. Let's hope it's all for the good."

"You're kidding," Paige murmured, torn between disbelief and unease. "Tell me you're making it up."

"I swear I'm not," Charlotte insisted. "Oliver was there on Saturday, helping to look for you."

Paige's face remained pale. "Did you talk to him?"

"No. Actually, I only saw him from a distance, but it was definitely him, because Cullum was there too, and their dad."

Not sure whether she wanted to curl up with embarrassment

or allow herself to feel pleased, Paige said, "Do you think some-one made him come?"

"I've got no idea. I'm just telling you, he was there." Charlotte glanced at the time. "I have to go," she sighed. "I've probably already missed the bus, but your grandma said she'd drive me to school. I just had to come and see you for myself. So we're good now? All the bad things forgotten?"

"Definitely," Paige assured her, feeling certain they would be just as soon as she got her head properly straightened out. "Thanks for standing by me all the times you did," she remembered to add.

Charlotte regarded her sardonically. "You didn't always make it easy," she told her. "Anyway, we should find out sometime this week if Kelly Durham's being suspended or expelled. Let's hope it's expelled."

Instantly feeling anxious, Paige said, "If she is, she'll find a way to make me pay."

"No way, we won't let her. She's history from now on. She's the sinking ship no one wants to go down with."

"What about Bethany and Matilda?"

Charlotte shrugged. "The Durmites are over without her. Are you staying in bed today?"

"I don't know. Mum wants to have a chat, *of course,* and I just know Dad will want one too."

Charlotte pulled a sympathy face. "At least he came back from the States," she pointed out.

"Big deal."

"You'd have been hurt if he didn't."

Letting her head fall back, Paige said, "I don't know what to say to him."

"So let him do the talking. He's the one who's in the wrong, so you don't have to do anything."

After a while Paige's eyes went back to Charlotte, a sheepish glint flickering in their depths. "Do you swear you're not winding me up about Oliver?"

Charlotte grinned. "Cross my heart. I know—why don't you text and say thank you?"

Paige immediately shrank from that. "No way am I going to be in touch with him."

"Up to you, but I would be if it were me."

Reminded of how different they were at times, Paige gave her a hug and watched her walk to the door.

Turning back, Charlotte said, "By the way, have you been in touch with *Julie* since all this happened?"

Paige's lips tightened as she shook her head. Lying back against the pillows as Charlotte left, she closed her eyes. She'd messaged Julie dozens of times since her phone had recharged, asking why she hadn't come and what sort of friend would leave someone out in the woods on their own for two nights in a row, but she hadn't received a single reply. She wasn't going to bother trying again. In truth, she didn't want to have any more to do with her. She didn't even care who she really was, although she'd definitely like to know, if only to expose her to everyone else.

How could she have allowed herself to be talked into what she'd done? It didn't seem credible now, yet she hadn't forgotten how comforted she'd felt when they were in touch. It really had seemed as though Julie was her only friend in the world, and that she'd be there for her when no one else would.

Except that hadn't happened, had it?

As if on cue, Waffle nosed his way in through the door. Breaking into a smile, Paige patted the bed for him to come and join her. "We're not dead," she whispered in his ear. "I know I said we were yesterday, but we're here, and everyone can see us, just like we can see them."

Seeming to enjoy this idea, he gave her a hearty lick.

"I thought I saw him sneak in," her mother said, putting her head round. "Charlotte gone?"

"Just."

Coming to sit on the bed, Jenna said, "So how are you feeling this morning?"

Paige simply shrugged. She didn't want to talk about anything, but at the same time she didn't want to hurt her mum any more than she already had. So in the end she finally admitted to being a bit mixed up. "Like one minute I'm fine and the next I'm all kind of . . . you know."

Jenna's eyebrows rose. "Do you want to try another way of explaining that?"

Paige sighed. "I don't know the words. It's just, like, weird, as though I've been someone else for a while, and I'm kind of back, but not."

"You've been through a pretty harrowing time, which is why it'll be a good idea to talk it through with someone."

"I'm talking to you."

"I mean a professional."

Paige's eyes went down. "I just want to forget it now," she said.

"I know, sweetheart, and I understand that, but we need to find out how much harm those girls might have caused, and what this business with Julie Morris and all those dreadful websites might have added to it."

"It was dark," Paige mumbled, "like really, seriously dark. Those chat rooms . . . I don't ever want to go there again, but it felt kind of OK while I was doing it. It was like everyone was my friend and they all understood me."

"But you know now that's not true?"

"I guess so, except a lot of the people I connected to are being bullied, the same as me, some of them even worse, so they did understand."

"OK, but they need to be helped, not encouraged by others in the chat room to take extreme ways out."

"I never encouraged anyone, I swear it."

"But you *were* encouraged, especially by Julie, and if she hadn't decided to let you down, I'm not sure where we'd be now."

Paige's eyes drifted as she pictured herself back at Whiteford Sands. "I kind of wanted to do it," she said, "but then I didn't. I was thinking about you and everyone. . . . I kept wanting you to come, but it was like I had to wait for Julie, so I couldn't come home."

"Why did you think you had to wait for her?"

"I'm not sure really. I mean, it wasn't only that—I didn't want to come back because it would mean either having to go to school or carry on riding round on buses all day. . . . The police asked me yesterday if I got a bus to Rhossili on Friday, but I didn't."

"It wasn't you? I had a feeling it wasn't."

"But you went to look for me anyway?"

"Of course, I had to. My instincts might have been wrong. They were right yesterday, though. I'm so pleased we took Waffle. He made very short work of it all."

Smiling as she ruffled his fur, Paige said, "When he came in it made me think of that part in *The Lovely Bones* where the girl realizes her dog can see her, so she knows he's dead. It was so weird. Then you were there and you could see me too and I got all confused. . . . I didn't want to come back, but I did."

Jenna took her hand. "Are you glad to be back now?"

Paige nodded but didn't look up.

Entwining their fingers, Jenna said, "I'm sorry I didn't realize sooner what you were going through. I can see now that you tried to tell me, but I was so wrapped up in what was happening with Dad. . . ."

Paige's head came up. "Has he gone back to Martha yet?"

"No. He's very worried about you, and I'm sure he won't be going anywhere until you've agreed to see him."

Heat rose in Paige's cheeks. "I don't want to," she said.

"I know, but I think you should. All those dreadful things Kelly Durham and her friends wrote . . ."

"None of it's true."

"No one believes it was." She didn't have to tell Paige about the police enquiries; they'd had a job to do, and it was over now, with no harm done—apart from to Jack, possibly, but he'd have to take care of himself. "And he really didn't leave because of you," Jenna added forcefully.

"He left because he found someone who matters more than us," Paige cried angrily.

"More than *me*," Jenna corrected, "not you or the others."

"See, that's what I can't stand," Paige seethed, her fist hitting the bed, "that he could let someone matter more than you."

Jenna smiled sadly. "I know it's hard for you, and I won't lie, it is for me too, but we can get through it. Almost losing you has taught me a lot of things, and the first is that nothing and no one matters more than you, Josh, and the twins."

Paige drew back. *"Them!"* she scoffed. "I thought I was number one."

Jenna laughed. "You are in that you're my firstborn, and I think it's been more difficult for you than I'd realized, having to share me and Dad since Josh came along. You'd got used to having us all to yourself until then."

"But I wanted brothers and sisters."

"I know, just a bit sooner than it happened. It might not have been as much of a shock if there hadn't been such an age gap, but we don't always get to choose these things." She looked down as Paige's phone bleeped with a text.

Just heard KD being expelled. Yay! Cx

"She's not even at school yet," Paige said, showing her mother the message, "so I expect it's still a rumor."

"I think there'll be quite a thorough investigation before any decisions like that are made, but there has to be some kind of punishment for the way she's behaved. And frankly, I don't want you in the same school as someone who'd treat anyone the way she treated you," Jenna told her.

"So I could leave?"

"Do you want to?"

Paige shrugged. "I'm scared she'll come after me if it all goes wrong for her," she admitted.

"If she does, at the very first sign of it you know what you have to do."

Paige swallowed.

"You have to come to me," Jenna insisted. "You can't allow yourself to go through it again. You're not a victim, Paige.

That's not who you are, so you mustn't let her turn you into one."

"I don't want to, but she has all these friends, and her family's, like . . . really tough."

Judging it wiser not to mention anything about Wendy Durham's visit, Jenna said, "I've heard about them, but we have the school on our side, and the police, and I think you'll find when you go back that you have a lot more friends than you realize."

Paige didn't look convinced. "They'll call me saddo and loser for trying to kill myself."

"No they won't, because it's not what you did. You thought about it, and when the time came you had the courage to pull back and see things through."

After a while Paige gave a weak sort of smile. "You always find a way to turn me into the heroine of the piece," she stated.

Jenna's eyebrows rose. "Because that's who you are."

"Like yeah."

"Like yeah, and if I know you, which I do, in time you'll find a way to turn this into a positive experience."

"How the heck am I going to do that?"

"Like I said, you'll find a way, but right now I can see that's hard to believe."

Paige's eyes narrowed suspiciously. "You're brainwashing me," she accused. "You're using the power of suggestion to get me to do what you want."

Jenna laughed. "If only I had such a gift."

After sitting quietly for a few minutes, Paige said, "Did anyone find out who Julie Morris really is?"

Sighing, Jenna said, "Yes, they did, but we don't have to talk about it now."

"I want to. Who is she?"

As Paige's eyes came to hers, Jenna decided there was no point in holding back. It would have to be dealt with sooner or later, and if she didn't tell her, chances were Charlotte would find out and deliver the news herself. "OK," she said, "she's Olivia Masters, Owen's sister."

Paige blinked in amazement. Confusion, anger, and disbelief chased across her face. The quiet, almost ethereal beauty who wafted around the school like a ghost, saying very little, playing her violin like an angel, hating her for posting lies about Owen . . . it just wasn't adding up. "I don't get it," she told Jenna. "She said she was bullied too. She understood what I was going through. She told me she'd been Kelly Durham's victim."

"Maybe it's true."

"But Charlotte would have known."

"Then I'm afraid I can't explain what was going through her mind. But I do have some more news about her . . ."

Paige's expression turned wary.

"She tried to take her own life on Saturday night," Jenna said softly.

Paige froze in shock. So she really had meant it. She'd actually wanted to die. It was why she'd had to wait for the girl who called herself Julie, she realized—to try to stop her. At least that was how it was feeling to her now. "She didn't succeed," she said, making it more of a statement than a question.

Jenna shook her head.

"So how did she . . . I mean, what did she . . . ?"

"She took an overdose."

"How do you know about it?"

"The police told me. As far as I'm aware, she's still in the hospital."

"The same one I was in?"

Jenna nodded.

Paige thought about it. "Is she going to be all right?" Did she care? She wasn't sure, but supposed she did.

"I'm not sure, but I expect we can find out."

Paige was still trying to get her head round it. Olivia Masters, Owen's sister. She remembered the time she'd gone up to her in school and asked her to tell Owen that she wasn't responsible for the post saying he was gay. Olivia had looked at her as though she despised her, and yet at the same time she was using an alter ego to befriend her. "She told me her mother was dead," she mumbled, "but it's not true. Owen's mother is alive."

Unable to explain that, Jenna said, "I'm sure we'll get to the bottom of it sooner or later. Meantime, do you feel like getting up?"

Paige wasn't sure. "What are we doing today?" she asked. "I don't want to go back to school."

"You don't have to, but Mr. Charles is asking if he can come here with Miss Willis from the pastoral team to have a chat with you."

Paige drew back. That was way too much. "Do I have to see them?" she protested.

"Not right away, but they'll need to hear your side of what's happened at some point, and so will the police."

Though she understood that, Paige still just wanted it all to go away so she could forget any of it had ever happened. It didn't matter that she couldn't think about anything else, especially Olivia now, and Oliver looking for her . . . She could hardly get her head round either of those things, although Mr. Charles and Miss Willis wouldn't be coming here to talk about them. They'd want to focus on the bullying and what had driven her to the suicide sites, and the last thing she needed was to play a part in whatever action they decided to take about Kelly Durham. "Can I just stay in bed today?" she asked miserably.

"Of course," her mother responded. "I'll call the school and tell them they'll have to wait."

Though Jenna was putting on a good front for Paige, inside she was burning with rage over the Durham child's appalling cruelty. She'd seen enough of the social network postings now, the doctored photographs, the name-calling, and the horrendous accusations concerning Jack to make her determined that not a single one of that despicable gang should be allowed to get away with what they'd done. Which was why she'd left a message for DS Mariner to call back as soon as possible so they could discuss bringing charges.

"I'm not sure we're going to get very far," Hanna remarked, looking up from her laptop. "I've just been researching it, and I can't find much in the way of consequences for bullies."

"There has to be some kind of punishment," Jenna insisted. "No one, not even a child, should be allowed to get away with the kind of things that were done to Paige."

"If you read some of this, you'll see it can be a whole lot worse, but so far I haven't managed to turn up a single case of a bully being prosecuted."

"We can't let that stop us. I don't care what kind of family the girl comes from—she needs to know there is a price to pay for her actions."

"Richard's our man," Hanna decided. "He'll know how to go about things."

"Of course," Jenna agreed. "He's in court today, but I'll

speak to him later. At the very least we should be able to get an antisocial-behavior order against her."

Hanna wrinkled her nose. "An ASBO? I'm not sure they hand them out for bullying, or if they even still exist. Weren't the Tories going to do away with them when they took office?"

"As it's not the kind of circle we normally move in, I can't answer that, but knowing what we do about the Durhams, they'd probably consider an ASBO a badge of honor. So it has to be criminal proceedings, something that'll go on the girl's record for as long as the effects of her actions stay with her victims."

"Which would be an unquantifiable amount of time. However, in principle I like the idea."

Jenna was scrolling through all the texts she'd received over the weekend, wanting to make sure she hadn't missed anything vital. Finding a message from her agent that had arrived on Saturday, she reluctantly opened it. The idea of having to empty her bank account and start asking Jack for money was something she really didn't want to start dealing with now.

Jenna, have seen the news. Really sorry to hear what's happening. I'm sure you'll find her soon. My thoughts are with you. Let me know if there's anything I can do. Call when you can.

Profoundly relieved that he wasn't intending to embroil her in any difficulties in the immediate future, she continued the search, erasing, saving, and forwarding where necessary, until she came to the most recent message from Jack.

How is she this morning? Can I come over?

Showing it to Hanna, she said, "She doesn't want to see him."

"Frankly, none of us do."

Jenna's eyebrows rose. "Not helpful. I can't just exclude him from what's happening. He cares very much, and I'd like his support for a prosecution."

"Which you're likely to get, but how much thought have you given to Paige and how she's going to feel if it turns out you *can* bring criminal charges?"

Jenna eyed her worriedly. "Probably not as much as I ought to have," she conceded. "I guess I should discuss it with her first."

"I think so, and knowing my niece, I expect she'll have her own views on what should happen to bullies."

Jenna nodded slowly as she reached to answer her buzzing phone. "Hello, Jenna Moore speaking."

"Mrs. Moore, it's Mr. Charles at The Landings. I've just been told that Paige isn't up to seeing us today."

"She still needs to rest."

"I understand, of course. She's been through quite an ordeal, and once again I'm very sorry that this was allowed to go as far as it did—in fact, that it was allowed to happen at all. We have a strict anti-bullying policy in place that follows the government guidelines, but it's obviously failed us badly in this instance, and of course we'll be looking into it."

"That's good to hear," she said coolly. As far as she was concerned, the school was as culpable as she was for not having stopped this right at the start, and she would be making that very point just as soon as the time was right.

"I'm sure you understand," he continued, "that it's not possible for us to monitor what goes on outside of school hours, but I'm aware that much of the intimidation happened while Paige was here, so please be assured that appropriate action will be taken. We will be deciding on what that should be once we've heard all sides of the story."

Wincing at his use of the word *story*, as if this were some little anecdote that could be passed around until a better one came along, Jenna said, "Do you have any news about Olivia Masters?"

"Apparently she's still in the hospital, but I'm told by the doctor that she's awake and sitting up. I've tried calling her parents, but they haven't got back to me. I'm not sure at this point if the police have been more successful."

"Is Owen at school today?"

"No, he isn't."

Unsurprised, she said, "OK, I'll let you know when Paige is ready to see you." Ringing off, she switched to another incoming call.

"Lesley Mariner here. I got your message."

"Ah yes, thanks for ringing me back." Jenna turned to Hanna, mouthing who it was. "I've been giving this some thought, and I'd like to know if it's possible to bring charges against Kelly Durham and her parents."

Hanna's eyebrows rose. "Parents?" she echoed.

Jenna nodded. In her book they were as responsible as anyone else for the way their daughter had behaved, probably even more so.

DS Mariner sighed. "I was afraid you might be thinking that way, and I wish I could be more helpful, but the only laws we have to cover cases like this fall under stalking and harassment."

"Then that's where we should start."

"However, the Crown Prosecution Service is rarely willing

to consider them for bullying—especially when it could end up criminalizing a child."

Jenna's temper flared. "So it's all right for my daughter to suffer at their hands, but not all right for them to face the consequences? Is that what you're saying?"

"I understand where you're coming from, truly I do, and in your shoes I'd feel exactly the same, but I've been here before, so I know how the CPS will view the case. They prefer the situation to be handled by parents, or the school, or social services."

"And if Paige had ended up actually committing suicide? What would the CPS do then?"

"It's highly possible that the same would apply, as no criminal act would be involved in a suicide, unless of course someone is given physical assistance."

"So these kids can go on websites or send texts to anyone they like encouraging them to do away with themselves, and the law does nothing about it?"

"Mrs. Moore, I swear I feel as frustrated as you do—"

"I don't think so."

"—but all I can do is tell you how it is, not how I want it to be. If you're asking me do I think they should be held to account, then the answer's yes, in some cases I certainly do. Having to face the full force of the law might make them think twice before they picked on someone again. But the power isn't with me, I'm afraid. It's with you and your MP and all the action groups that exist out there who are trying to come up with a better way of dealing with this."

Realizing she was heading up a dead end, and mindful of the fact that she wasn't going to do anything without speaking to Paige first anyway, Jenna said, "I appreciate your candor. Thank you. I have one more question before you go. If we end up deciding that we do want to take it further, can we bring a private prosecution?"

"Well, I don't see why not, but that's something you'd need to discuss with a lawyer."

After ringing off, Jenna said to Hanna, "I'd never be able to afford it, of course, but I needed to know."

"I could," Hanna reminded her, "and I promise you, if it's the way Paige wants to go, I'll back her all the way."

Touched, Jenna said, "I'll have to pick my moment to bring it up, and I guess I ought to talk to Richard first to make sure it's a viable option, because we can't have her deciding to go for it and then being told it can't happen."

"I have to advise against it," Richard told them later that evening. "Not because I don't believe you have a case—under Sections 2 and 4 of the Protection from Harassment Act you probably do—but the CPS won't like it, and you also need to consider the amount of pressure it would put on Paige, when she's already suffered enough."

"And she's my first concern," Jenna assured him. "I just want to know if it's possible to bring a suit if she decides it's the way she wants to go."

"Well, you have my answer, but I think you also need to take into consideration the kind of family you'd be up against."

"I'm not going to let them intimidate me," Jenna hotly informed him. "People who've committed crimes need to pay like anyone else."

No one looked at Jack, who was sitting quietly in one of the armchairs, but Jenna could sense his discomfort. She wondered when he'd ever seemed more pathetic, more out of tune with his surroundings. It was as though he was collapsing in on himself, with only the shell intact.

"All this is academic until we've consulted Paige," Hanna reminded them.

Richard nodded. "How is she today?"

"She's slept quite a lot," Jenna replied, "and she's been eating, so I'm going to take both as good signs."

"She's concerned about Olivia Masters," Kay reminded her.

Jenna said to Richard, "We haven't got to the bottom of it yet, but apparently Julie Morris is really Olivia Masters, Owen Masters's sister. Do you happen to know the parents?"

Richard shook his head. "I can't say I do. I'm not even sure I've ever seen them."

Jenna looked at her mother and Hanna.

"Well, what we do know," Hanna stated, "is that something strange is clearly going on with the girl, but I don't suppose we're going to find out much more until they let her out of the hospital."

"I guess I should be going," Jack said a couple of hours later. Richard had left a while ago, as had Kay and Hanna. The time since then had been spent getting the younger ones off to sleep, which had taken far longer than usual.

Picking up on his despondency, Jenna said, "She'll come round."

He nodded and reached for his coat.

"What do you really think of bringing a private prosecution?" she asked as he put it on. "I know you said you were for it earlier, but you haven't passed any comment since."

"What's there to say?" he replied. "You've already decided, and if it's what Paige wants, it's what we'll do."

"But? I'm sensing a but."

He took a moment, seeming to decide whether to go further, and then said, "OK, what I really think is that *you* want a lawsuit to prove to yourself, and the rest of the world, that you're a great mother who'll go to any lengths to punish those who mess with her daughter. The trouble is, we've already failed her, and everyone knows it. We weren't there, either of us, when she needed us, and no court case or public hanging is ever going to change that."

Jenna stared at him hard. He'd hit a truth even she hadn't seen, and she wasn't liking it much.

"You asked," he told her.

"You're right," she eventually conceded. "I'm making it about me and my need for revenge, and I'd still give anything to get it, but I promise you it's not going to happen if Paige doesn't want it."

His eyes remained on hers as he said, "I'm not doubting you. And for the record, you *are* a great mother."

She didn't agree, but to try to lighten things she replied, "Is that my cue to say you're a great dad?"

His eyes clouded again. "We both know that's not true, so let's not go there."

"You always used to be."

"Until I screwed up."

How could she deny it?

As he turned to leave, she said, "Am I sensing regret?"

Keeping his back to her, he said, "I'll always regret hurting you."

"But you'd do it again?"

In the end he turned to face her. "I'd try to handle it differently," he admitted.

She swallowed hard and tried to smile past the pain. Despite all they'd just been through, he'd still rather be with Martha than with them.

"Are you and Richard . . . ?" he asked.

"We're friends."

"He seems a good bloke."

"I'm not looking for your approval."

"Sorry, I wasn't trying to give it."

For a while he stood staring off to one side as if there were more he wanted to say and he just didn't know how to come out with it.

"Mum!" Wills suddenly wailed from the top of the stairs. "I've got a toothache."

As they looked at each other, Jack raised a single eyebrow. Picking up his keys, he said, "I'll call you tomorrow."

Chapter 22

Two days later Jenna was in the hallowed territory of the school principal's sitting room, facing Olivia Masters across a hearth filled with dried flowers. Also present were Mr. Charles, Miss Willis, head of the pastoral team, and an elegantly dressed woman who'd been introduced as Judith Merchant, Olivia's aunt.

The call inviting Jenna to attend the start of what was being termed restorative justice proceedings had come late yesterday afternoon.

"But I thought restorative justice was supposed to be about seeing someone face-to-face," Paige had protested when Jenna had told her about it, "so why can't I be there?"

"All I can tell you," Jenna replied, "is that Olivia's asked to see only me at this stage. But apparently this is just the start, so I'm sure you'll be included further down the line."

"What about Dad? Is he going?"

"No. Just me."

"So who else will be there?"

"I don't know at the moment."

Now, as Jenna gazed at Olivia's pale, almost translucent complexion, taking in how stiffly she was holding herself—back ramrod straight, hands clasped together in her lap—she couldn't help noticing how distant, or perhaps detached, she seemed. She was certainly a beautiful girl, with lustrous blond hair hanging loosely about her shoulders and a perfect oval face, yet the glimpses Jenna had caught of her almond-shaped eyes had shown a girl who seemed disturbingly empty inside.

Empty and cruel?

Apparently suicidal.

With everyone seated, Mr. Charles opened the proceedings. "Olivia wants to explain her part in what happened to Paige. When you've heard what she has to say, I'm sure you'll realize, Mrs. Moore, what tremendous courage it is taking for her to be here today." To Olivia he said, "If at any time you want to stop, you must simply give the word."

Olivia's eyes stayed down as she gave a barely perceptible nod.

Not thrilled by the way this girl, who'd tried to persuade Paige to end her life, was receiving so much consideration, almost being treated as a victim herself, Jenna regarded her coolly. She guessed she was the victim of something if she'd tried to end her life.

Judith Merchant whispered something into her niece's ear. Whatever it was, it seemed to make Olivia shudder. A moment later the girl nodded again.

"My niece would like me to speak on her behalf," Judith said to Jenna. "If you want to ask any questions, either she or I will be happy to answer if we can."

As Jenna looked from one to the other she couldn't help

wondering why Olivia's parents weren't attending this meeting, lending the support their daughter so clearly needed.

"The reason Olivia befriended your daughter through an alias," Judith began, "is complicated, though I believe not hard to understand." She let a moment pass as she squeezed Olivia's hand. "She singled Paige out because she was jealous of her," she stated.

Jenna felt a beat of confusion.

"To explain," Judith continued, "Paige has everything Olivia has always dreamed of: she's pretty, popular, intelligent, and has a way of bonding with others that Olivia has long craved but never had the confidence to attempt."

Though Jenna wanted to point out that the girl was exceptionally pretty and a gifted student where music was concerned, she sensed that confidence was probably more of an issue than looks or ability.

"Paige is also part of a close and loving family," Judith went on. "It's this blessing, perhaps more than anything else, that drew Olivia to your daughter. She wanted to *be* Paige, or connect with her in a way she'd never managed with anyone else, but coming from the place she was in, she was afraid to get close. So her brother, Owen, befriended Paige in the hope of helping his sister in a somewhat vicarious way to get to know Paige. He'd talk to Olivia about her and what he knew of the relationship she had with you and your family, how happy you all seemed, what a noisy and loving house Paige lived in with her brothers and sister. As far as Olivia was concerned, Paige had the perfect life, and the kind of character she admired above all others. She wasn't afraid to stand up and be noticed at school; she wasn't too nervous to answer questions, or take part in a drama, or play on a sports team, or do whatever else was asked of her. Anything she became engaged in had the backing of her friends and, most importantly, of her parents."

As Jenna watched Olivia, so still and withdrawn, she was starting to pick up on a dispiriting remoteness, a kind of darkness even, that seemed to swallow her.

What was it with this girl?

"Olivia wanted desperately to be a part of Paige's world," Judith pressed on. "She wanted to matter to Paige in a way she felt she didn't to anyone else. So she came up with the only way she could think of to make Paige interested in her. Or perhaps I should say, to make Paige depend on her. She thought if she could turn everyone against Paige, that Paige would eventually start to believe that Julie Morris—the name Olivia gave herself—was her only friend."

Jenna was still staring at Olivia, waiting for the girl to look at her, but Olivia didn't lift her head.

"Olivia began her efforts," Judith went on, "by hacking into Paige's Facebook account to make it look as though Paige was accusing Owen of being gay. Owen knew what she was doing and helped her, even though he was terrified of revealing his personal truth. It wasn't so much his friends' reaction he was afraid of as how his father would take it, but I'll come to that. To continue with the posting, Olivia's plan to befriend Paige could have backfired right there, and probably would have if Kelly Durham, the school bully, hadn't jumped on it and started a campaign against Paige that apparently gained its own momentum."

Jenna said nothing, simply waited for the woman to continue.

"So Olivia outed her brother on Facebook, and instead of turning against *him*, everyone turned against the friend they thought had betrayed him. It was what Olivia hoped would happen, because it provided her with a way of offering friend-ship."

Jenna was quietly stunned. How could a girl of Olivia's age be capable of devising such Machiavellian manipulation, never mind carrying it out? "Where on earth did you think all this was going to lead you?" she asked Olivia curtly.

Though Olivia's eyes came briefly to hers, she didn't answer.

"I'm not sure Olivia had really thought it through at that point," Judith said for her.

Jenna waited for Olivia to contradict or confirm that, but she was apparently going to do neither.

Judith continued, "It was largely through Owen, who be-came a part of Kelly Durham's set, that Olivia was able to warn Paige what was about to happen to her, or offer comfort after it happened."

"Why didn't you just report it?" Jenna demanded forcefully. "You'd brought about a dreadful, terrifying situation for my daughter. How could you possibly call yourself a friend? You weren't even who you were claiming to be."

Though Olivia flushed, she didn't reply. Her aunt said, "I need to explain my niece's home situation. For many years she has been the victim of her parents' bullying, as has Owen, though it's been worse for Olivia. So bad that she doesn't always evaluate situations the way the rest of us do. She has been se-verely affected by the abuse, which is both mental, physical, and sexual. The damage it's done . . ." She took a breath that was almost a sob. "I've had my suspicions, of course, but living so far away . . ."

Jenna's eyes moved to Olivia. Naturally she felt pity for what she'd been through, but she couldn't ignore what she'd done to Paige.

"It was after a particularly brutal episode at home," Judith continued, "that Olivia was online with Paige and Paige began saying that she couldn't take any more of the bullying. This was when Olivia suggested they should take a way out of their misery together."

Jenna looked at Olivia again. No matter how damaged the girl was, she had to be made to understand that it wasn't possible to get away with what she'd almost done.

"After Olivia arranged to meet Paige last Friday morning," Judith was saying, "she took a bus to Rhossili, in spite of having told Paige to go to Whiteford Sands. Olivia wanted to pay a last visit to her grandmother's grave at St. Mary's. While she was there her father found her and took her home, where he shut her in her room, confiscated her phone and computer, and left her there while he and his wife, my sister, drove Owen to a healer in North Wales to have him cleansed of his sins—his sins being his homosexuality."

Jenna shuddered inwardly. What kind of parents were they, for God's sake? How could they behave in such a monstrous way to their own children? *Cleansed* for being a homosexual? Raping their own daughter?

"It was Saturday evening before Olivia managed to break out of her room," Judith continued. "When she did, she went to the bathroom, smashed open the cabinets, and swallowed every pill she could find. Her parents returned early the next morning with Owen. When they realized what had happened they refused to call for help. Whether they'd actually have allowed Olivia to die I can't say, but thank God Owen snatched his father's phone, locked himself in a downstairs bathroom, and dialed 999. He was still in the bathroom when the police and ambulance services turned up, and he wouldn't come out until they'd managed to convince him his parents had gone."

As a deep and terrible silence fell over the room, Jenna watched tears sliding silently down Olivia's cheeks. To her surprise the girl spoke then, her voice soft and feathery, her hand still holding tightly to her aunt's.

"I'd have gone to Paige that night if I could," she said, "not to carry out what we'd planned, but to see her, persuade her that it wasn't the right way out for her. I was going to tell her about me, what my parents have been doing to me and Owen. I wanted to ask her to tell someone, but it was too late. There were no buses at that time of night and I had no other means of getting there. I tried to find my phone and computer, but I couldn't, and we don't have a landline at home. So I sat down and wrote a note for my aunt Judith that she never got. I guess my parents destroyed it before anyone could find it."

"I haven't been allowed to see my niece and nephew since my mother died," Judith told Jenna, "and that was over ten years ago." She tried to swallow. "The abuse has been going on since then," she said shakily. "As I said, I was always afraid of it, but I had no proof, and my brother-in-law, being a senior executive at the council, knows how to deal with social services. Nevertheless, I should have tried harder. I suppose I just couldn't make myself believe that my own sister would go along with it. I know now that she was as bad as him." As she put an arm around Olivia, Jenna noticed the girl stiffen before she relaxed.

"Olivia and Owen were incredibly brave on Monday," Judith continued. "They spent most of the day talking to the police, telling them everything that had happened to them. Owen had contacted me on Sunday, so I was with them while they were interviewed, and it's being arranged now for them to come and live with me."

Jenna's eyes moved to the headmaster. This would clearly release him from having to take any action over Olivia's part in what had happened to Paige. He'd be relieved about that. Whether she was too, she'd only know when she'd had time to digest it all. "What's happened to your sister and her husband?" she asked Judith.

"They were arrested on Monday," Judith told her, "and they're probably going to be charged sometime today. If they're bailed out, it's very probable a restraining order will be issued to keep them away from the children. However, we don't want to run any risks, so we've decided it would be best for Olivia and Owen to be as far away from here as I can take them, just in case their parents are released."

"Where do you live?" Jenna asked.

"In Kent, close to Deal. There's a lovely school not too far away where Olivia can continue with her music, and hopefully she and Owen will be able to make a fresh start in a new environment with new friends and an aunt who's desperate to give them all the love they deserve."

Jenna hoped they could receive some therapy too, while wondering if they could ever fully recover from such a terrible start in life. She looked at Mr. Charles and Miss Willis before saying to Olivia, "I'd like to tell Paige what I've heard here today. I think she has a right to know."

Olivia regarded her with wary, haunted eyes.

"You said you were going to tell her yourself," Jenna reminded her.

"It's going to come out sooner or later," Judith said softly to her niece, "and I know you don't want Paige to suffer any more than she already has. An explanation could be very helpful."

Olivia turned back to Jenna. "OK," she whispered shakily.

As the girl leaned in to her aunt's shoulder, Jenna could see how tired she was, and heaven only knew what else was going on inside her. Deciding there was nothing to be gained from prolonging this any further, she got to her feet. "Thank you for your honesty," she said, sounding both gentle and firm. "I realize this can't have been easy for you."

Olivia didn't respond; her head was down again.

"Knowing Paige," Jenna continued, "there's a chance she'll want to see you once I've told her what you've been through. Would you allow it?"

Olivia looked up at her aunt.

"You don't have to if you don't want to," Judith murmured.

To Jenna, Olivia said, "Please tell Paige that I'm very sorry for everything. I wish we could have been proper friends. She's someone . . . she's . . ." As her voice failed, fragmented with tears, her aunt pulled her into a closer embrace.

Outside in the corridor Miss Willis said to Jenna, "Thank you for coming today."

Jenna turned to her. "As affected as I am by all I've heard, I'm sure you realize that Paige is still my main concern."

"She's ours too," Miss Willis assured her, "but we can only take this process one step at a time. Please try to understand that."

"I do, but I'd like to know that a part of that process doesn't involve Paige sitting in a room with Kelly Durham to engage in restorative justice."

"I'll admit it's been discussed," Miss Willis told her, "but so far Kelly and her mother are resisting."

Unsurprised and relieved, Jenna said, "I think I should make it clear that if Kelly Durham stays at this school, Paige won't be coming back."

"I understand your feelings, of course, but we have to give children a chance, even those who have as long a history as Kelly's of intimidation and harassment."

"Bullying," Jenna corrected. "Please let's call it what it is. And I can't help wondering how big a role her grandfather's donations to the school play in keeping her here. I imagine he's already made another to try to brush this under the carpet too."

Miss Willis flushed. "You're right, he has, and I can tell you that it has been refused."

Impressed, and hoping it was true, Jenna eyed her closely, waiting for more.

Sighing, Miss Willis said, "It's sad but undeniable that some children derive a certain amount of pleasure from cruelty. Whether that's down to their upbringing or to a psychological or psychiatric disorder isn't always possible to say. It's also true that some grow out of it, while others don't."

"Kelly Durham is fifteen going on sixteen and you've just said yourself that she has a long history of bullying, so do you think she's going to grow out of it?"

Clearly discomfited, Miss Willis said, "That's not for me to say. Hopefully, though, speaking to Olivia has shown you how complex the problem of bullying can be, especially when it comes to punishment."

"In Olivia's case I understand that punishment is difficult, but she still needs to know that what she did was wrong."

"I agree, and I want to assure you that we aren't just letting it go. As for Kelly . . . There are several options open to us, but, of course, we need to carry out extensive enquiries before any decisive action can be taken."

Angrily Jenna said, "I'm glad you've got Kelly's welfare so close to your heart. Now tell me where Paige's is, because she was the victim in all of this, and just about everyone at this school knows it. So exactly what sort of message do you think it's going to send to other bullies if you keep Kelly here or drag out some pointless investigation into the kind of cruelty that *has* to be punished?"

Miss Willis was finally moved to say, "It would be a wrong message, of course, and between us it's more or less certain that Kelly will be asked to leave. I just don't like to give up on a child until all avenues of rescue have been explored."

"Which is admirable, and your job. It's also your job to make sure my daughter is safe while she's on these premises."

"Indeed, and I want you to feel assured that we greatly value Paige here at The Landings. I know she hasn't been here as long as most, but her contribution has always been a hundred percent whether in her studies, her community projects, or the various other ways she involves herself in representing the school, which is why we most certainly don't want to lose her."

"Then you really have to make sure that the right decisions are taken before the start of next term," Jenna retorted, and with a polite but cool little nod she left.

"I'd give Kelly Durham the chance if she wanted to go face-to-face," Paige declared rashly, after Jenna had finished telling her about her visit to the school.

"You'd sit down in the same room as that girl and—"

"Listen to her explain herself and apologize? Yes, why not? She wouldn't mean it, but I think she ought at least to be made to do it."

Exasperated, and yet unable to suppress a smile, Jenna said, "Well, it seems she's not willing, so at the moment it's not likely to happen."

Paige merely shrugged, and after a while her eyes took on the intense, oddly baffled look they'd had while Jenna had been telling her about Olivia. "It's a shame Olivia doesn't want to meet," she remarked, "but I'm not sure what I'd say to her if we did. It's really terrible what she's been through. I mean, we always thought their parents were a bit strange, you know, never speaking to anyone or allowing anyone into the house. Do you think they had a special place where they did all the abuse? Do you know what sort of . . . ?"

"No, I don't know the details of what they did, and we certainly don't need to be making them up for ourselves. It's enough to know that it happened, and that those dreadful people are going to be made to pay for their crimes."

Paige nodded vaguely. "I understand now why she said her mum was dead," she commented. "It's because she wished it was true." Her eyes came to Jenna's. "It's funny—well, sad, actually—that she picked on me because she thought our family was so perfect. I suppose Dad hadn't gone then, so she didn't know it was all an illusion."

"What she probably didn't realize," Jenna said, "is that no one's family is as perfect as they might seem from the outside. Everyone has their issues."

"Charlotte's family seems pretty up together," Paige replied. "So does Cullum's."

"Cullum lost his mother a couple of years ago," Jenna reminded her, "and I happen to know they've all had quite a struggle trying to get over it."

"Because Richard told you?"

"Yes."

"He seems a really nice man."

"He is."

Paige drifted again, apparently losing herself to more inner reflections. "That still leaves Charlotte," she pointed out in the end.

Jenna's smile was wry. "Not everyone has to be dealing with issues all of the time," she responded, "and if we're really lucky, they hardly come along at all."

"So we're not very lucky."

"Not lately, but it'll change. In fact, I have some news I can share with you, if you like, that I think you might want to hear."

Paige eyed her carefully, clearly still too bruised by her experiences to allow herself to think positively.

"Actually there are two pieces of news," Jenna corrected. "The first won't interest you quite as much, but here goes: I spoke to my agent on the way home, and apparently an American film company wants to buy an option on *Poetry Emotion*."

Paige frowned. "What does that mean?"

"It means they're interested in turning it into a movie, provided they can raise the money."

Paige's eyes rounded. "That is totally awesome," she cried. "Oh my God, does it mean we'll be going to Hollywood?"

"Wouldn't that be wonderful?" Jenna laughed.

"I know—let's go through the book and decide who we think they should cast."

Liking the sound of that, Jenna hugged her tightly. Suspecting the best way to handle the next piece of news would be to treat it as if it were no big deal, she began unloading the dishwasher as she said, "The other call I received on my way home was from Oliver Pryce. He's wondering if he can come and see you."

Paige's jaw dropped as she stared at her mother in disbelief.

Jenna pretended not to notice. "I said to come about five," she added casually. "I hope that's OK."

"You did what? Mum! You said *what*?"

Jenna regarded her, all innocence. "Would you like me to change it?" she offered.

"No! I mean, *yes*. Josh and the twins'll be home by then."

"No they won't. Dad's taking them to TGI Fridays."

At the mention of her stepfather Paige's face clouded, but only for a moment. "Oh my God," she said, gulping, as she tried to think what to do. "Mum, do you have any idea . . . ? I mean, I never told you this, but he is like . . ."

"It's OK, I know." Jenna smiled.

"What? How do you know?"

"I'm your mother. Mothers know everything."

Paige's eyes narrowed. "That would be seriously spooky if I didn't know it wasn't true."

Laughing, Jenna said, "You've got an hour to make yourself presentable."

"That is *so* not long enough." Dashing up the stairs with Waffle hard on her heels, Paige almost shut him out in her haste to FaceTime Charlotte while she put on her makeup and tried to decide what the heck she was going to wear—never mind what she was going to say!

*　*　*

It was five minutes to five when Paige reappeared in the kitchen, her makeup so carefully applied it might have been done by a professional, and her white ruched top and her best jeans, the ones with rips in the knees, enjoying their first outing since purchase. She was so nervous and excited she almost squeezed her grandmother as Kay came in the door, asking what Richard's son was doing hanging around outside.

"He's already here?" Paige gasped.

"He's obviously keen to see you," Jenna commented.

"Don't say that," Paige snapped. "Just don't."

Jenna held up her hands. "You look lovely," she told her.

"Are you sure? I couldn't make up my mind between this top and the red one we got in New Look. I thought this one made me look a bit more . . . you know."

"Definitely," Jenna assured her.

"What do you think, Grandma?"

"Oh yes, definitely," Kay agreed. "Very you know."

Since her grandma's jokes were rare and almost never funny, Paige didn't even pick up on it. "Shall I invite him in?" she asked.

"I think you should," Jenna replied.

"But where can we go without everyone listening?"

"There's only me and Grandma here," Jenna pointed out, "but if you insist, we can always go and sit in the car."

"Don't you dare," Paige growled, missing the irony again. "Oh my God, I am so nervous. What am I going to say to him?"

"Why don't you ask what his favorite hobbies are?" Kay suggested.

Paige gawped at her. "Like I'm really going . . . What are you doing?" she protested as Jenna began steering her toward the door.

"He's waiting," her mother reminded her, "and Grandma and I will stay here in the kitchen if you want to bring him in the front door and take him into the sitting room."

Moments later, wanting the ground to open up and swallow her as a mortifying rush of embarrassment turned her cheeks an unflattering puce, Paige stood staring at Oliver, not sure what to say or do. Since he was leaning against his car with his head down as he texted or checked his phone, he didn't realize she was there at first. As soon as he did he put his phone away.

"Hi," he said, starting toward her. "Thanks for agreeing to see me."

He was so utterly and completely drop-dead that she had no idea how she managed such a casual little shrug as she said, "No problem. I mean, I think my mum agreed for me, but that's OK."

With the lift of an eyebrow she'd seen him do on his video when he was singing the words "Are those smiles meant for me," he said, "Cullum wanted to come with me, you know, to say sorry and everything, but I told him to pick his own time."

Paige gave a choked laugh, though she wasn't sure why.

"So how are you doing?" he asked.

"I'm cool. I mean, it was all a bit . . . you know . . ."

"Sure. You had us all pretty worried."

He was worried about me. "It was just dumb," she said. "Kind of a spur-of-the-moment thing that got out of hand."

He nodded and came to lean against the wall next to her.

"Do you want to come in?" she offered. It was freezing out

here, but no way was she going to put a coat on and cover up what she was wearing.

"I'm here to apologize," he said, as though he hadn't heard the invite. "I should have realized what was happening. . . . I mean, I did. Cullum told me, and obviously I got that Kelly and her mates were making out they were you sending messages, putting stuff on my Facebook page, and all that. I should have done something about it, but I didn't, and so I definitely owe you an apology."

"It's OK," she assured him, her heart so full she could hardly speak. He'd understood it wasn't her, and now he felt bad for not coming to her rescue, which meant he wished he had. She wished he had too. "It wasn't up to you to look out for me," she said.

"Yes it was. I can't stand it when people are picked on, it really gets to me, and I could have made it stop. Honest to God, I kept meaning to, but there was like this other part of me that kept saying, 'They're just messing around, trying to get your attention, don't rise to it.'"

"I don't blame you for thinking that."

"Kind of arrogant, though."

"Depends which way you look at it."

He cast her a glance, and when he smiled she felt her heart turn inside out. "Are you going back to school before the end of term?" he asked.

She shrugged. "I don't think so. Apparently I don't have to, but that kind of feels like running away."

"No one would blame you if you wanted to hang loose for a while. Apart from my brother, who's desperate for you to do the part of First Voice in the production on Good Friday."

Paige smiled. "Because if I don't he'll have to?"

"I think that's how it goes. He told me to tell you he'd pay you whatever you asked if you'd agree to do it."

Though Paige wanted to say she would, if only to prove to Oliver that she was coping with everything, she truly didn't know if she could face it. "Tell him he's not rich enough," she quipped.

Oliver laughed. "OK, I will. It's kind of unusual having a girl in the part," he added.

"I'm down for other roles as well, but only minor ones."

He nodded. "I could never really get my head round that piece."

Not wanting to sound like a swot, she simply said, "I know what you mean."

After an awkward pause she went on, "It's really good of you to come."

"It seemed the right thing to do, and now I'm glad I did."

Knowing she'd read massive amounts into that later, she said, "So where are you going now?"

"Home, I guess. I've got a load of reviewing to do."

"When do your exams start?"

"Middle of May, so not long."

"Will you take a gap year before going to uni?"

"You bet. I'm ready to get away from this place, see a bit more of the world."

Filled with dismay at the thought of him looking forward to leaving, she said, "Who will you go with?"

"Liam, I expect, and a couple of others."

It was out before she could stop it. "Lindsay?"

He shook his head. "We're not together anymore."

Paige's heart felt like it was trying to leap out of her body. "Oh, I'm sorry to hear that."

"It's cool. It was kind of coming for a while." He turned to look at her. "That's not to say . . . I mean, you and me . . ." He was clearly embarrassed and starting to blush.

"No, no, it's fine," she assured him. "It's not what I was thinking."

"It's just you're only fifteen, and I . . . Well, you get what I'm saying?"

"Sure, I get it," she said, somehow not blurting out that she was nearly sixteen, and Liam didn't seem to mind about Charlotte being fifteen. It would look too desperate and really put him on the spot, which would make everything a thousand times worse.

"I'd kind of like it if we were friends, though," he said. "Or I could be like the older brother you always wished you had."

Paige tried to smile. *Friend? Brother?* "What makes you think I always wished that?"

He shrugged. "Just a hunch. But also it might help you to know you've always got someone to turn to if anything like this starts up again. I mean, it shouldn't, because she's being expelled, isn't she?"

"I don't know. Anyway, I'm not sure that'll stop her coming after me."

"The first sign of it, you've got my number. Cullum's going to be on the lookout, so he'll keep me informed even if you don't."

Finding herself suddenly horribly close to tears, Paige said, "I probably ought to go in now."

Pushing himself away from the wall, he said, "Sure. Thanks for coming out."

"No big deal."

As she started to walk away he asked, "Hey, if you do decide to do the play on Good Friday, would it be OK if I came?"

She couldn't turn round or he'd see how upset she was. "I don't expect I will," she mumbled, "but I'm sure I'll see you around."

Minutes later she was in her mother's arms, sobbing as though her heart would break. "I wanted him to like me," she gasped, "but he thinks I'm just a kid."

"Well, you are three years younger."

"So what? That's nothing, and it hasn't stopped Liam being with Charlotte. He doesn't fancy me; he just doesn't want to say so."

"He wants to be friends, though, and lots of relationships have started that way."

"No, he wants to be like a brother. That's different altogether."

"Not really, because he isn't your brother and never will be, no matter how close you might become."

"How are we going to get close if I don't ever see him?"

"He's already said he'll come to the play if you do it," Jenna reminded her, "so you'd see him then. And we could always invite him and his family over to the Pitcher and Piano after to celebrate."

"Who says we're going to the Pitcher and Piano? It's the first I've heard of it."

"Dad thought it would be a nice idea, if it was what you wanted."

"So Dad's coming to the play?"

"Of course. You know he wouldn't miss any play you're in."

"Won't he be gone back to the States by then?"

"Apparently not."

Paige's expression remained mutinous. "I haven't said I'm going to do it," she pointed out heatedly, "and now I feel I'm being forced into it."

"That's not the case at all. The decision's entirely yours. I'm just saying that if you do feel up to doing it, we could all go for a little party after to toast your success."

"You mean after everyone's booed and shouted at me to get off, or howled because of how bad I sound?"

Jenna frowned. "You read that part beautifully. Everyone thinks so, especially Miss Kendrick, who, by the way, wants to come and see you tomorrow."

"No way! I want everyone to stop coming to see me. It's just making everything worse."

"OK, OK . . ."

"She's only going to try and talk me into being in her stupid production, and I don't want to do it."

"I promise she won't pressure you, and actually it's not why she's coming. She wants to say sorry for not going to Mr. Charles when you first told her what was happening with Kelly Durham."

Paige stared desperately at her mother. "I don't want to see her," she cried. "I really, really just want to forget all about it."

"Then that's what we'll do for now, but I'm afraid you still have to see a specialist for an assessment of—"

"All right, if I have to I will. I just don't want to make the whole of the rest of my life about this, because I can't see how that will help at all." Tearing herself away, she ran upstairs to FaceTime Charlotte, who'd understand better than anyone how she felt about Oliver not wanting to go out with her, even though he wasn't with Lindsay anymore.

* * *

"I was thinking," Jack said later that evening after bringing the children home, "I could sit down outside her door and refuse to move until she speaks to me."

Jenna raised an eyebrow. "She's out with Waffle at the moment, so it wouldn't do you much good."

"You know what I'm saying."

"Yes, and I know it's worked in the past, but she's older now and this is a little different."

He nodded dejectedly. "I'm running out of ideas here, so if you've got any . . ."

Sighing, Jenna said, "Look, I know you're in a hurry to try and make amends, but she still needs time."

"How much time?"

"I've no idea. These things don't run according to a schedule, and she's been very hurt by your leaving."

Kay said, "Why don't you write her a letter? Or send her an email?"

"Saying what?"

"Whatever it is you want to say when she's ready to talk. If she knows in advance, she might be more willing to listen."

"Or not," Hanna muttered.

"Hanna," Jenna chided.

"Well, what's he going to do," Hanna cried, "explain to her that he's fallen for another woman, so he's not going to be living with you and the family anymore? She already knows that, so reading it or hearing it isn't going to make her feel any better about it."

"She needs to know that his feelings for her haven't changed," Jenna told her.

"And you think that'll help?"

"It can't do any harm."

"She's not a child. He can't just palm her off with words that aren't going to mean anything when he's gone again."

"So what do you suggest?" Jack asked her helplessly.

Hanna threw out her hands. "It might be a start if you told her you'd made a colossal mistake and want to come home."

Jenna looked at Jack and decided not to come to his rescue, in spite of not being sure she'd want him back now anyway. She might still love him and wish it was possible to erase these last few months, but she was beginning to realize that she'd lost respect for him, and without that—and trust—they were never going to stand a chance.

"I have to be true to myself," Jack said quietly.

Hanna's temper flared again. "And being true to yourself is blowing my sister's inheritance, almost getting her charged with fraud, making her afraid she was about to lose her home—oh, and shacking up with another woman when you've got four children at home. How are you liking that truth, Jack? How well is it working for you? Because I can tell you this, it's not working for me at all."

Jack eyed her darkly. "You've always had too much to say for yourself, too high an opinion of—"

"Stop," Jenna cut in sharply, "both of you. The younger ones are just on the other side of that door, and frankly I don't want to listen to any more of this. All that matters to me is that my children are safe. I understand that matters to you too, Jack—"

"Which is why he shot off to the States," Hanna interjected.

"And he came back when Paige was in trouble," Jenna pointed out. "He has a lot of ground to make up with her, there's no doubt about that, and I'm not paving the way for you, Jack. I'll do what I can to help her through everything, obviously, and as soon as I feel that a rift between you is having a detrimental effect on her I will get on the case. Until then, think about what she's just been through, remind yourself that everything's about her, not you, and for God's sake start taking her rejection like a man instead of hanging around here feeling sorry for yourself all the time. Oh, and let's be perfectly clear about this: the real reason you want to hurry up and get back on terms with her is so you can return to the States to be with your mistress."

"*Yes,*" Hanna whispered behind her.

Jenna turned to glare at her.

"It needed to be said," Hanna pointed out.

Kay came to pat her back. "Yes it did, Jenna," she told her. "I'm sorry, Jack, but it really did."

"So you're all ganging up on me now," he said sourly.

"Yes, we are," Paige told him from the back door.

As everyone turned round, Jenna asked. "How long have you been there?"

"Long enough," Paige replied, hanging Waffle's lead on its hook. "Mum's right, Dad, you're only staying until I've said it's all right that you fell for someone else and that I understand, but I'm never going to understand it. Perhaps one day it won't matter anymore, but right now it does and I'm not going to pretend it doesn't. You've hurt the person I love most in the world, and she really didn't deserve it. You've hurt all of us too, me, Josh, and the twins, and we didn't deserve it either. That's not to say I don't love you, because I know that on some level I still do, but it'll never be the same between us again, and that's what I'm finding really hard. You've ruined what we had, but instead of understanding that, you seem to think everything'll be all right just as long as we play by your new rules. Well, it's not going to happen. It can't, because what you've done has changed everything. I'm Mum's best friend now, not you, and she's mine. You can be a part of it, but you'll never be at the center of it the way you used to be. I expect it'll be easier for you with Josh and the twins, because they're younger, but don't think they won't know as they get older that you put someone else before them. That's not me saying I'll tell them you did, because I won't; they'll work it out for themselves, and they'll realize that we have the best mum in the world who loves us more than anything and would do anything for us, and a dad who loves us and would do anything for us provided it doesn't get in the way of what he wants. Good luck with that, Dad. I hope it goes well for you, but don't ask me to forgive you right now, because I can't." Leaving them all speechless, she clicked her fingers for Waffle to follow and took herself off upstairs.

Jack's face was even paler than Jenna's as he stared at the empty doorway.

In the end, Jenna said, "I hope, when you've stopped thinking about how this is affecting you, Jack, that you'll spare a moment to feel proud of her for being able to speak her mind the way she just did."

Jack's eyes came to hers as he said, "I think I already do."

Chapter 23

Paige was in her mother's car outside the Dylan Thomas Centre. Her grandma, Bena, and Auntie Hanna were in the car behind, while Josh, the twins, and Waffle were at home being looked after by Mrs. Keys from the village. The children were too young to come to a play like this, even though they'd been mad keen to see their sister perform.

"I expect you're going to be famous after," Flora told her so earnestly that her little glasses steamed up with the excitement of it, "and everyone will want your autograph. Can I have it now so I'll be the first?"

Paige had dutifully signed the back of a drawing, the only piece of paper Flora had been able to find. Josh and Wills were next in line, with an old envelope in Josh's case and a birthday card in Wills's.

In truth, Paige still wasn't sure she could go through with it. Though she'd been attending rehearsals for the past week, which had all gone well, it wasn't the same as having to stand up in front of an audience that the recently expelled Kelly Durham or one of the Durmites might have snuck into.

On the other hand, she was determined not to let them win.
She wanted to do this. She loved the play and knew how much
it would mean to her mother to see her in the lead role. Oliver
was coming, and that meant a lot to her, even if he didn't want
to go out with her. She'd feel a proper loser if she backed out
now, and yet the truth was she desperately wanted to.

"Are you OK?" her mother asked gently.

Paige nodded. She was glad they were in the car park next to
the river, well past the hotel she'd seen her dad coming out of
with Martha the last time she was here. They'd obviously been
in there screwing, which made her feel sick and angry with him
all over again.

He probably wouldn't come tonight after the way she'd spoken to him the last time she'd seen him.

Good. She didn't want him here anyway. He wasn't a part of
their lives anymore.

Swallowing the tears that suddenly threatened, she said to
her mother, "Did you know that Olivia was supposed to be performing Stravinsky's memorial piece tonight?"

"You mean 'Do Not Go Gentle into That Good Night'?" her
mother replied. "No, I didn't know that."

"She's not now. Miss Kendrick confirmed today that she'd
pulled out. I wonder if she and Owen might come to see the
play anyway."

"It's probably more likely that they've already gone to Kent
with their aunt," Jenna reminded her.

Paige wasn't entirely sure why, but it made her feel horribly
sad to realize she might never see them again. "I keep thinking
about her," she admitted, "and wishing she'd had the courage
to make friends in the proper way. We'd have made her feel a
part of our family—and shown her what we're really like."

Smiling at the irony, Jenna said, "I'm afraid she wasn't capable of connecting in a normal way, which is a great pity. She probably could have been a lovely friend."

"When I think about all those vile things people said about me and Dad and then I think about her . . . She was really going through it, and he's her *real* dad, for God's sake. It's so horrible, and her mum was a part of it. Can you imagine how bad it must have been? I hope they get sent to prison for the rest of their lives."

"I don't think the sentence is as long as that," Jenna responded, "but it ought to be." After smoothing Paige's hair, she said, "Are you ready to go in now?"

"I guess so," Paige replied, feeling another surge of nerves swamping her resolve.

When she didn't move, Jenna said, "If you've changed your mind . . ."

"I haven't. I just . . ." Spotting Auntie Hanna and Bena waiting out in the cold, she opened the car door. "I'm going in now," she declared to her mother. "You don't have to come with me."

Since they'd brought Paige early for costume and makeup, Jenna said, "We'll probably go across the road for a drink, but I'll keep my phone turned on in case you need me."

"OK. Thanks, but don't worry, I'll be fine."

Famous last words.

An hour and a half later Paige was at the side of the stage with Captain Cat, Rosie Probert, and the five drowned sailors ready to begin at the beginning. Cullum and Charlotte, who were playing Mr. Edwards and Miss Price, were still hanging back, but they didn't need to be ready for their cues yet. Paige's opening speech was a long one, and though she knew it by heart, right now she couldn't think of a single word.

"Breathe," Miss Kendrick whispered in her ear. "Nice deep breaths."

Doing as she was told, Paige felt the lines slowly reassembling, all the richly witty and outlandish adjectives, the strange and thrilling use of verbs, the poetic conjuring of the sleeping town of Llareggub. From the other side of the curtain she could hear the burble of voices, and she tried to picture where her mother was sitting, and Oliver, and Kelly Durham if she'd managed to sneak in. Once the lights went up she wouldn't be able to see the audience, so she wouldn't know where anyone was, which might be a good thing.

What was she going to do if everyone started catcalling and booing?

Die and never put herself in this position again.

"OK, make with the dry ice," Miss Kendrick instructed Lloyd Brace, one of the stagehands.

As the predawn mist began to billow over the stage, Paige felt a sudden, desperate urge to flee. She might have done so, were she not frozen to the spot in panic.

Breathe. Just keep breathing.

Captain Cat—aka Tom Parsons the class clown—was going onstage to lie on his bunk.

As he disappeared in the mist Miss Kendrick's hand touched Paige's arm, gently easing her into position.

When the curtain went up she would be performing solo for a full three minutes. Everyone would be watching her, listening to her delivery of the world-famous lines, assessing her understanding of how they should be spoken, judging how worthy she was of this great honor. A female almost never took on the role of First Voice; it had been written for a man, and the

Thomas diehards, the purists, would want to see and hear it performed by a man.

They were going to hate her, boo her, and shout her off.

From the corner of her eye she caught Miss Kendrick's arm going down, Lloyd's cue to raise the curtain, and hers to begin at the beginning.

She heard herself speaking the words: "To begin at the beginning: It is spring, moonless night in the small town . . ." The audience could see her now, a girl, an impostor seeming to float in a groundswell of fog, an apparition in Llareggub. ". . . starless and bible-black, the cobblestreets silent . . ."

There wasn't a murmur in the room; the only sound was her, speaking softly, lyrically, wryly, with Captain Cat, asleep on his bunk, being slowly revealed.

She wasn't sure at which point she lost the sense of herself and became totally immersed in the bizarre and wonderful tragicomedy; she only knew on a level too distant to touch that there was nothing apart from the hilarious and intriguing oddities of the characters, their dreams, rivalries, disappointments, passions, and the day they were spending "Under waking Wood."

Until finally Polly Garter met Mr. Waldo in the forest, and "the thin night darkens" and Llareggub was quiet again.

As the cast took the applause Paige could feel herself shaking so violently that it was hard to smile, even to move forward to take a bow. She'd landed back in reality with a crashing thud. She couldn't believe that they were at the end of the play, that she'd got through it, that it was over and no one had howled, cackled, or done anything but laugh in all the right places and hang on to each and every word. A sea of faces was bobbing in front of her, one indistinguishable from another, as hands pounded together and whistles flew like cheers through the air.

She spotted her mother sitting with Richard, Auntie Hanna, and Bena, Grandma with Oliver just in front, and so much pride welled up in her that she was ready to burst. Then she saw two figures standing at the back, both blond and looking right at her. Her heart caught with surprise, but even as their eyes connected Olivia and Owen turned like ghosts and left.

It was time for her single bow. She stepped forward, smiling so hard it kept turning to sobs of laughter. Her eyes swept the audience again and again and stopped when they found her dad sitting alone, near the back. Now he was standing, hands held high as he clapped, pride oozing from every part of him.

He'd come, and though she'd felt sure he would, she hadn't realized how happy that would make her too.

You were totally awesome. O.

She showed Charlotte the text in the dressing room, her heart thundering with excitement, adrenaline still pumping through her veins.

"Oliver? Olivia? Owen?" Paige cried above the din of the other actors. "I've no idea which one of them it might be."

"Check the number," Charlotte shouted. Paige did and felt a beat of surprise.

"So?" Charlotte prompted.

"It's not Owen or Oliver," Paige told her, "so it must be Olivia."

Seeing how perplexed and uncertain she was, Charlotte hugged her. "It's probably her way of trying to make up for things."

Paige nodded as she wondered if she should text back or ignore it. She'd make up her mind tomorrow, she decided.

Charlotte pulled a teasing face. "So you're not pissed off it wasn't from Oliver?"

Paige's eyes lit up. "Not a bit, because he's coming to the Pitcher and Piano, so let's grab our stuff and get the hell out of here."

Six weeks later Jenna was in the dining room, surrounded by children's clutter, with the French doors open to the garden and sunshine pouring in as frivolously and insistently as good spirits at a happy celebration. Her laptop was open in front of her, the screen filled with words she had written in a heady burst of inspiration that had lasted for most of the day. There were five entire pages of text, and having finished laying down this first chapter for now, she was very clear in her mind about where the book was going next.

What she wasn't so sure about was what had freed her from the block, why words and ideas and characters had begun to stretch, yawn, limber up, and then to flow with a life force all their own, although she could hazard a few guesses. It would be a mix of things. There was emotional distress, which had a knack of transforming itself into creativity. She remembered her own words to Paige: *You're not a victim. That's not who you are, so you mustn't let her turn you into one.* That, she realized, was what she'd allowed the author Natalie West to do to her with her cruel put-downs. Another thing—and this was the biggie—was the mind-blowing reception she'd received for the two children's books she'd completed in less than a month.

To be fair, they were only twenty pages each, or would be once the illustrations were added, but according to her new publisher, *Billy the Bully* and *Meanie Monica* were exactly the kind of early-learning books they'd been looking for—and that the nation needed.

"This subject is constantly in the news," Tina Nash, her enthusiastic young editor, had declared excitedly, "and what's important is to catch kids when they're very young to drum it into them that bullying isn't where they want to go. No one would want to be Billy or Monica after reading these books, and if we can get schools to accept them for pre-kindergarten years . . . You know, this could be ripe for an animated TV adaptation. Actually, we could have a whole franchise on our hands here if you were able to come up with more."

Jenna was still thinking about that. Writing for the very young wasn't necessarily a field she wanted to get into; however, if part of the proceeds of her efforts could go to Kidscape, the anti-bullying charity she and Paige had recently become involved with, she might be tempted.

Until that was sorted out, she was keen to remain an adult-fiction writer, and could even start calling herself one again now that words were finally starting to flow in a very encouraging fashion. This was the third day running that she'd managed to sit at her computer and create five straight pages that truly felt like the start of something—well, something that would have a middle and end to add to the beginning, which was a definite improvement on where she'd been a month ago. Moreover, the funds she'd received for the film option on *Poetry Emotion* had enabled her to pay back her last advance, so she no longer had a deadline hanging over her like a sword of Damocles.

So it could be said that life was finally taking a turn for the better, at least on the financial and creative fronts. As far as family and personal matters were concerned, there were still days when she found being a single mum and deserted wife so difficult and dispiriting that it was a struggle to get through them. However, she managed it, mainly because she had to. A depressed mother was a burden her children really didn't need, particularly when Paige's recovery from her own experiences still had some way to go. Paige could seem very up one day, but the next it could become evident that her confidence, along with her ability to trust either herself or anyone else, was floundering.

The success of *Under Milk Wood* had been a perfect example of how fragile she still was—on the performance night, the praise for how well she'd handled the role had given her a tremendous boost. However, after the high had come the low, which had sent her crashing back to earth in a way that had lasted far longer than either of them had expected. Still, the one-on-one counseling was definitely helping, as were the group therapy sessions run by Kidscape that she'd attended in London over Easter while staying with Hanna. Hearing about other people's experiences, as well as sharing her own, seemed to be making her feel much more positive about life, especially now she knew that such luminaries as Barack Obama, Rihanna, David and Victoria Beckham, and Will Young had all experienced some form of bullying—and look where they were now. Having such role models was driving Paige to help those who were still suffering; she was even planning to give a talk at school later in the term about what had happened to her, why she thought it had happened, how she'd felt during the worst of it—and how important it was to seek help as soon as it became obvious that the abuse was getting out of hand. "Don't Be a Victim" was the title of the speech she was preparing.

"We can't allow anyone to hold back because they're afraid

it'll get worse if they tell," she'd declared to her mother the last time they'd worked on her talk. "That's what I did, and OK, it did get worse, but only because I didn't make it clear to Miss Kendrick just how bad it was. If I had, the school would have put a stop to it there and then."

Whether that was true they'd never know now, but what mattered was that Paige believed it, and though she could be a little evangelical at times in her determination to stamp out "this evil menace," as she called it, Jenna would far rather see her like that than struggling to overcome it.

At the same time, Jenna had to concede that Paige was one of the lucky ones, for, having been blessed with a strong character—an attribute Jenna insisted was all her own, nothing to do with either parent—she was recovering far more quickly than others who'd been in her situation. As for Jack, his relationship with Paige might be slowly starting to improve (largely because Paige, in her words, was more tolerant of weakness now than she used to be), but the dynamic between them had definitely changed.

Though Jack continued on occasion to try to blame Jenna for the rift, saying she was turning Paige against him, Jenna had learned to stop rising to it. Nothing would come from such a futile argument when he already knew that he'd created the problem himself. So the furthest she would go to hit back was to remind him, in a very sweetly cutting way, that this was the price he was paying for choosing himself and his needs over his children's. However, it apparently mattered greatly to him that he should remain a part of his stepdaughter's life. If nothing else commended him, that certainly did.

Exactly how his relationship with Martha was going, Jenna

had no idea, nor did she care—unless it was badly, in which case she wouldn't mind knowing every last detail. However, when he was around, which wasn't nearly as often as he'd promised the children he would be, no mention was ever made of his other life, nor had anyone yet been invited to take part in it. (Lucky them, she always thought.) Paige wouldn't be interested anyway, but Josh and the twins might be if it meant spending more time with their father. However, Jack clearly wasn't listening to the hints Jenna frequently dropped.

"Martha's not interested in children," her mother, whose own therapy had so far helped her to progress from a pat on the back to an occasional rub, would often comment. "She doesn't want to spend her precious weekends at petting zoos, or swimmers' club, or kiddie athletics, much less taking them for a haircut or to buy new shoes." And the newly talkative Kay would sometimes continue, "He was a decent enough father for the time he was here, but that was because it suited him. Now it doesn't, so he's happy to do what he can when it doesn't get in the way of anything else he wants to do. If it does, it's down to you."

Though the truth of that grated on Jenna, she had to admit that maybe she preferred it that way. Of course it had been easier when Jack was around doing whatever fatherly activities he did, which actually amounted to quite a lot, but these days it was definitely simpler to be in control of what the younger ones were doing and where they needed to be without having to rely on him. Relying on her mother, however, was a whole different story, since she certainly wouldn't be able to manage without her, nor would she want to when it meant so much to Kay to feel needed. There was also the invaluable Bena, who was constantly offering her services as chauffeur, babysitter, or drinking companion on the evenings they could manage to fit in a glass or two.

Suddenly deciding she felt like celebrating her day's work—and the sunshine, and the wonderful sense of freedom that was hers for about another half an hour—she went into the kitchen to put on the kettle. One of the best parts of being her these days, she was coming to realize, was not having to wonder where Jack was all the time, or show an interest in his new hobbies, or—more importantly—ask him for money. He still provided for the children, of course, but not regularly, and when his contribution did come it was often short of what it should have been. Since he'd never been mean, she could only conclude that he wasn't earning as much as he'd like as a director of Gwynne and Associates.

Shame.

She was doing quite well herself. Well enough, in fact, to think about taking the children and her mother to Disney World next year. Charlotte too, if she wanted to come and keep Paige company.

"Hey, Mum! Did you remember to wash my black top?" Paige asked, appearing out of nowhere and catching a happy Waffle as he leapt at her.

Still getting over the shock of someone suddenly being there, Jenna said, "What are you doing home already?"

Paige went to the fridge. "Didn't you get my text? Last lesson was canceled. Mrs. Brain fainted, so they decided to call it a day."

"Fainted? What's wrong with her?"

"I think she's pregnant. Anyway, my black top?"

"Is on your bed."

"Cool. Oh, by the way, what are you doing for your birthday next Friday?"

Jenna shrugged, as though she'd all but forgotten. "I haven't given it much thought," she replied. "Maybe we could all go to the King for something to eat. Do you fancy it? Would you come?"

Paige didn't look thrilled. "So how about you come to where I'm going?" she suggested.

"Which is where?"

At that, Paige's expression turned mischievous. "Well, since you ask, Oliver's doing a gig at the Cross Keys and he's offered me some tickets."

Understanding that she ought to look suitably impressed, Jenna did her best. "That's very kind of him," she said, "but I'm sure you don't want to take me."

"Oh no, I definitely don't," Paige confirmed, "but Richard's going to be there and we thought you two oldies might like to keep each other company."

Laughing, Jenna went to give her a hug. "If I didn't know better, I'd think you were trying to do a little matchmaking," she accused.

"And if I didn't know better, I'd think you were interested."

Jenna's eyes narrowed.

"Oh come on, Mum, everyone knows you two fancy each other to hell and back."

"Mm, wouldn't it be better to be taken to heaven and back?"

"Too tame."

Jenna had to laugh.

"Does that mean you'll come?"

Jenna pretended to give it some thought. "I will," she decided, "with the proviso that you don't get in my face, invade my space, or cramp my style."

Paige groaned desperately. "I know you're trying to speak my language, but honestly, don't."

Laughing as she cupped her daughter's face, Jenna said, "You know, I'm thinking I might turn you into a novel."

Paige seemed to like the idea of that. "Cool," she declared, her eyes widening with interest. "Can my name be Florence? And can I have a love interest who's an awesome musician?"

"Yes to everything," Jenna concurred, "just as long as we make sure it has a happy ending."

Acknowledgments

An enormous thank-you to Harriet Ferris for helping to start the journey of this book during the writing of her dissertation.

Also to Megan Wiltshire and her friends Chloe Bragg, Hannah Day, Aimee Woodhouse, Emilia James, and Kayleigh Griffee of Brimsham Green School, who at age fifteen offered their inspirational insights. Also to school librarian Becky Harrison for arranging my visit, and for the hugely appreciated backup that followed.

Another enormous thank-you to Dick Knill of South Wales Police, and to Jonathan and Buffy Lee.

Thank you to Dan Norris for putting me in touch with Claude Knights of Kidscape, who gave so generously of her time with much expert knowledge and guidance.

A thousand times thank you to Christine McCarthy for introducing me to parts of the Gower I'd never have otherwise found. Also to Julie Dixon for pointing me in so many right directions.

Last, but by no means least, love and thanks to my stepson, Michael Garrett, for the lyrics included in this book. And to the Lambert family, especially Max, for helping out with the children!

I should also thank Verbena Forse and her daughter Sarah for the generous donation made to the children's charity CLIC

Sargent in return for having Verbena's name featured in this book.

If you are the victim of bullying or if you know someone who is, then please don't hesitate to ask for help. Someone will always be there for you.

The number for Kidscape is 020 7730 3300. Or you can contact them at www.kidscape.org.uk.

Too Close
to Home

A Novel

SUSAN LEWIS

A Reader's Guide

Susan Lewis *on* Too Close to Home

Dear Reader,

*As many of you already know, my books often have a
serious theme to them, and* Too Close to Home *is no ex-
ception. This time I have explored some of the devastating effects bullying can have on victims and their
families.*

*Bullying is an issue that raises its monstrous head in
so many lives and in so many ways. In this case it claims
fifteen-year-old Paige Moore as its victim, and we see
how easily it goes undetected as her mother struggles to
deal with a broken marriage.*

*In preparation for this book I spent some time with
an MA student who is writing a thesis on the subject of
bullying, as well as a select group of fifteen-year-old girls
who've had their own experiences, either firsthand or
through friends, of peer intimidation and devastating
forms of jealousy and spite. They were very sobering
sessions, and in many ways deeply shocking—until
then I hadn't fully realized just how cruel and relentless
and even life-threatening bullies can be. In some tragic
cases, as we know, the victims have been driven to take
their own lives, feeling it to be the only way to escape*

their tormentor(s). Of course, social media plays a huge part in perpetuating and worsening the misery of innocent victims as it allows the bully to carry out his or her sadistic attacks twenty-four hours a day. (There must, of course, be a profound disturbance in the mind of someone who does this, maybe the subject for another book!)

Since publishing the hardback in the UK, it has been extremely encouraging to discover just how many of you have been moved by the story and how greatly you care about this issue. I agree with you that we need to talk about it more in order to get to its heart and attempt to overcome it. A way of doing this can be to get in touch with anti-bullying charities, such as www.stopbullying. gov. In the UK, Kidscape is a great organization to support, and they also provided an exceptional amount of support and guidance while I was writing this book. Their contact details, along with an interview with the head of Kidscape, Claude Knights, can be found on the following pages, as well as on my Facebook page and on my website. You will find that this interview provides some invaluable information for those who want to learn more about how to deal with the issue, particularly parents and victims.

While dealing with the extremely thorny and complex subject of bullying, I have also explored the consequences of family breakdown and betrayal. We see how Jenna, Paige's mother, becomes so wrapped up in her own problems that she doesn't see what's happening right in front of her. I wonder how many of us have been in that posi-

tion? For those who are lucky enough to have escaped it, perhaps this book will help convey what it feels like to be in such a challenging and heartbreaking situation.

I really hope Too Close to Home *has touched you in some way and that you will be sharing it with your friends and family, and if you know someone who's suffering, I hope this will help you to find a way to reach them.*

Thank you to all of you who have shared your reviews with me already and for those who've just reached these end pages, I'd be very interested to hear your thoughts, too!

The Research Behind Too Close to Home

An Interview with Kidscape

As many of you may already know, *Too Close to Home* deals with the difficult, even toxic issue of bullying. Its main focus is Paige Moore who, aged fifteen, moves to a new school in Wales where her life is turned into a living hell.

When writing this book Susan wanted to present very real scenarios experienced by children who are bullied. Dealing with such a sensitive issue, she had to be sure the research was thorough and was, therefore, extremely grateful to be put in touch with Claude Knights, CEO of Kidscape.

Kidscape is an anti-bullying charity in the UK that supports children from ages six to nineteen and we hope that after reading this you, too, will think more closely about this subject and those who may be in need.

In Susan's book, fifteen-year-old Paige Moore falls victim to some ferocious bullying, both face-to-face at school and around the clock online. Have you noticed a significant increase in bullying since the advent of social media?
Social media has certainly added another dimension to the bullying landscape. The 24/7 aspect of online bullying as well as the sheer number of platforms add to the opportunities to

dish out abuse. The disinhibition experienced by the bullies because they do not have to face the pain of their targets makes for very raw, thoughtless and relentless cruelty. At Kidscape we have found that young people who are vulnerable offline are often targeted online. Too many incidents of bullying remain unreported, but as there are an increasing number of channels for disclosing occurrences statistics would seem to point to an increase.

One recent study indicates that 69 percent of young people aged between thirteen and twenty-two had experienced cyber bullying and that 20 percent of those reported it as extreme. A robust finding across much recent research into the prevalence of bullying per se is that 46 percent of all children report that they have experienced some form of bullying during their time at school.

What are the signs that you advise parents to look out for?
The ability to identify the signs and symptoms of bullying is crucial as it can lead to prevention and early intervention. A child who is being bullied may exhibit some of the following signs and symptoms: they may be frightened of walking to or from school; refuse to attend school; feel ill in the mornings or on certain days discernible by a pattern; be truant; show a marked deterioration in their schoolwork; become anxious after using their mobile phone or computer; may become distressed or withdrawn; start stealing money (to pay the bully); refuse to admit that anything is wrong; have unexplained bruises or cuts; may become aggressive and unreasonable; and give improbable excuses for any of the above.

Do you feel schools are vigilant enough?
Schools vary hugely in terms of how they acknowledge, respond to, and deal with bullying behavior. The support given to targets of bullying and their families has improved over the past decade, but there are still too many establishments that value exam results and reputation above the creation of an environment that does not tolerate bullying in any form and that investigates incidents that take place beyond the school gate. Schools have a duty of care to all their pupils that entails providing them with an environment that guarantees their safety and in which they can pursue their studies free of anxiety. Anti-bullying policies are mandatory, but to be meaningful in an active sense, they need to be understood and enforced by the whole school community. Pupils need to understand that bullying in all its forms is wrong and that there will be consequences if any anyone engages in this destructive behavior. At Kidscape we still have to deal with too many examples of bullying situations that have slipped beneath the radar and which have not come to light until a crisis point has been reached. There remains a real need to provide additional training in preventative strategies for teachers as well as the resources to sustain peer-support initiatives and workshops for parents.

What sort of advice do you give young people who contact you for help?
We urge young people who are being bullied not to suffer in silence. If their school ignores the bullying, we tell them not to be resigned to becoming a target. We also suggest a wide

range of strategies that include: telling a friend (A supportive friend can keep bullies away.); saying "No" assertively; not giving a reaction to taunts, giving the impression that you don't care; thinking up creative responses in advance; trying to avoid being alone in places where you know the bully is likely to pick on you; practicing "walking tall" and looking confident so that the bully finds it harder to identify you as a target—even if you feel small inside; and keeping a written record of all incidents. Advice specific to online bullying is also given, and this includes never sharing passwords; activating privacy settings; never sending out provocative or cruel messages yourself; and reporting abuse to the service provider and retaining evidence.

In the book, Paige's mother, Jenna, is distracted by problems in her marriage. Do you find that children will try to protect their parents by keeping their own pain to themselves?

We can quote a number of cases where children and young people have channeled much effort into protecting their parents by hiding the agonies caused by bullies for months and even years. In such cases the parent finds out what is going on once a crisis point has been reached, e.g., an escalation into self-harm, attempted suicide, risky behaviors, etc. One memorable case study is one where the mother was suffering from breast cancer and her ten-year-old daughter, who was enduring extreme face-to-face bullying, was determined not to disclose her pain as she felt that there was already too much anxiety in the home. The mother found out the extent of her child's agony when she happened to see her in the bathroom (the door was normally locked), and she caught sight of bruises, cuts, and cigarette burns on her back and legs. This revelation resulted in an anguished call to Kidscape. Some children tell us that they are ashamed to tell their parents, and that they feel that they are somehow to blame for the abuse.

If a parent contacts you wanting to know how to help their child, what advice do you give?
The advice would depend on the nature of the bullying, but information essential to all bullying situations would include the need for parents to encourage their child to disclose what they are going through by ensuring full support and a real sense that they are believed. The parent needs to find out the details of what has been happening, which entails talking to teachers, probably the head of school. Parents can help to "bully-proof" their child by emphasizing a positive outlook, including assertive body language and firm eye contact. Well-developed social skills, including the ability to listen to others, to ask questions, to smile when appropriate can be modeled and encouraged by parents. These are all protective behaviors, which help to prevent being assessed as a potential target of bullying.

Do you ever counsel the bullies themselves? If not, are there organizations that do?
Some of the young people who attend Kidscape therapeutic sessions are both target and bully in different settings. Our literature addresses issues that underlie bullying and aims to stimulate reflection and provide strategies and motivation for changing that behavior. One of our major projects works specifically with young people who tend toward aggressive and

antisocial behavior. The content includes modules on anger management, conflict resolution, and the development of self-awareness. It is a sad fact that in comparison to targets of bullying very few bullies come forward to ask for help. Kidscape's aim is early intervention. If we are to challenge bullying, we need to work with both bullies and victims. There is certainly a need for more interventions that address the underlying issues that lead young people to satisfy specific needs through bullying.

Questions and Topics for Discussion

1. Have you, or has someone you know, ever experienced bullying?

2. In what ways do you think the Internet and social media change the bullying culture in schools?

3. What can be done about this issue, in schools or at home? Do schools have a responsibility to get involved? To what extent?

4. What do you think prompts bullying behavior in teenagers? Can it be stopped?

5. Discuss Jack and Jenna's relationship. What changed between them after the move to Wales? Could they have handled their affairs differently? How would you have handled it?

6. What sort of consequences do you think bullies should face for their actions?

7. Why do you think the bullies chose to target Paige specifically?

8. Discuss the mother-daughter relationship at the heart of this novel. What did you think of Jenna's parenting? How could she have handled Paige's situation differently?

9. Discuss Paige's relationship with Jack. How does the fact that he's her stepfather influence the family dynamic?

10. Paige has a very complicated home life: her mother's marriage is in jeopardy, they recently moved to Wales, finances are tight, etc. What other aspects of her home life may have heightened the stress Paige was under?

If you enjoyed

Too Close to Home by Susan Lewis,

you won't want to miss

The Girl Who Came Back

coming in March 2016

It wasn't right to feel this way.

Not about her own daughter.

The child was only nine, for God's sake. She was an innocent, a tender young soul still trying to find her way in the world. Except that wasn't how she seemed, innocent and tender, or how she behaved.

She wasn't like other children. She didn't run or skip or play childish games. She didn't sing or tease or sleep like an angel.

She didn't look at people, she stared; she didn't laugh, or when she did the sound was false, jarring, sadly humorless. Olivia had never heard girlish giggles erupting from bubbles of happiness or excitement inside Amelia. Little seemed to amuse her, or even please her, although she was often fascinated by things: insects, small animals, dolls; tools, gadgets, other children's toys. She always wanted what wasn't hers, which perhaps didn't make her so very different from other children; Olivia had come across plenty of kids like that.

Amelia didn't speak very much either, at least not to her mother.

She chatted away with her father when he made time for her.

She was the apple of his eye, when he remembered she was there.

As far as he was concerned, nothing was too much for his girl, provided it didn't get in the way of his other commitments.

Olivia felt sure that Amelia was the only human being her husband had ever come close to loving, although she'd thought he loved her once.

That seemed a very long time ago.

She wondered how she'd ended up in this marriage, how she'd allowed herself to become the victim of such an egotistical man with such a dismissive air toward those he considered of little use.

Olivia was never entirely sure how useful she was to him.

In a material sense she wanted for nothing. They lived in a large, imposing house a stone's throw from Chelsea Bridge. She had her own suite of rooms, a fancy car, a generous allowance, and all the freedoms she could wish for.

She also had a daughter who was healthy and intelligent, meticulously clean and tidy, but instead of joyful and open-hearted was sullen and sly.

Yes, really—sullen and sly.

Olivia had never voiced her feelings about Amelia to anyone, least of all to her husband, Anton. Of course he would say the problem, if there was one and he probably wouldn't admit that there was, lay entirely with her. She was Amelia's mother, therefore she was the person Amelia spent the most time with (when she wasn't away at school), so it stood to reason that she was the biggest influence on Amelia's life.

Amelia was on her third school now, fifth if Olivia counted the two kindergartens she'd attended.

Amelia couldn't settle. Other children didn't warm to her,

or were afraid of her, or ruthlessly tormented her. Olivia felt sorry for her when she was bullied and tried to soothe her, but Amelia hated being babied.

What was to become of her?

Would she change as she got older, and start to understand that she needed to be more like others if she wanted to be accepted by them? It was pointless trying to have the conversation with her; she simply got up and walked away. Or she'd tell her mother to shut up, or to leave her alone she was busy.

Anton's parents were bewildered by the girl, although most things bewildered them these days.

As for Olivia's parents; they'd separated a long time ago and she hadn't seen either of them in a very long while. She didn't even know where they were living now, though she guessed she could find out easily enough if she tried.

She'd felt so painfully alone since marrying Anton, which wasn't how she'd felt before, when she was still single. She'd had lots of friends then, a career as a legal secretary, a great social life, and she'd always been up for something new. Anton had been like that, too, dashing and daring, successful, romantic, and always attentive.

So what had changed him?

Maybe his irresistible charm had been an act that he'd simply dropped once he'd made her his wife, seeing no need to go on pleasing her in the ways he used to.

She had no idea if he ever had affairs, but she hoped he did; they would provide her with a solid excuse to leave when the time was right.

Wasn't the time right now?

Not while Amelia was still so young.

So you see, I'm not such a bad person. I really do care about my daughter, I want what's best for her, I'll never turn my back on her, I'm determined to find a way through to her heart.

In the meantime Anton could ridicule and humiliate, neglect and even beat her, but only until Amelia was able to make her own way in the world, that was when Olivia would go and never come back.

Looking around for Amelia now, she found her staring at her from an upper deck of their cruiser. The breeze was ruffling her mousy hair; the sun was burning her freckled cheeks.

"Have you used sun block?" she called out.

Amelia held up a tube, presumably to show that she had.

"Are you going to swim?" Olivia asked.

"Only if you do."

Olivia's heart twisted around her conscience. "You know I can't."

"Why not?"

"Because I've never learned."

"That's just stupid."

"Yes, it is." Olivia didn't admit that she was afraid of the water, if she did Amelia would ask why and Olivia could never find a good enough answer to that. Or not one that would satisfy Amelia.

"Where's Daddy?" Amelia demanded.

"Inside, sleeping. Or working."

Amelia turned away and a few minutes later she was on the deck beside her mother. "I want you to swim," she told her bluntly.

"One of these days I'll learn," Olivia promised.

"I want you to do it now."

"It doesn't happen just like that. I need someone to teach me."

"I can teach you."

"OK, but not here. We're too far from the shore, and I'll need to be able to touch the bottom in case I panic." She smiled, hoping that Amelia might, too, but she didn't.

"Are you afraid of drowning?" Amelia asked.

"Of course. It would be a horrible way to die."

Amelia seemed to think about that, then suddenly pulling back her arms she gave her mother an almighty shove sending her over the edge into the sea.

Olivia was too startled to scream. Her hands and legs flailed desperately in the water. "Amelia," she tried to gulp. "Throw . . . throw me . . . the lifebelt."

Amelia only watched her.

"Amelia! Please."

Amelia turned away and went to sit at the table where she'd left the book she was reading.

Fifteen or so minutes later her father appeared from the cabin.

"Hello, sweetie," he yawned, ruffling her hair. "Are you OK?"

Amelia nodded.

He looked around, taking in the fresh sea air, calm waters, and distant shore. "Where's your mother?" he asked.

Amelia shrugged and carried on reading.

SUSAN LEWIS is the internationally bestselling author of thirty-three novels. She is also the author of *Just One More Day* and *One Day at a Time,* the deeply moving and often hilarious memoirs of her childhood in Bristol. She lives in Gloucestershire, United Kingdom.

Sign up for her newsletter at susanlewis.com
Facebook.com/SusanLewisBooks
@susandlewis

Chat.
Comment.
Connect.

Visit our online book club community at
Facebook.com/RHReadersCircle

Chat
Meet fellow book lovers and discuss what you're reading.

Comment
Post reviews of books, ask—and answer—thought-provoking
questions, or give and receive book club ideas.

Connect
Find an author on tour, visit our author blog, or invite one of
our 150 available authors to chat with your group on the phone.

Explore
Also visit our site for discussion questions, excerpts, author
interviews, videos, free books, news on the latest releases,
and more.

Books are better with buddies.
Facebook.com/RHReadersCircle

RANDOM  HOUSE